POOL HOUSE

ALSO BY MARY H.K. CHOI

Emergency Contact

Permanent Record

Yolk

POOL HOUSE

A Novel

MARY H.K. CHOI

FLATIRON
BOOKS
NEW YORK

This is a work of fiction. All the names, characters, organizations, places, and events portrayed in this work are either products of the author's imagination or used fictitiously.

Printed in the United States of America. For information, address Flatiron Books, 120 Broadway, New York, NY 10271. EU Representative: Macmillan Publishers Ireland Ltd., 1st Floor, The Liffey Trust Centre, 117–126 Sheriff Street Upper, Dublin 1, D01 YC43.

www.flatironbooks.com

Grateful acknowledgment is made for permission to reproduce from the following:

Hands Clean
Words and Music by Alanis Morissette
Copyright © 2004 UNIVERSAL MUSIC CORP. and 1974 MUSIC
All Rights Administered by UNIVERSAL MUSIC CORP.
All Rights Reserved Used by Permission
Reprinted by Permission of Hal Leonard LLC

Designed by Leah Carlson-Stanisic

Library of Congress Cataloging-in-Publication Data

Names: Choi, Mary H.K., author.
Title: Pool house : a novel / Mary H.K. Choi.
Description: First edition. | New York : Flatiron Books, 2026.
Identifiers: LCCN 2026004097 | ISBN 9781250800442 (hardcover) |
ISBN 9781250800435 (ebook)
Subjects: LCSH: Mothers and daughters | LCGFT: Novels
Classification: LCC PS3603.H6546 P66 2026 | DDC 813/.6—dc23/eng/20260203
LC record available at https://lccn.loc.gov/2026004097

First Edition: 2026

10 9 8 7 6 5 4 3 2 1

For Sam

AND NO ONE KNOWS EXCEPT THE BOTH OF US.

—Alanis Morissette

PART I

DAY ONE

STEVIE

Stevie has been usurped. She's rounded the corner at Ralphs to catch Moon, her mother, speaking to a young tattooed Asian woman in the cereal aisle. The angle of the other woman's head and the way Moon uses her hands as she speaks, gaining speed, indicates that some deep and abiding imprinting is taking place. Moon has orchestrated this, trawled *Rock N Roll Ralphs*, as she cringingly still refers to the grocery store on Sunset, switching her famous face on for her dopamine hit, a hoovering vortex of want.

Stevie retreats into the endcap of the aisle, to hide behind chips the size of feed bags, and this is how Stevie is sick in the head. She has the thought, clear as day, that her mother is *cheating on her*. The term that springs to mind is *cuckold*, and while she is aware that this isn't even the definition of the word, she also yearns for her mother to a clinical degree. It was Mother Hunger, self-diagnosed but very real. And her circumstances were a perfect storm of absence, workaholism, and her mother's own ungovernable appetite for anyone who wasn't Stevie.

Delilah Moon (Theresa Moon on her passport) had not been a household name. Though coming up in the nineties at exactly the moment of the paparazzi boom and unprecedented *Us Weekly* sales, she'd burned bright, especially for the time on a red carpet where she'd been virtually naked and astonishingly pregnant, the same year Björk wore a swan dress. She'd had an athletic and well-received run in several B movies as a kind of Murder Lolita, as well as a handful of Miramax pictures that were all "of a time," predictably with heavy sapphic overtones. She played the same home-wrecking kinderwhore, au pairs in bad wigs and unexplained martial arts training, deployed usually to avenge some murdered (male) family member back in some shitstain rural village in Asia.

For Stevie, this created the very specific experience of growing up knowing that most of the boys at her elite private school, as well as the male teachers, had seen Moon naked. Mostly her boobs but sometimes her bush, and it was purported—though never confirmed (and Stevie had always been too mortified to ask)—Moon had even had live, actual, unsimulated penetrative sex in that first film. Definitely at least one of the blowjobs had been real, and the joke was you didn't need a Moon sex tape to leak, they were all already out there. This was why it was the dads who stopped to talk to Moon. Increasingly the granddads. Or else they wouldn't say anything at all, backing into Moon with their iPads flapped open, held up for the world's most obvious creepshot.

But this Stevie could tolerate. She was proud of her mother. Moon was a trailblazer and iconoclast. Many VH1 talking heads shows agreed on this. And they could minimally rely on a few speaking fees around AAPI month, which meant that by June her mother would get upset about the mid-face deep plane lift she couldn't afford because being referred to unerringly as a legend made her feel old.

Lately, with the return of the Y2K scumbag aesthetic, there was also a certain breed of alt Asian Baby Girl who loved Moon and unfailingly made efforts to impress her. They were all unequivocally cooler than Stevie. With better clothes. Confident and usually near-naked. Goths who vaped, e-girls with tattoos and neon racing stripes on their shredded, oversized jeans. Narrow-hipped girls from Torrance. Cinephiles from Riverside. Letterboxd was their Tumblr. All as much fans of softcore nineties femme fatale films as experimental cinema. It was these girls who tormented Stevie most. She knew from their striving vocal fry and the unprompted recitations of their LinkedIn accomplishments that they didn't actually care about Moon. But optically, at least from a branding perspective, even Stevie had to admit they were all much more convincing as stand-ins for the role of Moon's daughter.

It wasn't fair. Stevie had been beautiful too once but had outgrown it. Generals had been set up with agents. She'd even modeled briefly, earning $4,000 for a weekend, about as much as she makes now in two months, after taxes. At twenty, Stevie's features float vaguely in the growing puddle of her face. Her looks were watered down and her ratios have proven unlovely. *She's got a face for background*, she's heard Moon say to a friend. *It's probably a blessing*. She's also a foot taller than her mother with wide shoulders. If they were Russian nesting dolls, they would be separated by at least three sizes. Stevie did have good breasts, though, they were probably her best quality, but they lend a biological functionality to her appearance that makes her seem stolid. Moon shimmers with volatility. Frailty. In the heyday of her career, her choppy hair, flat chest, sickly pallor, and large darting eyes were a manic pixie dream. As zany and wistful as Faye Wong, only shorter. Even now, at almost fifty, her mother looks half her age with an ethereal, unreliable quality that screams to be looked after.

Watching Moon and this better daughter, Stevie fantasizes about walking out of the store and vanishing. Not caring where she winds up or what happens next, just going. But then, there it is. Moon angles her chin and the light dims in her eyes. It is sudden. The drop in interest as abrupt as falling blood sugar. Moon is bored. Or she has been offended. It doesn't matter. Stevie's seen it happen so many times that the choreography of it lives inside her body. Killing her a little each time to have the look turned on her.

So she swoops in for the rescue, Moon's eye brightening with relief, and she's introduced to Julie, a teacup Korean in a sheer dress, with one million razor-sharp teeth in her child-sized skull, and tiny marsupial hands that give off broad psychotic gestures. Julie, who'd received an MFA at USC, who'd written her thesis on Moon, and has inch-long, pencil-eraser nipples that exactly resemble her mother's.

"Now I run this diasporic Asian cultural fund," she tells Stevie, and

Stevie tells her in the supercilious manner of someone on Moon's payroll, "I love that for you." Also, that they have to go.

"Can we get a picture?" Julie asks, holding out a phone. A nagging pressure builds in Stevie's forehead. The woman's phone is encased in an undulating rubbery glitter sculpture with tiny portraits of K-pop idols suspended inside. And even as it physically pains her, Stevie draws them away from the cruel backlighting of the refrigerated shelves, frames the shot, and shoots in bursts. Hundreds of photos with her mother and this woman.

* * *

At work, hours later, at Pee Wee's, a farm-to-table, fast-casual burrito restaurant that is the namesake of some baseball legend and the fifth fastest-growing food franchise behind Cava, Stevie's gloved hands send a warm parcel of burrito shushing down the stainless steel countertop on a tray. She scans the next ticket, reaches for a fresh tray and bowl, then checks the time. At Pee Wee's, she's surrounded by clocks. There is a digital one on the wall behind the line, others on the foot of the menu displays, on each ticket, again on the monitor of every register, and a regular analog clock with hands by the front door that only the older people on staff know how to read.

Her wrist shudders as her mother's winking cartoon avatar rises up from the screen of her watch. *Incoming Call from Moon.* Panic sails up from her asshole to her mouth. Her mother has been out of her sight for less than four hours but now she's convinced that Moon's dead. She's dead and someone from a teaching hospital has called the most dialed contact on her phone to see about harvesting her organs.

The call disengages and Stevie's gloved fingers move along independently of her, sprinkling exactly two ounces of charred chicken into the bowl, one palm cupped to corral the bouncy bits of protein from straying. *Probably a butt-dial,* she tells herself, annoyed, as another, more insulting thought flits through her head which is that they would never think to call Stevie first because Stevie is not even her mother's emergency contact.

Her watch pulses again.

Moon: FaceTime Video.

OK, so Moon is alive. Her mother disconnects. Then repeats the process as cortisol surges through Stevie's system with unremitting rigor, her body still convinced that they're calling about Moon's cornea and heart. They would not want her liver. Stevie exhales as slow as she can, the air hissing out audibly as her hands fill single-use plastic condiment containers for a takeout order. But the small satisfaction of the snapping lids can't penetrate the exquisite and familiar rage traveling across her extremities. Another call thrums up her arm with a voice message that reads: *Call me, it's urgent.* Stevie shuts her eyes. Her outrage is so pure that her vision trembles.

MOON

Sitting in the driveway, Moon is vaguely aware she is in shock. Or that she might be. She's giddily impressed rather than sad, and while she's worried about this, what it says about her that excitement is the dominant feeling, she is also concerned by how convinced she is that if she called him right now, he would pick up. He would pick up because it was her.

But he's dead. She can't believe it. He's dead. It's incredible that he's dead. Mac. *Her Mac*, as the reporter had described him on the phone. She hadn't cried on the call, but she cries now. It's unfathomable. There's no official press yet. Corinna, Mac's wife, has issued a statement on social media, but that's it. No details beyond respecting the family's privacy during this difficult time. There's no cause of death circulating, but Moon knows. The reporter had a source at Port Police. They're holding the identity of the body until they can tell his elderly mother somewhere in the Outer Hebrides. There is no suspicion of foul play. There were eyewitnesses. And a bridge.

Sweating in her baking car, an old thrill rumbles through her body. The intrigue of arriving change. Moon has instincts around this like animals in apocalypse films. Something is coming. She's almost glad she skipped her AA meeting, choosing instead to wander around the Grove in the stifling afternoon, the festiveness of the outdoor mall reliably depressing in a way that recalls Christmas in the wrong season, reminding her of Texas. She wouldn't have taken the call if she'd been in her meeting, upstairs in the community room of the Farmers Market, so this feels fated somehow.

She wipes her lipstick on the back of her hand; it leaves a garish, greasy smear. She remembers swimming in Lake Lucerne. Mac cannonballing. Bobbing up, laughing, spitting water out in an arc like an angel pissing in a fountain. How he'd declared the water delicious, tasting like *fucking Volvic*. The tug of his arms pulling her into his lap. The way he'd frolic in the room after sex to make her laugh, fat and sublimely confident, arms raised, flaccid penis dangling. The look of him cleaning. Always cleaning. Listening to the Stone Roses. The smell of him. The skin at his temple, the scent of uncooked rice. The nightly drone-hiss of the CPAP machine that he kept hidden even from his staff.

None of it makes sense. She blows her nose on a crumpled napkin and pulls out her phone before she realizes. Again, she's thinking to call him. She wants to gossip about what she's heard. She wants to hear him laugh about it. She wants to resume being angry at him instead of heavy and sad and regretful.

She gets out of the car, passing the mailbox and the front door of the house, proceeding through the white, mechanized side gate, and thinks back to a decade ago. A near-miss. The small heart attack that they'd referred to as *mini* and then the bigger one that should have taken him out. They'd reconciled then. Again. The fourth time. Fifth. It didn't matter. But he'd looked diminished and exhausted in the hospital bed. Properly old to her for the first time until his eyes snapped open and he grabbed her by the waist to ransack her bag for cigarettes.

He wouldn't kill himself. He was too petty to allow his enemies to keep living, beating him, eating beautiful meals while he lay there, eyes sewn shut.

Moon knocks on her own kitchen door. She knocks again. It is the back door, or the side rather, glass-paneled and up a flight of stairs. The house is unoccupied but she wants to make sure. She plugs in the passcode and slips inside. The shades are up, the sun pools golden in the room, and as she hears the click of the central AC, she looks around her magnificent kitchen. It is incomprehensible to her that she won't get fucked up now. That she will have to do this sober.

She should call her sponsor, but instead she takes off her bra. Natori. And her pants. The Row. Thousand-dollar pants. She slings them over the back of a Danish leather bar stool by the marble counters that are spectacularly veined like a great wedge of Stilton. The room evokes words like *hearth*, *biodynamic wine*, and *Marcella Hazan chicken*, all those bougie white-people words. Southern Californian status words. She even has one of those brushed gold faucets on a jointed arm that juts out from the backsplash to fill pots for pasta. As if she eats fucking pasta.

She wonders what will happen next. Whether there will be press requests, and the old reptilian instincts kick in, what she will wear, glam, the expenses of getting a facial, Botox, RF microneedling. She may need to bleach her teeth. Whatever comes, she will have to lose weight. She wonders how this will have changed the course of her life in a month. A year. Ten.

She hates him for doing this to her, and in thinking this, she cries. That selfish fucker. He'd told her not to buy this house, she remembers now. All her money is in the house. He told her it wasn't *prudent*, his word, puckering his pretty little mouth in a flautist's embouchure. *Prudent, prudent, prudent.* A real naggy word. His accent furring the r's. She'd done it anyway. Possibly because he hadn't approved. The pain in her throat does a collapsing thing into her chest when she thinks of Corinna. She wonders how alone she must feel in that house in Malibu. Barely thirty. And then she's furious to be thinking protectively about Mac's new wife at all.

A bridge. Christ. She's surprised he'd had the balls. And then, unkindly, she imagines that final topple as an accident. A slip. An undignified little wobble with dancing, frantic hands. Or maybe he had meant it. The drama of it reeks of petulance. Wanting the world to know of his unhappiness. To wonder about it.

She checks the time, wanting Stevie. She wants warmth. A body. Even as she's distantly aware that she can no longer hold Stevie with abandon as she once had. She calls her daughter. FaceTimes. Calls again. Leaves a message. She circles the kitchen island, vision blurred with tears, running her fingers along the cool surface of the stone. She picks up a box of cauliflower-based snack cracker. Dairy, gluten, and tree-nut free according to the box and somehow costing twenty-two dollars.

There are other cues throughout the room that hint at a particular caste of lodger. The interlopers she despises. The details seem to glow in the kitchen that she doesn't always recognize as hers. The cheap citrus-scented reed diffusers from Home Goods, the gilded bowl filled with cashed vape cartridges. An abandoned bamboo matcha whisk that she will add to the others.

The last tenant's name had been Howie Yoo. She'd fallen into the obvious joke two weeks ago.

Howie Yoo, he'd said, hand held out.

Fine, Moon replied, annoyed.

She hates dealing with her patrons, these assholes that live in her house, these *creatives* and *thought leaders* that book the whole thing through an app for weeks, sometimes months, for thousands and thousands of dollars that now pay her mortgage.

A week ago, Howie had texted to see if she had any USB mics *floating around*, and annoyingly she did. She'd gone over with the whole IKEA bag of plastic Amazon'd flotsam that the others left behind. The waste of these *digital nomads* shocks her. Metric tons of plastic—Theraguns, ring lights, yoga mats, cables, milk frothers—all trailing in their wake.

A company had booked the house, so she'd been surprised when the tenant was Asian. He'd worn a Fleetwood Mac 1977 Rumours concert tee despite obviously being born in the nineties. His faded flannel pajama pants recalled college boys and by dint of him being visibly Korean and therefore feeling slightly less abstracted to her, she wished she'd worn a bra. When he found the mic, he'd looped the cable around its base and taken a step back, hand shooting up to his chest. She'd worried he was having some kind of medical event but then saw as he held her gaze, maroon splotching across his face, that he recognized her.

Two perfect silver droplets sprang out of his wide eyes like mercury and he made a snotty, gurgling sound as he swiped his forearm across his face and groaned. *Holy shit*, he said, face screwing into a full sob. *You're Delilah Moon.*

She remembers she'd taken his hand. It was plump, soft, and sticky to the touch like a child's, and the warm intimacy of it reminded her of handling wet money. The unanticipated effect of this sudden, fierce reverence stunned her with the shimmering, air-conditioned quality of very pure MDMA. The hit of uncut emotion flooded her with the euphoria of being picked first round for team sports. Of receiving a very public apology. The relief was overwhelming. She felt like herself again. She led him inside. His damp eyes in the kitchen light were dark gray.

Wabi-Sabi *helped me get through my parents' divorce*, he'd said of the network sitcom that had, at least according to certain critics, killed Moon's more serious film prospects.

He'd gasped when she kissed him. And when she took him in her mouth he shuddered and came almost instantly. He apologized and then thanked her. After, when he offered his hand to help her off her knees, she was so insulted by the gesture and its necessity, that she laughed then thanked him. She should have fucked him, she thinks now. She can't believe she hadn't fucked him. He'd been a deft kisser, lips soft, warm, and pliant, and when his fingers dug into her hair, she heard herself moan. She felt his erection at her belly and was aroused by the darkening dot of pre-cum on the dingy grosgrain drawstring of his pajama bottoms, but then remembered the reality of herself—the pilling nude seamless panties, the wild, coarse state of her pubic hair, the vaginal dryness that accompanied the night sweats—and dropped to her knees.

How old were you when your parents split up? she'd asked, pulling his pants down. Her other hand rooted in her own underpants where she felt heat and triumphant wetness.

Ten, he'd said, watching her.

If she'd slept with Howie, the last person she'd slept with wouldn't be Mac. A man who is now dead and who at the time had been freshly engaged to someone else. It all feels heavy and terrible now. Mac is not even Mac anymore but a waterlogged corpse and it feels like a contagion, his deadness. She thinks of maggots crawling inside her ears, thick cottony layers of mycological hoar eating through her skull. She touches her hair absentmindedly, thinking of cobwebs but also her silvery roots and how she will not only have to get a haircut but have it dyed.

Howie Yoo had left a week early, citing a work emergency through the app. The next tenant is a family from Carroll Gardens with two kids. They've stayed with them before. They don't arrive until next month but this time they want it for eight weeks. Two months without worry. Enough for the mortgage, pool cleaning, insurance, with some left over. Only the family's a pain in the ass. Covertly high-maintenance in the way of artists and leftists where they seek constant reassurance that they are easy. This time they're asking Moon and Stevie to leave the property entirely. They will pay extra off-app for the trouble of an empty pool house because they feel more comfortable this way. For privacy. She'd been tempted to deny their request, but now a new plan forms. She blows a raspberry with her lips, warming up, then makes the call. Her heart is pounding. She has no idea what time it is in Hong Kong. She hopes he is awake.

Unlike her daughter, he answers on the second ring. Of course he does. Her sweet, sweet boy. She needs him to come. It's time for him to come home. To her house. To be close.

"Dano?"

"Moonie," he says, and her heart cracks wide. She looks at the dipping light in her window. It will be early where he is.

"Baby? I have something to tell you," she says, and hearing his voice she is able to calm her thoughts.

"What is it?"

"It's about Mac," she says. "Our Mac."

"What?"

She exhales completely and feels steady now.

She gets to be the one who tells him.

The release of it borders on erotic.

WABI-SABI
[2012–2019]

Search the Wikipedia entry for *Wabi-Sabi*, the show where Mac played Moon's husband and Adam Dano played her son, and you'd learn that it followed the foibles of the blended military family at its center, the Sato-Connors. Stationed on a fictitious Air Force base on an unnamed island somewhere in Hawaii, *Wabi-Sabi* aired from 2012 to 2017, a culturally specific time in television that engendered zero reservations about using the same three shots of Diamond Head State Monument to establish exteriors and shooting almost entirely on a soundstage in Burbank, ensuring no work for local *ohana*.

Borrowing its title from a Japanese design term that centered on the acceptance of imperfection within nature and the impermanence of existence, *Wabi-Sabi* aired just long enough to be syndicated, with a holiday special that finale year with another hour-long reunion show two years later. But the swiftest business for the series was still conducted over DVD, the way porn is for old people. The residuals were healthy but erratic, with merch and box set sales providing the lion's share of the revenue especially at military base PXs and Costcos during the holidays.

As appropriated catchphrases went, *Wabi-Sabi* didn't quite achieve the traction of an *umami*, what with white America's obsession with cooking food that doesn't belong to them, and even now, the term mostly served as a coddling bulwark against the well-intentioned efforts of crafty hobbyists. Mostly seen as an aesthetic potentiated by third-career ceramicists in pockets of Marin County with a penchant for wobbly mugs featuring overlarge handles.

The show was broad. Multi-cam. It featured a laugh track and was largely considered unserious pablum, TV Muzak, best binged in the background of other activities. It was suited for elliptical machines with captions on and sound off. The humor orbited around a single bit. Mac was old, his wife was young, and his son from a previous marriage, Todd-Michael Sato-Connor played by Adam Dano, wanted to bang his hot Asian stepmom. Family relations were depicted as a virtuosic barrage of boner jokes set against the context of military sex worker jokes and its overtly racist and colonialist premise was neutralized only because it was also blatantly sexist and unerringly homophobic. That Moon, a Korean woman, was cast as Japanese didn't remotely chart as an issue.

The true mastery lay in how the writers somehow managed to exploit both Moon and Dano equally, providing few opportunities for either to keep their clothes on.

By all measures, the show was a hit. It had been a *Jeopardy!* clue twice. Once for the show title and another for Moon's name. And the cast rang the opening bell at the stock exchange. For an entire summer in 2013, New Yorkers were treated to a man on the street segment aired in a loop on the seat-backs of yellow cab TV screens. The segment ran every thirteen minutes and revealed that a large portion of the show's viewers assumed *wabi-sabi* was a made-up term. When asked to define it, one woman said it was *the green stuff in sushi, you know, that isn't avocado*. Others assumed it was a catchy non-word, *doodad* or else *jibber-jabber*, market-tested for appealing mouthfeel by TV executives.

Many of those questioned said it had to do with Asians because: *You know, Asians!* The guess was usually delivered with a sly, sheepish smile, an innocent eye roll, and an uncannily persistent wobbling gesture, a shimmy at the shoulders with raised hands. It was as though they were all conveying a universally pervasive conceit: The incomprehensible weirdness of Asians.

They did not interview any Asians for the segment.

ADAM

When Adam Dano's TV mother called to say his TV dad was dead, he'd known but pretended he hadn't. He was only thirty-two, still capable of change, and he'd promised himself in Hong Kong that he was done with half-truths and exactly these sorts of petard-hoistings. It's just that Moon rarely cried—almost never—and it was her startling vulnerability, the heartrending quavering of her voice that had made it seem kinder just to hold space, to listen, let her unload, instead of interrupting to gloat that he'd already found out from Mac's brother Callum. Adam had been in crisis over it. He might have been the last of them to see Mac alive, and the thought fills him with unalloyed panic.

This next part is where Adam questions whether he is even a good person. Moon wanted him to come to L.A. She'd even offered to pay for his ticket from Asia. But not only had Adam already known about Mac, he'd already been in town, specifically in Silver Lake, at his friend Kip's not fifteen minutes south of Moon's, and hadn't thought to call her. Still, when she summoned him, the pull to the woman he loved more than his actual mother was immediate and powerful. She'd used the words that drove right into his gut. *I need you.* Words he would never hear from his own shrewd and capable mother, Katherine. As Moon wept softly, the serotonin flooded him like a narcotic. He told her he'd be on the next flight out, refusing her money, feeling disgusting and thrilled. Pumped full of stolen valor.

So now, forty-eight hours deep in L.A., Adam's returned to the dog-breath atmosphere of Inglewood, waiting for Moon outside the arrivals terminal. It is almost ten a.m. Traffic is likely horrendous and he feels sick that she insisted on picking him up because he's *come all this way*. His phone vibrates. It's his mother, his *actual* mother, reminding him that while he hasn't exactly lied to her yet, it will be awkward and difficult not to. He sighs. Sweat blooms at the base of his spine and on the top half of his butt cheeks. His stomach creaks ominously. Lately, there is always a strong likelihood he will shit his pants when he leaves the house. His stomach has been fucked since Hong Kong and he feels shame about this as though it is an indictment of his excruciating whiteness. Exhaling with purpose, he clenches. He carries a Ziploc snack bag of wet wipes and a spare pair of neatly folded boxers in a different, second Ziploc bag. And he feels moderately reassured by this as he scans the haze and beetling cars surrounding him, filled with the sense that he's in hostile territory. He scratches his cheek, the beard making him crazy. His phone pulses again, alerting him to a message that he will not listen to.

Originally, he'd been on his way to New York for his mother's birthday. Chek Lap Kok to JFK. Except that business was oversold on the direct and coach was a nonstarter so he'd gone with a ninety-minute layover in L.A. But living in Asia for a year, he'd somehow forgotten about the shitfuck clownshow that was LAX. He had Diamond status, Amex Platinum, Sapphire Reserve, Global Entry, Clear, but there was nothing to be done about delays. He'd had a glass of wine at the lounge. Then two more. It had been morning-morning and he hadn't liked what the booze indicated about him philosophically. He skulled a double espresso and then went to sit on a toilet for a while, not before laying down a complicated lattice of seat liners, then downloaded Instagram again. Also, Raya. He mindlessly liked his agent Rory's story of his dog Maxwell, the two of them hiking on Runyon. Then matched with Sylvic, a recently divorced folk singer, just as Rory texted him about lunch.

He didn't want to go to lunch. He didn't want to be in L.A. But then he noticed the 118 unread notifications from the WhatsApp group chat about Liverpool FC. He rarely checked the group chat since it mostly functioned as a friendship beard for Mac and Callum, so the two otherwise estranged Maclean siblings could talk without having to acknowledge their disaffection. But the activity was unusual, and as he scanned the condolences, funeral details, heart hammering, scrolling frantically, he accidentally double-tapped the news of Mac's death—sending a heart—his vision pinholing before his frozen fingers could undo it. His first thought had been overdose or accident. Mac's vomit-caked face. The drunk waspish figure of him lurching into traffic. Dead? It wasn't possible. Mac had looked fantastic when he'd seen him not ten days earlier. He'd lost weight and was tanned; in fact, he'd been insufferably smug about it. Restored to the vision of himself when the show first started.

Adam had idolized him back then. They all had. The thick, leonine red hair. Muscular and broad, looking bearish in suits but moving with startling elegance on his swift, small feet. He'd been first on the call sheet and could wear an earwig to have his lines piped into his head without ridicule, whereas Adam was rolled head to toe in bronzer, his abs airbrushed into an eight-pack each day. Mac could be an unrepentant prick but he could also be kind and gruffly avuncular. But when he'd shown up unannounced at his door in Hong Kong, laughing at Adam's shock, duty-free bags clinking, Adam had not welcomed him.

When he learned Mac was dead, Adam walked out of the bathroom, then straight out of the airport, disregarding his connecting flight. He'd gone to Kip's in a daze, guts emptied, lightheaded, thinking only of the Erewhon within walking distance, the capaciousness of bright, sunny skies. Of bee pollen on his smoothies. Kip was shooting a werewolf movie in Bulgaria and Adam had been trapped in an edit for months, hunched over a desk in the dark in Lan Kwai, his movie in utter shambles. He needed a beat. He couldn't face his mother just yet. Not like this.

Presently, he watches a man smoking beneath a no smoking sign. He's been stoned for days. He'd smoked Kip's diabolically powerful weed and most of the cigarettes in his freezer, filling his head with internet. He thinks how he's teetering on the brink of proper depression.

The film had been doomed from the start, he knows this now. But he could picture it, a retelling of Buñuel's *Exterminating Angel* that would flout National Security Law, skewering China's "one country; two systems" policy about Hong Kong's reintegration into the Mainland, setting the action in a surrealistic, allegorical hellscape that nobody could leave. He'd been swept up by the romance, the colonial grandeur, the Foreign Correspondents' club, the old-timey police station in Central, head full of Merchant Ivory, James Clavell, Wong Kar-wai. Stooped over a folding table on a plastic stool on the street, mowing through a brothy bowl of noodles, smiling at his own hungover reflection in the pools of spicy oil on the surface of his soup, he'd felt capable of anything.

They'd asked him to direct but mostly he was being extorted for cash. He'd tried ignoring their calls and texts until Benny, quiet Benny, one of the drivers, showed up at his apartment at two in the morning, and had been there a while judging from the multiple cigarette butts at his feet, white plastic 7-Eleven bag dangling from his wrist. Adam had the clear thought that Benny was there to kill him and found it excruciatingly cool that he'd appeared so sanguine about it. They'd trudged up to the Hong Kong Shanghai Bank together as Adam felt like a constitutionally anemic little princeling; a fish-bellied little bitch that he kept drawing more money from his trust than he felt comfortable with.

As he handed Benny another HKD $20,000, he noticed the email from his mother. An Evite of all things. He clicked on it, the animation of an envelope revealing cream stationery with a digitally rendered deckled edge and swooping calligraphy. It was as funny as his mother ever got since Katherine exclusively handwrote her letters using hundred-pound, bright white, matte, individually cut cards with clean edges. It was a lighthearted indictment of his distance, an invitation to her birthday dinner, a personal entreaty for filial niceties despite their chilly correspondence since his departure. But more importantly it was an out. A good excuse to leave again.

There's no way he can tell Moon that this was the extent of his Hong Kong adventure. That after Benny robbed him, he'd shaken the

7-Eleven bag for Adam to take. Inside was a packet of microwaveable shrimp cheung fun and a cold milk tea that he'd not only carried home but angrily eaten.

He thinks back to when he first met Moon. At a table reading in Culver City. He'd been eighteen and had never felt uglier or more out of his element. He'd worn the same shorts that were secretly a bathing suit, because his regular clothes were wrong. No one wore dark basketball shorts or regular jeans in L.A. Everything at the time was screen-printed or painted or embroidered. His hair was brittle and brassy, bleached so violently that his scalp was crusted with scabs. And when Moon approached, he'd been so absorbed by his forensic efforts to determine whether she was wearing a bra that by the time she was saying hello, he was operating on a delay. She seemed amused but then looked him dead in the eye before whispering, *It's you and me, kid, OK?* and squeezed his arm.

Moon's car approaches. The same black Porsche. She is almost hit by a Flyaway bus as she veers and Adam has the quick, powerful thought that this is a bad idea, but then she is parked and he sees her small figure fly out of the car, leaving the door hanging open, and he runs to her and picks her up the way they've always done.

FOR YOUR CONSIDERATION

[SUMMER 2012]

The first time Stevie met Adam Dano on set—his hair and teeth freshly bleached, shirtless, waiting for his spray-tan to dry—she felt the first real stirrings of sexual desire. It had been a revelation. She thought he looked exactly like Ryan Gosling. And this had been particularly overwhelming at seven years old, since she'd just watched the 2004 cinematic opus based on the Nicholas Sparks bestseller by the same name—*The Notebook*.

When she happened upon the battered, white-sleeved For Your Consideration screener DVD among her mother's things, it gave no hints as to the secrets it contained. But when she put it on, she'd known by instinct—guided by the glistening pink of the lovers' mouths, Allie's pearls, Noah's hair, all that rain—how to shift in her seat, cross-legged on the carpeted living room floor, grinding purposefully like a dog with worms, *stirring-stirring-stirring*, the dreadful, almost itchy frothing in her belly gaining, coalescing, thickening—high-traffic polymer rug fibers prickling through the cotton gusset of her underpants, and her mother's name DELILAH MOON pulsing across the screen in large watermarked block letters at the exact instance the sensation hitched, hiccupped, then shot out of her in hot, sticky webbing that smelled strangely of butter.

She was spent, elated, and amid the jumble of fervid emotions, awakened a new kind of loneliness, one that spoke to a lack of romantic love. The single thing Moon, who had everything, didn't seem to possess. So when Stevie met Adam, supposedly her brother, it's not like she wanted to have sex with him, more that she would watch if he asked.

Even at a young age, Stevie was not entirely uninitiated to the vagaries of fame. She knew it was only a matter of time before Adam would no longer be meaningfully accessible to her, and inspired by *The Notebook*, she handwrote a letter on actual paper, admitting that she was young but not too young and that she was willing to play the long game. She knew enough not to ask him to wait. Men were impatient and fickle. She didn't have to grow up as the daughter to a C-list actress to know. And she'd considered signing the letter *Love, Stevie*, but it had felt too brazen and unserious, too emotionally tawdry for her capacity for deep feeling, so she wrote *Yours Cordially, Stevie Moon* instead. It sounded polite but meaningful.

She'd sealed the envelope with spit, closing her eyes as she pressed her flattened tongue against the salty strip of mucilage, wondering how it would taste to kiss him, then added the extra security measure of washi tape because Moon would have to deliver it to him at work. Even still, Moon betrayed her. And the next time Stevie saw Adam, her mother asked him to hand her a piece of gum from Crafty, *Please, Yours Cordially, Delilah Moon*, and Adam had colored, unable to look directly at either of them.

The last time Stevie saw her fake brother had been at Christmas. Six years ago. She'd been fifteen to his twenty-six and they were all in Canada shooting the final reunion special. Production had put them up at Sutton Place, that great pink sanitarium-looking hotel that everyone inventively referred to as *Slutton Place* because shoots overlapped and people fucked. It was Olympic Village except with smoking and a lot more lower back pain. Still, it was surprisingly festive in the wood-paneled bar. The multiple fireplaces had been lit and Mariah was screaming about not wanting a lot for Christmas, and even though the bullshit turnaround made it impossible for anyone to visit their families and Mac had left earlier on a private jet and offered a ride to no one else, people were in good spirits. They didn't even start a pool on the odds of the storm striking the rich, fat bastard straight out of the sky.

Stevie had been handling a decoy gift plucked from the base of the tree when Adam snuck up on her. She'd known the gift-wrapped box was empty but the impulse had been too powerful. But when Adam said her name, she'd thrown it down and wiped her glitter-covered palms on the black velvet skirt of her party dress.

He'd been training for a role in a superhero franchise and had transformed into a hulking great slab of a movie star. Fortified by whey isolate, hypertrophy, and HGH, it was as though they'd pumped him up with binding agents to form a human chicken nugget with star power. Even still, Stevie could see him in there. Adam Dano. Behind his eyes. Trapped in all that mass in his now too-small head. Teeth so white they glowed blue at the edges. Stunned by the hard-packed enormity of him all these years later, embarrassed to be caught shaking a present like a child, Stevie told him he looked disfigured and he'd laughed.

All night, she monitored the micro-expressions flitting across his face, the thready reluctance in his broad smiles. She felt both pity and envy. It was comedically obscene how much speculative groping his size invited. Grown men squaring their jaws, practically tiptoeing as they smacked him appraisingly on the shoulders, going for his middle without warning. The women mostly touched their own faces, lips parted, eyes roving down his torso as he spoke. At all the attention, Adam seemed panicked, as though he'd wandered into a surprise party thrown for him at great expense by people he'd never met. And when he told her he wanted to go outside for a smoke, the air was so cold that it rushed out of her in a gasp and he'd removed his shearling coat to arrange around her shoulders.

When she returned to her hotel room, she'd kicked off her shoes, recalling the heaviness of his jacket and how it fell pleasantly in a weighted embrace. She climbed the king-sized bed and summoned the oblique blue scent of boy deodorant and remembered how when she handed back the coat, his hand had been warm. She'd shoved all the clothes and the hard plastic blow dryer off the bed, onto the floor, closing her eyes, sticking her fingers in her mouth. She swirled her tongue around them and palmed herself between her legs, squeezing her thighs when she came into her hand, toes pointed, thrusting herself forward, rising off the bed to sit up with the force of her orgasm. And then, when she fell back on the mattress, she laughed. It was all so stupid. Jerking off over Adam Dano required a special kind of focus. He was so dumb. It was like masturbating over a cow.

DAY TWO

STEVIE

The atmosphere is a brilliant, deepening blue, and on the bus Stevie sits at the window with the middle-aged man beside her dozing, listing with each stop, threatening to graze her shoulder with his oily blond head. All day at work, she's been rehearsing what to say. At varying points in the service line, she'd imagined turning to Freddie, her work wife, to say that her father was dead. Or even Arvin, her other colleague, or Xan, their boss, and every time, fresh anguish would twist in her chest, eyes threatening to stream, nose clogging until she had to excuse herself for becoming a hygiene issue.

She is stunned by the news. Her most powerful ally gone. The only man in her life that found her both compelling and capable. Who hadn't thought of her as surplus to her mother. The first time she'd met Mac had been at Olive and Berries thirteen years ago, a restaurant known for shareable mains, edible flowers, using tiles instead of plates, and a very public divorce between the owners that centered on the custody battle over a pygmy donkey named Regalia. Stevie had loved Mac immediately.

Interestingly, he hadn't been handsome. He had a big, bulbous head and a small pink cherubic mouth, reminding her of an oil-painted ginger Santa Claus. He was nothing like Moon's other paramours, the writers and directors who seemed to hate Moon for the very real manic vulnerability that attracted them in the first place. Instead he was attentive and intelligent, never once glancing at his phone, asking after her tastes in music and literature. He made Stevie feel sophisticated. As though she were better at being a person by the grace of his conversational sportsmanship.

He'd also given her an understanding of power. And how it lived in the gray of his bespoke suit that carried hints of the deep green of his cufflinks. The way the waitstaff knew to move around him in the choreography of bees and speak his name as though the word tasted delicious in their mouths. And when Stevie, by tacit calculation, knew to spurn Mac's date and chide Moon's lack of appetite, eating with zeal, swallowing back her gag reflex for the roasted artichoke dip that resembled badly cooked sick, she learned not only to court but how to win Mac's favor. She understood the competition inherent to being a woman in the presence of a man. It was the first time she had bested Moon and the occasion was stamped indelibly onto her psyche.

In subsequent years whenever Mac and Moon broke up and reconciled, Stevie's fealties remained neatly apportioned among the camps. Untainted by the other. A twin Popsicle snapped cleanly in half for each of them, leaving nothing for herself, the way it was for a single mother of two, which is how Stevie sometimes felt about the turbulent couple.

But now he is gone.

Last night, Stevie clung to her mother, weeping, so full of remorse that she'd refused to call her back at work. For even dawdling a while after her shift for no particular reason other than pique. She'd felt her heart throbbing in her hot, miserable face, throat aching and all cried out, but then quieted at the gruesome realization that she was stuck now with Moon. Alone. Sole custody. Holding the Moon bag all by herself. Her knees almost buckled, the fast-moving carousel of terror-inducing images that had previously been jettisoned to some far-off box in the darkest regions of her mind galloping back in as fresh concerns.

Her mother's thin bruised thigh as she got her steps in, feet slapping the tiled kitchen floor, suffused with the wired agitation of someone who's been up all night on god knows what. Stevie with her bare ass hitched over the Pool House kitchen sink to piss, ablaze with shame, unable to go in the yard for fear the tenants would see, shaking with terror that she couldn't break the bathroom door down without crushing Moon on the other side, who was unresponsive and probably dead right there of hypoxic brain injury or vomit asphyxiation, going white then blue.

Then there'd been the time they were kicked out of the Pool House and then displaced again from their motel room. Moon had declared it a *classic L.A. adventure* as they filed out with another exhausted, beleaguered family, leaving their one-star accommodations for a full day after four weeks—the infamous, highly illegal twenty-eight-day-shuffle—so motel owners wouldn't have to extend tenant rights under California law for housing anyone for a full month. They'd decamped for WiSpa, the twenty-four-hour Korean 찜질방, stowing all their valuables in the lockers, storing everything else in Moon's car, ignoring how cruisey the saunas became after midnight.

Moon is an actor. She trades in make-believe. Drama. But suddenly, Stevie couldn't get over Moon's breathless theatricality when she'd proclaimed Mac dead. She'd seemed almost excited to tell her that Mac, *Our Sweet Mac*, had *passed*. She'd sounded almost Southern. And still holding her mother's small frame, her torso the exact circumference of a medium movie theater fountain soda, Stevie recalled that Moon had once played Maggie from *Cat on a Hot Tin Roof* for a community theater fundraiser somewhere in the Valley, and imagining the slow, listing fan, the wicker furniture in the cheap local production, Stevie was leached of all feeling, the door in her heart sliding shut. She'd stepped away from her mother, tears dry, convinced that she was watching Moon watch herself. That Moon was delivering lines.

Stevie had stared at her, excused herself, showered, then gone to bed without speaking to her again, sneaking out early for her shift. Stevie has always wanted to look more like her mother, but it scares her at times to think how much of Moon she contains.

She gets off the bus now at her stop to walk up the hill, the night air cool, legs pumping, taking slow steps, feeling the cars whoosh past so close the wake turbulence pushes against her soft body. She wants her mother now. She has questions. She also imagines getting picked off at the big blind bend by a speeding vehicle and flying into a ravine, her mother crying at the back-to-back funerals and how this might make everything easier.

She wants to know if he's left them a note, knowing that he hasn't—that he wouldn't—and how embarrassing it is that she even wants one. The only reports of Mac's death lead back to his social media, onto main, a gallery of smiling photos, from the set of his new show, the one with dragons already on its third season where he plays a mad king with daughters, the show where he'd met his new young wife who has written a brick of a caption about the preciousness of their short time together. There is nothing about Moon or Stevie, and this cuts straight to the wound of her confusion.

It was Mac who'd taught her to drive, who texted on her birthday, and who'd given her—mostly terrible—life advice. It's Mac who came to tell her Moon had wrecked her car and been involuntarily admitted for a seventy-two-hour hold. It's how Stevie had learned that her mother's emergency contact was still her former TV husband and not her daughter. She'd been surprised at the time but also relieved. It was the closest she'd felt to being part of a larger family even if it was just the three of them.

Stevie opens the white side gate to trudge down the lawn. She is just so tired. She passes the Big House under the picture window with her head down, not wanting to be summoned for some missing amenity by the tenant standing there. But there's something familiar about the figure, stood dead center, a flight up from the paved patio, seeming to be onstage while she is relegated to the orchestra pit. He's telling some story that calls for moving his hands in radiating motions around his head and that's when her heart hurls itself against her sternum as though banging down a door.

It's Adam Dano.

The great love of her life.

And also her brother.

Although not technically on either count.

Most significantly, he is Moon's son. The one Moon loves best. Her *sweet, precious boy.* Stevie quickens her step to the Pool House, to scurry and hide, but a flat, dulled thump rings out from behind, and when she turns, his large hand is flat against the glass. Wearing a weird pale outfit, bearded, looking like a bedraggled Protestant Jesus but definitely him, now waving. For a moment she stands there, unsmiling, unblinking, but then raises her hand. And in the next moment her mother is beside him, beckoning.

"Stevie, look!" says Moon with ta-da hands once Stevie's come inside, as though she's performed a magic trick.

"What is he doing here?" Stevie asks in a deadpan.

Moon's smile falters.

She'd expected to see Adam at the funeral but this makes no sense. Him in the Big House. It smells maddeningly delicious. Of onions dissolving in fat over time. Stevie hates being an improv partner in Moon's schemes but she's prodigiously good at it. And the prompts are all there. Moon in Mom Drag, a fitted high-necked maroon dress, severe but professionally feminine, like a stewardess, with the added prop of an apron tied at her neck, left open in the back so as not to wrinkle the *look*. The archetypes are heavy-handed. Mother: fatted calf; prodigal son. Stevie: shit disposition; stinking uniform.

"How're you liking Pee Wee's?" He nods with too much brightness at her purple polyester work polo, and Stevie knows instantly that they've been talking about her. She looks down on instinct and spots a crumbly bit of what could be dried avocado on her chest.

"It's a job," she says, deadening her gaze.

"At least someone around here's got one, right?" he quips from the other side of the kitchen island, forklifting a gigantic pile of meat from an elaborate charcuterie board into his mouth, then sliding across the terrazzo in his socked feet.

"Bring it in, Stephen," he says, going for a hug. The sudden contact almost winds her, she's so starved for comfort, tears immediately standing in her eyes. She feels the hard nudge of his chin on her head as he chews and she holds her breath, hoping he can't smell the stale fry-oil in her hair.

"Not really loving the beard there, Dano," she says, pulling away, but when he laughs, her insides warm, even as he throws his head back and she can see the food in his mouth. "It's giving prepper rather than professorial," she continues, hating that she's mugging for him, and when he laughs again, she adds, "Like, big-time Second Amendment energy."

Behind him, Moon opens the oven door to pierce the browned roast chicken with a meat thermometer and Stevie's sense of reality lurches. Moon hasn't cooked meaningfully in years; in fact, her mother cooking in the Big House, using the actual oven, is as uncanny as someone switching on the cardboard TV from an IKEA display to watch a game. Again, the pervasive sense is one of performance, so when Moon pulls out new white tapers and carries them to the adjoining dining room, where the table has been set, Stevie's jaw tightens. Mac has killed himself and now Stevie's being conscripted to playact as a family in the Big House, to welcome Adam as if he were home for the holidays.

Lighting the candles with an air of ceremony, Moon glances over, finally sensing Stevie's silent contempt, and shoots her a questioning look. A challenging look. Heat gathers in Stevie's eyes.

"What?" prompts Moon, and sensing Adam's attention on her now, Stevie shakes her head.

"Wash your hands," her mother says in a hard tone. And as much as she wants to call Moon out, to humiliate her in front of the audience of her fake son, she shuffles to the kitchen sink.

Her gaze travels across the lawn, down a slight hill, landing on the darkened outline of the Pool House. It looks different to her, the facade altered in some way but then her vision shifts. The Big House kitchen window becomes a mirror and behind her, as the water runs too hot, scalding her hands, the reflection of Adam slides toward Moon, catching the fridge door before it shuts, as Moon ducks under his arm, to return to the stove, and the smooth choreography reveals a physical familiarity, a synchronicity, a closeness that is as pleasing to watch as it is painful in its exclusion of her.

But when Adam twists off the top of a beer, Stevie shuts off the water and turns, her alarm instant and colossal.

"Is that beer?" she asks, drying her hands on herself, then turns to her mother. "You let him bring beer here?"

"Calm down," says Moon. "They must have been here from last time."

And the breeziness of this, as though one of their friends had just left them from a dinner, some chill, casual hang, and not some rich asshole living in their house, threatens to tip Stevie over the edge. She begs Moon silently to tell him everything, that she's a drunk, that they're broke, but Moon gazes back with innocent curiosity. Because the Moon Adam gets is TV Moon. The Moon who would never let him stay in a hotel. The Moon who will protect him from ever knowing about the sick, sad squalor of their real lives. And then it occurs to Stevie, heart crushed to powder, that not only does Adam get the best of Moon but Stevie will always get the worst.

"You know what?" Stevie says. "I already ate." She grabs her backpack, heart thundering, ignoring Adam's curious looks, stumbling down the stairs, face screwed, tears spilling as she strides toward the glass box. Once again retreating.

THE POOL HOUSE

[2019–PRESENT]

A later addition to Moon's property, the Pool House, hewn from steel and glass, was about the size of a two-car garage with a pitched polycarbonate roof that rattled spectacularly during thunderstorms. Brittle and hostile as an environment, it was Harlow's wire rhesus monkey mother experiment as shelter and designed mostly for sitting in performative reflection or as an enviable Zoom background. Conceptually, it was beautiful. Architectural. Reminiscent of a glass corporate award or I. M. Pei's pyramid were it dropped from a great height onto a lawn.

The austere structure gave first-time visitors an instant foreboding, as it would be with a boarded-up well or an overgrown maze on the grounds, there was just something about it that seemed too obvious a scene for a future crime.

It was ill-advised from the start. A total money pit. And none of the soaring metal joists were as weight bearing as initial calculus hoped, which meant none of the windows opened, even if this didn't preclude a creeping draft from stealing in, carrying a fine silt that coated lungs, irritated throats, and chilled bones. Not that it was particularly cool either. Without the pair of black damask shower curtains from Home Goods that Moon and Stevie hastily glue-gunned directly onto a hanging beam, inhabitants would roast like insects under the magnifying glass of the facade, against the southern exposure.

Which is to say no one had intended to stay there long term. And the Pool House with two adult women living inside was a particular diorama. In the same way that the Pool House upset the essential spirit of the grounds, evoking an alien landing beside the lemon tree and the hippie-dippy mossy grotto, Stevie and Moon upset any ambitions the Pool House may have had for itself. It seemed embarrassed and unhappy, the way animals were when you put outfits on them. And it exacted vengeance in small but devastating ways.

It was a sadistic aesthetic choice to have the furniture be see-through. The acrylic Louis XVI ghost chairs, Lucite Italian pedestals, and a Noguchi coffee table with a tempered glass base that didn't so much as feature an air bubble to warn unsuspecting shins. The artful objects existed as long-con assassination attempts should either of them trip, rushing headlong into panes of glass, shredding their bodies into ribbons, spattering all the priceless vintage furniture, that, bless, could at least be cleaned with a bit of Windex. As defense, mother and daughter parked bras, cups, socks, and towels on all the various levitating, otherwise invisible hazards, serving as those brightly colored warning stickers placed on glass sliding doors to alert birds, children, and drunk guests.

As a result, the Pool House that was intended to be ethereal, the crown jewel of the yard, mostly evokes a fish tank with a load of laundry tossed in that has been vigorously shaken. Partly, it's a parable about ambition. Without the cost of the Pool House, Moon and Stevie might have been able to live in the Big House at least a while longer. And to further salt the earth, the invisible box that has them trapped together is what's keeping them apart.

DAY THREE

STEVIE

Stevie doesn't know how many more trespasses against her self-esteem she can endure without becoming mutilated beyond redemption. At work, she is newly determined and pokes her head into Xan's office. Xan, her boss, is anywhere from twenty-five to forty-five, skinny, with a small high butt and hair the same flat wheat hue of her skin, and she's at her desk in her black manager's polo, finishing breakfast, sitting at her large, putty-colored computer that Stevie could swear is a decoy like those hardback books that are secretly a stash box for drugs.

Xan waves her in even as Stevie wants to recoil from the windowless cell that is breathtakingly filled with the sulfurous odor of egg being chewed audibly. Wetly. Stevie sits, the aromatic assault unbearable even as she forces her face to appear avid and confident.

"I've thought about it," she tells Xan, taking small sips of air through her mouth. "I want to do Yarmouth." She'd been hoping to be dispatched somewhere warm, Flagstaff or Johnson City, Texas, two locations where they need assistant managers, but she'd learned that Yarmouth will be ready first. Yarmouth sounds actively cold, like Norway, but Stevie needs to leave. Immediately.

Last night, she'd watched the Big House for hours, vibrating with spite, longing for her mother's chicken but eating the leftover burrito from staff meal in her Tupperware instead, the avocado browned. Stevie knows now what about the Pool House has changed. Moon had thoughtlessly torn down the blackout curtains, forcing Stevie to gaze up at them, mother and son. She imagined the two of them carving the bird, the candlelight casting shadows attractively on their skin as they chatted companionably. It had been almost one in the morning before the lights downstairs switched off. And the whole time as Stevie trawled the internal Pee Wee's job boards, she thought how she'd already be assistant manager if it weren't for Moon. She's been at Pee Wee's three years, a lifetime for the Fairfax flagship where most of the employees were hoping to be plucked by casting directors of various unscripted series, not elevated from a purple polo to a maroon one. But the thing about Fairfax was that it was the first of its kind, the way it was for the Forever 21 that had once been on Figueroa. You had to relocate to advance and Stevie couldn't leave Moon then. She'd have been leaving her for dead.

Moon was brittle. Frail. She was *talent*. Her mother was head of household yet Stevie was the *man*. Holding Moon's purse. Opening doors. Stevie's the one who deals with the tenants. Just as it's her duty to dispatch larger insects that wander inside or any animals that wind up dead in the pool. Stevie will never forget the time Moon accidentally set a dish towel on fire and covered her ears as the smoke alarm went off leaving Stevie alone to put out the small blaze.

It would be one thing if Moon were grateful, but she's oblivious. Stevie can just imagine Moon making herself out to be some long-suffering mother with a deadbeat, drop-out boomerang kid. Telling Adam how worried she is about college. About Stevie's future, never once disclosing her own role in it all. But it's over now. They both lose. Stevie can't do it anymore. She's done.

Xan opens a drawer and fishes around to pull out a tube of lotion that she uncaps. "I wouldn't go googling anything about Yarmouth," she says, and then begins to moisturize her arms up past her elbow in slow, circular motions in a surprisingly intimate ritual. "All you'll get is that it's the opioid capital of America, but it's not. It's just one of them. There's a ton. And if you go looking for something bad, nine times out of ten you'll find it."

"Yeah, that makes sense," says Stevie, casting around the black box, recalling how it was Xan's depressing converted office that had given her the idea to pop out the white ELFA shelving in the linen closet of the Pool House to fit a thin foam mattress on the floor.

At least in Yarmouth she'll have a bed again.

Xan kneads her lotioned forearms, commending Stevie's wisdom in diversifying her search since Johnson City might not ever come through, most of the Southwest patch has *gone robo*, become automated. "They always say whatever work you'd do for free is your dream job," says Xan, flapping her arms up and down slowly to dry them. "I dream of this job sometimes," she continues with a small eye roll, going on to say that, while it's definitely not her dream job, even in her dreams, she likes knowing what she's doing.

When Stevie first started out at Pee Wee's right out of high school, she'd decided to find it hilarious. It was performance art to get up at 4:45 a.m. on truck days, wearing gloves and still having to wash her hands so often that sheets of skin peeled off her fingers like dried Elmer's glue. She'd thought of it as preparing for a role, that she was in the montage stage of her life. To stay focused, she'd had to archive her group chats and mute her friends' socials, the lank-haired daughters of producers and directors who read vintage classic paperbacks, drank collagen smoothies, and exclusively attended the second weekend at Coachella. Most of them were at college on the East Coast, away from their families, some of them would be graduating soon, but that has nothing to do with Stevie anymore. She knows what Xan means about dreaming of the job. There's something monastic about knowing what to do. And when she yields to the quiet, balletic movements, the utter anonymity of this nothing role, she feels stupid in a good way. The way she imagines purebred dogs feel.

Once Xan excuses her, Stevie passes through the kitchen. The air is close, thick and warming. Dinner protein is on. And in a near stockpot, so big it's giving racist cannibalism jokes in old-timey cartoons, the bubbles tell her that the water is the requisite 208 degrees to blanch vegetables for five seconds to kill off surface bacteria. Stevie has made employee of the month not just for their location but the entire 149 Southern California Patch. She received a perfect score on the food handling safety protocol. Right now she makes just a dollar above California minimum wage, and while her biggest expense is car service because she doesn't drive, she tries to save everything else. She has just over nine thousand dollars saved in her bank account, and while she doesn't know if it's enough, she knows Moon moved to L.A. with much, much less. Besides, as an assistant manager full time, she'd make $20.56 an hour as well as tuition reimbursement if she went to night school. It would all unfold like clockwork. And then, when she's a general manager, she'll make a yearly salary that works out to actually less than $20.56 an hour but with benefits. Only two more rungs and she's in six figures. They even match retirement.

She washes her hands, checks the format, sees that she's stationed next to Freddie, and slides in beside her.

"You were in there a while," says Freddie, still stinking of sweet vape smoke. Her gigantic talons threaten to pierce through the fingers of her gloves as she sprinkles cheese over her tray.

The thing about Freddie is she doesn't treat the job seriously. She doesn't have to. The worst thing that's ever happened to her is that her parents moved from Westwood to La Cañada. So Stevie doesn't respond, scanning the ticket in front of her. She loves bowls. Bowls forgive all structural sins and moisture mishaps.

"She was grooming you, wasn't she?" whispers Freddie. Freddie says there's something about Xan that reeks of a lifetime of being overlooked, *kicked like a dog*, is how she puts it. And Stevie can never tell if Freddie is just describing Xan or pointing out their similarities in some diabolical girl-way of bullying.

"We should go out tonight," says Freddie, and Stevie turns her head in degrees, desperately not wanting to. Again, she imagines saying she can't, that she's sad because her fake dad is dead and her mother is in love with her TV brother, but then a customer walks in distracting them both and it's *The Regular*. "Hey *Jen*," he says to Stevie, and

Freddie laughs but covers it up with a fake cough that causes her customer to look up in alarm. "Calm down," says Freddie, "it's allergies."

Stevie nods at The Regular, emptying her head, keeping her face impassive even as she senses Freddie's interest. Freddie calls him *Double Protein* and knows nothing about the date Stevie once had with him. Meanwhile, *Jennifer* is Stevie's Starbucks name. As in, the name Stevie uses at Starbucks since they can't seem to reconcile *Stevie* with her face. Even the Asian baristas. So when The Regular asked for Stevie's name, she'd said Jen.

Stevie can never remember what he looks like unless he is standing right in front of her. He wears trousers that are too tight and too short in a way that seems bad but intentional. She doesn't remember his job, something in tech or marketing. But even now when he smiles, the signal for her to begin his order, she feels glad for his confidence in her capabilities.

His order is unchanging: bowl, rice, black beans, adobada chicken rather than asado, Christmas salsa (red and green), no cheese, no crema, jalapeños on the side. He comes in two to three times a week. Occasionally he comes in twice a day if he's getting dinner, which is when he gets Double Protein. For years Stevie fostered a crush on him, supported by the intricate scaffolding of fantasy, where her main preoccupation was populating his life with highly specific details, basically playing *Animal Crossing*, like how he'd have a Yamaha G1 Baby Grand, a telescope, hardwood floors, floor-to-ceiling bookcases that were built in, a dog he lied about being a rescue, and a white, blond wife who played tennis.

When he abruptly asked her out and waited an hour until she'd closed, she'd presumed they'd have sex. They went to an Ethiopian restaurant in his neighborhood that stayed open surprisingly late and featured red tablecloths. When he knew the proprietors is when she'd decided he wasn't going to murder her. Stevie had never been on a proper date before and imagined herself telling someone, possibly a lover in the future, and making jokes about it.

He talked about the finals for a sport with the presumption that she followed it, and then told her about special running shoes that mimicked the health benefits of running barefoot. She'd told him her real name but he kept calling her Jen anyway. She'd fantasized about fucking him in his car but instead he took her to his house. A bungalow in Mid-Wilshire that was just perfect and when he opened the door, she'd held her breath, trembling with anticipation for the life that she'd envisioned. But the house was empty. As if he'd been robbed. She was drunk by then, having bolted three glasses of wine at dinner. And the wholesale obliteration of her fantasy—no piano, no dining table, not even a proper couch—only a gigantic TV mounted on the wall—was so dramatic and uncalled for that she wanted to cry.

He'd gone to his room to change, explaining that he'd just moved, that he'd gotten a divorce, and when he returned in a gray T-shirt and sweats, he was so violently unhandsome that Stevie was stunned. He held out a circular contraption the size and shape of a toilet seat, a blown glass dragon that was nestled in a spray of flowers. *It's a bong*, he told her. And in that moment, she made the mistake of looking down past the dragon's green bead eyes, to his naked feet, at the bare pallor, the long digits of his toes, and been so repulsed that she had to claim sudden illness and leave. And only when her car arrived did she recognize the music he'd been playing as Maroon 5.

So now when The Regular comes in, Stevie doesn't think of the lonely TV. Or that he had a single, black leather bar stool at his kitchen counter. She looks only at how nice his teeth are. How they gleam with a subtle uniformity that she understands to be wealth, marveling at the wild swings of intimacy a person can experience with another. She had once stood in his house ready to fall in love with him and now she has been returned to the other side of the sneeze guard, put in her place, not even allowed to touch his food with her bare hands again. She sends his order down and The Regular proceeds along the line. When she leaves, he might wonder about her, remembering her only as Jen. And by then Stevie will have become someone else entirely.

KIDNAPPING

[SPRING 2013]

Whenever people came over, they would comment on the picture. In it, Stevie is eight. She's wearing neon purple leggings and a matching shirt and Moon is in a black halter-neck catsuit that ripples across the ribs of her taut, braless torso. They're smiling. Both doing Little Teapots, arms on jutted hips, mirroring each other. That the image is printed out, presented in an old-fashioned silver frame, one of the only photos in the house, seems significant. Conspicuous. The sort of souvenir the camera sweeps across wistfully to denote that circumstances have changed.

It's from when I foiled a kidnapping, says Moon to whoever zeroes in on the bait. She refers to it as a conversation piece. To Stevie the photo signals a significant demarcation in her understanding of her mother. Of Moon's unfailing need for attention and her selective memory. It had been taken at the Getty Center because admission was free and it was Moon who'd approached the man. Tapped him on the shoulder with her phone because he had a camera slung around his neck and asked him to take their picture. She leaves out this part. That she had talked to him first and that he was exactly her type. Medium-build with dark hair and dark eyes that seemed to be thinking something totally different from what his mouth was saying.

Stevie was reading Judy Blume's *Forever* that day, and Moon had walked off in search of better flowers for her selfies, the azaleas growing in concentric circles, or the six kinds of roses, but when Stevie looked up she was gone. Properly lost amongst the throng of tourists wearing cotton separates and Stevie felt a stab of anger at how often she was looking for her mom and not the other way around.

That's when she saw him again. The man. He'd told her she looked lost and this rankled her. They walked toward the museum, the man insisting he was headed that way anyway when her mother pushed past him from behind. Moon's hot hand clamped around Stevie's arm, yanking so hard they both lurched forward, legs tangling.

Get away from her! Moon screamed, calling him a pervert, screaming *Help!* and then *Fire!* to onlookers who could easily see it was neither. Her mother's breath was sour and hot, yeasty, as the taste of metal exploded in Stevie's mouth when she bit her tongue as the ground leapt up to meet her. The man backed away, alarmed, palms exposed, no fault, and Stevie ignored the crowd, especially the boy who'd screamed, *World Star!* with his phone raised. She helped her mother up, her mother who'd gone slack by then, her pancake makeup beading with sebum, beginning to slide. Moon had tuckered herself out, the tang of her mixing with the roses and gasoline scent of her perfume, and even as Stevie wondered how and when she'd gotten so wasted, she'd understood that inside her mother was a howling black hole. The pull was relentless. It would never stop. Her mother hadn't saved her from a kidnapping. It was life with Moon that was the hostage situation.

DAY FOUR

ADAM

He sails through the produce section gathering lemons, limes, ginger, blueberries, kale, peppers, the fake rain misting the back of his hand as he arranges everything into his cart. There's no doubt in his mind that Moon's household is in crisis. Nothing is as he'd remembered it. There's no food, no books, and she's changed the artwork to feel starkly impersonal and gaudy. It is a subtle alteration, an uncanny wrongness, like how the contents of the cabinets can't be tied to the rhythms of a healthy family, mostly a surfeit of themed serving ware. It could just be an Ozempic kitchen with its general indifference to sustenance. She hasn't cooked since that first dinner and even then mostly pushed her meal around her plate, clearly upset about Stevie. But it's the neglect that troubles him. The multiple boxes of opened pasta, an expired can of hominy, two sacks of flour, again, all opened, and a half-plundered holiday gift basket with various packages of rancid nuts and oxidized chocolates. Even the fridge is puzzlingly configurated, no milk or coffee, and five bottles of various ketchups all going at once.

And then there's Stevie. He wants to be tactful, but there'd been an unmistakable acetic, moldy dishrag scent to her when they'd hugged, and he'd been stunned and concerned, feeling as though it spoke to some larger sign of neglect that he can't help but at least partially blame Moon for. He can't believe she'd let Stevie live in the pool house.

He adds another tray of pasture-raised eggs into the cart, as well as ginger shots, fresh juice, chia seeds. They both need to be fed. They need fat, good fat, and as he turns the corner wondering what else he can fill their bodies with to restore them, he thinks of how drastically Stevie has physically changed. As recently as a few years ago when they were closer, he might have made fun of her because his fake little sister has filled out almost to the point of satire. But the way she keeps tugging at her shirt, rearranging and adjusting for her expanded chest, makes his heart well with fondness and compassion.

Moon too is different. Dimmed. She smells the same, of skin and flowers and this other slightly bitter, caustic undertone that he equates with medicine. But the brittleness of her dyed hair, the fine tributaries of lines at her eyes are new. Mac had often joked about her eyes, *Manson Lamps,* he'd called them, but the electricity of her gaze has been altered. She isn't drinking, a revelatory development that would have been ridiculed had it happened during the show, but now he doesn't even want to ask. They'd talked about the funeral, who they thought would attend, and he'd confided that he hadn't gone to Mac's wedding. *I saw*, she'd told him, cradling a mug of tea, admitting she'd only seen because she'd searched through all the photos.

Why didn't you? she'd wanted to know.

He'd shrugged. A two-day affair with over three hundred guests for Mac's fourth wedding had simply been too overwhelming at the time.

Honestly, I thought there'd be another one.

She'd smiled sadly. *I can't believe he's going to be dead at his own funeral. God he'd hate that so much.*

When they'd retired to bed, he'd had the wholesome sense that he was in the country or on family vacation. And when he went downstairs later, to check the locks a second time, he'd glanced across the lawn at the pool house, overtaken by the pleasant thought that he would look after them both. That he would fix this.

Crossing the parking lot with his shopping now, he stops. His stomach creaks ominously. He exhales with purpose, clenching, sweating viciously, and proceeds with care, scanning the sun-bleached parking lot, allowing a car to turn ahead of him before continuing, the rumbling wheels of the shopping cart emphasizing the querulous vibrations in his gut. He scratches his itchy face with the back of a clammy hand just as his phone flashes.

His mother's timing is flawless.

He can't possibly speak to her now.

And as another zipline of pain shoots across his midsection, he pulls his hat down, trying to physically hide from her.

He knows he's doing it again, not showing up and not giving an explanation. He'd done it to Mac, but the way he sees it, staying in L.A. now for the funeral is penance. And funerals outrank weddings, which outrank birthdays. He can't suffer the same catered affair at his parents' Upper West Side home with the usual batch of his mother's friends, many of them genuinely glamorous or interesting, some in the industry. The idea of making small talk on the state of his career with Donna Karan and some lesser real estate Kushner is unbearable to him. As is the polite conversation with whichever upwardly mobile young woman his mother would attempt to set him up with. He genuinely can't expend the serotonin.

He could text Katherine but this would only enrage her and in turn terrorize the help. He pictures his clipboard-wielding mother and thinks how he'd be in the laundry room if he were there, window cracked open, smoking weed furtively just to get through the night. He will call her after the services.

He gets in the car, thinking how much his mother had disliked Mac. She'll be annoyed once she hears about his passing from someone else, mostly because she'll have wanted to send flowers, even for that *odious vulgarian*. Katherine is nothing if not decorous especially for those she finds morally irredeemable.

Adam lays his forehead down on the hot steering wheel between his hands. He can't believe that Mac is dead and that he is going to his funeral and afterward he will have to go to New York and probably attend some benefit with his mother to make up for his absence at her birthday. He is in his thirties and this is his chief concern. This and not soiling himself.

By the time he pulls into Moon's curved driveway, to the front door overgrown with shrieking pink dahlias, he is almost blacked out from relief.

He runs up the stairs to the side door of the kitchen, two at a time, his body taut. He retires to the bathroom, strips completely naked the way he'd done as a child, and, in a cold sweat, empties himself noisily on the commode and wonders with utter dejection if this is who he'll be forever. Two weeks ago, a Chinese herbalist in Sham Shui Po prescribed him a tonic for blood circulation. Adam had shown him his tongue only to be informed that he was depleting his essence from an overabundance of sex. It was his constant fucking that was causing him to age prematurely. He was told to expect shutdowns throughout his major organs. Skin, stomach, cock. The guy had been Mac's guy and Mac had laughed at the diagnosis, pounding a hammy paw on his shoulder, and even now Adam doesn't know if everyone was just fucking with him.

He doesn't know why Mac had shown up at his door. And he doesn't know what happened between then and the moment on the bridge, only that the desire to end a life can arrive suddenly. He'd always thought Mac would live to a hundred. He'd been rich enough to be a hypochondriac, the way anyone with enough self-importance, privilege, and Catholic guilt expected to be smote. He'd practically crinkled from the supplements, herbs, and roots that were apportioned in fat, knobby paper packets that he kept in his pockets. And he'd been an early investor to med-tech start-ups and anti-aging companies. He'd had his genome sequenced, bloodwork every month, quarterly biomarker checks, the thick silver ring on his finger telling him when to sleep, drink, walk, how anxious to feel at any given moment. As far as Adam knew, there were no incipient malignancies, dysplasia, no pathogen or vector unanticipated by Mac's vigilance. Any sickness, he'd been determined to detect in its infancy. Every life-saving health intervention he wanted.

Crack a rib, crack them all, get his heartbeat back at all costs. Just save his life. Mac was suspicious of teaching hospitals, wasn't an organ donor, but now he was dead.

Sitting on the toilet at Moon's house, faint from exertion, he feels haunted. Everything about Mac depresses him. Like some Christmas Ghost of the Future. He is desperate to avoid his fate. The discreet hair transplant and *daddy do-over*, the lipo, tummy tuck, and gynecomastia surgery, for his *bitch tits*. He'll never forget the first dinner at Mac's with Corinna and a few of her friends. All perfectly nice, holding fishbowl-sized wineglasses, smoking weed. And how at one point, Corinna had tipped her face up to kiss Mac with an air of determination as though answering to a dare set forth by her friends, one of whom Adam had once matched with on a dating app.

He will have to take his last beta blocker to get through this funeral. But Moon needs him. So does Stevie, he senses. Then to New York. A town overrun with bodies. Just like Hong Kong. New York's twin flame in rhythm, urgency, congestion, the pedestrian bottlenecks in Causeway Bay, like darting shoals of fish, the crush in some ways worse than New York, truly suffocating.

What he craves is clean, fresh air. Summer camp. Trees. He longs for the childish excitement of scaring yourself in the pitch-black and running to the safety of the light. What he wants is Fisheries. Not The Fisheries but Fisheries, the 450-acre wooded property upstate that belongs to his mother's family, the Fishers. With a reservoir and a smallish lake, it is memorialized in prose and immortalized in lyrics and has been run as an artist colony for over a hundred years.

He recalls the smell of deciduous trees, the clean, vast space. The sharp cold air. The mist. How when he was a boy he'd keep the beam of his flashlight close to his feet, on the path, too terrified to scan out and catch the pinpricks of yellow eyes in the fields beside him, the deer, the chipmunks, whatever animal made the screaming sound of babies that would make him break into a sprint, breathless and thrilled when he reached the cottage where his grandparents lived.

Open-air therapy. Forest bathing. Verdant abundance and the calm industry of a community dedicated to the service of artists. The picnic baskets assembled and left outside each studio door so as not to disrupt creation with the minor concern of lunch. It has been over ten years since he's visited despite its few hours' distance from Brooklyn. It's where he'd last read Thomas Mann's *The Magic Mountain*, right after his superhero movie tanked, and it's only there that he can believe he might be happier doing something other than acting.

He washes his hands, drying them on the stiff decorative towel in the downstairs bathroom, struck again by how certain L.A. homes never feel properly lived in. He wants to bring Moon and Stevie to Fisheries. They will play card games in the 150-year old cottage, read, take thick, sultry naps by the fire, and go for long, rambling walks. A reprieve from worldly concerns, it's what they could all use.

In the kitchen, he returns to the abandoned groceries, putting perishables in the fridge and washing the produce. He eats a blueberry, imagining all the antioxidants detonating in his system, replenishing him. He drinks activated charcoal water. He grills corn and steak, slicing bread and massaging kale with garlic, salt, pepper, and olive oil until it gleams invitingly. He adds lemon juice and chunks of parmesan. Moon doesn't emerge so he makes a plate for Stevie. The sun drills down on him as he crosses the damp lawn. He has a sense of trespass, that Moon wouldn't want him to go and that Stevie wouldn't welcome him, but he has to start somewhere.

But then he sees it. Christ, he hates the glass house on sight. The unwholesome cottage that is nothing like the ones on his family estate. It's cold and brittle. Still. Hostile. He walks toward it, a long, niggling crawling on his skin, the heebie-jeebies and the alien itch of his beard. He's close now. He can see clear through to the other end of it and the disarray shocks him, how it resembles a FEMA disaster site, trash bags pushed to the perimeter, clothes strewn all around. He'd expected girlish California decor, a pale fuzzy armchair, a lambskin area rug, but the extent of the chaos testifies to a perversion or pathology, a private family secret, like hoarding or the illegal breeding of wild animals in a studio apartment. It reminds him of a photo he saw once, in a gallery show in Chelsea, a portrait of a young girl chained by her neck to a tree in a yard surrounded by a fence.

He is not meant to know about this. This horrible box. This meager shelter. He looks behind him, toward the path and at the upstairs windows of the house, checking for Moon, but her shades are drawn. He attempts the pool house door, entering the code for the side gate, Stevie and Moon's shared birthday, and the bolt unlatches, the glass door popping open. He steps inside, shocked by the airless heat, the gust of fruit flies that swarm him. He turns toward the blinking microwave clock, zero:zero, the provisional kitchen, two burners, a miniature fridge, a single mug washed and upturned, and imagining Stevie living like this, washing the solitary mug, makes him want to weep.

He sets the plate down on the counter and turns toward the striped love seat overloaded with clothes. On the clear coffee table in front of it, under a layer of debris, he spots a blue lace bra twisted on top of a bright glint of metal. He picks up the picture frame to see Moon and Stevie laughing, the image as indelible to him as a famous movie poster, the way they don't face the camera but each other, once a fixture in Moon's trailer. But now, standing in the squalid room, he can't reconcile the image with the women they've become.

Beyond the sofa, he catches sight of the sad, small bathroom, the toilet seat so close to the basin of the sink, the shower an upright coffin, and beside it, the door ajar, he sees the closet, more clothes on the floor, but then he stills. He pushes the door wider, heart racing, recognizing the pillow on the floor, the floral pattern that exactly matches the ones in his room along with crumpled bedsheets atop a lamentable mattress, no larger than a yoga mat, and he understands that what he's looking at is a closet transformed into a bedroom.

He glances up at the ceiling, the hazardous clear roof, the tree branches hanging overhead, and his eyes adjust to see that the roof is covered by a yellow-green muck that is absolutely everywhere, and scanning the glass all around now, he learns that the invisible house is filthy, as though sprayed in brownish scum, festooned with large dirty swipes all over, and by the door, a clear, perfect handprint.

He swats at his arm, the black crush of fruit fly making him shudder, and he grabs the plate. She can't know what he's seen. He lets himself out and runs back.

WHEN MOON MET MAC

[2002]

Moon first met Mac at some CAA party in the hills. He'd been garrulous and red-faced, kissing her hand and introducing himself by his failed marriages. Moon had been twenty-four; Mac, almost forty. She'd called him Hank, after Henry Tudor, on account of his red hair and the wives. Plural. Though he'd joked how it was more of an Anne of Cleves situation than Anne Boleyn, since a discreet beheading cost slightly more than alimony.

Moon hadn't known anyone at that party. She'd worn a sheer silk Monah Li dress in black, a rarity for the ethereal designer, that Moon had intended to return. The cardboard hangtags were scratchy and dampening against her back. And she had to keep her hair in a certain position to keep them covered, but there was free food—raw bars, carving stations, champagne galore—and she'd been enthralled by the louche spectacle of it. It had all the trappings of an oligarch's wedding. This was a time before the mergers, when there were multiple competing networks, when theaters still made money. It had been a halcyon era. People weren't yet cancellable. IP wasn't yet the dominant genre of film. And *AI* was a movie with that kid from *Jerry Maguire*. She'd been invited by a mailroom clerk, a fan of her only film at the time, *The Hermitage Volumes.*

The art house movie was being shown on a loop in the backroom at Melt Comics and quickly gained a cultish dedication among Moritsugu, Lynch, and Araki fans, who, upon seeing Moon naked on screen, inevitably tried to shoot their shot.

She'd broken up with her boyfriend at the time, the director of *The Volumes,* and been functionally homeless, but at first she hadn't been attracted to Mac. There was something about him that too closely resembled the good ol' boys she'd left behind. His hair, the porcine flush, the sweating and the suits. But he did have size. Presence. Later she'd find out he'd been huge in the U.K. as a serious thespian. A real BAFTA-cadging, West End type who also happened to have a law degree from Kings College. This intimidated her. She had no formal training, she'd barely graduated from a public high school that was most famous for their 4-H program and their prize-winning heifers. But he wasn't Southern, rather Scottish. It was only recently that he'd become renowned for playing a mob boss in the remake of a heist film from the '70s.

By the time Moon saw him again, Stevie was one. Her other movies had come out. She'd made it to the Oscars once, to the real thing, not just the parties. And the Met Ball. She'd done the cover of *Vanity Fair*, the Young Hollywood issue with the gatefold, and made it onto page one. She had a manager, an agent, a lawyer, and a mysterious pregnancy that had created a maelstrom of speculation as to the identity of the father, but then, as everyone had warned, work got quiet. She'd been at Musso & Frank to be introduced to another actor who bore an unsettling resemblance to her when she saw Mac in the horseshoe booth right next to theirs on the dining room side. He'd been with another man, older. And Moon had been with Tali, her manager, this other actor, and Stevie in a Bjorn, despite several attempts by the staff to seat them on the grill side with the families.

She'd draped a napkin on Stevie so she wouldn't drip blue cheese dressing onto her head. At least that's what she'd told herself. But when she saw Mac, she'd briefly considered leaving with her baby's face covered, as though this would somehow disguise her too.

She'd eaten quickly and was outside, fumbling for the valet ticket that had fallen somewhere within the caverns of the Stephen Sprouse Louis Neverfull masquerading as a diaper bag, when Mac approached and said hello. Moon glanced up, flustered but never betraying it, handing Stevie over to him so she could root more thoroughly in her purse, discreetly wiping her damp brow with the burp cloth in her bag. Mac took it in stride, wordlessly accepting her baby without fuss or hesitation, walking her around in small circles, and later Moon would be surprised to learn that he had no children despite all those wives and desperately wanting them. When Moon's car emerged, he'd taken her keys from the valet, tipped him two hundred dollars, left his own car, and driven Moon and Stevie back to her apartment share in K-Town, where he stayed for two days, buying hundreds of dollars in groceries before he left.

That night, when they slept together, it had been slow and imploring. It was Moon's first time since giving birth, still somewhat incontinent, nipples weeping, C-section scar tender and puffy. Nothing like their final time, the joyless pneumatic pumping, the two of them unable to look at each other. He'd been good to her and was engaged again by then, which made things easier. Straightforward. He would see them infrequently but was willing to change diapers, do feedings, and get up on the rare occasions he stayed over.

Four years into it, he called with his producers on the line. He was ready to make her an offer.

DAY SIX

MOON

MAC'S FUNERAL

Moon can tell from as far back as the Yoshinoya on Santa Monica Boulevard that the funeral will be a zoo. They're in the middle of a long, unbroken procession of gleaming electric SUVs with Dano behind the wheel. His car, a ridiculous white ovule of an electric sedan, a real yeast infection suppository-looking thing, had been delivered earlier that morning via flatbed truck.

When Stevie clears her throat, Moon casts a sidelong glance at her. It's been days of silence. Stevie had even refused to get in front with Dano, making a chauffeur of him as she sits with Moon in the back. Her hair is pulled into a half pony, baby hairs wisping becomingly at her temples. She's pale, with shadows under her eyes, but it gives the touching effect that she is worn out from the efforts of growing, she is so tender, coltish, right on the cusp of ripeness. She's worn the vintage dress that Moon set out for her. The dress Moon had worn when she met Mac. A dress she'd failed to return when he noticed the tags and she'd been too flustered to tell him the truth. It's kept well. Black, bias-cut, with a fluttery hem that fits Stevie beautifully. And it's incomprehensible that Stevie is old enough to wear a dress that Moon had worn around her age and that they are on the way to Mac's funeral.

She looks down at her knees, then at Stevie's. She shifts, her left fingers numb. She's been riding with her clawed hand wedged beneath her seat belt to rescue the delicate silk of her dress from wrinkling, but with her right hand she impulsively reaches to cover Stevie's. And when her daughter doesn't pull away, a lump forms in Moon's throat.

Still, there is a small, sour worry in her heart. She doesn't want anyone asking what Stevie's been doing these past years. And she doesn't want Stevie answering honestly.

She turns to Stevie, smiling as pleasantly as she can. "Thanks for taking the day off," she says, and Stevie withdraws her hand to tug at her own dress.

"I didn't take the day off for you," she says.

Moon looks up, catching Dano's eyes in the rearview, a gesture Stevie also spots, crossing her arms at her chest to sigh and look out her window.

"Are we even invited to this thing?" Stevie asks.

"Of course we are," Moon answers quickly, sounding defensive to her own ears, then reaches out to smooth some bunching at Stevie's shoulder. "There's no guest list. It's a funeral."

Stevie shifts away. "Yeah, but are we wanted there?"

Moon stares at her daughter's quarter profile, saying nothing, heart thundering. The slubby, fat wrinkles of the white tee that Stevie's worn for modesty under the dress breaks up the lines. It's all wrong. It invites more attention to her large breasts than diverts it, the white cotton straining beneath the bodice. Moon reaches out again, this time with both hands so the armscye lies flat. "This should have been a bodysuit," Moon tells her of the shirt, wishing Stevie would stop ruining things she knows nothing about.

Finally, Dano turns the car in to the black wrought-iron gates of Hollywood Forever to ease toward the valet station. The car stops and Moon's door is flung open, a gust of heat engulfing her as she swivels her hips to set one platform-heeled shoe on the ground. The valet offers a beefy forearm to hoist her out without upsetting the temperamental fabric of her dress and she is flustered by the sudden closeness of the man, his warmth, the whorls of arm hair, the sun-baked clean smell of his skin, neck, shorn scalp, and finally, the Pachuco crosses tattooed on his hands. When he releases her to Dano, he bows slightly as he steps away, making a quick, wry sign of the cross as he takes in her dress, a runway Galliano from '92, black, slippery silk, with a high priest's collar and a train, slashed in places at her thighs, her hips, and her ribs. On her feet, Alexander McQueen armadillos in python that she cannot walk in without help. The purse is the only thing she'd had to buy, a small hard black clutch she'd looted her checking account for that she assures herself she will resell, vintage McQueen, among the first minaudières, with a skull at the closure, jewels as eyes.

Over the past handful of years, Moon has had to liquidate her investments, then her retirement. Each month the margin narrows, but she just about makes her mortgage. She's not proud that she rents her house out, but it says something about her character that she is willing to make sacrifices. She's nothing if not hardy. She's never relied on parents, or a man; she has her kid and herself and she makes it work. She will not be made to feel shame for her choices even if it means selling some jewelry, a watch, and a cluster of status purses, no matter how surly and ungrateful her adult child is about any of it.

Most of her clothing she has tried to keep together. She wants it as a collection. As an archive. As part of her legacy. Moon had left Texas with nothing. Her mother, Sunny, had burned it all—clothes, books, and CDs—incinerated at a church gathering, a radical act of parochial zeal that enraged and frightened Moon enough to leave. None of her pieces had been expensive but they were lovingly collected, pristinely maintained, and mostly one-of-a-kind vintage, tailored to fit her exactly. But now in a deep closet off-set from the upstairs lounge, with a lock and an additional bolt, away from the renters, in PEVA garment bags sprayed in pyrethrin to repel moths, she keeps her collection chronologically organized—all the former versions of herself, everything she's worn for red carpets, interviews, shoots, and productions, from designers, many of them bought by Mac who'd never buy her jewelry or furs but whose own clotheshorse tendencies migrated to the occasional piece of women's couture at auction or else straight from the runway.

He loved to dress her in canny little suits, wasp-waisted Mugler, Ghesquière shoulders, Stella McCartney satin bustiers, tiny and slightly tarted up, the clothes of a business-minded brothel madame ready to transition from day to night as was the trend of the time. He'd been partial to intricate, fussy, sculptural Philip Treacy hats, which were not at all Moon's style, given her massive Korean head, but she loved them for the craftsmanship. And whenever she removes the lid from a hat box with all the acid-free tissue inside to lift out a polychrome fascinator of shimmering butterflies, never worn, she recalls how happy they'd made him.

He'd never cared for grunge, never understood Marc Jacobs. Anna Sui. Todd Oldham. He'd loved Mr. Armani, and later would pretend he'd always loved Prada when this absolutely had not been the case during the designer's more militaristic utilitarian years that he referred to as *mannish*. He openly disliked the flashy Italians Moon favored—Versace, Cavalli, Moschino, Dolce & Gabbana—the outré designers, but they could always agree on McQueen, Westwood, and most of all, Galliano.

Moon hopes one day her collection will increase in cultural value once her own stock rises, and she often imagines these moments, casually rewearing a highly photographed dress at the exact perfect occasion so when they make the comp of past and present, it will be seen as significant. Minimally it will be noticed on someone's Substack or a particularly in-depth podcast by staggeringly fashionable men. Possibly *Las Culturistas*. She can also imagine herself auctioning off an infamous look for charity. She still has the naked Alaïa dress, for example. And when she can't fall asleep, this is what she thinks about behind her eyes, switching out details at night in bed.

This is exactly such a moment. Mac's funeral. She has never worn the Galliano publicly. She is as nervous as she would be on the first day of a big job. And she knows exactly what part to play.

The grounds are hysterically green. A testament to a lawn watering schedule that can't be legal, and Moon notices that the valet wears a kilt in the Maclean family tartan. That they all do. Everyone on staff. The iPad-wielding event team, the photographers, even a few family members that Moon vaguely recognizes, and this gives them an instant servile quality or a sycophantic air, as though Mac will smile down and remember them in his will. She also notices a step-and-repeat to their left that she finds distasteful even as she reflexively considers which outlets would have thought to send press, whether they are industry-facing or editorial, and the tension in her shoulders migrates to the base of her skull.

The scene is operatic. Blank eyes glint below tulle mourning veils and arrowing feathers. Everyone is dressed for exactly the opposite time of day, exuding the deranged chaos of red carpet events. Attempts by ushers to herd them into formation are brushed off, everyone chatting in stubborn clumps. She puts on her sunglasses and watches Dano and Stevie do the same. She is glad Dano shaved off the ridiculous beard before she'd had to tell him to. But mostly she wants a propranolol. Or a Cymbalta. Even a Wellbutrin. Her organs shift beneath the tourniquet of her foundation garments. She has lost feeling from mid-rib to the tops of her knees and her sensorium redirects its efforts to her feet that have become swollen and hot. It is the kind of turgid, all-encompassing heat that pairs gloriously with Klonopin. Indica. It is weather that invites doubling down and going hard on brown liquors in the thick of the afternoon. Armagnac at 2 p.m. She is almost high on her own disbelief to be sober in this moment. She feels faint, with a vertiginous wooziness that makes her feel not quite real. She hasn't eaten in days, but when a BFA photographer gestures for Moon's attention, she regrets nothing.

She releases Dano's arm to call Stevie to her left. She urges Stevie slightly behind, at an angle that flatters her daughter's broad shoulders, and pulls Dano to her right and fore because this is his better side. As she extends a leg, angling her chin, altering her smile as she sways back and forth on her feet to lend a spontaneous sense of movement to each captured image, she thinks about the call with Tali, the manager who'd been on the brink of quitting Moon but will now stay on, at least for the upticked interest and a possible reinvention.

Moon has been sleepless with adrenaline, rehearsing this moment. All three of them in dark clothes, Stevie's shirt actually tying things together, Moon sees now, Dano's suit with a starched white Nehru collared shirt mimicking the collar of her own.

And when the photographer reaches for a second camera in his harness for more images, asking Stevie to step out of frame, for just the actors, Moon spots Mac's second wife, a woman with whom she's exchanged choice words on the street outside of Kitson and again in the crowded locker area of the Beverly Hills SoulCycle some twelve years ago.

"Mac was like a father to her," she tells the photographer, tugging Stevie closer. "We're family." And even as Stevie stiffens, attempting to pull away, Moon's hand is a vise grip. It is vital that they all see it. All the wives. Their friends. Today Moon is the matriarch of the family that matters. The one memorialized from TV.

The spindly shaggy-topped palm trees pierce a cloudless sky overhead and within a many-headed undulating menagerie of dark clothes, she spots Dano's agent, a celebrity chef, and various executives and actors. They all know of her personal relationship with Mac, even across the wives, but only some of them know that she wasn't solely his muse, that she was his consigliere, his most trusted advisor, that it was she who'd bullied him into returning to the stage for Bryden's final mounting of *Uncle Vanya*, a role for which he'd won his only Olivier. And it was Moon who had told him that regardless of the money, he would hate himself if he did the show with the dragons. What she just hadn't known was that he would meet his fourth wife there. Or that it would all end here.

And when an explosion of caterwauling bagpipes breaks out, she is startled by the force of what she can only describe as acute self-loathing, a wadded mass of shame and guilt that pushes its way through her. He'd called her over and over. Left messages she'd deleted unheard before eventually blocking him. She'd been furious, not that he'd married the girl, but at his credulousness, that he'd believed she could change him, that she would save him. She gulps for air, helpless, as she clutches Stevie's arm. Stevie gives her a questioning look, her white face awash with concern, but Moon squeezes tighter, telling her to keep going.

The other guests are divvied into golf carts to make their ways to the lower lawn but Moon walks, weeping openly, holding on to Dano and Stevie on each side. She watches her feet with a curious sense of remove, the incomprehensible physics of the lobster-clawed instep of each shoe resembling mallets, and she has the sense that she is playing a large complicated instrument rather than walking, until they find themselves at the reflecting pool, chairs arranged on either side in rows.

That's when Moon smells her. Jasmine so powerful she can taste it. Danica Williams-Jones captures her in a floral embrace, gathering one of her hands into both of hers, smashing Moon's knuckles with cocktail rings. "Oh, sweet girl," she says, wiping at Moon's wet face with a wadded Kleenex, then turning to Stevie to cup her cheek. "You poor, poor dears," Dani says, giving them a look to suggest that in Mac's death Moon and Stevie have been afflicted with a terrible wasting disease. Dani played Mac's mother on the show despite being only six years older than him in life, and despite her antagonistic role as Moon's mother-in-law, Moon is happy to see her now. It's been years, at least five by a quick count.

Dani is the crypt-keeper thin of the very wealthy and her dark bouclé designer suit rises off her shoulders as she moves, like the carapace of a beetle, singling out the scrawniness of her neck, and Moon can't help but admire this hardscrabble attempt to evade death by simply being too thin to detect. Her hair is teased high in a fine burnished froth, like copper filaments or orange cotton candy, and Moon can see the gleaming contour of her skull as the sun shines through, and her handsome face, in a similar terra-cotta hue, appears to have been fired in a kiln then dusted with lanugo, the protective peach fuzz that marks the body's attempts to warm itself from a lifetime of caloric restriction.

"I can't believe he did this to you," says Dani, shaking her head. She draws Moon into another embrace, then pulls her away to get a good look at her. She rummages in her gold-tone Chanel 19 for another tissue with one hand, clutching Moon's shoulder with anorexic grip strength. "He should have married you," she says, voicing what Moon has longed to hear but stuns her now. "It's all anyone talked about at the wedding," she says, a thick vein rising in her forehead. "He should have married you and left you everything."

Moon is struck dumb. She hasn't allowed herself to dwell on this. The troubles she could have avoided if she'd kept him in her life. What Stevie would have stood to gain in this moment. But before she can respond, Dani shakes her head, face contorting as mass quantities of fluid pour out of her eyes. "He must have been in so much pain," she wails, and there is something so incongruous about the sudden volume of wet exiting the woman's desiccated body that Moon is powerless against hugging Dani again with genuine compassion, the old woman's torso as brittle and porous as a scarecrow.

And then, face mottled and damp, Dani turns to Stevie and in a higher, breathier register says, "You'll have to look after your mother now. She's all alone."

When Stevie doesn't respond, Dani gives her an assessing look. "Oh, but you must be off at school. Where did you wind up?"

"NYU," says Stevie quickly, and the half lie pains Moon despite the reward of the changed subject and Dani's altered demeanor. The other woman brightens, swiping her Kleenex across her nose as she enumerates all her favorite places in New York (Met Breuer, Barney Greengrass, Lincoln Center) and everything Stevie would do best to avoid (anything below the park).

But then, an eruption of chittering machinery, cameras thrust upward, signaling the arrival of someone significant. Kilt-wearing headsetted ushers swarm the commotion, eyes gleaming and brazen, and Moon finds herself suddenly in a collision path with security, expecting to be body checked, shoved out of the way, but then she sees him. Flanked by broad torsos in dark suits, a man with blond hair, face imbued with the pedigreed oatmealish slack of an insulated genealogy that could have used a few invasions. His hair is thinner in real life despite the considerable resources available to him and he keeps his head down, his downy pate as vulnerable as a newborn's, seeming to hurry as though late for a flight, as though there existed a plane in the world that wouldn't wait for him.

Stevie tightens her grip on Moon's forearm, eyes wide. He is a minor royal, but the only one they have in L.A., and Moon can't help but be dazzled by what a considerable show of posthumous pull it is that Mac has persuaded him to come to pay his respects. She spins to locate Dano but instead locks eyes with Corinna, Mac's new wife, who Moon has never met, but who she has studied in social media posts. Her expression is unguarded, a look of pure wonder. At all of twenty-five, her youth is an assault. The way the light hits, gilding her silhouette, caressing her taut erect frame, pale hair and skin transmuting with the cream of her dress, an interesting, canny choice of palette, Mac's widow is overwhelming in her tragic splendor.

Moon hates her in that moment with an intensity that shocks her, assailed by the promise of her. All that future. Pale, stunning, tall, with a guileless unimaginative face. She can picture the rest of Corinna's career with vivid clarity, a few small, humorless supporting roles in faultless ensembles that capitalize on her breathless, unmarred youth, then possibly an addict, a transformation into something monstrous or gritty with full nudity for a worthy script by an auteur, possibly; preferably foreign.

Corinna is encircled by a retinue of over-fillered skeleton friends and one of them, upon seeing Moon, scowls and pulls Corinna away as the crowd shifts to reveal the Royal, who looks up and locks eyes with Moon as recognition alights in his limpid gaze. He stops. Smiles. For a moment Moon is transported. Levitating above herself, no longer hot or uncomfortable, beyond hunger, forgetting even Corinna, and she senses rather than sees the press of his hand as she fights to keep her eyes open against the explosion of flashes. The crowd nudges against her back and she hears him say, "I'm sorry for your loss," in his soft accent, and she tilts her head toward him. "Thank you for coming," she says, miraculously remembering to open herself up, presenting them both to the audience of the world, as a final torrent of light detonates around her.

When it's over, she swings around to see who's seen and she catches Dano with a dark-haired woman in high, high heels and a shrewdly cut suit that evokes Italian bombshells, Loren, Vitti, Bellucci, but Moon keeps turning, searching still, and that's when she understands that she is looking for Mac, and a horrible ballooning presses against her diaphragm. Her composure shatters, the adrenaline leaving her as she blinks into the inky tide of waterproof makeup that dissolves into shards to pepper her tear ducts. She cannot breathe, feels the ground lurching where she stands, and then Stevie is suddenly beside her, hoisting her up.

They are directed to a preferential area under a small scalene triangle of shade, and she slumps into her seat. She peers through the murk of her vision at the Tiffany blue cardstock of the program. *He would hate it*, she thinks. It is sentimental and prosaic. Befitting a wedding or a child's christening. She sobs, touching the lines of his face in the black-and-white portrait, recalling back to his heart attack, how he'd begged her to get him a Diet Coke and when she'd returned, asked her to marry him. He didn't have a ring, lying there, ashen in the hospital gown, hair standing up in tufts, and now she'll never know if he'd meant it.

Seeing the pearlized gray box in front, she shudders. It's all so wrong. He'd wanted to be cremated and scattered into Loch Marree. He would have hated the music. *No Mahler*, he'd told her once, *none of this Barber Adagio for Strings*. She should have taken him to Scotland. She could have done this for him. She imagines blue-gray, fog-laden waters and the mineral-rich scent of the land and she looks around, desperate for recourse, anything, but then there is movement and it is Mac's mother, a woman Moon only knows from pictures, being wheeled into position, tartan blanket covering her lap. Her dark eyes are fixed on the box and she is unbearably old, gaunt, with skin that is translucent and bruised, lips drawn back, parted, in a mask of terror, frozen in anguish, and to Moon she looks like she's silently screaming.

STEVIE

Her sunglasses keep sliding off her nose and her dress clings at her ribs, the small of her back, her legs, anywhere sweat has soaked through. They've completed the onerous parts of the funeral, the horrible box, the sermons, and the incense. She has been asked about college by a half dozen people she barely knows and she's lied each time and doesn't care. What's most baffling to her, too ludicrous to reconcile, is that all of this is happening at Hollywood Forever, a venue she knows from outdoor movies on picnic blankets and the Halloween party. She can't tell what is more profane, that they have parties over the bodies or that there are bodies buried where the parties are held. She keeps forgetting what they're all doing there. It's hot and confusing. The photos. The recognizable faces. Carrying her sobbing, ragdoll mother to the reception. She is moved by Moon's anguish, the power and sincerity, but is also conflicted by it. And as Moon bolsters her hot grip on Stevie's forearm, Stevie wonders if she'll ever be able to leave.

They proceed to the main administration building for the reception, across the shadeless, unrelenting expanse. Stevie staggers in her heels, Moon unsteadily clutching with the full force of her weight, and when Stevie accidentally catches Adam's eye, her mother's other crutch, beardless again and as beautiful as he's ever been, she looks away unsmiling. For days, she's witnessed his life with Moon through the picture window of the Big House. Cooking dinner, grilling outside. Sometimes the two of them work side by side with their laptops open on lawn chairs, laughing like stock photos, all of it in excruciating, goading panorama. And Stevie has to tug hard at the leash of her impulsive, eager heart, at that old tender desire that wants so badly to join in because the provocation is too enticing, too much like the show she has been excluded from her whole life. But the one thing that keeps her focused is that she will need to stay away in order to leave. Because what she resents most about Adam is that one day, very soon, he gets to.

Stevie knows she's been weak and stupid her whole life. Delusional to what must have been a willful degree. She'd never questioned that she'd chart the same course as all her friends. She was aware that some of her friends were richer than others, she wasn't a complete idiot, but admittedly she'd had no real curiosity of her and Moon's finances. Stevie figured she'd done her part, keeping up her excellent grades and maintaining her "spike" for admissions, a zine she'd begun in middle school about leading an artistic life. It's only when she was accepted into NYU early decision that she began to think about money but only in the oblique way that she felt strongly that it was Moon's job to figure it out. And that Mac would help.

If there's a single, distinct demarcation in a person's life that splits into a before and after, that cleaves them irretrievably from a former understanding of themselves, the following is Stevie's. They were already staying at the motel by then. And for some reason, Stevie's faith in Moon extended to believing that conditions would be *temporary*, that they were getting work done on the house. Even when she saw the rental app open on Moon's iPad with their house listed on the page.

Even when they arrived at the waterlogged accommodations that stank of mildew, two awful twin beds in a single room, Stevie had mostly bitched about the weak Wi-Fi, and worried about the social humiliation of her friends finding out. She'd still believed it was all provisional and largely annoying. The way it had been as a kid when Moon left her for weeks with her nanny, and later when they could no longer afford childcare, with randos when traveling for work. Or when she'd had to peel Moon off the couch or the floor after a Big Night, rolling her eyes at her incorrigible mother when her robe flapped open. But when Stevie got into NYU, to the liberal studies program that cost $86,000 a year, she'd felt nothing but a strange coldness in her face and hands. She'd closed out the email without making a sound. She'd pictured the moment, imagining herself screaming, jumping, crying the way the girls did in their reaction videos on TikTok. Moon had been on the other bed doing a sudoku puzzle and Stevie must have told her because in the next instant Moon looked up, eyes wide, then rushed toward her and burst into tears. *My baby's going to college!*

The numb, enclosed feeling fell away. It wasn't even joy she experienced, it was relief. She'd feared that Moon might be angry, she would be going so far away. She'd even worried that Moon would be jealous that Stevie would be going to college when her mother hadn't had the chance.

Except that night Moon didn't return to the motel. Not answering her phone or texts. If Stevie hadn't skipped school the following day, she would have missed her mother skulking in for a change of clothes the next afternoon, haggard, sallow, and wretchedly hungover. Moon had tried to rush past her, twitchily claiming she was late, that she had an important meeting that she absolutely couldn't miss, something big, *really exciting actually*, but Stevie had stood in her way, blocking the door.

Moon grinned at first but then balked when Stevie still wouldn't move. Then she'd cast about the motel room, wild-eyed, grabbing the clothing iron that had been holstered onto the wall by the sink, raising it above her head. It would have been comedic, slapstick, or vaudevillian had they both not been so angry. All night, she'd thought Moon was dead, convinced she was lying shattered in some hospital bed or throttled by some maniac. And as Moon lunged, roaring about what little Stevie knew of working for a living, that she knew nothing of the world, Stevie kicked her. It wasn't a blow so much as a shove backward with her foot, but Moon had bounced off the far side bed, seemingly in slow motion, her head snapping back before springing forward, her neck doing that pencil trick when you waggled it between lightly held fingers, appearing rubberized. They'd both been shocked.

In that moment they'd understood what they'd known but been

reluctant to admit, which was that Stevie was bigger and could not be overpowered. Moon's primacy had unraveled. And as Moon demanded Stevie's faith in steering the ship of their lives, Stevie wouldn't do it anymore. Stevie did know something of the world. She'd learned it covering for her mother. All the times Moon had gotten a pick-up schedule wrong or forgotten themed dress-up days or money for class trips, Stevie lied to her friends and teachers. She'd borrowed money, forged signatures, or else convinced them that school yearbooks were immature, that overnight ski trips weren't her thing.

And as she looked up at her own warped reflection in the metal base of the iron, something in her brain broke. The sight of her puny mother was suddenly ridiculous. She'd laughed, horrified by the precarity of their lives. How scared she'd been for most of it. Like when she'd been left with Moon's makeup artist and her husband in Topanga for two days at thirteen, with no way to get to school. How the husband had been muscled and vain, never putting on a shirt, tracking Stevie's movements in the house, asking about her boyfriends, sitting so close that she'd felt the heat of him on the couch. And how fitfully she'd slept, door locked, chair wedged under the knob, holding her pee until morning.

In the end, Moon had dropped the iron. Jolting as though waking from a dream. They'd stood there mute, stunned from exhaustion. It was Stevie who'd apologized first, then Moon. *I'm sorry. I'm sorry.* There'd been no further conversation and for the rest of their time at the motel Stevie stayed home. At night, she slept in front of the door, lying on that filthy carpet laid thick with dead skin, dust mite shit, human shit probably, dried flecks of semen, body curled up like a fist, freezing, with a cold draft traveling all up her back from under the hard, metal door, wearing all her clothes, Moon's car keys in hand, shoes on her feet, ready to give chase, ready to fight if Moon tried to escape again. In the day, they didn't discuss it, watching TV companionably on their respective beds.

Once they returned home, not to the Big House but to the Pool House, Stevie went back to school and for several days normalcy seemed to resume. A few weeks after that, Moon got into her wreck.

None of this Adam knows. This Moon is kept secret. It's why Moon's left all her unsavory utilities in the Pool House—Preparation H wipes, testosterone cream, the dingy stained bathrobe used to dye her hair—because the Moon across the yard is unburdened by age or perimenopause. So while Adam might appear loyal to the funeralgoers, receiving warm smiles for his dedication in keeping Moon upright in her preposterous shoes, it's Stevie who's spared nothing. Helping Moon all day with her bathrooming, dressing her, shimmying the black garment over her mother's denuded body, her tiny frame compressed into a flesh-colored Spanx catsuit, eerily devoid of hair, nipples, belly button but featuring a peek-a-boo gash for peeing. It is the stuff of nightmares. And what Stevie must disabuse her heart of is this feeling, this painful belief that the only love she deserves from her mother is a one-sided parasitic intimacy.

Finally, they approach the two-story stone structure where the reception is held, and as Stevie trudges alongside Moon who clings to her, she looks down at her bound feet and reminds herself that it's her mother's vanity that hobbles them all.

In that moment, a golf cart eases by with Corinna in the rear seat, alone, riding backward. Mac's widow faces the three of them, her cart now moving excruciatingly slow, almost at the pace at which they walk, and it strikes Stevie as strange, if heavy-handed, that Corinna's dressed in white and Moon in black.

When they'd first met, she'd been aghast at how close they were in age. Stevie had been seventeen, Corinna barely twenty-two. And she could tell from the bright pink headband Corinna had brought as a gift that Corinna had thought she'd be younger the way she'd expected Corinna to be older. After that meeting, she'd had nightmares. Vivid dreams that were troubling for how pedestrian they felt, how utterly unfantastic. In them, Stevie was married to Mac in scenes depicting various everyday situations. Stevie with Mac at breakfast, pouring him tea, fussing over his eggs. Sometimes Moon was there, complicit. Her presence there a blessing. And despite the dull familiarity of the configuration, the three of them sharing a meal, passing the salt or lifting a napkin, Stevie's horror flapped inside her like bats, confined but thrashing.

So now when Corinna dismounts shakily from the golf cart and her pale shawl slips free of her neck, Stevie can't help but release her mother, to bolt toward the young widow to help, to say something, to see if beneath the grief Corinna feels relief because Stevie would understand it. And for a second Corinna looks up, right at her, but only before taking the scarf proffered to her by the valet who'd caught it and turning into the building without so much as a nod.

Cheeks burning, Stevie faces her mother. But Moon ignores her, lifting her skirt, and for a few steps, head held high, she walks unaided with miraculous grace, a paralytic in Bethesda compelled by the miracle of Jesus. But when she wobbles, both Stevie and Adam advance to catch her, only Moon shakes Stevie off, jilted.

When Moon and Adam disappear inside, Stevie crosses the road, away from everyone else. And once under tree cover, she looks down at the headstones, smaller monuments that she hadn't noticed before, memorials set flush against the ground like pavestones. One bears a man's name, the date of his birth and death, and beside it, a stone that reads only *Mother*. No name. No surname. Just the role she'd played.

She proceeds toward a monument, a kind of stone temple that evokes Rome or Greece, places she has never been. Once inside, she listens to the crisp click of her heels. It is cool, reminiscent of a church. And as she passes statues of men in robes, under an archway and into a hall, she spots shelves encased in glass—memorials—dioramas, terrariums containing entire lifetimes, whole personalities reduced to trinkets. Photos, some from school, headshots—hairdos over decades—newspaper clippings, medals, small toys, matchbox cars, baseball cards, even a candy bar with the candy still inside. To Stevie they seem like the contents of hastily emptied pockets, and in thinking of what she'll carry, what she'll bring with her where she's going next, she considers all the pool houses that traffic helicopters and drone pilots must see from above. All those clear boxes and miniaturized human lives.

She advances deeper into the crypt, reflecting on how Mac can see her now, that he can read her disloyal thoughts of him. And that as much as she loves him, she hadn't trusted him, and how in the end she'd been right. She will never forgive him for leaving them like this, the male cliché of a bridge, akin to shooting yourself in the head but putting on a military uniform and saluting yourself in the mirror before doing it. A Michael Mann movie she has no interest in. All she knows is that whatever unprocessed trauma arises from the occasion, the money shot she will imagine the rest of her life will sit like grit in her cells, rolling around until they calcify and harden. But when she turns a corner into what looks like a hall, she's bowled over by the brilliant light, the cascade pouring from the skylights onto her upturned face. Her eyes fill with tears. The room is resplendent with purple orchids in square planters, one on each waist-high column, a half dozen in the room, and Stevie can sense something, God, Mac, some sweeping hope that there will be moments after *this* moment, that tides can turn, that circumstances will change, and with wet cheeks, she keeps walking.

She proceeds into another hallway, where the families are all grouped together, where the wealth is apparent in their numbers and the patrician, Protestant-sounding surnames, and she continues into an alcove with a stained-glass window and wooden bench. Her feet hurt but she passes it. But when there is another one, another chance, she sits, ignoring the feeling of trespass. This window is somehow even more beautiful than the last, the warm amber light a balm. She doesn't know if someone will ask her to leave, if the seating is only for the rich families, but she undoes the clasps of her shoes and removes them anyway, pressing her stinging soles on the cold stone floor. She crosses her arms to hold herself together, and her head aches, pressure encircling her teeth in a dull, insistent pain. She closes her eyes, wondering if it counts as praying and if she even knows how to pray and what she would ask for, but then she hears footsteps.

ADAM

Adam follows the dark-haired woman into the crypt, with a mystified sense of predestiny. Even as he'd dressed that morning, sliding on his new summer-weight The Row suit, slipping into his calfskin loafers, it had been with the promise of intrigue. There'd always been the probability of seeing her, but no way to know if they would share more than a cool nod from across the green, in front of her husband and son who is now taller than her by several inches, gangling and sullen, absorbed in an iPad as though he were a child at a restaurant.

He'd met Rana a decade ago; they'd been in a play together in New York. LaBute. She'd been married then too. To the same man. The first time they'd met alone in a crowded Italian restaurant in Carroll Gardens, she'd spoken of her husband's business conquests and ate with pornographic gusto. He'd been sick with desire. At first he'd been struck stupid by her reputation, her fame in certain circles, but ultimately it had been about her. The emotional output of the production had been merciless. He was twenty-two and she was forty-nine.

Watching her move now, he recalls how she would comment on his qualities as a lover with the same brusque manner as she would his scene work. She'd made all the decisions. When and where they'd meet. What they'd eat. What music they would listen to. How, sitting at the edge of her kitchen table, peering down, she would teach him to push up against her pubis to lift the hood of her clit as he ate her out slowly, fucking her with the entire length of his hand as she would bear down to squirt across his astonished cheek.

When the play wrapped, with no reason to meet again, he'd throbbed with longing, dashing into Saks, then Bergdorf's one fevered afternoon, to find her perfume, and he'd sprayed his clothes, his sheets, his hands. And it was in missing her, moving through the contours of his heartache as though digging a tongue into the warm, salty socket of a missing tooth, that he'd first learned to weep on command. They've seen each other once since, at an agency event in L.A.; she'd been leaving as he'd arrived, but she'd long been friends with Mac and he'd hoped she would come.

Now as they walk deeper into the cool tomb, exchanging small talk about travel, as though they are strangers meeting at a hotel bar, he finds himself eliding that he is staying with Moon or how long he'll be in town. He watches his actions from afar, remote and strangely inexorable. And when she turns down a hall to reveal another, more secluded dead end where a bench appears, he sits without question. His response to her is swift and urgent. She positions herself to face him, kneeling, astride him and when she lifts her skirt, revealing the red marks from the fastenings of her stocking at the tops of her thighs, he sees floaters in his eyes from the blood rushing to his cock.

He moves his hands under the fine wool fabric of her skirt that is bunched at her waist, her warm bare ass filling his palms, and presses his mouth to her breast. Burying himself into her, he fucks her with an old devotion. Performing with her had required the same attunement. He was aware of his shortcomings as an actor. His manneristic cheats. How he kissed the same way, lunging with a hand raised to her face to suggest passion, repeating the motion each time, the lines escaping his thoughts when he didn't lift his arm to the exact height, revealing the sequence as an unbroken chain, the memorization exposed in the inevitability. The lines. The actors. The stage.

Smelling her, touching her presently, it is as though he is sliding into her with the hydraulic intensity of his youth, and he closes his eyes, all thought mercifully quiet in service of his mechanical responses, his blood flooding deterministically away from his mind. His response to her touches him. How guileless he feels, how much he wants to be led.

He feels the same intimidation he has always. A complete enthrallment. He wonders if he's in love with her.

But then he hears the clipped taut beat of shoes striking marble and remembers himself. He shifts away from the stained glass and golden light, peering through the cascade of Rana's dark hair to catch the slender figure of Stevie passing in the hall and he is incredulous, as though he has summoned her like an apparition. She keeps her gaze forward and walks with the propriety of a child balancing a book on her head. He is slick, still inside Rana, pants hanging open. He hadn't intended on finishing but the momentary amazement almost topples him over the edge. And when Rana grabs his face, redirecting his gaze, he is unsure of what he's seen, so shocked but roused by his ability to sustain his ministrations that he feels close, too close, sucking his pinky to nestle into Rana's ass, and only once she's tightened around him, screaming soundlessly, a click in the back of her throat, shuddering against his shoulder, does he allow himself to come.

Once outside, there's a ringing low in his ears. He yawns in the bright sun, irritable and exhausted. He descends the wide-set stone steps of the mausoleum and checks the time. And again, as though part of a larger sequence, he spots Stevie as he suspected he would, out by the lake, and they could have been at a golf course if not for the recognizable celebrity monuments. She stands alone as though waiting, shielding her eyes with a raised hand, as though saluting, and he can sense her awareness of her appearance, how she looks to him, the poignant figure she cuts. A group of workers in wide-brimmed hats stack chairs on a lawn far out to the left, and Adam falters. She's made it clear she can barely tolerate him. And he can't imagine what she thinks of him now. Now that she's seen this disturbing side of him, prostrate and worshipful, debilitated with need. He is desperate to redeem himself, wondering if it's even possible. All he can think to do is clean. Scrub the entire pool house. Get down on his knees until it gleams.

"Hey," he says.

She glances past him before turning back toward the lake. "Where's Moon?" she asks. The water is a dark green, almost milky, with half-hearted fountains and a floating island hosting a smaller mausoleum, a replica of the one they've just left.

"Back with Dani and some people."

He stands beside her, then stoops down to rip up some grass to have something to do with his hands, then releases the pieces to the ground.

She watches him, then, remarkably, does the same.

They stand silent a while, the sun boring down on their heads.

"So do you go back to Hong Kong now or?" she asks, squinting, without any acknowledgment for what she's seen beyond how it seems to have neutralized any animus that she'd felt for him before. She stoops to rip up more grass and then yawns, covering her mouth with the back of her hand.

"I'll head to New York first." In the distance, he watches the hatted workers climb onto a golf cart. "It was my mom's birthday."

"When?"

"Couple days ago."

He still hasn't called her.

She stares ahead, unblinking. "So you come running when Moon calls but you blow off your actual mom's birthday. You know you don't have to try so hard, Adam. Like, don't worry. You're her favorite by a lot."

She says this without bitterness, as though she's accepted it as fact, and it pains him to be seen as an interloper.

"I was here already," he says, wondering if he should have just gone on to the City, avoided all of this. "I tried to tell her but . . ." He doesn't know if this is strictly true.

Stevie turns to him. "But it ruins the plot," she says, "the lore." She shakes her head with a small, sad smile. "You're so alike," she adds, but then her gaze flicks up and when he turns, Rana is exiting the mausoleum. Her head is bowed and the studied care with which she navigates the stairs in heels reveals her age and Adam can't avert his gaze, too worried that she'll fall.

Watching her, he's bewildered. At this remove, he cannot locate attraction for her, leaving him only with regret and a faint sense of injury. Mostly, he feels shame and the deep conviction that he's done something wrong. Toward Rana, Stevie, but oddly, also himself. He watches Rana approach a small crowd, likely to locate her family, and with her back to him, her walk still suggestive but with a distinct unsteadiness, she is no longer the vision immortalized in his twenty-year-old fantasies. He can admit to himself now that she's ruined her face and that it's a tragedy. The surgical adjustments are fine work, shrewd and subtle, but up close, just as it had been with her breasts, the planes are unnaturally rigid, tensile, with a cubist's severity that beggars what had once been a profile with consonance, wit. He would have loved to have seen her old.

When he turns back to Stevie she is watching him.

"Who was that?"

"We used to work together," he says.

Stevie nods as if understanding something new about him. And only then does he realize that Rana is the exact age of his mother. That they were born the same year. He hadn't been aware of the special relationship between the two women before and wonders what this means. The biographical fact and his ignorance of it.

"You know they were still together, right?" Stevie asks, and he cannot imagine who she is talking about. "Moon and Mac," she clarifies after a beat.

This surprises him, even as he doesn't know why it would.

"The last time I saw him he was sneaking out of our house and he pretended not to see me."

"Jesus," he says, wondering if the rekindling was a recent development, or if it had never completely gone away. He feels betrayed not to have known but also deeply annoyed by whatever efforts were taken to conceal it from him, as though he would still care.

He doesn't get it. Why women are attracted to Mac, a man he loves like a father but knows far too much about, possibly more like some wayward, oversharing uncle.

But then again, they had all three of them been too close.

Three makes for difficult stability. It encouraged jockeying, taking sides, a constant paranoia of who would fall out of favor or be left behind, a preoccupation with loyalties. Moon worried about the boys closing ranks. Adam wary of the couple. And Mac was threatened by their comparative youth, how the two of them were more alike in character. Adam might have thought Moon was using Mac for the strategic alliance, if it hadn't been for all the embittered, tearful conversations in her trailer, especially that first year when he'd been the only one to know, passing messages between them like the only child of divorcing parents. He'd seen the careless way Mac treated her, outright ignoring her or ridiculing her, and he'd vowed he would never turn out like him. A bully when it came to the people he worked with but also spiteful to women. And as much as he worries about his own failure to maintain a relationship, to ever stay in love, Adam is reassured that not only does he love women, he also truly likes them. He pictures Mac leaving Moon's house, hair mussed, shirt untucked, feigning absorption in his phone as he skulks out the door.

"When was that?" he asks.

"Right before the wedding," she says.

"And he still got married?"

"Yup." Stevie sniffs, the heel of her hand pressed to her eye. "I thought for sure Moon would go first," she says. "When she had her wreck, he's who came and told me."

Adam nods, arranging his face carefully as though he recalls any details of Moon's accident. "You should have seen him," she continues. "He kept checking his pulse. I swear, I thought he was going to pass out. He's all peaky, talking about his blood sugar and honestly I thought Moon was dead because he couldn't just get to the fucking point." She laughs, then sighs. "The whole time I kept thinking he was useless but at least I wasn't alone. But then of course he left right after."

She laughs again, a mirthless miserable burble. He doesn't even know when this would be. He ransacks his memory for details of the accident, but it is like searching for a lost receipt in a morass of paperwork. He doesn't know if he'd talked to Moon afterward. Or Mac. Or Stevie. He can't locate even the foggiest mental image of himself picking up his phone with any of their numbers displayed, or even reading the news, he had been so caught up with his own vanities and grievances, and he wonders if there is something fundamentally wrong with him that an event so significant to the people he claims to love is so inconsequential to him. That he can be so self-centered.

Stevie takes another long, juddering breath, face full of misleading angles, the coldness of her gaze belying the still plush softness of her cheeks. She must have been so scared, he thinks, as he checks his jacket pockets for tissues despite knowing they'll be empty. And in that moment, he sees that in this way, he is everything like Mac. Useless. Bumbling. And completely unaware of what anyone else is going through.

"We should get Moon," she says after a moment, and he nods, following her.

DAY EIGHT

MOON

At an AA meeting two days later, Moon gazes around at the circle of faces, at the women's slow blinks and the motes of dust suspended in the shaft of midafternoon light. Camille J. is speaking. Camille J. is a newcomer and her face carries the soft bloat of fresh sobriety. The proving dough of her cheeks is pale, tender as though full of milk. The bright floret of her lipsticked mouth puckering out of the blanched flesh like a belly button.

Wherever it is that Camille J. has moved from, presumably New York because she keeps mentioning it without mentioning it, is nothing like L.A. "The problem is all of California," says Camille J. reasonably. Camille J. dubs it a *humanitarian crisis*, that there's hard liquor available in grocery stores, alongside baby formula, even at Target. "They could at least give us a chance," she says, hair balayaged in a soft gray, bag costing $2,200. She is recently divorced and living with her mother in Mar Vista, though she is quick to distinguish that her mother has moved in with her, not the other way around.

Camille J.'s disdain for her mother needles Moon, recalling the self-tape she'd sent before leaving the house in a hurry. It is a reprisal of a role from a mid-budget streamer three years ago. The movie had performed startlingly well as in-flight entertainment where she'd played the agitated nutcase wife of a man who through grit and resourcefulness rescues their daughter from a kidnapping, killing everyone else. She has no idea why it's being resuscitated as a franchise now and while she needs the work, any work, a helpless hysterical mother isn't what she'd had in mind. Especially one with a brutally short haircut and agonizingly prosaic wardrobe choices like madras knee-shorts and sleeveless poplin button-downs.

As she set up her phone on a tripod to record, angled to the window on a surprisingly sturdy gimble that one of the tenants had left, Moon wondered what it would take for a total reinvention. The photos from the funeral are circulating widely, of her and the Royal, and she looks tall and pale and slightly deranged, a departure from her most defining role on a half-hour multi-cam sitcom. She looks like a film star. Minimally, hour-long prestige TV. But she needs to do more. She should start her own production company and command real agency in whatever she is to do next. She'll read widely. There have to be better roles out there no matter how few archetypes are available to women as they age. The evil stepmothers or mothers-in-law are bush league grotesqueries. It's not until you age into proper genre—sea hags, witches, and ghosts—that you can take big, interesting swings. And if Moon has to play a monster, she wants to be mythic.

It kills her that in the best shot of her and the Royal, Corinna is in the background, her bright face rising like a pearl from the mass of black-clad relics around her. Moon thinks how sympathetic she'd looked. How many decades she has before she has to play the mother. As a widow, Corinna's youth cuts a tragic figure. Despite however much of Mac's estate she now stands to inherit. Moon remembers how she'd once been the upstart, the ingenue, recalling with an acid twinge in her windpipe how even Stevie had rushed to help the younger woman. Practically pushing Moon aside to catch her scarf, in front of all those people, mere feet from the woman who plays Mac's wife on his new show, all those photographers poised and hungry. That single moment, if captured, could have ruined it all.

She hates how desperate Stevie is. So eager to curry favor. To people-please. As if it isn't Corinna who had robbed her of Mac's attentions over the years, who will continue to live in his house. There will have been a prenup but Moon could just as easily see there not being one as a grand gesture to distinguish this marriage from the others. Corinna has everything already, Moon doesn't see why Stevie also has to fawn over her while rebuffing every single one of Moon's efforts to spend time together. It is treasonous and weak.

The truth is, neither of her children had impressed her at the funeral, Dano disappearing for over an hour, leaving her at the mercy of his agent, an inconsequential little man who hadn't even known Dano was in Hong Kong let alone making a movie.

She really should be making her own projects. A part with teeth. Not unlike the films from her twenties. Sexy, troubling, and perverse. Nothing like this mom role. For the original, they'd given her a perm to age her up and in the artwork to promote the film, the father and daughter are locked in a steamy, desperate embrace while Moon's outline, tiny and shadowed, is only recognizable by her hair, giving the impression that the movie is about a love triangle where the mom is the villain and father and daughter are lovers. But what nettles her most is that the casting fuels one of her biggest career regrets, of allowing her onscreen persona to bleed behind the scenes and imply that Moon is a bad mother in life.

It had begun as a legitimate scheduling crisis. Stevie's preschool was closed and Moon had an interview. With no alternative, Moon brought a three-year-old Stevie to the poolside bar of the Standard Hotel. And the scene of a child set up with crayons beside a Lucite box containing a woman in a bikini—since it was customary at various hotspots then to install models in boxes, fish tanks, and cages—became the lead of the magazine piece. Moon's ditzy negligence as a mother became her entire persona, inspiring the shoot where she'd worn a lace apron with curlers in her hair, cigarette dangling from her mouth over a smoking saucepan, holding the one Asian American Girl Doll upside down in the crook of an arm, magnum of champagne in the other. Moon OK'd the concept without hesitation. The photographer had been Ellen von Unwerth, the images quickly became iconic, and the bit stuck.

Finally, Camille J. is wrapping things up, a cool twenty seconds after Marci L., the timer for the three-minute shares, signals her. Camille J. blames her mother for her regression to adolescence and her pernicious weight gain, despite telling them all that she listens to podcasts at 1.7x speed to give her the impression of velocity while she sits in traffic, keeping time with her jaw, once eating a whole pound of raw almonds, anything that requires dedicated, forceful chewing as though her eating is the motor for the car and her life. Somehow this is still her mother's fault. "She wants me fat," says Camille. "That way I'll be with her forever."

Moon goes very still, experiencing a flutter of apprehension around telling Stevie about the newest tenants. They're arriving in three weeks, then she and Stevie have to vacate for two months. It's not as if Moon enjoys it either. So close to their birthday. The idea of another family crawling into her house like hermit crabs, the couple fucking in her bed, the entire family wearing shoes in the house despite the rules, kicking their filthy soles up onto her sofas, all of it makes her sick.

She wishes she could get away. What she wants most is to be on set. The provisional life. Not having to be the mom. Once they'd shot an indie at a real summer camp for five weeks and it had felt exactly like summer camp, partying all night in front of a large bonfire. It wasn't just the pleasure of time sequestered from real life, bills, doctor's appointments, family, groceries, it was the time together, a return to youth. Moon loved observing the fiefdoms, her sisters and brothers, how the camera department always had drugs and were cooler than everyone else, while the sound guys were the bass players of the band, reserved, shyer, but also snobbier, quietly believing themselves to be the smartest of the lot. She loved the set crushes and the gossip and the loyalties and the work. And she'd wondered if this was how college felt. Or grad school. Or even high school if she hadn't worked through it and only spent time with boyfriends.

Right after she'd had Stevie, trapped in that bleary interminable smear of months before Stevie was a person, before her little girl laughed and recognized Moon as her mother, she'd been dazed and horrified for the blankness she'd felt. Bereft for no longer being pregnant. She'd been overwhelmed by the sense of absence and failure, dumbstruck that it took hours to even coordinate an outing to see another adult even if it was only to say hello and hand over insulated shopping bags to a supermarket cashier. Raising Stevie was somehow more solitary than even being alone. She'd wept steadily, her sense of herself leaching out of her at every orifice, and once, sitting in a bathroom stall at Target, arms trembling from the effort to hold Stevie over her lap in her bassinet as she peed, pale thighs crushed under the weight of her daughter's plastic throne, Moon vowed she would get back to her community. Her other family.

Before Stevie was born she'd sometimes resented the sense of invasion during production. How she'd peer down at herself, feeling like a Hieronymus Bosch depiction of a body in a hellscape, an eggshell hollow figure with demons and humans trudging in and out pawing, grooming, carrying out their varied unionized chores for her upkeep and for their health insurance. Once, a makeup artist had crossed the threshold of Moon's mouth while fixing her lipstick and Moon could taste the Funyuns on the woman's fingers and been disgusted by the forced intimacy but then later craved exactly this, becoming a part of a larger unit with blurred boundaries, surrounded by an extended family, all those people concerned for her whereabouts, constantly underfoot, wanting *eyes on Moon* at all times.

It's been too long since she's been seen. Properly looked at and looked after. She is dying to go somewhere for twenty-some-odd days, to pour herself into the confines of a wholly fabricated other person, created by someone else, hitting her marks, saying the words, being with others engaged in the trust fall of doing precisely the same demented thing right back at her.

In the early days of motherhood, when all her nerve endings were exposed, Moon had wondered if she would leave the business entirely. Production was grueling, long, the schedule impossible to coordinate.

Then there was the necromancy and dissonance of promotion, of pretending to care deeply about something that was dead to her by then, her curiosity extinguished months or years earlier when they'd shot the thing, when she'd practically been a different person. And the ending of the jobs too. Disbanding a family every time, the sting of heartache dulling with each separation, distancing her more and more from sincere sentiment.

Now she's mostly desperate to know if her "last fuckable day" has come and gone. She has no idea where she stands in this dogma. The day may have passed without acknowledgment or awareness in much the same way her mother had died. And she mourns this with a cavernous, howling ache. She will miss being hot so much.

Once the meeting concludes Moon goes to her car, passing Camille J. fellowshipping with Cara P. in the parking lot. "And every Mother's Day, I'm just happy she's dead," says Cara P., a translucent woman with white eyelashes who has always reminded Moon of a ghostly Shelley Duvall.

"I don't even feel bad about it," she continues. "It actively makes me happy that I don't have to call or make plans. It's different for my brother," she says. "He's ten years younger and my mother doted on him, just really babied him. She took baths with him until he was ten."

Moon hurries past the women, reflexively glancing at Cara P.'s left hand to confirm that she isn't wearing a wedding band.

And once she in the car, door closed, a headache settles in her eyes. She knows it's a problem in her own thinking, but she can't fight the impulse to separate herself from all these women. There was just something unsexed and hardened about them. Just full of cortisol and thick, yellow, organ-enveloping visceral fat, the kind of fat you can't lipo or work off even with GLP-1s. They had slack upper arms and sloppy lower bellies that they made minimal efforts to conceal, belly buttons spreading like an em dash, disappearing right into the horizon crease of a stomach roll.

Moon wasn't going down like that. She checks her face in her mirror as she heads down Hyperion, glad to have kept her makeup on from the self-tape. There's no way these women have ever been as critical of their fathers. Stevie's the same way. She'll only romanticize Mac even more now. It's so typical that Stevie only recalls Moon's misdeeds with forensic and sectarian detail.

She thinks how good it would feel to bring home a box of See's Candies again, like all those times in the past, their silly little tradition. How this time they might laugh about it.

Moon switches lanes, ignoring the car she's cut off even as it leans on the horn and the driver gesticulates wildly in her rearview. She must get through the next few days. Just until her sober anniversary. One year of no drinking. According to her sponsor, the first year is the worst. Anniversaries in general tend to be fraught. A time of relapses. There is depression. Stuck grief. Massive apprehension that from now on the galloping, awful dread will simply rip through your life without any anesthesia.

Her audition tape had been good at least. She'd had to balance sympathy and dignity, to create credible tension while being unlikable enough for the husband, the hero, the Agamemnon in the Electra complex, to shine. She'd made herself look elegant and frail. Deserving of protection. She must be exactly what she is, the most poignant thing of all, a former beauty. But then it occurs to her, that maybe in the sequel, the mother might actually be behind the kidnapping. They might even kill her off. And she smiles thinking about it, welcoming it, envisioning the final, glorious close-up.

SEE'S CANDIES
[2008–PRESENT]

Stevie doesn't remember how it started, but whenever Moon had to leave town for work and Stevie had to stay behind, her mother would return with a tray of Pecan Buds from the See's Candies stands at LAX. It didn't matter if she'd gone to Atlanta or Hawaii or Prague, she would come back with the same gift, the same nut-filled pralines, announcing, "엄마 왔다!" when she got to the door, and Stevie would run into her arms screaming, overcome by her mother's arrival. It was tradition in their house for so long that when she was small Stevie had believed Moon worked at the airport given the provenance of the sweets.

Once Stevie became a young teen, she'd hated being left with strangers, especially on school nights. And one afternoon after promising she would only be gone for a few hours, Moon left Stevie with their neighbor, a single mother of four, but by then Stevie knew well enough to lie to the woman, go home, and wait for Moon there. Moon was gone three nights. And this time when Moon did come back, she didn't call out, leaving the candy on the kitchen counter, in a bag with a receipt from the See's Candies at the Grove still inside. Moon insisted there'd been a misprint, swearing that she'd been to Atlanta while failing to produce her flight information, and when Stevie handed back the box, she'd said, *You know I never liked these.* That was the last time she pretended to be happy when her mother returned.

DAY NINE

STEVIE

When Stevie arrives to work, the sky is brooding and dark, presaging a downpour, and the mood is alert, giddy, the sense of school when regular programming has been disrupted by a special assembly or an active shooter drill. There's an audible crack of thunder and the customers jolt and titter, turning toward the glass storefront as sheets of water pummel the sidewalk and a couple runs in holding a jacket over them, breathless, laughing and shiny with rain. "Guess we're having burritos for lunch *and* dinner," remarks an older man to Stevie, but when she doesn't react, he says it again louder, booming, until the woman next to him gives him a weak laugh and says, "Seriously," pacifying him.

She wouldn't have predicted the weather earlier that morning beyond the sense of disturbance in the pressure in her head. She couldn't sleep, too hot, too flummoxed by the events of the day. She can't stop thinking of Adam in the crypt, how beautiful he'd looked, and all night she'd wondered what it would be to be desired, to be so consumed while utterly surrendered. The woman had been sophisticated, regal. And as Stevie hurried past them, even she could see that the sex was transactive. She's enthralled by the mutual exploitation. This idea that they could each take what they wanted, rutting with abandon, with rigor. For sport. Stevie wants this. Closeness without stakes. Without loss. Without compromising or giving any part of herself, and she newly considers her reaction at The Regular's house, seeing that her fright hadn't been immature or unwarranted. She'd been powerfully turned off and her body had known before she had. This insight gives her hope, opening up the possibility that the converse might be true, that while she may not know the instant she is in love, that she might cognitively fail to recognize it, some mysterious lurking wisdom will alert her once she's ready.

As she'd begun preparing for her day, blinking into the half light, she'd heard noises. Splashing. Wondering if an animal had fallen into the pool, she'd looked outside only to see Adam swimming. It was a strange revelation that made her laugh audibly, alone in the Pool House. They mostly ignored the pool, they being the other tenants, despite the considerable expense to have it cleaned. Everyone understood it to be largely decorative, an inconsequential body of water, shallow and irregularly shaped, only ever good for wading into with sunglasses and a sunhat, holding a drink. It was a pool made for iPads. But there was Adam, the glowing white submarine length of him sawing through its surface, doing laps.

His movements were dignified. He'd obviously taken lessons, there was something lovely and productive about his form, efficient. And she enjoyed watching his long pale arms lifting, lowering, the *o* of his mouth appearing every third stroke, and the way he disappeared for a measure, remarkably, to produce an underwater flip.

She'd been delighted, liable to clap if it hadn't been for the stunning disclosure that he was naked. The aurora of his exposed haunch was luminous as it rose out of the tide and it had been breathtaking to anticipate the dark coils of pubic hair, the undignified lump of a penis in cold water, but the bulge was hidden to her, blurred as if censored, and she'd felt cheated until she understood that her view had been obstructed by pale shorts the color of his thighs.

But then, another movement. This time in the fore. The stirring of what Stevie assumed were blinds but instead was her mother in the bay window of the Big House, wearing her good white bathrobe like an ermine cape over her shoulders. Moon was holding herself, watching him, and her stillness and attention were astounding, her unprecedented quietude, the totality of her repose. Stevie had been struck by her mother's elegance. The jut of her midsection, the angle of her neck, the way she hugged herself, one hand touching the side of her face, her mouth slightly open.

* * *

At their break, it's still raining and she and Freddie stand under the awning of the bar next door so that Xan won't see them smoking through the storefront glass.

"OK but look at this," says Freddie without preamble, pulling out her phone, adjusting the dimness. The dick is thick, uncircumcised, and unmistakably photogenic. Flash-blown like a trendy food photo, with a hand wrapped around its base, springing out of the screen like an IMAX warhead. As Freddie unlocks the orientation to landscape, she tells her about a new dating app that encourages sexts. The penis looks unduly pleased with itself.

"Invitation only, obviously," says Freddie.

"Obviously."

Stevie has previously never understood the tradition of sending around photos of body parts unless they are literally detached from the body for ransom, but even she can see that this penis seemed eager and well-meaning, the kind of kid who'd wear bow ties on picture day. And now she cannot stop thinking of Adam's penis. Wondering how big it is, since it's purported to be huge, or how attractive. Hoping it isn't frightening or too closely resemble an unshelled mollusc. Freddie swipes, revealing a man that is neither skinny nor fat, with brown hair, white or white-passing, in his thirties or forties, wearing a blue button-down.

"Totally generic whatever. Peloton guy, listens to I don't know, The Chainsmokers, some shit," says Freddie. "But . . ." She swipes back to the penis. Then swipes back and forth. Dick. Guy. Dick. Guy. "Crazy, right?

Hundred percent you'd think he had noodle dick," she continues. "Not even al dente but like chickpea pasta disintegrating shit, right? Anatomy is a mystery."

Stevie puts her cigarette out, flustered.

"Wait, are you offended?" Freddie wants to know. "Did I just hostile workplace environment you?"

Stevie laughs but then becomes distracted by a car service that stops a few feet away, and Melody, a girl from the cupcake boutique down the street, gets out wearing a short, pleated schoolgirl skirt with lacy black thigh-highs but with the disaffected boredom of someone wearing a uniform that she personally finds corny. According to Freddie, Mel makes money from OnlyFans but keeps her job for added visibility, to prove she's not AI, the cupcake store acting like a showroom where people, *psychos probably*, can view her in real life. It is understood that Stevie and Freddie are lower on the social order since they are in fast food and Pee Wee's is corporate-owned, but Mel nods to them and Freddie makes a noncommittal sound even though Stevie knows Freddie is pumped to be acknowledged, and as Mel fixes a stocking and slams the car door, the thought pops into Stevie's mind: *Mel fucks.*

In the employee bathroom later, looking at herself under the brutally unforgiving lights, Stevie thinks how it's not even the way Mel dresses or her makeup that sexualizes her, it's another elemental quality. An essence or smell. Stevie knows fucking is related to confidence. But in the mirror, her reflection is somehow both dull and oily and wearing a polo that makes her resemble someone liable to burst into song as part of an ensemble hired to celebrate children's birthdays. There is something non-erotic about her. A kind of neutering erosion has taken place. She has had sex with four different people under varying circumstances so the data remains inconclusive. Stevie rubs at the makeup under her eyes, but the dark smudges are her, sickly and unmoving.

What she most wants to know is what Adam thinks of her. Adam who also definitely fucks. She'd always been aware of this. She's kept track of his conquests over the years, at least the ones that were publicly known, a costar or two, a popstar, and once a librarian he'd famously met on a flight. She ties her hair high on top of her head in a messy bun and then blots her skin with a square of toilet paper. She wonders how much sex he is having, but watching his movements both in the crypt and that morning in the pool, it has to be a lot. She thinks of the word *thoroughbred*, recalling the penis Freddie had shown her, and she feels herself grow flushed.

She can't unsee it, that Adam knows how to have sex in a way that reminds her of expensive precision machinery or watching crayons being manufactured in a factory. Her childhood crush had been about kissing mostly. Ignoring the details of his anatomy, assigning him a Ken-doll bump. But now she is desperate to see it all.

Stevie lifts her shirt above her breasts to reveal a black sports bra that is so worn it is almost sheer. There is a small angry red patch on top of her left boob, a rash, and she feels tenderness rise up in her. She cannot remember the last time she looked at herself naked—there isn't a full-length mirror anywhere in the Pool House—and standing there holding her shirt up at her armpits, she wonders how much uglier she's become in the last year and if this is something she can repair. And just as she has the thought to lift up her bra to look at her bare breasts, itchy at her rib cage where the elastic's bitten, a knock rings out.

Stevie jolts.

"I'm in here!"

Xan responds, "I know," as if knowingly intruding on another person's private bathroom time is a normal thing to do.

Stevie rearranges herself, running the water to wash her hands despite not having peed, despite now needing to.

"Sorry," she says as she exits, but instead of going into the bathroom, Xan gestures for Stevie to follow her into her office and shuts the door.

"They're scheduling you for your interview with corporate. It's basically a formality, you should have heard all the nice things I said about you."

Stevie is immediately lightheaded. Xan is standing weirdly close.

"This other kid," Xan barrels on, "the one I didn't tell you about who was 99.9 percent going to be promoted from within, failed his pee test." Her boss makes jazz hands at her. "Isn't that incredible?"

Stevie nods, then swallows so hard she has to cough. "Yeah," she chokes. "Incredible."

"Yarmouth!" Xan says, raising a fist.

"Yarmouth!" says Stevie, mirroring her and wanting to die.

Stevie washes her hands a second time to rejoin the line. The interview will be in a week, she'll have management training either in Long Beach or in Boston after she moves. She has no sense of what Boston is like. It even takes a moment for her to register that Boston is in the state of Massachusetts and not a state in its own right. It is all moving so quickly. She will leave L.A. Moon will be alone. And then Stevie will too. In her own apartment for the first time. She imagines herself in the future, a vivid premonition, possibly around the holidays, in many years' time, wearing a good East Coast coat, perfect skin and hair, returning to town and bringing Xan a present to the store. An expensive Italian espresso machine with a gigantic red bow on top like they have on cars in commercials. Or something artistic like a paperweight. Freddie will still be there. So will Arvin. Maybe she'll even see Mel. And they'll all come to appreciate who Stevie had always been, right under their noses.

DAY TEN

ADAM

When Adam's date Sylvie emerges from the bathroom in a short robe, climbing on him with her powerful tanned legs to kiss him on the neck, she reminds him that they have "maybe forty minutes." She says this in the same breath as her encouragement to "stab her with his thick, hard cock." He pulls out his phone from his back pocket to set it on the uncomfortable teal sofa and reminds himself not to leave it there. He tries to focus. Sylvie is attractive. A shaggy-haired blonde with broad shoulders and terrific natural breasts, someone his mother would have described as *strapping* to indicate that she is at least thirty pounds overweight. Sylvie is Australian. And according to her profile she's also a folk singer with labored personal branding and, according to her apartment with its unfortunate Joybird couch, baskets of toys, children's books, and Scandinavian pedal-less bike splayed out on her living room floor, a mom.

Staring at the bike, at the chipped blue paint on the seat, he wonders if the forty minutes refers to when her son will be home, and the thought of her kid walking in encourages a spongey remoteness to invade the length of his penis. As Sylvie grinds on top, he thinks of anything to rouse himself. Rana's mouth. Two women kissing. Young Rana kissing Young Moon. White panties. White nightgowns. Stockinged feet. Tits of all sizes. Wet, slick thighs. A threesome he had in

Kreuzberg. But when he pictures Stevie's breasts under her white shirt at the funeral, he is so taken aback that he hears himself say, "Hold on," in a breathy, laughing tone, feeling himself wither completely inside his pants, and when she reaches down for him, he lifts her off his lap. It's not because she's a mom, he wants to tell her. In fact, he loves moms. They're actually sort of his thing. "I'm sorry," he says instead, raking the hair off his face and grabbing his phone. "I can't do this. My dad died."

He gets in his car and plugs in Moon's address. He is overcome with shame but also a dazzling sense of relief, of a fate narrowly avoided. But then he texts Rana before he can think, despite her not responding to his earlier text. And as he sits, sweltering in his parked car, he has enough presence of mind to see how pathological it is that he texted Rana after his failure with Sylvie.

The Chinese Medicine doctor's diagnosis is now all true. His chi diverted to flow straight out of him. And he can't stop making things worse.

He knows there is something wrong with him. He's been to meetings for sex and love addiction but the meetings were always crowded with women, many of them attractive, especially together like that, convened and capitulated, and he'd sensed their collective attention as a pleasurable hum on his skin. Sitting there, among them, he'd secretly become aroused like a real degenerate, getting sexually charged, bouncing his leg to take the edge off, keenly aware of the other men in there, usually two, and how much more attractive and stronger he was. His thoughts would sharpen and his breathing would shallow, but then, talking about God, higher power, sobriety, he'd feel the exact locus of headache, down to the taste in his mouth, of the crashing worthlessness he always felt right after he fucked someone just to see if he could, to see if he felt different after, envisioning a supercut of his own gigantic face pulsing in his mind, his words, the practiced candor, the disarming grin as he walked them all out of his small Silver Lake house to the Uber he would pay for, up the slight hill, a neutral zone, far enough away from his door but not as far down as Intelligentsia, as he kissed them on the forehead and told them under no uncertain terms that he was grateful for their time together but that their road had come to an end.

There is just something underhanded and seedy about him as a person. And now goose bumps break out on his arms and a burbling, high-pitched sound escapes from his trembling wet lips as he begins to cry. His dick is broken. And it's his fault. He broke it. His dick is broken and his stomach is fucked and despite sex being the only area of his life where he's known true peace and freedom, a total lack of self-consciousness, where he'd never once had to question his ability or intellect, it's all ruined now. He is so sorry to his penis. His sense of his penis, the kinesthetic sensitivity, the securely attached affection he'd always had for it, might be permanently altered. And he is devastated.

Now he believes he is being punished. And he hates thinking this way. This superstitious, karmic, provincial, unintellectual way, but he's not an unspiritual person and this is what he deserves. He should have been kinder to Mac. To his Hong Kong crew. He used people and the scary thing is that he doesn't even know when he's doing it. Mac had delivered himself to Adam in Hong Kong for a reason, as a test, and he'd failed. He'd spurned him as though Mac had shown up expressly to distract or sabotage him. He'd spent the whole day with his former TV dad being dragged from his herbalist to his tailor in TST, having lunch, then drinking for hours, but instead of taking Mac back to the Mandarin Oriental in a cab, Adam had left with CiCi. And it wasn't until he was standing in the kitchen of the high-rise Tsuen Wan apartment that CiCi shared with her mother, hand clamped over her mouth, that Adam was struck by the incomprehensible vision of himself.

He hadn't even been attracted to CiCi. He didn't even like her. CiCi was a zany, birdlike woman with a bawdy laugh who the DP, apparently a well-known sex pest, had hired as an associate producer without Adam's approval out of what Adam would later learn was an act of penance. Because CiCi, despite being forty years younger than the DP, was also his ex. It was CiCi Mac had spent the whole night whispering to, buying drinks for, humiliating himself to show her pictures of him as a young man onstage at the Palladium in black-and-white photos, and it annoyed Adam powerfully to have this embarrassing interloper from his old life rappel in and throw his weight around, buying his crew drinks, pulling at the bill with such vigor that Adam had almost let go at the last minute just to see him stumble.

Adam hated who he became when Mac was around. Had for years. And as Adam pounded CiCi, delivering his thrusts quickly so as not to wake her mother, her underwear pulled down only to her knees, rust-stained panty liner scrunched at the crotch, he'd heard birdsong from the open window of the stifling apartment, marveling at the perverse scene as though he had nothing to do with it, wondering why it was that the whole debacle had seemed grimly foreordained, akin to running over a dog with a car and then having to smash its head out of mercy with a rock. It was while fucking her that he shat himself, hot diarrhea somehow seeping into his socks but miraculously bypassing his pants. And from that moment he hasn't had a peaceful shit or come since.

He'd thought he'd redeemed himself with Rana. But it's obvious now she'd been an outlier. He must've responded to her with such spectacular propulsion because he'd summoned a younger, more vigorous twentysomething version of himself through sense memory, influencing his erection in a misleadingly positive way.

He pulls himself together now to begin the drive home, morose and disoriented. He can't go on like this. He feels a terrible, dizzying momentum, all his thoughts colliding into each other at erratic intervals. He drives past the Petersen Museum, the striated undulating hideousness feeling almost personally offensive, and suddenly he pictures Mac laughing at him. Throwing his head back, the raucous cackling exposing his molars because Mac can see everything now.

Mac's just witnessed Adam's fumbled sexual attempts, ghostly X-ray vision peering straight into his heart, mocking his purposelessness. Mac sees it all. And now Adam weeps, chastened. He shouldn't have come back here. He should have gone straight to New York. He could be in Fisheries by now. Home. He needs to beg for his mother's forgiveness. He needs to sort himself out. But he also can't stand the thought of being alone. He wants to be told what to do. He would give anything to feel the gruff squeeze of Mac's hand on the back of his neck, at the scruff, where baby animals are carried by mouth. He's so sorry. How could he have ever scorned Mac for wanting to see him? He missed the way he looked when he peered over his glasses at table readings. The way he cracked both thumb knuckles with his middle fingers before starting a scene. The kindness of his attention at times. And he thinks with rising torment of their last moment. A sad old vision of Mac with his head down on his forearms at the bar. A caricature of a red-faced expat. Mumbling and plastered.

He can imagine it precisely, how he could have been different. He pictures them in the cab. How Mac would have leaned heavily on the window, pressing his sloppy face against the glass. He can envision it, the massive fashion ads of Central throwing shards of crimson light on Mac's hand. It's so vivid it's cruel that Adam can't make it real. They would have had breakfast at the hotel buffet. Maybe gone to the spa. Mac might even be alive. And now new images flit behind his eyes. The red socks. Mac's red socks. When he'd talked to Mac's brother at the funeral he'd told Adam about Mac's socks. The shoes they'd never found, lost on impact, but he'd managed to keep both his socks. *The flashiest fucking ankles*, his brother remarked wistfully. And now Adam dreams about the socks on Mac's small feet. And Mac's hand. Blue, not red. Bloated and bobbing in the East Basin Channel. And Adam just wants more than anything for Mac to forgive him. To love him again.

THE FLIES

[2024—PRESENT]

It is a lie that fruit flies live for a day. Depending on the kind, they can endure for about forty. Fungus gnats for eight. The Pool House crawled with them. There'd been several valiant attempts at hobbies and interests in the early days of Moon's sobriety: cooking, crochet, Ashtanga, but then there'd been Siggi, a tawny-haired six-foot Swede who owned Sill, an overpriced plant store off York in Highland Park that also sold CBD products for dogs during Fourth of July fireworks.

He'd sold her many new companions—snake plants, a trio of ZZ's, pothos—and had them delivered to the Pool House. Their interest in each other waned fast—Moon and Siggi were addicts quickly addicted to other things—but hordes of unkillable stowaways hid in the soil of the hardy plants that thrived on benign neglect. Legions of fungus gnats and spider mites emerged like Trojans while Moon and Stevie slept. And once they swarmed, attracted to any source of moisture, they unremittingly bashed themselves against phone screens at dusk and dive-bombed just-poured glasses of water. They were relentless. They'd hover at their mouths while they talked and more than once, sensing a tickle in her nose, Stevie pressed a pinky deep into her nostril to retrieve a still wriggling, wet fly.

They aren't just a nuisance, they are a plague.

DAY ELEVEN

STEVIE

It is the pain that wakes her. The entire hemisphere of her skull has tightened to a point that when Stevie brings her hand to her face, panting, she expects to feel something nightmarish, gore. She'd been dreaming of sex. Not the immediate act but its aftermath. The horrible feeling of being pinned down, being flattened by an unrelenting mass of wide shoulders, that post-nut deadweight of a gigantic man, as dense as extraterrestrial rock. It is an awful nightmare and she senses with the knowing of dreams that the man is dead.

There is a loud crashing static in her ears, of her brain pulsing against the interior of her skull so forcefully that she isn't sure she can see, and she hears herself make a plaintive bleat, her brain hemorrhaging from the inside. She wants her mother but her mother is away, too far, so instead she rolls to her side in the airless closet, miserably hot, wet, and in pain. She is unable to take a full breath. Panicked, she pulls at her nightclothes, her T-shirt is bound to her, swung around her torso like a torniquet. Effortfully, she sits up, whimpering again, missing her phone, wanting to call Moon but instead pulling her shirt over her shoulders, careful not to agitate her throbbing head, and when her underwear feels scratchy, digging into her ass with toothy laced edges, she struggles out of them too. She rises to her feet, holding a blind hand out for the wall, keeping her head still as she stoops down, groping for her sheet.

Out of the sleeping closet, it is cooler. It's the rain that accounts for the noise. A hundred thousand droplets strike the angled transparent roof above, and when Stevie understands that she is under siege, that the explosions aren't coming from behind her eyes, she calms. She sits on the plastic-covered love seat, grateful for the cold of it under her bare ass, and carefully lies down, covering herself with the sheet, heavy with exhaustion. And as she drifts, fatigue lapping at the contours of her consciousness, she thinks forlornly of how abandoned she feels.

She's only been asleep for what feels like minutes when she hears beeps and the unmistakable metal *thunk* of the Pool House lock turning. Even rising out of dreams she grasps its significance immediately. Someone has come in. The rain has stopped, her head still aches but without the devastating urgency from before. She keeps still, peeking through the spidery slit of her lashes, spying the gleaming pale mound of her exposed breast, keenly aware that she is naked, that her sheet has slid off her and onto the floor. Stevie knows she won't be able to scream. She has never been able to scream the way other girls can. Not on roller coasters or at jump scares in movies or when her friends hid around dark corners to lunge for her, shrieking. In this moment, Stevie's voice retreats deeper inside her, cowers and takes cover.

On her back, supine, all parts of her displayed completely, she plays dead. The intruder is backlit and holds something large and flat, held in front with both hands. And when he is fully inside, she sees from his length and shape that it is Adam. She is naked. Too naked. Fleshy and anatomical like a corpse. She wills herself to sit up, to pull up the sheet, not make it weird, laugh and kick him out, but another more insistent part of her is curious about the purposefulness of his movements. And even in the surreal liminal space between sleep and total wakefulness, she knows to submit. It will all be over soon if she just waits.

He stills, facing her, watchful, and she closes her eyes, evening her breath, clinging to the guise of sleep. She hears rhythmic, dull clinking. There is a chore-like quality to the noise as though he is tidying, and she wonders briefly if Moon has sent him. He is to the left of her and slightly above, away from her field of vision, and his absorption in his efforts makes her nudity feel incidental. She is embarrassed again but in a different way, she is nothing more than furniture.

He seems to look at her and she wills herself to keep her eyelids from trembling as she peeks. He steps into a shard of light and she prays he won't see the flush traveling over her, he is watching her now so intently. And then, horror, she feels a whisper of hair, a tickle, the awful crawling of a fruit fly high on her thigh. Powerless against the impulse, she scratches herself, shifting and sighing, heart pounding so hard she wonders if it is visible in her chest. She shuts her eyes but not so tight to reveal herself and, sensing him approach, she waits for him to say her name. She imagines his exasperated voice, telling her to get up, but instead she feels heat. His breath close on her bare hip. If she held her hand out, she could reach for his hair, touch his cheek.

And then it is over, the cool shush of sheet draped onto her. Covering her to the neck, blanketing her feet. He moves around the room, not even trying to be quiet, with a manner rote enough to make her feel as though she's the one corrupting an innocent task, making a spectacle of herself without his consent.

Miraculously she falls asleep again and wakes this time with sun streaming into the room and a terrible stiffness in her neck. The sky is wild. Storm clouds slit through with bright white light. Her headache seems to be better but she is assaulted by a strange smell. It scorches the hairs in her nostrils and drives into her saliva ducts. It's a smell so acrid and substantive that she stands in an effort to distance herself from it. She blinks, eyes straining, putting on a pair of shorts from the floor, a faint echo of headache still ringing around her skull, and in scanning the room for her work shirt, she recalls she is not working today and then thinks of Adam.

Her gaze roves around the room for clues, to see what's changed, trying to understand, aghast by how the sunlight reveals the filth of the house. She looks up at the ceiling splattered by bird shit, aphid shit, and tree sap, a worm's-eye view of effluvia, and she feels woozy with shame that he's seen this, that he knows how she is living. She understands now how he must have looked at her nakedness with clinical, anthropological dispassion, and turns on the faucet in the kitchen, letting the water run so it will cool, but it won't cool, so she pulls her hair back to drink from the metallic, tepid stream, envisioning poisonous particles rushing into her blood. Head tipped sideways, she spots a turquoise plastic tumbler on the counter, the cheap Target cups they set out for pool use. Then, another on the coffee table by the love seat. Twelve such cups scattered around her. Vinegar unmistakably. Sealed off with a square of Saran Wrap and held in place by an elastic band with small holes poked through the film, pricked by a toothpick.

It is bizarre, this invention. And effective. Inside is a traffic of trapped gnats rattling under the cling film like bluebottles against a windowpane, the vinegar below littered with the dark scum of dead flies. They are not so unlike the Pool House, she realizes, this smelly, stifling death-aquarium, and she is touched but confused by the gesture. She imagines Adam watching a YouTube tutorial or else knowing how to do this because of some enchanting aspect of his life that is unknown to her. But the overpowering feeling is one of care. That he has put forth such an overt gesture, one that announces how much he thinks of her, alters her flattened perceptions of him—TV brother, sex maniac, swimmer—all shifting in a way that stirs her.

She shuffles into her Vans, trap in hand, but stops short, catching sight of her mother across the lawn, dressed somewhat formally in a collared blouse and skirt, standing at the foot of the outside stairs, smoking. Moon hasn't smoked in years and immediately Stevie's apprehensive, cycling through what this could possibly signify. No way it's good. Probably a court date or some other bureaucratic interview for which Moon has to resemble a tax-paying adult. It's possible that it's for a part. That Moon might be going out for things again but this is its own headache—wild swings in mood, caustic, single-word responses, dissociation. Or else it's to do with Adam, an outing they've planned, and the prospect of being left alone agitates her. Moon fans the air as Stevie crosses the yard, still holding the plastic cup, and she has the sense that they are meeting in the middle of the lawn for a duel.

"You look fancy," Stevie remarks, sounding sarcastic without meaning to. On Moon's feet are a pair of Stevie's old shower slides. It reminds her of how kids' Halloween costumes often end at the shoes. Shrek in sneakers or a Mira from *KPop Demon Hunters* with Crocs.

"What is that?" Moon nods at her hand.

Stevie holds the cup out to her.

"Vinegar trap," she says, tearing off the plastic wrap. "For the fruit flies."

"What kind of vinegar?" Moon asks, implying there's a wrong kind and that Stevie has definitely used it.

Instead of responding, Stevie peels the plastic wrap off the top and slowly pours it out into the yard.

"I'm sure the lawn really appreciates that," says Moon, and Stevie laughs dryly. "It's just not good for the grass," Moon adds in a softer tone.

"Ask Dano," says Stevie, "about the vinegar. He made them." Moon's gaze travels to the Pool House over Stevie's shoulder. And Stevie shakes out the remainder of the liquid, flicking a dead bug off the rim with a finger.

"Just come inside already," says Moon, as though Stevie has taken to sleeping in the yard for the novelty. "Or at least take care of the Pool House if you're going to keep staying there. I'm sick of seeing all your clothes on the floor and leftover bits of burrito in the drain. No wonder it's crawling with bugs."

Stevie just stares at her. Standing there in her weird clothes. Moon would pass a polygraph right now if she were asked about her part in the flies. Or Stevie's cause for living in the Pool House. Stevie can see that she has zero recollection of the corny blond plant store dude and can almost summon pity for her. It must be completely disorienting to be this delusional.

But suddenly Adam is above them, standing in the picture window, watching. Wearing basketball shorts and a T-shirt, hair rucked up in the back. He's just woken up, evidently uninvolved in Moon's plans, and this gives Stevie a lick of satisfaction. Wherever Moon is going with her mood and her smoking and her outfit, she's going alone. Stevie might even hang out with him in the Big House, steal his lunch, go for a swim, and watch him unwatched.

Stevie smiles, holds up the empty glass to him in a toast, then turns back to her mother with a blank gaze. "You leaving soon?" she asks, pointedly refusing to inquire where Moon is headed or when she'll return.

Moon nods, then checks the time again.

But Moon doesn't go. And Stevie, who is usually so attuned to her mother's tempers, has no idea what is going on. Moon is obviously dawdling. And as her small hand travels up to brush aside a strand of hair, Stevie notices Moon pressing the meaty part of her palm to the corner of her eye. She's crying. And regarding the tiny figure of her mother dressed like a preacher's wife, how shrunken she appears when she is disguised as someone else, all at once Stevie remembers. Where Moon is going, the significance of the date, and why Stevie had the day off in the first place.

THE WRECK
[THREE SUMMERS AGO]

3:32 p.m.

Mounted to the soffit of the Eagle Rock ranch house, under the eaves of the garage, the Nest Cam shows the top of a black vintage Porsche 911 easing past the Mini in the driveway to proceed downhill, gaining speed ever so slightly to traverse the road, jump a small curb, crumple an old wood fence, and stop once it's wedged at the base of a granite birdbath. The low door swings open and a woman emerges, rearing backward to free herself from her seat belt, stumbling. She rights herself, then stills, looking up at the shadowy figure of a hawk perched on a metal balcony railing of the three-story house next door.

What the woman doesn't know, since she is not from the neighborhood and isn't signed up to the private Facebook group, is that the hawk is not real. It is a metal effigy mounted to the railing to ward off lesser birds and other nuisances, and while dogs will occasionally do a double take, pigeons have long become inured to its presence, often standing right beside the hawk in groups, treating it as a conversation piece rather than a threat. At times finding occasion to defecate on its head.

A different surveillance camera, this one belonging to the neighbor who keeps unsanctioned chickens, shows an angle of the woman from the front. She is wearing cutoff jean shorts and a tatty T-shirt of the expensive and deliberately distressed mien that reads "sci-fi fantasy," germane not only to this neighborhood but also a few adjacent ones. Her purse, which she'd automatically shouldered, is also visibly expensive, allaying the fears of the community who would come to view the footage later, identifying first the three-thousand-dollar bag, then the actor attached to it. A few of the neighbors had heard of her or else known her face but not her name, conflating her with a handful of other Asian actors who they also claimed to absolutely love while largely considering them all to be character actors.

The woman shakes her head, only once looking back at the birdbath, and then proceeds toward the house without surveying the wreckage of her car. And here a different camera shows her from behind, visibly wobbling, her gait stuttering and precarious. Front lit, she is a silhouette, outline shimmering. Her five-inch block heels veer treacherously to one side, her figure slight, resembling a newly born foal, all limbs and large head, ungainly until she careens too far to the left and then falls suddenly out of frame. There is no audio in the footage but there is an awful particular crack in real life, the wet pulp impact of stone rushing to meet Moon's mouth. At this point, she rolls sideways to reveal the gore of the hole in her head, and here there are no cameras, but what Stevie imagines is the frame pulling all the way out, into infinity until Moon is a dot and then we fade to black.

Moon remembers very little. She's since learned from the report that she'd not only wet herself but bitten the paramedic who'd arrived on the scene. After her 5150, the seventy-two-hour involuntary psych hold, there'd been a 5250 for treatment, for up to a fortnight, of which she could afford twelve days after her legal fees. All told, her minor fiasco set her back fourteen thousand for fines and lawyers, given this was her second wet reckless. She'd also blown a .31, a staggering blood alcohol level and a personal best.

Then, there'd been property damage and car repairs to the tune of another twenty grand. Never mind the hours and hours of paperwork. Many people, including Moon to a degree, expected this to be her bottom, but it hadn't been. They'd wanted her in proper rehab. Thirty days at sixty thousand bucks, six if she'd had real health insurance, but she'd lost SAG coverage for the minimums, exhausted COBRA as well as the extensions, and was only covered for *catastrophes* for which nobody believed daily therapy and catered meals qualified. She'd gone to her court-ordered AA meetings but had taken umbrage that a for-profit carceral system could tell her to attend meetings that discussed God and that, in turn, AA could designate themselves babysitters for private citizens on behalf of an outfit as corrupt as the California judicial system. Other than a few dental implants, she'd been unhurt and hadn't injured anyone else and even briefly trended locally on Twitter for fans believing her to be dead and non-fans wanting to know who she even was.

So there's no telling why the last time Moon got wasted had been the last time. Or why all of the significant dates of her life are convened around the same three weeks in the fall. Mac's death, Moon's sobriety, Moon's mother's death, ending on Moon and Stevie's birthday in early November. There's also no significance behind why the crash happened in Eagle Rock either, but with the steep hills and blind turns, it's a miracle that Moon was unharmed. Or possibly the miracle would have been for her to get injured just enough to get scared straight, but providence rarely works the way anyone wants.

ADAM

He watches a Mylar balloon, a festive little #1, bobble on its leash, attached to a foil-wrapped weight on their table. There are eight women including Moon, women of diverging ages, who otherwise wouldn't belong to each other judging from their shoes or hair. Outwardly, the earnest gathering resembles a child's birthday party were it attended by randomly selected jurors for a misdemeanor case. And this makes sense because from what Adam gathers, the event is Moon's first sober anniversary with her AA home group. They've convened at the picnic tables on the lawn at Brand Park, in Glendale, but another group, all with dogs, have commandeered the area between theirs, relegating him and Stevie to the kids' table, while Moon and the others collect at the table closer to the trail head.

He and Stevie are sitting on the picnic table top, feet on the bench, next to stacked cases of sparkling water, a to-go coffee traveler, and a tray of golf-ball-sized cupcakes. In the sober light of day, casting sidelong glances at Stevie, he has no idea why he'd felt such a pressing urge to lay the traps last night. He'd been in the kitchen, searching for magnesium supplements, a Tylenol PM, anything to help him sleep when he'd spotted the apple cider vinegar and recalled Eckhart, the groundskeeper at Fisheries, and his tumblers of vinegar and dish soap that he'd lay out by the sinks.

"You know what I keep thinking?" she asks him.

He gives her an impassive shrug, even as a panicky, cornered feeling arises. “What?” he asks, poised to blurt out that he hadn’t known she’d be naked.

She turns to him fully. “If it had been anyone else’s funeral and they’d seen each other, he’d definitely be here right now. They’d definitely be back together.”

“Probably,” he says, relieved to be talking about Mac.

“He’d hate this,” she adds with a laugh, and he pictures it, Mac nodding and listening politely to the witchy woman in Chacos with gray hair all the way down to her hips.

“You know she still hasn’t told me she’s in AA,” he says, watching Moon chat with a petite blonde wearing a primary-colored jumpsuit native to young mothers on the East Side. “I mean, I can see why you freaked out about the beer that first night.”

“I didn’t ‘freak out.’”

“Not ‘freak out,’ but . . .” He shakes his head. “I just wish I’d known.”

“Trust me, you’re better off not knowing anything,” she says, reaching for the balloon string, throttling it.

They both watch Moon.

“That’s Pam, her sponsor,” says Stevie, about the blonde. “You’re supposed to pick someone who ‘has what you want.’” Adding, “What do you think that’s about?”

The early-thirties white woman is decently attractive in an L.A. way. Feathered bangs, expensive teeth, possibly secret-wealthy enough to be an anti-vaxxer and a fiscal Republican but enough of an ally to make land acknowledgments before an event.

Stevie goes quiet for a while, surveying the other women, but then says, “I’m definitely going to be some kind of addict, right? Like, I’m fucked?”

“No,” he says quickly, but she gives him a hard look. “Maybe,” he says.

“Statistically, genetically, definitely,” she argues. “It’s so weird we’re throwing her a little party about it. Like, culturally, I get commemorating the occasion, but really? A celebration? It’s like Mac’s thing. What *was* that? We're really all just going to ignore how he killed himself because somewhere along the line, one of us, or all of us, basically failed him?"

She keeps eyeing him as though dubious of trusting him, but when he doesn't disagree with her, she continues. "And today? Am I really supposed to be *proud* of her for doing the most basic minimum shit of not getting trashed every day? How much of an accomplishment is that really?"

She drains the rest of her seltzer, her long neck working as she swallows hard. "I sound like an asshole."

"You sound angry."

"I'm not angry." She flicks the balloon with disgust. "I don't know, maybe. But it's like . . ." She lowers her voice and leans in closer. "How pathetic is all this? I mean, I'm sure these people are nice, but we agree this is depressing, right?" She widens her eyes at the cupcakes, the women, the soda. "How is Moon not better than this?"

She looks to him as though for reproach, but stays silent.

"And what does today even mean?" she continues. "Is she *better* now? Are we supposed to *be good*? She made an amends to me or whatever, but Jesus Christ . . ." She looks at him expectantly. "Has anyone done an amends at you?"

He nods. It had been an ex. "Once."

"So you know, right? It's the weirdest fucking thing. It's like an apology grenade. She was reading it off a piece of paper, just thing after thing, crying so hard, and half the shit, I'm not even kidding, I don't even remember, it's all Complex PTSD blacked out. But can I forgive her? Ever, truly? I don't want her to get fucked up, sure, but how is this not forgiveness blackmail?"

Adam's seen their fights. The way they scream at each other, launching blisteringly abusive invectives until one of them bursts into tears, or, more terrifying, they both start laughing. He wonders where all of Stevie's rage will wind up.

"It's only been a year," he says, meaning for her to go easy on Moon, but when she nods empathically and says, "Exactly," he doesn't know what point they've agreed on and doesn't ask.

She reaches for another cupcake, chocolate, and peels back the liner, glancing down without relish but biting into it anyway. "But what else can you do, I guess, other than pretend it's her fucking birthday?" she says with her mouth full.

It's possibly the most Stevie's said to him in a go. Incongruously, she's dressed as though for a first communion, in a white blouse with a large collar, and he has the dislocating sense that he is seeing her for the first time. That she's pulled back her face to reveal the pulsing core of herself and he is touched to be trusted but also unnerved by how bitter she sounds.

The worst part is, she's right. Chances are, she will be an addict. She will make some questionable choices. And in allowing for this, the image of Stevie's naked body pulses once in his head, and even as he instantly banishes it, there's a lingering echo of this other feeling, the conviction he'd felt of her awareness, that on some level he knows she'd been awake. He'd felt it from her tense curiosity and the tautness of her pretense. He'd known instantly, the way a camera picks up on unnatural stillness. From how hard it is to fake sleep in a take.

He wants to do something for her. To give her something. Stevie has always been astute and slightly scary but in this moment, he also keenly feels her vulnerability. He knows he can't successfully bullshit her but he feels a need to guide her toward a healthier, less dauntingly grim course of thinking. She isn't even close to being ruined.

"You're probably going to be very specifically fucked up about all of this," he says. "You probably won't know for years exactly how."

"Great," she says. "Can't wait."

"It's a lot," he agrees. "But everybody gets super fucked, without exception. And it's all a question of what you do with it."

She nods at this.

"And this is going to sound patronizing and unhelpful, but you will learn how to cope. It's why people become artists or philosophers or go to school for a thousand years, to understand why they are the way they are. It's also how addicts and despots are made. And, I don't know, narcissists who get married four times." He takes a deep breath and it occurs to him that he can't even account for how Mac will have fucked him up in the future either.

"Do you really think he was a narcissist?" she asks. "Or was he just a brat?"

"What's the difference?" he asks.

"A bridge but no note? Is that a premeditated fuck-you or just a big tantrum? I keep going back and forth."

"Fuck you to who, though?"

"Everyone. If he's a narcissist it's all of us. I read somewhere that suicides are a hate crime against surviving family," she adds, "but I think that gives us too much credit. I don't think it was that deep. He was too emo to do that to us and mean it." She doesn't say anything more, running her thumb along the cupcake liner, scraping a white line with her nail, the focus parting her lips. She sucks her thumb and glances up at him.

A shriek erupts from behind them and they both startle, turning toward the parking lot, to see kids, not children exactly, but two girls around Stevie's age, one smacking the other on the shoulder, scream-laughing in the way young women do, a cry for attention disguised as protest. The girls gather around a phone and a quick negotiation follows, and the girl holding the phone gestures, pointing at a yellow Bugatti as the other positions herself in front of the car to squat low with a serious expression.

The Mylar balloon thwacks him on the shoulder.

"Keep it in your pants," she says but with a smile as the balloon bobs back toward her. His mouth is indescribably dry. He doesn't know if she's now referring to the night before. Or the time in the crypt. Possibly both.

"You know all my friends used to look like that," says Stevie, nodding over at the two girls, and the whiplash in his thoughts is so abrupt that he has to clear his throat. "Not exactly like that but that general idea." Her gaze flicks up in embarrassment. "Whatever. What I mean is there used to be this, like, power when I was with them. And I was so scared that they'd stop being friends with me and it would go away, but now I don't care. We're all strangers now. And it feels fascinating, maybe even good, but also like I lost my mind. Or that I'm completely unreliable to myself. And I'll think about their hair and their skin and their bones and their teeth and how none of it matters because everyone is interchangeable and we're all going to die. Like, I thought for sure Moon and Mac were going to end up together but he's a literal corpse. Not even a corpse. Sludge. Like, that was it. And none of it matters. It's like how I forgot about how today was this special day because on some level I don't care about it. Even though Moon cares so much. Like, one day she will stop caring about me. And I might stop caring about her. It could happen."

"You can't think like that," he tells her. "And it's different. You're family."

"No, you're not listening to me," she says with a sad smile, eyes bright with tears. "I'm saying, it might be a good thing. Maybe it's better this way."

Activity breaks out among the women then. Two of them, the gray-haired one with the sandals and Pam the sponsor, approach Moon, carrying a paper plate shakily between them, with a cupcake, covering the shuddering flame of a single candle with their hands.

Moon stands and they all begin singing "Happy Birthday" as Adam and Stevie are summoned to gather closer and Stevie blows her nose on her cupcake napkin. They sing, "Moon M.," for her name, which makes Stevie glance up, smirking even as her face is red from crying, both of them thinking the same thing, that Moon's name is Moon Moon to these people, but also that Moon looks happy. Basking in their ardor, hugging the women, Moon moves to stand beside Pam.

"I'm Moon M., and I'm an alcoholic," she says.

And sure enough, they go, "Hi, Moon."

"OK," she says, exhaling slowly, hand flat on her heart as though calming a horse. "I'm just going to tell you what it was like, what happened, and what it's like now." She smiles ruefully and Adam thinks how he's always been attracted to the magnetic zeal of the sober, the seeking hunger that never seems to diminish.

"I was an inconvenient baby," Moon begins, pausing, radiantly as though to tell a joke, but instead letting out a shaky breath. She speaks plainly. Of her pregnant mother, Sunny, twenty-three, freshly in Texas, and praying Moon would be the right man's baby. But Moon had been born two months early, fully grown, a full-blood Korean, not a lick of Irish in her. Not anything like the military man who'd married Sunny and brought her home.

Adam glances at Stevie, not knowing where any of this will go.

"I know they did their *best*," says Moon, and at this the small crowd laughs knowingly. "He wasn't cruel or violent, he wasn't anything. Just looked straight through me like I didn't exist."

Moon never talks about her family. In all the years he's known her, she's brought them up once. Only to mention she never went home for the holidays. That she'd never once been back there at all. And as her head tilts up, as dogs bark around them, the length of her neck pale and exposed, eyes squeezed shut, there is a genuine humility that is new to him. He has never questioned Moon's capabilities as an actor. Her stage presence is undeniable, an asset to any ensemble, professional, affable; but he's also always known that neither of them was a true talent.

Once, over a lunch at Urth Caffé, he'd overheard someone refer to her as "unwatchable and unfuckable," seemingly without malice, as if these were plain biographical facts, and when Adam turned, it hadn't been some over-proteined, day-player piece of shit in a hat, but a prominent director. He'd turned back around surprised, even a little jealous, that the director knew who she was. He'd been aware of Moon's predictability as a scene partner, how she holds her face when she waits to speak, the way she comes in early and how big and vaudevillian her movements become when she's unsure, but now, watching her, he's transfixed.

"When I left home for good, it felt wonderful," she remembers. "I wasn't just running away but moving toward something. All that highway in front of me. All that promise."

Staring into middle distance, she tells them how she'd been homeless when she first arrived. How she'd stumbled into her first project, the work that had established her and exploited her. He listens with his heart in his throat, knowing how the chapter ends but afraid for her in the moment, at that age, at that diabolical mixture of youth, sex appeal, and a desperation to be seen.

And as planes fly low overhead and Moon glances at them, there's something about her that appears seized, as though she's receiving transmissions directly from heaven. She is searching, beseeching, her story unfurling in juddering increments, pacing as canonical as a Beckett monologue, and he is astonished by it. Wanting it for himself. The lack of vanity or shame. He recalls that first day they'd met, what he'd mistook for self-possession. How famous she'd seemed to him already. White shirt. Hair up. He understands for the first time how young she'd been. And by the way she tells it, how frightened.

"My mom died a year ago," Moon continues, face crumpling. "Except she actually died way before that." She lets out a dry staccato laugh. "My stepdad just didn't tell me. Cancer, apparently. It was fast. But the whole time I thought, how fast? If she knew she was dying, why didn't she come see me? What mother could stay away?" She sobs and someone reaches out with a Kleenex and Moon smiles through her tears as she takes it.

"There's this part in the Big Book I loathe," she says, "'To Wives.' It's so depressing. 'As animals on a treadmill, we have patiently and wearily climbed,'" she quotes. "'The wife who trembles in fear . . . driven to maudlin sympathy, to bitter resentment . . . unselfish, self-sacrificing. We have prayed, we have begged, we have been patient. We have struck out viciously. We have run away. We have been hysterical. We have been terror stricken.'

"Everything a wife does is in response to the husband, the alcoholic. Every action a reaction. And I'd always thought of my mother. Her duty to this man. The wife he made of her and how I never wanted that for myself," she says. "But then I think about my kid."

Her voice breaks and Stevie stiffens beside him.

"And everything I've put her through. And I know I made a wife of my daughter," she says, pausing for a sharp intake of breath, and the tears stream down her cheeks in a way that seems involuntary and guileless, her expression unchanging. "It's unforgivable because I'm the mom. But finally I'm ready to be a part of her life. Instead of forcing her to be a part of mine. And it doesn't matter how old she is or how big she gets. Nothing can drive me away. I'm done leaving. I'm here now. If she'll have me."

Moon nods. She's finished. And as she gazes at her daughter, eyes gleaming, the small crowd turns to face Stevie as they applaud. Stevie offers a small tight smile and Adam's heart stops. The moment is as fraught as a public proposal. Frozen, expectant faces on a Jumbotron. The moment stretches out, Stevie's expression remaining inscrutable, neither smiling nor scowling, unblinking, he feels the women around him straining, practically bouncing on their toes with unconcealed encouragement, faces wet with tears, a collective sense of coercion that isn't fair to Stevie but so poignant.

But then, Stevie touches her lip, kneading it with her fingertips. Her eyes well, then spill and instead of backing away, she advances, slowly, shyly, toward Moon, the others clearing a path, a white-woman Red Sea parting ways for Stevie's Moses, and soon mother and daughter are hugging, weeping, laughing that they are weeping. Moon wipes her daughter's eyes before they embrace. And now Adam is laughing too, relieved, they're all laughing as though they've suffered an ordeal together. And imagining Mac's red beaming face, giving a furtive blot to his tears with the sleeve of his shirt, Adam allows himself a secret gladness that the other man isn't there. The brat or the narcissist. That from here on out, it's only ever going to be the three of them.

PART II

DAY THIRTEEN

STEVIE

She tips her head back, dunking her hair in the cold, chlorinated water. The air is redolent with charcoal, the grill is going, and she can hear Adam and Moon, the adults, making arrangements for their dinner. She touches her face with damp wrinkled fingers and sinks below the water to sit cross-legged at the bottom of the pool, churning her arms to stay submerged. She feels foolish denying herself this for the past week. And there is a residual sting of guilt that she'll be leaving, that she'd forgotten Moon's sober birthday, but for this moment everything is as it should be.

She recalls the way the crowd of women had turned toward her that morning. She'd known some of their names but only vaguely, their faces belonging to a TV show she doesn't watch. She's accompanied Moon to meetings before, remained unfazed if not outright resentful for the portion of the share when Moon talks about her, when Moon enlists her for the supporting role, the long-suffering family, the reverse shot of the acceptance speech at the fake awards show of Moon's mind, but this time, when Moon cried, Stevie was struck by how it could be the last time. That this could be it. And even as she felt herself soften, become sentimental, possibly embarrassing herself, she'd allowed herself to be swept up by future nostalgia, following the feeling, because all daughters left their mothers, and either of them could die at any moment. So instead of releasing Moon's gaze, she'd held it, shone it back, imagining she would never see her again, and something inside her shifted, easing into place, answering to whatever it was inside Moon, and the other women had seen it too, felt it, she could tell, and they radiated unalloyed love back at her, admiration it seemed, and she'd let herself be pulled by the current, unworried, unashamed in front of these shabby women with no makeup and weird shoes just eating it up, worshipful, one of them with broken blood vessels blossoming at her nose reaching out to touch Stevie's arm, staring at her intently, wanting something back, so Stevie squeezed her hand, transmitting love because the woman needed it, lacked it, and then finally, she let go and went to Moon. Stevie wanted to be mothered. She wanted to take from her. For once, she answered the call and sucked it for all it was worth.

She floats up in the water now, then swims to the edge closest to the house, gripping the side to hoist herself up to peek at them, the grown-ups, and again she's struck by the wholesome tableau, the way they resemble a cozy, bingeable sitcom. Moon wearing a vintage Opening Ceremony tee and jean cutoffs, a young cool mom, large sunhat on her head, holding a platter, making space for it on the table. And Adam in the navy apron Moon wore that first night, tongs in hand, sipping a seltzer as they talk. They are a beautiful mixed-race couple in a national spot for conscientiously traded mutual funds, with Stevie in the pool as their child.

The first morning she'd woken up in her old bedroom, sprawled sideways on the queen pillowtop, blackout curtains drawn, sheets soft, snuggled beneath a down comforter in the climate-controlled cold of the Big House, she'd blinked, reveling at the blackness of the room and the dark behind her eyes, joyfully unable to detect the difference. The room has been cleared of all her possessions, tumbled rocks now inside a meaningless tray on the built-in shelf, Moon's Peloton where her desk had once been, all anonymized. Stevie's things are stowed away in the locked closet with Moon's clothes and Stevie marvels at how much she doesn't miss them. She can almost pretend she has no memories there. She will barely have to pack.

She also loves the door and the thickness of the walls. The feeling of enclosure. The safety of being contained. She can't even hear her family moving around in the house in their rooms or downstairs, nor the persistent construction of the homes around them, the additions, the remodels, the constant upkeep of the lawns, the droning leaf blowers and mowers. Even the dogs.

After the park, there'd been no formal discussion that Stevie would return to the house. Her mother had beckoned her and she'd answered and she'll stay with them as long as she can. Each day is costing them, but Moon can worry about the next tenants, the mortgage, all of it. She'd had dinner with them that night, then retired upstairs, showering for a long time before putting herself to bed.

Now, clinging to the poolside wall with her legs up, the baked stone perimeter hot against her wet calves as she floats on her back, her heart beats heavily and healthfully inside her. She closes her eyes, blotches of red pulsing across her vision, and then peeks down at the scandal of her body, the bikini borrowed from Moon that barely contains her chest, her nipples erect as her breasts list toward her armpits. She checks the tie at her neck, tightening the sodden knot.

Bobbing there, she thinks how fascinating it is to have a man in the house. It is intimate and abrupt. She feels sheepish in the aftermath of her talk with him. When she'd blathered on about high school and death. It was so stupid but mostly she'd wanted him to find her thoughtful and mature, completely different from the hot girls in the parking lot, even while wanting him to find her as attractive. Now that they live together, he seems to taunt her, shouting in her face with his large maleness. During breakfast he'd thundered downstairs to appear beside her without warning, shirtless, the sudden breadth of his chest imposing and obscene in its nippled bulk. He'd asked her an inane question about laundry and the dullness and sincerity of the conversation lent a plausible innocence to his ludicrous nakedness, and she'd stared unblinkingly into his eyes, wondering if he was fucking with her, afraid that if she reacted in any way, averting her gaze or reaching for her phone, she'd come off prudish and clumsy.

At work, Stevie's wondered about how he spends his time, and now that she's witnessed his habits, she can't imagine it would be any other way. He is busy but with small, self-imposed chores. He hadn't worked all day yesterday or earlier that morning or afternoon. He'd taken a call before lunch, going outside to pace, but there'd been an ease in his rolling gait and an idle playfulness to the way he'd pivoted on his heel to walk back. Still, he is constantly moving. He gets up at six, leaving the kitchen smelling of coffee from mail-order frozen pods that are overnighted to him, to step out onto the lawn barefoot where he thrusts and squats, grunting as he lifts, pulling large black weights toward him, or jumping in furious bursts, hands held out in front of him like claws. All morning she'd spied on him unseen. Tucking herself behind a wall or else peering down from her room while he sprawls by the pool like a lizard, an arm or leg dangling into the water as though to keep the rest of him cool. She's called in sick today, something she's never done before, without telling either of them. And she wonders how it would feel to be so unburdened by the concept of labor, without each hour signifying a certain dollar amount after taxes. She also wonders how long all of this can possibly last, but for now it gives her the sense of summer vacation. Of rest earned.

Getting hungry, she swims to the shallow side. She pulls herself up as water sluices off her strong legs and she steps up, keenly aware of her round fullness, the way she bulges out of the bottom of her bikini, ass cheeks gobbling up the scrap of textile, bare feet hot on limestone. She reaches for her striped towel, wraps herself in it, as Moon and Adam discuss a woman they both know. "Twins at fifty-five," hisses Moon from behind dark glasses, gesturing in the air with a large fork. "And she wanted a home birth, *surrounded by family*." Stevie takes a seat next to hers, facing them.

Beyond Moon, Adam's grilling, wearing long linen pants, apron strings tied at his back. He looks overwarm and subdued and Stevie wonders what's led them to this discussion or how invested Adam could possibly be. She removes her towel and arranges herself on top, adjusting the lawn chair to lean back.

"Her oldest is twenty-two," continues Moon. "What twenty-two-year-old needs to see his mother in that state?" Moon points toward her midsection. "And when those little ones are twenty-two, she's going to be seventy-seven, wait, is that right? Yeah, seventy-seven. I mean, Jesus fucking Christ, just because you can, do you necessarily need to?"

"That'll never be me," Stevie says. Her mother turns to her, her expression concealed by the sunglasses, reminding Stevie of the hard glint of security cameras at work. Their attention on her body registers as pressure.

"Jesus, beanie," Moon exclaims, glancing at Adam for corroboration. "This suit's a little, *little*, don't you think? Not that there's anything wrong with your body, your body's wonderful. It's just, is that even comfortable? There's no support." Moon gestures toward her chest with both hands.

"Who cares," Stevie says, cheeks burning. "It's just us."

She'd worried Moon would recognize the suit since she'd stolen it from her closet, out of a white plastic bin full of bikinis, at least twenty different swimsuits that she knows her mother hasn't thought about in years.

"Wait, so no kids for you?" Adam asks. "At all?"

"This can't surprise you," she says. "After everything we've talked about." Stevie senses her mother's curiosity but Moon doesn't condescend to ask.

Moon continues on. "I guess it's the twenty-two-year-old who's fucked. Taking care of all of them when they're forty." She lifts a Diet Coke to her mouth, throwing her head back, shaking the can when she's finished with it.

"Fridge cigarette," remarks Stevie, and her mother stops talking, expression soft. Open.

"Fridge cigarette," Moon says with a small frown. "I was just talking about that. Didn't I say the same thing to you?" she calls out to Adam, lifting the empty can. She squeezes Stevie's foot with affection.

It was Mac's favorite vice, beloved more than even his whiskey, the one thing he was sensitive about, finding it tasteless and American to be addicted to Diet Cokes of all things, sharing a habit with some low-class mom from a square state. He'd make it until the afternoon, after lunch, to have his first, preferably in a mini can, with a proper straw that he would chew to bits. And then, depending on the day, he would take down two or three more before dinner.

Adam approaches and removes an actual cigarette from the pale blue pack on the table. He puts it in his mouth, using the long lighter for the grill, tilting his head, scowling as he lights it.

"Kinder bar," says Adam, plucking the smoke from his mouth to exhale.

"God," Moon says, looking up at him and laughing. "Such a man-orexic."

Kinder bar wasn't the German chocolate. It was exactly half a Kind bar. Mac was constantly on a diet, and the dad joke was that a snack was only made kinder if you had half. It was Stevie who usually had the other half, even if they never split satisfactorily, shards of nut flying everywhere.

She glances up at Adam and he's watching her, looking rakish and rumpled as he smokes. And she remembers the last time he'd smoked with her, how long ago it had been, and how different he looks now. Bare feet, standing in the bright heat of late summer. She wonders if it'll be another six years before she sees him again. She'll basically be thirty at that point, which is outrageous. And he'll be properly old. Married with kids from the sound of it.

That night at the Christmas party, she'd asked for a drag, stepping closer to him, heart racing, but he'd laughed at her, white puff of steam rising from his mouth. *Fuck no*, he'd said, laughing, calling her a baby.

Presently, he waves at the air with pursed lips, the long lighter still in his hands, as if to dispel the smoke. Moon reaches up to take the cigarette from him, but Stevie extends her longer arm to intercept it. "Can I have some?"

He gives Moon a questioning look.

"I'm basically twenty-one," she reminds them. Moon's lips thin, but she nods, adding, "Don't go crazy," before Adam hands it to her. Stevie takes it, her pruned fingers touching his, and when she lifts the filter to her lips, she is aware that she is putting her mouth where his had been, before Moon could. And again, she loves this closeness. The three of them with her in the middle. Wishing it could last forever.

They both watch her and she revels in it. Lapping up their undivided attention. The way both their gazes are fixed on her. She takes a tentative puff and it catches immediately at the back of her throat, and she chokes, coughs, rising to her feet.

"Easy," he says, watching her as Moon gets up to pound her on the back.

Stevie laughs, eyes watering, embarrassed but gratified as Moon laughs too.

"See," says her mother, pointing. "It's a sign. It's a terrible disgusting habit. Never do it again. Don't stay in your bathing suit all day, pee after sex, never pluck your eyebrows. And never ever, ever smoke. It'll make you old before your time."

"I've smoked before," Stevie croaks, still choking, sounding like a child.

"Yeah, you're a real pro," says Moon, sticking the butt between her teeth and immediately looking cool. And when Moon gets up, the backs of her thighs reveal the lined pattern of the lawn chair, and Stevie marvels at her prim tidiness, the prepossession radiating off her no matter what her mother's doing or how she's dressed.

Moon peers at the meat on the grill, prods it, then lifts it onto a cutting board with her large fork. And Stevie thinks how she'll never tire of watching her. That Moon will always be her favorite show.

"I'm hungry," Stevie calls out. Adam warns them that the meat has to rest but Moon saws off an end piece, cigarette angled out from her lips, and when Stevie opens her mouth like a baby bird, her mother feeds her. The meat explodes with fat and salt and tastes like love.

"Overdone?" Moon asks with concern, and Stevie shakes her head, bursting with bittersweet sorrow. She longs to hoard however much of her mother as she can before she leaves. She wants to swallow her whole and carry her around in her mouth.

"No, it's perfect," says Stevie, and then, in a sudden unchecked burst of giddiness, wanting to be closer, Stevie opens her towel like a flasher to bundle her mother against her wet body, and Moon shrieks, running away as Stevie chases.

DAY FIFTEEN

ADAM

He holds the damp purple fabric up to his nose and inhales. It is clean, the clean of colorfast bleach, of name-brand detergent. He holds it out to eyeball its size, triumphant that he'd sent it back into the hot cycle with an extra rinse and it hasn't shrunk. Stevie's work shirt had been disgusting. Malodorous, practically crinkly with grime, and when he'd seen it hanging on the back of a chair, he couldn't resist. Even as he'd privately judged Moon that she would never think to wash it herself.

With Stevie in the room next door, he feels a sense of relief. During the day, he mostly stays indoors, completing an errand in the mid-afternoon, then going for a run after dinner, but all without the urgency and anxiety that would have consumed him in New York. In New York he'd felt that he was doing the wrong thing at the incorrect time and was constantly late, everyone else seeming to be plugged into different migratory patterns.

Here, he finds satisfaction in small household achievements and experiences the fullness of trips to the grocery store and farmers markets in service of feeding his family. The routine and regularity of their meals settles his nervous system and his stomach. He's deleted the dating apps, as well as the social media apps he reluctantly keeps up for work, eliminating any comparisons of his life to others'. He has even archived the group chat from the Hong Kong crew and is sleeping soundly through the night, finally, his new tracking ring consistently reporting sleep scores in the high eighties. Plus, he isn't drinking and feels clear-eyed and lighter for it. And finally, he has taken to masturbating only once a day, less an act of pleasure than ablution, a clearing out, trying not to dwell on details such as duration or the consistency of his erection.

He's enjoying these honeyed L.A. days, and as he lays Stevie's shirt flat on a pool towel on top of the dryer, Stevie passes the laundry room but then backtracks.

"Is that mine?" She's wearing soccer shorts and a white bra, barefaced with her hair up. She snatches it, feeling for damp. "It's wet," she says, dismayed. "I have to leave for work, like, now to catch the bus." She glares at him, then throws it into the dryer, and when she bends over, there are stretch marks high on her thighs.

"What time is it?" she asks, and he keeps his attention securely north of her chest.

"Almost seven," he says.

She pushes past him and he follows her into the kitchen. She opens the fridge to remove a glass dish of last night's leftovers and peels off the silicone lid.

"Why doesn't Google Maps ever tell you when a bus is coming? Like, if a bus is late, they just tell you how late it is, like minus however many minutes from the time it was supposed to arrive. But they never tell you how many more minutes it's going to be. Why tell us how late it is? We know how late it is. We're standing right there. Just admit you lost the thing and that you fucking hate bus people."

As she talks, she fishes out a large piece of steak with her fingers to pop into her mouth, a charred piece of greenery falling between her breasts, leaving a snail trail on her cleavage. He was about to tell her to get a plate but now wants to tell her to put on a shirt. He'd overheard her say to Moon at the pool, *It's just us*, and he's pleased that she's so comfortable around him but now as she roots around in her bra with her mouth full, he wonders if there's such a thing as too comfortable.

He turns away to grab a paper towel and is annoyed but unsurprised to find only a half-sheet left on the bared cardboard tube.

"Do you want a ride?" he asks, heading to the pantry for another roll.

She looks up, smiling, the manipulation plain on her face, and pops another oily morsel into her mouth. "Yeah," she says. And watching him replenish the paper towels to hand her a sheet, she adds, "Thanks, Dad," and smiles.

She's kidding. He knows she's kidding but he's strangely affected by it.

She sets the bowl down, chewing juicily. "See, that's what Moon doesn't get. It feels good to take care of people. It's what I like about my job."

He thinks of Stevie's foul shirt. "Moon takes care of people in different ways," he says diplomatically and she gives him a hard look that makes him laugh.

"So you like your job," he says levelly, and she nods. Adding, "You know I got a promotion?"

"That's amazing," he says, meaning it, and she lights up. She tells him the job is surprisingly pedantic. "Harder than you'd think," she says. There are protocols for everything: thick, bound folders of information that they are expected to memorize, as well as exams. Speaking animatedly, there's something infectious and delightful about her enthusiasm, and he thinks that this is how he'll broach the subject of Fisheries when he sees his mother. He'd gotten an email about their annual benefit picnic; they were honoring a Chilean filmmaker that year, with a letter from the outgoing executive director. He would be wildly underqualified for such a senior position, but he could bring renewed vigor to their fundraising efforts. An outsider could be good for them. In fact, if there was a total reorg, how outrageous would it be for him to be considered for leadership?

"We should celebrate," he says, feeling suddenly optimistic, but Stevie waves off the suggestion.

"Don't tell Moon," she says.

"You can't be so pessimistic," he says. Stevie is too inexperienced to know how persuasive conviction can be. "You have to give her a chance to come around."

He imagines the quote his mother would supply for the press release. Tactful but thrilled.

"I'm serious," she says. "Don't say anything. We're in a good place right now." He starts to argue but she raises her hand to cut him off.

"Don't do that," she says, smile hardening. "Don't tell me about my life."

She pulls off the domed lid of the cake stand and picks up a cut slice of apple cake with her hands and takes a bite. "Like, the baking, the cleaning, I appreciate all of it, but don't act like you'll always be here. I'm not like you guys with the *pretending*. You can't just tell me things because you like hearing yourself say them or it's *interesting* to see where I'll take it." She takes another bite. "I'm not trying to be harsh, but it's true," she says with her mouth full.

She eats without pleasure. As though beating a buzzer or filling a hole. And he finds himself thinking of the pool house, the sad bunched sheets on the floor, and wonders if she'll return there when he leaves. He can't bear the idea of it. He reaches for a cabinet and takes out a glass and as he fills it with water, he ruminates on how different her life could be.

It is undeniable that Stevie is healthier under his care. It's as if they're getting better together. It's like watching illness leave her body, the way the hollows at her eyes have filled. She showers now with regularity. And he's convinced that the longer he stays the more she'll improve. He's aware she's been conditioned for disappointment but he isn't Mac or Moon and she needs to know that.

"Fine," he tells her. "I'm here now, though, what do you need?"

"Water," she says, looking down at the one in his hand.

He laughs and gives it to her.

She drinks in big, childish gulps, exhaling noisily when she comes up for air.

"What else?" he asks.

"A car."

"Take mine," he says.

"To have?"

"To use."

She nods with a dry expression as though he's haggling with her.

"I thought you couldn't drive," he says.

"I can drive, I just don't."

In the car, he shows her how to adjust the seat. The mirrors. The wheel. Lights. He explains the varied tones of the low beeps, showing her the aerial views of the car on the tablet display. At first she is nervous, unused to the absence of idling in an electric car, that she has to keep a foot on the accelerator. *The brakes are too sensitive*, she complains, lurching violently as they leave the driveway. At a stop—a beep filling the cavern of the vehicle—the other car passes before Stevie understands that it's the shrubbery beside her that has set off the sensors. "This car is kind of dumb," she whispers, but they circle the block several times, advancing as far as Los Feliz Boulevard before Adam takes over and drives her to work.

"Mac was a terrible driving instructor," she tells him, and he privately wonders how he stacks up. "He had absolutely zero faith in me. Like I was going to get us killed, which is actually a really unhelpful energy. You should have seen how scared he was. He would jolt, like physically jump." She startles out of her seat to show him, grabbing the door. "And then he'd slam the floor on his side." She demonstrates again, bringing her foot down. "As if a brake would magically appear, and it would scare the shit out of me.

"Every time we were done, he'd be so happy," she recalls with a headshake. "And I'd have to thank him like, '*Great Job!*' like he was a little kid, because he so obviously needed it, even if he'd just screamed in my face for twenty minutes. It was amazing. I swear to god, to this day, he thinks he dadded the shit out of the driving thing."

She laughs, then abruptly looks toward the sky. "Sorry, Mac," she says, then turns to Adam. "Was he like that with you? Mean but needy?"

"All the time."

"It's weird but I never thought about what a nightmare he must have been to work with."

They pass the shaggy heads of palm trees planted beside low-boughed Christmassy cedars, evergreens that have never seen cold climates, and Adam considers Mac's rages. How his furies were violent but quick. The worst was that once it was over, no matter how abusive he'd been, he would be sheepishly penitent and expect to be forgiven. Adam has seen Mac launch himself across the table to scream directly in the face of a casting director, a woman who'd not so much as blinked as he yelled, and when she'd refused to hug it out, he'd found a way to fire her.

The man couldn't stand lingering resentments. Whenever he was late to set, he would send his assistant ahead of him peeling hundred-dollar bills off a thick knot with his apologies. And the crew would be forced to cheer when he finally arrived, not that they were mollified, but because the first AD would beg them to. If anyone ever seemed sullen or resentful at all, Mac would find every excuse to keep wasting time.

Adam hadn't grown up in a screaming house. It was deemed low-rent. The more physical exertion a sentiment required, the more brutish and base it was considered. Theirs was a house of withholding. Of icing out. Of outright ignoring unless there was an audience, in front of whom excoriating humiliation in the name of fun was par for the course. But the one time Mac screamed and Adam raged back, he'd seen excitement light the man's face and it chilled him to see the bloodlust in his eyes. It's why Adam mostly took to evasion.

But in Hong Kong, Adam had left with CiCi and as easily as he could have put her in a cab and sent her away, he'd gotten in with her. He'd done it to fuck with Mac. Out of contempt. And this will have been his final act toward a man he'd loved. And he'd even exploited a woman in the exchange for good measure.

"I can't stop thinking about the driving," says Stevie. "That he definitely didn't want to die."

It's what troubles him most too. The inconsistency of the permanence. How unlike Mac it is to do something that couldn't immediately be undone.

He pulls up in front of Stevie's store, suddenly so exhausted that there's a tremor in his hands.

"Can I ask for one more thing?" she asks.

He nods.

"Don't disappear. I know you have to go to New York, but don't just be gone one day. I want notice."

"OK."

She searches his expression to see if he means it, then unhooks her seat belt. "I know what I said earlier but you're actually a really stable force in my life right now," she says. "Unlike either of them."

She waves at him through the window, and once her back is turned, he swallows, wondering how she could have known how desperately he'd needed to hear that. And how he's definitely going to fuck this up.

THE HERMITAGE VOLUMES

[1997]

The Hermitage Volumes is Moon's first movie. Technically sixteen movies. Also, *The Sex Tape*, so to speak. Made on a Canon XL-1, when she was squatting at the rambling house downtown that now hosts weddings and corporate off-sites called The Hermitage. The director and Moon's boyfriend at the time, had likened it to Warhol's Factory, if parking had been the presiding concern.

Moon had arrived in L.A. by bus, spent the week at Holiday Lodge, and rapidly run out of money. The motel, not incidentally the same motel she'd stayed at with Stevie the last time the tenants displaced them, was walking distance from the Greyhound station. And as Moon dragged her suitcase behind her, desperate for a sign, she'd looked up to see such a sign. A fabulously deco, mid-century neon testament to sun-bleached Hollywood glamour, and despite the leathery inhabitants that gathered to chain-smoke on plastic chairs in the parking lot, Moon took it to be auspicious.

She'd been standing right under the sign, scratching a mosquito bite on her leg, pancake ass hanging out of a smocked boob tube she'd worn as a dress, cat's-eye glasses and bloodred lipstick, all of eighteen—appalling for Moon to think of now—and the director, mixed-race, short, and wearing a daisy-print shirt, had backed up in his antacid yellow 1973 Chrysler Imperial. And even as her heart hammered, she'd kept it cool, laughing when he'd lowered his sunglasses and said, *Quick, get in.*

She'd lowered her sunglasses right back, *Well, what took you so long?* And climbed in because it felt like a movie. Because she's always just wanted her life to be a movie.

The Volumes themselves are 960 minutes of recorded surveillance footage of Moon and two other squatters divided into sixty-minute cassettes. It has since become a cult classic among fans of endurance video art such as *Logistics*, the 2012 Swedish documentary that runs 857 hours, and *La Flor*, an Argentinian drama running thirteen hours that was shot over ten years, with six episodes, four actors.

This was when people were still going to the movies. With big box office weekends. *Titanic. Men in Black. The Lost World: Jurassic Park.* The sorts of transportive, four-quadrant fun for the whole family that would allay fears and quash misgivings about the Heaven's Gate mass suicide, the death of Princess Diana, and the Asian market crash. And Moon, having taken no college courses or spent meaningful time with other artists, was swept up by the desire to make something slow, quiet, and oppressively mundane and be high-minded about it.

Because this is what life feels like, it's art imitating life, but this is our life only because we are making art, she'd said during a particularly bracing conversation that she'd only later learn was the by-product of the weed in the blunt she was smoking being dipped in sherm, or embalming fluid, also known as liquid PCP.

And the director, giving no indication that they would essentially be ripping off another artist's thesis project during his MFA at Bard, hammered on about class and status. *It's like, anti Windows 95 and pro the Unabomber manifesto,* he said dreamily, and how they as *disenfranchised poor people are holding attention hostage and taking back power.* Except no one with a job or semblance of upward mobility watched *The Volumes* in their entirety. And Moon would also later learn at his funeral in a sprawling Protestant megachurch in Diamond Bar that the unhoused gonzo filmmaker was a trust-fund baby with real-estate-mogul parents who were, actually, early investors in Microsoft.

The Hermitage Volumes were about nonviolence. And a pointed lack of planning. It was as much a film as Warhol's *Sleep*, the five hours of looped footage of his lover sleeping, but theirs would not be looped. They would do it for real, shooting over five weeks. They would eat breakfast. Exercise. Lie on the floor. Lie on the couch. Lie on the couch with their legs up against the wall. Race around the living room with one of them on a rolling office chair. Sing songs in front of the industrial fan on the floor since they had no AC. Sometimes one of them would be sick in bed and the camera would remain with them. Other times there was no one in the frame for almost an hour. Filmed without sound and grainy, it was deliberately voyeuristic as though to suggest the camera was hidden.

The director had been obsessed with legacy. And right before he died of lymphoma, he'd released *The Volumes* under a Creative Commons license. This was seen as part of his genius. He was considered disruptive and innovative. Open-source before open-source. Some real secret-rich-kid Robin Hood behavior. Meanwhile, it was Moon who'd gotten fucked.

But in other moments Moon thinks of *The Volumes* as exposure therapy for white America. She is the lead. The only person to look at for much of it. Doing all the things at home that everyone does in theirs. She'd had more screen time than either of the boys. Than the boys combined. It was a decade before the first iPhone. Same with YouTube. Long before social media and OnlyFans. She hadn't imagined there would be a way to monetize the footage or that surveillance would become the most profitable global entertainment machine. She'd been prescient but not cynical enough.

DAY SIXTEEN

MOON

TWO WEEKS UNTIL THE NEW TENANTS

"I have good news," says Tali, her manager, over Zoom. "They want to remake *The Chronicles*."

She always calls it the wrong thing.

Moon's sitting outside on the stairs, eyeing the half cigarette perched in a terra-cotta plant saucer wishing she could just smoke, but Tali, a two-pack-a-day diehard at her peak, is decimating a tea tree oil toothpick with her teeth, so Moon leaves it.

"It's not *The Chronicles*, it's *The Volumes*," she says.

There are two other squares on the call, *Michelle* and *TaliAsst*, blacked out, cameras off, with a little red symbol to denote they're muted but listening. She hates the unseen audience of them, knowing they're all probably in the same air-conditioned office, on the same floor, mere feet from each other but not interacting. Even Tali's sight line, the preening pout of her lips, suggests that she's talking to her own reflection.

It makes a difference, Moon thinks. To meet in person, be forced to embrace, remind themselves of their humanity, their legs, the texture of their hair, to at least ask about each other's families before getting parking validated.

"What else have they done?" Moon asks, and Tali's shoulders collapse slightly, her irritation obvious. "They're very dynamic," says Tali. "Both women, new to film but very culturally relevant, young and exciting. One's a playwright, the other a curator."

Another voice comes on, *TaliAsst*, the red border around her still-black square pulsing. She haltingly recites names that Moon does not recognize and a few other proper nouns from what Moon gathers is from the women's CVs, but with a few more questions, it's established that they are more famously known as the twentysomething daughter of a record producer and the granddaughter of a literal former American vice president.

"But they're so much more," enthuses Tali, rattling off the statistics of the girls' social media followings as well as their other ventures—a prebiotic soda, protein ice cream, and a cosmetics line. Tali reminds Moon they don't technically need her participation or blessing. "They're doing it as 'inspired by,' not 'based on a true story,'" she says. As if Moon needs to be reminded. She's well aware that her role in *The Hermitage Volumes* is often cited as a landmark case in fair use and clearance. But while they don't need her life rights, they're eager to give her a speaking role. "They're being really empowering," says Tali. "They're fans." Moon imagines the casting updates from *Deadline*, the haggard photo of her at some daytime function for the comp spliced beside whatever tender Asian talent—likely Waysian—would play her.

Revulsion settles around her shoulders. The assistants are probably rolling their eyes. And why wouldn't they pity her? For her branding fuck-up. For fumbling her bag. Every zillennial is an expert at marketing and self-promotion. The less Moon's heard of someone the more famous they are. Influencers with milquetoast faces are signed to CAA and launch consumer businesses that sell for billions. Meanwhile, at eighteen, Moon hadn't even signed a release.

She can't believe the funeral, the photos, the moment with the Royal has only amounted to this. She'd been expecting calls, lunches, anything to signal the next right step. She could have made more efforts on social but the prospect of it had made her morbidly depressed.

“What’s the deal like?” she asks finally.

“Business affairs is still talking,” says Tali, and Moon watches her agent’s eyes migrate to the part of her screen where her emails must be open.

“It’ll get you in front of a whole new audience,” says Tali. “It’s good news.”

After the call, Moon lights the cigarette. It tastes like shit; anything would, she is on the second day of a period that only comes every four months and her sense of smell is superhuman. The scorching afternoon is suffused with the scent of rotting leaves from the rains during the week and the toasted fresh hay of cut grass. Earlier as she was peeing, she’d dislodged a menacing blood clot that looked *knuckly*, the ferrous tang almost knocking her back.

She stubs the smoke out, exhales, and absently checks Howie’s Instagram account. The old lodger, *Howie Yoo? Fine.* He still hasn’t asked for a refund, hasn’t updated his feed since October 2021, and she finds it impossible that he wouldn’t have heard about Mac or seen the pictures. She feels wounded that he hasn’t contacted her, and then laughs when she realizes this. She is definitely on her period.

She goes back inside, setting both hands on the cool surface of the stone countertop, then spreads her arms, nudging the fruit bowl aside, pushing her coffee mug out of the way until her left cheek, breasts, entire torso is flattened, pressed up against the cold. She lies there for a moment. Thrilled to be home alone. She’ll do the job. She closes her eyes, cringing at Tali’s reaction, the exact way her assistant had sounded breathless, eager, yet somehow with the condescending patience of a young person talking to a very old person. She shifts her head up, gaze landing on the cheap gilt bowl purchased from Home Goods. There are moments throughout the day when she looks around her house and is insulted to think that anyone, Dano, the tenants, even Howie would think that she would decorate this way.

She lifts the bowl; it still features a dusty price tag stuck to the bottom of it. They leave things in it, coins, car keys, vape cartridges, once a dog chew, some heinous piece of pig cartilage with scalloped white teeth marks in it. She'd had a beautiful, burled maple vessel that had been hand turned by an artist in San Luis Obispo but someone had left a sumo orange to rot in it for three weeks and Moon had thrown it out.

The new tenants have contacted her on the app again. They take turns, the wife and the husband, asking her various questions, whether the pool is heated, if she has a spare Pack 'n Play. It's all but presumed that Moon and Stevie will be off the premises. They're negotiating whether or not they can bring their dog. A pet fee through the app is an extra two hundred dollars a day as well as a thousand-dollar deposit, but they've offered five thousand cash all in, up front, to keep the animal in the Pool House. But only if that's OK. Otherwise, *we might have to make other arrangements ☹*.

They're normal people, they keep insisting. *Regular Brooklynites*, as it says on their bio. Their arrival is imminent. She has to tell Stevie soon. She'll get an earful about the timing but they don't have a choice. She tries to think what she did for her twenty-first birthday but can't recall. And for all she knows Stevie's made plans that don't include her. Which, fine. But she'll have to at least help clean, which also means they'll have to kick Dano out soon.

There is no tactful way to do it and on certain days it seems that he has no intention of ever leaving. She peels herself off the counter and looks around the spacious kitchen, staring at the gold faucet on the backsplash, trying to remember how much it cost. She'd had to run water as well as gas behind that wall. It had to have been something stupid but how much? Two thousand? Five? Ten? She has absolutely no idea anymore.

She'd remodeled the house with the thought to own it forever. Her sofa is custom, her bed too. Sitcom money feels like a fever dream now. The regularity and abundance. She goes upstairs, trailing the wallpaper with her fingertips, recalling those early days of couch surfing. When she'd slept in her car and hung out at Canters, nursing free refills of coffee to hustle whatever lonely dandruffy dude into buying her a hot sandwich in the small hours or split their crêpes Suzette. She'd slept with a few of them, more than she'd care to remember and sometimes just to use their shower. But she doesn't talk or think about it. She's just glad Stevie won't ever have to make any of the same choices.

But when she pushes open Stevie's bedroom door, she's appalled by the state of it. Unmade bed. Clothes all over the floor. A pool towel clumped in a heap. She picks it up to find it wet, grunting as she rises, then steps onto the corner of something plastic and unyielding, her knee almost crumpling. She lifts up some sweats, exposing the offending phone charging cube and kicks it angrily, watching it ricochet off the wall, leaving a mark, and then drops the pants to discover a lime-green thong that has wormily felted itself to one of the legs. Moon stares at it, genuinely disturbed by its crotchy soiled tawdriness. She bends down, wishing she had a capped pen like a detective at a crime scene, repulsed, wondering who the underpants are for.

They'd always been frank about sex. She'd raised Stevie without the puritanical shame of most Americans. Stevie had been well-supplied with books on growing bodies, periods, masturbation, and sex. She'd read the entire Judy Blume canon by the time she was ten. They'd even shared a hardback journal where Stevie could write in questions that Moon would answer and they never had to talk about it face-to-face unless Stevie wanted to.

But with the arrival of breasts, Moon watched Stevie become inhibited, uncomfortable, constantly tugging at her clothes, her body a calling card for the worst sorts, squelching her youth, heralding an adulthood that she seemed squeamish about. It had been an ostentatious shock, Stevie's body. Full C-cups out of nowhere at fifteen, her legs lengthening beyond Moon's, fleshy curves leavening, and Moon, who'd never experienced such a dramatic puberty herself, felt something akin to estrangement. Certainly overwhelm. Stevie's body recalled the Russian territories in the board game Risk. A foolish terrain to even attempt to protect with Moon's own small frame. She's felt estranged from her daughter's body. Even a sense of betrayal at the genes that so clearly were not her own. The Korean father whose pedigree is as mysterious to Moon as her own father's.

The underwear feels like an invasion. An artless, vulgar intrusion. It is the underwear of third-world sex workers. The fake lace hewn from plastic extrusion fibers that should carry a P65 health warning, and a lewd flash spikes through Moon's thoughts, of Stevie arcing her back, robotically mimicking the moans and motions from porn. Stevie is definitely having sex. Sex of posturing and commerce, of ads and marketing and subjugation, and she now wonders where Stevie is.

With her hands full of laundry, peevishly folding the sweatpants to avoid handling the panties, Moon draws the curtains back, opening the windows to clear the air.

Twenty-one. Older than Moon when she began her career. She has no prospects. No plans. A girl like Stevie is supposed to be in school making interesting friends, hooking up with sheltered boys she will fall in and out of love with, realizing her own ambitions and joining a scene. Stevie is soft. Hopelessly uninitiated.

Looking around the room, it dawns on her that she's spoiled Stevie. She's as coddled as veal from a childhood of comfort and luxury. She feels frantic at the thought. And when she turns to go, Moon sees on the doorknob a tangle of white strung on it, recognizing it as Stevie's bikini. She shakes her head, recalling the salacious strips of textile, but when she reaches for it to launder, knowing it will have been abandoned still wet, left to mildew, she feels the square acrylic beads on the ties. The memory arrives at once. Of the suit that matches the ludicrously expensive coverup she'd bought on Via Della Spiga in Milan before Stevie was even born. It is Moon's bathing suit that Stevie borrowed and never mentioned and now Moon's fear blooms to fury.

She walks straight out of the room, down the hall, across the upstairs living room to her walk-in closet, surveying the room full of hanging bags, looking around with a sense of outrage. She's given Stevie everything and now her daughter values nothing. She imagines her daughter clumsily pulling on too-small priceless garments, the seams straining across her back, when she would have gladly loaned Stevie whatever she wanted. To think she'd felt so guilty about the tenants. All while Stevie was stealing from her.

Moon is not a monster. She isn't screaming about wire hangers. And now she recalls that Stevie hadn't even returned the dress from the funeral. She storms downstairs in search of her phone—she will make Stevie tear apart her bedroom until she finds it and force her to dry-clean it—and as Moon circles the living room, Dano's car pulls into the driveway. She marches out her front door, barefoot, impatient for him to approach and call her phone, but as the shadows of the eaves reduce the glare in the windshield, she sees Stevie's hands on the wheel, face hidden but unmistakably her, and Moon forces herself to get a grip. To exhale slowly at the new information.

So she's driving again. This time with Dano as she once had with Mac. And before she can even ask herself why, Moon ducks back into the house before either of them sees her, to watch them.

THE WEDDING

[LAST FALL]

The Ojai Valley Inn would not have been Mac's choice to have a wedding. But he'd been married in a castle in the Scottish Highlands, at Hotel du Cap-Eden-Roc, as well as at City Hall in New York, and it seemed only fair to defer to his new wife since it was the first and hopefully only time she would be married. Corinna, the second oldest of six, all the siblings with names beginning with C, had always been sentimental. She'd wanted to get married where her parents had. Since her parents' wedding, the inn had expanded, adding a spa, and this was all her father talked about, not once mentioning, at least not on the day, that Mac was a year older than him and six years older than his wife. By all accounts it was a lovely affair. In fact, of the 268 attendees, *lovely* was the most deployed description for the nuptials.

They were married on the Orchard Lawn, with the reception held at the Hacienda Ballroom. The bride wore custom Valentino and Jimmy Choo and a vintage silk slip for the after-party reminiscent of the one Carolyn Bessette-Kennedy wore, a personal style hero of Corinna's, but not her older sister who was actually named Carolyn.

Corinna wanted to walk down the aisle to an Evanescence song, but Mac vetoed it on the basis of it having lyrics but also because he couldn't stand the thought. Stevie would have loved it. Despite her choice in men, Stevie thought Corinna had excellent taste. She was willowy but wore deliberately ugly designer shoes as well as owlish glasses to indicate that she was beautiful but found it embarrassing at times. And while her acting career was holding steady as the attractive girl in a party scene with one line, she also had a DJ career that was just ironic enough to befit celebrity friends' parties, like the prom that a pair of fashion designer sisters held annually, as well as the birthday party of another designer who had also made a recent foray into Japanese listening bars.

Corinna has always made Adam uneasy. The first time they'd met, they'd quickly figured out that they'd been at some of the same parties. In fact, she'd told him that he'd dated one of her friends but wouldn't tell him which one, implying that she hadn't approved of his conduct. When he didn't attend their wedding, she'd texted him despite not having his number, which meant that Mac had given it to her. She was unsettlingly forthright in a way that Adam associated with being gorgeous and well-adjusted. And also entitled. It was as if she felt whatever authority Mac claimed over him to have been transferred to her by marriage. As though she could bully or reprimand Adam as easily as Mac and he resented this. She'd grown up in Santa Barbara, possessing the outdoorsy ease of Southern Californians, with none of the anxiety or even manufactured taste that L.A. transplants have to exude. She was photogenic and privileged enough to be confidently basic, wearing outfits that were flattering but utterly devoid of reference or attunement to the finer aspects of what was happening in silhouette or texture in the current season. She claimed not to get fashion while being given clothes that flattered her. Adam resented this also. The groom wore Brunello Cucinelli. The reception did not go into overtime. Most of Corinna's friends did not drink. Moon would have had a terrible time beyond the gloating.

DAY SEVENTEEN

STEVIE

Stevie feels so fucking future. She feels beautiful and excited, already nostalgic for the night, the amazing time she's going to have. She's wearing archival Gaultier from 2004, pilfered from Moon, a mesh top swirling with butterflies that she's seen reselling on auction sites for three hundred dollars, which thrills her. And when she'd changed in the Pee Wee's bathroom, even under the sickly lighting, she'd looked at herself in the mirror with a sense of recognition. This was who she was meant to be. This was Stevie living her life. Moon had said so herself, it was time for Moon to be part of Stevie's life, not the other way around.

She gazes up at the power lines, then down at Freddie, seized by wistfulness. She will miss the drama of Freddie's face, the animated eyebrows, the insistent, muscular movements of her mouth when she speaks. There are fifteen or so of them standing around like cows by a spray-painted dumpster in the alley that runs the length of Fairfax, smoking weed with music playing at a volume low enough to skirt both noise ordinance and normal human acoustic detection. They're still close enough to work to catch the Pee Wee's Wi-Fi, but she tries not to dwell on this, instead focusing on feeling young and carefree, wishing it felt more glamorous.

It's an unprecedented series of events that has brought them there.

Mel from the cupcake boutique had sought Stevie out and gone, *Stevie, right?* and when Stevie nodded, Mel went, *I saw you on Deux Moi with the Royal,* tactfully adding, *I'm sorry for your loss.* Stevie was shocked to be confronted by her other life in this way. It seemed insane to talk about Mac while wearing her Pee Wee's uniform to Mel, of all people.

Freddie had been astounded but Stevie, who'd always found Mel unbothered and cool, thought it was also possible that Mel wasn't as cool as she'd previously thought. And after, when Freddie said, *She's not as pretty up close, right?* Stevie had known exactly what she meant. Mel wasn't beautiful, she only gave the suggestion of beauty. And Stevie marveled at this, wondering how she could pull off the same trick. Mel's skin was congested and the track of false lashes on her right eye had been crooked, lending her the impression of a mangled doll or a scary old woman who had lost her mind.

So now here they are. Stevie mimicking cool, dressed like her mother. It is perfect timing. It might even be the first and last time Stevie will have this. Earlier that day, she'd had her interview with Pee Wee's corporate. It had been uneventful and conducted online. She'd been nervous all morning, sweating with her door closed, sick with anxiety that Moon would barge in and find her, but the moment she saw the other two women on the screen, their backgrounds as provisional and spare as hers, she was filled with utter detachment. They asked about scheduling, whether or not she was still in school, and she found herself telling them that the job was her main priority and that if she considered school it would only be to take business courses to *upskill* if her new post required it.

At varying intervals during their short interview, one of the women, a blonde with intensely drawn eyebrows, would sigh or else her dog would bark, enlarging her window and muting the others, causing her to become flustered and muting herself at all the wrong moments. It all reminded Stevie of high school French, where all she had to do was parrot back most of the question in agreement, *Do you like going to the library? Yes, I like going to the library*, modulating the overall sentiment and only asking follow-up questions if they seemed excited or concerned. The idea that they were somehow superior to her, that they might hold sway in her future, seemed conceptually oblique.

She has the same sense now. That nothing is quite real. That everyone is playing a part but unconvincingly. She'd sensed from the moment they'd ended the call that the job is hers, but she can't grasp how she feels about it. And as she watches Freddie, who's changed into a Sade T-shirt that looks vintage even though it isn't, holding her phone up to Mel, her glossy mouth forming the words, *Anatomy is a mystery*, Stevie abhors the thought of starting from scratch all over again.

The gathering begins to disperse, presumably to embark on a second, more exclusive location. Stevie looks down at her shoes while Freddie scrolls on her phone, both of them knowing to tactfully avoid eye contact so they're not humiliated when they're left behind, but when Mel asks for Stevie's phone number and drops a pin, Stevie hugs her.

Back in the car, Stevie clicks through the carousel of aerial drone shots of the $4.2 million house where they're headed and she knows it's a spectacular failure of imagination that the fanciness of the staged photos, the pool area, the sunken living room with a fireplace, and the drone shots taken of the property during a Super Bloom placate her fears of being murdered at some stranger's house party like Sharon Tate, but they do.

* * *

The night is alive and the air crisp as they park at the bottom of a hill to walk up a driveway jammed with cars. The large wooden door is unlocked and there is a tinny noise that registers as music only once they're inside. The overhead lights are antiseptically harsh, giving the appearance of a place of business or a set, and as Stevie surveys the shag-covered sunken living room and the randomly placed columns, she recognizes the buzz of background music as Miley Cyrus's "Party in the USA," a selection almost hostile in how desultory it is.

Mel's in the kitchen with a friend, a young woman in a skirt with a waistband slung so low that it throws Stevie into anatomical confusion about the location of her genitals. They're talking about a literary zine

Mel is making. "It's like the opposite of AI," she says, widening the circle to allow Freddie and Stevie to join them. Mel tells them that all of the submissions are written by hand and printed that way and Stevie wonders about illegible penmanship or something written by ChatGPT but copied out by hand and fights the impulse to ask.

She allows her mind to wander, gazing at Freddie nodding at Mel, trying to imagine the multiverse version of the Freddie and Mel who live in the reality of Yarmouth. She wonders what their parties will be like or if she'll even be invited, and the thought fills her with such sadness that she immediately wants to go home to Moon and Adam, to make popcorn and watch movies. But she reminds herself that her current life isn't her life either. Soon, she and Moon will be back in the Pool House. And then Moon will be back alone. She imagines the Pool House on the afternoon she's left for Yarmouth and how lonely her mother will feel. No Mac. Dano. Or Stevie. The thought wrenches her insides and she wishes everything could be different.

She gazes out at the spacious living room past the kitchen struck with a sense of bitterness. She knows whoever lives here won't stay long. A house like this would have once been referred to as a "content house," one of those clout mansions that twentysomething TikTok influencers rent out in packs. Nowadays it would be referred to as a "coworking space and production studio." Just as cold, impermanent, and unloved.

She thinks of the family that could have lived there instead. Kids, grandkids, multiple generations gathering for the holidays. A real family. A normal fucking family.

Just then, Freddie squeezes her arm and says, "I'll be just a second," and disappears out of the kitchen, and Stevie knows she is searching for Sage Castro. Sage Castro is a skater who is famous depending on where you get your internet, and Stevie only knows him through the abstracted, distorted lens of Freddie's ardor. Meanwhile she's also pretty sure that Freddie has never spoken to him.

Stevie scans the large kitchen island littered with the dregs of remaindered bottles from chaotic BevMo! runs and on the other side of the counter, a tall bulky boy with shaggy brown hair watches three other shaggy-haired boys who are dancing shirtless and in unison in an adjoining area with an athletic Asian girl who wears a hoodie but no pants. They're smirking as though they find it all silly but there's a general lack of mirth to the proceedings.

Stevie locates a dry Solo cup and gives it a sniff before helping herself to a greenish bottle of Mezcal.

"You know we were gonna have a door charge for this," the boy says without looking away from the troupe.

"Oh," says Stevie, surveying the empty room. The boy's profile is studded with cystic acne, his mouth hanging slack with a sheen of visible wet on his lower lip as he watches the dancers, and Stevie is struck with the thought that she and Thor together now represent a less hot version of the other group.

"You want me to pay for this or something?" she asks, swirling the contents of her cup with her finger. The boy shakes his head, still watching the others.

Stevie is moved by his yearning, imagining the exact tenor of whimper a boy like him would make as he comes onto his belly after jerking off and wiping it with a sock that he leaves on the floor for his mother to launder. "Nah, we're good but next time look out for the pre-sale drop or you won't get in," he says. "I'm Thor by the way."

The dancers stop to gather around the iPhone mounted to a tripod and watch until one of the boys guffaws, for being cooked, apologizing as the others groan with good cheer, delivering encouraging slaps to his shoulders as they position themselves to run it back. "I'm Stevie," she says.

"Stevie, huh?" Thor asks, and Stevie knows what's coming. "Wonder or Nicks?"

Stevie looks at him, disbelieving of her own restraint with *Thor*.

"Well, I'll Valhalla at you later," she says, walking away with her disgusting cocktail.

For the next ninety minutes, Stevie pretends to read a book off her phone but mostly rehearses a speech to Freddie about loyalty and how feminism works. Eventually, when Freddie stumbles down the stairs, she rushes toward her, taking an ungainly knee beside Stevie on the carpet and saying, "Dude, don't murder me, but I can't take you home. My dad's super pissed. He's, like, shitting I'm so late."

Stevie knows that they are, at best, situational friends, but this is bullshit. "Did you at least find Sage Castro?" she asks, whispering the name, but Freddie shakes her head. Stevie rolls her eyes and checks her phone. Ride shares are surging, it will be at least eighty dollars for Stevie to get home, and as Freddie jaws open her bucket bag, raking through the contents, she can barely keep her eyes open.

"Bro, you can't drive," she tells Freddie with a careful laugh.

Freddie ignores this.

"Split a car with me," Stevie insists. "I'll drop you first. You'll get home just as fast. Probably faster. Your shit is parked so far and you're . . ."

Freddie shakes her head, finally finding the tub of gum in her bag. "It's just weed. I'm medically a better driver when I smoke because of my ADHD," she says, popping two chiclets in her mouth. "I swear, you should see me parallel park right now." Freddie holds her hand out to show how steady it is, and this makes Stevie irrationally furious. Freddie is an adult but Stevie can't believe how delusional and selfish she's being. As if killing a pedestrian or another driver is an outcome strictly reserved for people whose dads weren't *like, super pissed and shitting*. Freddie tilts her head with a severe frown, her bovine lashes flapping dramatically as "Party in the USA" repeats.

Stevie rises to her feet, trembling with anger. "Have fun with your DUI," she says, hearing the tremor in her voice.

"Why would you say that?" Freddie says, slapping Stevie's shoulder harder than what could strictly qualify as a joke, then turning in for a hug. "I'll text you when I get home. Don't stress." She sails out the door, leaving Stevie with a corkscrewing sensation high up in her chest, unable to take air into her lungs.

Stevie sits back down, eyes swimming. She checks her phone again. It is almost one a.m. and her battery is on 11 percent and when that old

Frank Ocean song about exactly the kind of bad party she is at comes on, she feels ridiculous. She leans up against the base of the couch, voiding her thoughts. She rests her phone on her tented legs and flattens her palms against the carpet, concentrating on how it feels. How the sensations travel up her arm. She looks at her shoes, focusing on keeping her breath even. She imagines her rage as a large bead of mercury in the center of her chest and it's helpful to envision it as a contained mass.

Before Moon wrecked her car, Stevie had called the whole thing. She'd expressly warned Mac about it. After a driving lesson and before they'd pulled away from the restaurant, literal Father's Fucking Office where they'd had lunch, she'd told Mac that Moon was out of control. And she'd been right. It was 108 degrees out and the AC was blasting and Stevie had to concentrate not to stare at Mac's nipples that stood rock hard under the tech fabric of his unusually tight shirt. Moon was drinking in the day. She wasn't even being subtle about the bottles anymore. And that's if she drank at home. The main issue was that she'd begun disappearing.

Stevie had agonized about telling him but Mac had only grinned at her. *It's not as bad as all that, is it?* he'd said. She remembered how hopeful he'd looked. His chin jutted out, eyes sparkling. He'd practically begged her to take it back, let him un-know it, release him from any responsibility, and when he said, *Moon's always partied*, her insides caught fire and her mouth tasted bile and she'd said, *I guess so*. He'd patted her shoulder, then squeezed it. As though he were proud of her. As though she were taking it like a champ.

The betrayal had been breathtaking. She'd told him out of desperation. Her own father was somewhere in Arizona. A programmer who didn't want anything to do with her, with a private Facebook page and a photo that included his white wife and their twin girls. Stevie had purposefully never been cute with Mac. Never girlie or precious. Didn't say *I love you*. Or *love ya*. *ILY*. They hugged rarely. Occasionally they shook hands like business associates as a bit. She didn't send any hearts, deliberately choosing a thumbs-up in response to a text. But he'd once given her his business card which she still keeps in her wallet, telling her to call if she needed him. She'd needed him and he'd dismissed her.

She discovered later that his new girlfriend was responsible for his weird shirt. And his distraction. He'd met her on his new show. She wasn't one of his daughters, *thank god*, rather a slave maiden who appeared topless in a handful of background scenes, usually saddled with some amphora or musical instrument.

Ultimately, Stevie couldn't blame him. Moon was a liability and Stevie was nothing more than an inconvenient little appendage. A sidecar of hassle. The hard shock of his rejection had left Stevie feeling fiendishly stupid. She should have known. Anyone else would have known.

At the party, there is no longer music playing, and there's something about the acoustics where Stevie can hear the conversation from clear across the room. On the other side of the large, irregularly shaped coffee table, one of the sweatshirted clump is telling the others that Hoobastank's 2004 single "The Reason" is the perfect song to accompany a dating profile because it's so specific as to betray zero information or personal interest. "You could be kidding or totally sincere," he insists, and Stevie becomes aware that with everything in life there's actually no difference.

MOON

THAT SAME NIGHT

When Moon comes downstairs, she finds Dano shirtless, in Warrior II in the middle of the kitchen, the furred nooks of his armpits and pepperoni nipples on full display, directly at Moon's sightline.

She checks the clock; it's past midnight. "Did you talk to Stevie?" she asks, irritated that she has to go through Dano for information on her daughter. She edges past him for a glass of water as he shakes his head before easing down into a chataranga, exhaling creakily into his updog. "She's still at work," he says, Adam's apple bobbing in his throat. "At least I think she is."

She wonders if she's supposed to be worried, it's unusually late, but then decides against it. Instead, she brightens the overhead lights in the living room before getting up so close to the mirror by the door that she's steaming the glass with her breath, close enough that she can see her pores, the squiggly veins in her eyes. She's still wearing her makeup from a different self-tape, another mom role, a neighborhood busybody, this time whose character description sounds suspiciously Asian (dark hair, dark eyes, could be thirty or fifty, *rule-following type*). She digs both hands into her hair, grabbing up by the roots and pulling until the slackness at her jaw and brows disappear, marveling how if she could only keep her hands this way, her nasolabial folds—the slalom of wrinkles that form a ventriloquist dummy hinge on either side of her mouth from her nostrils—would be gone and the defeated sag of her philtrum, the teardrop divot above her lip, would be shortened. Additionally she'd need an upper and lower blepharoplasty, a fat transfer below her eyes, plus a brow lift, the kind that Korea offers that hide scars in the eyebrows or even the hairline. She also wouldn't kick a neck lift out of bed but she'd need another set of hands to see those effects.

Foundationally she needs a deep plane face lift, but holding her skin up this way, her eyes appear cartoonish and slanted, evoking Jocelyn Wildenstein, that billionaire lady with the face like a cat.

Dano comes up behind her to look at himself. She hears the faraway screeching of tires and her pulse quickens, thinking of her audio, but then remembers that she isn't taping in that moment. She releases herself, scalp tingling, recalling in the nineties how European people, especially soccer teams for some reason, would make Chink Eyes for group photos and how bizarre that had been.

"You know what Mac once told me," Moon says, and Dano, who'd been flexing in the mirror, puts his arms down. "That the camera loves bipolar and that's the only reason I get cast." Actually, it hadn't been Mac, but a Polish cinematographer they'd had dinner with, but Mac had laughed and agreed with him. It was the eyes, they both said. Not the shape but her look, her *crazy eyes*.

"Yeah, well, he said I had the self-esteem of a molested kid," says Dano. She swings around to look at him. She knows exactly what Mac means but she can't believe he'd actually said it out loud.

"That's so fucked up," she says, but he only shrugs.

"Did I tell you I got a consult from Ben Telai? This was years ago," he says of the Beverly Hills plastic surgeon, shifting his nose to the left to be properly centered. "He showed me what I'd look like if they just . . ." He mushes down the tip slightly. "But I couldn't."

He scrutinizes himself, tilting his head back to look up his nostrils, and she considers how comfortable they both are doing this, that they used to do this all the time, have long rambling discussions about their appearance while staring in the mirror.

Once, years ago, a *New York* magazine writer had referred to him as *jolie laide*, "ugly pretty," describing how his huge, geometric nose seemed to prank the rest of his face, rendering his expressions too elastic, goofy, but that the contrast of his busted features with his large, muscled frame lent him BDE, rather, Big Dick Energy. The article had run alongside a gallery, close-ups of his gumby face interspersed with closer-up, slow-motion video clips of him walking in sweatpants and basketball shorts in New York.

She'd known how much this would have embarrassed him, so she texted him the link immediately and he'd responded with a meme of Moon in her pregnant red carpet dress and she'd felt her heart swell with love. They understood each other better than anyone. He'd never judge her. He'd even love her when she was old. At the funeral, in the harsh overhead lighting of the actual sun, everyone had seemed ravaged by time. Wrinkled, and skittish as if startled by the resolute truth of their bodies and faces, and the thing that aggrieves her most is that a full face from her preferred surgeon begins at $150,000 and that the most pronounced evidence of a lift is that you couldn't ever tell, only that a woman appeared 30 percent more well rested, generally not-poor, and infinitely less pissed off.

But it's never as easy as changing one thing, she thinks, looking at her wide-set eyes, and her still-full lips that feature a mildly simian protuberance that gives her face a point of interest, that prevents her from ever being conventionally pretty. There's impossible calculus in the harmony of a face. It had been that way when she began masseter Botox injections. While it softened the squareness of her jaw, it loosened the musculature that held up her cheeks, sliding them down to create the shadow of jowls from certain angles. One small alteration can dramatically shift everything else and you can never take it back. Behind her, her tall, silly son grins at her. She welcomes the warmth of him at her back.

"We're monsters," he says.

"We're disgusting," she agrees, and they both laugh.

* * *

They go swimming, the pool as warm as bathwater. He tells her he's been heating it since dinner, and the way he says it, as though wanting credit for his forethought, makes her consider the energy costs and resent the extravagance, even as she wonders why she would never think to do the same. Why heating the entire pool for herself would be too wasteful.

Gazing up at the sky, she wonders how she'll ask him to leave, feeling morose, thinking of endings, thinking of her mother. The pool lights cast them both in a soft pink hue, throwing dappled shadows across Dano's wet face.

"I can't believe my mom and Mac are in the same place," she says, sounding sentimental. "I'm not even sure *place* is the right word." She has an anxious dread that they'll meet. But she can also see them getting along. She can imagine Sunny enjoying Mac's charms, flirting with him, lighting up for his benefit.

"When did she actually die?" he asks softly, referring to her share at the park. And, staring at her pale palms underwater, knowing she's avoiding her sponsor, she thinks she might be over AA.

"Three years ago," she says. "I just wish Stevie could have met her."

She still keeps the laminated St. Francis prayer card from Sunny's funeral in her wallet that her stepfather had sent. It had been enclosed in the letter he'd written. This is the part she hasn't told anyone. The exact way she'd found out.

Over the years, Moon would mail money to her mother. And when Stevie was born, she began including photos. Their sole correspondence was Sunny cashing the checks, and Moon took this as a sign of gruff approval. She'd enjoyed the idea of Sunny socking the money away in a private account, buying herself a new pair of shoes or treating her church friends to a meal now and again.

She'd told herself that Sunny was grudgingly acknowledging her success and even at her most cash-strapped, she'd always send something, never less than a few hundred dollars until that letter when her stepfather confessed that he'd been intercepting the envelopes the whole time, well after Sunny had died.

In the letter, he reminded Moon of everything he'd paid for along the way, raising her as his own, enclosing the prayer card and a photo. He'd moved to Vietnam, he said. *To paradise.* And in the picture he was smiling, sitting in a plastic red chair in shorts, with his old, scrawny brown legs spread wide. His arm was slung around the waist of his new wife in a strapless white dress, standing beside him with a stiff smile of resolve on her young face. He'd congratulated Moon for her bountiful life, referring to her again as *Theresa*, leaving a Hotmail email address, in case she ever wanted to keep in touch.

She'd felt stupid for ever thinking Sunny would give her the satisfaction. And, shocked that in pocketing the money, her stepfather would have kept Stevie's pictures to himself. She couldn't stand this most of all, the photos being thrown away or worse, secreted in a dark, cool drawer with his most shameful, private things.

Mac was the only one she'd wanted to tell. And she'd told him everything. Showing him the photo of the revolting man, throwing it in Mac's face, brightly aware that it might humiliate him for its parallels to his life. Two ridiculous old men with their child brides, but instead of rebuking her or arguing, he'd held her. And then, she'd turned to him and they'd fucked themselves raw all afternoon and when he'd left to return to Corinna, she'd filled the howling cavernousness that remained with an insouciant little Pét Nat, an Adderall, an Oxy, some tequila, and then had apricot torte delivered to the house.

She'd had many days like this, where she was barely conscious between the pills and the pills to counteract the first pills, softening the incalculable cruelty of another 70-degree Los Angeles day with a sun that was indifferent to the news of her mother's death. And as Moon lay on a lawn chair, she thought how the sky had probably looked exactly the same, cloudless and goading, on the real day Sunny died.

The next morning she'd stopped drinking. *Struck sober*, as they called it in the rooms. A total severance from her past. Black. White. One. Zero. On. Off. Just like that. She'd known it was over. She'd woken up in emergency rooms before. One of her friends had even OD'd right in front of her, Hank Selman, one of the funniest guys she'd ever met, a real sweetheart with a family history and a pain disorder. His mouth had foamed, actually foamed, little bubbles sliding down his chin, his fingers making stiff horrid knots, the fat rails of what they'd both thought was coke still out on the coffee table as she'd held his head, crying, waiting for the paramedics to arrive but knowing it was too late when the beaded Ganesh curtain from Pier 1 moved in his shitty airless NoHo apartment the instant she no longer felt his presence in the room.

So many possible bottoms, but this one had been hers.

"The last time I talked to Mac," she tells Dano now, "he said I used people. He called me a succubus, which is so fucking Mac, he couldn't just call someone a vampire."

She thinks back to this moment often. She'd known that she'd hurt him but had chosen not to care. His pain was insignificant compared to hers, even calling attention to it seemed contemptible. Corinna's feelings she had not even considered.

She wipes her face with wet hands.

"Using people?" repeats Dano. "I don't know how innocent anyone is on that count." He turns away to swim to the far side of the pool. A flicker of firelight illuminates his face, cigarette dangling from his mouth. He swims back, hand held aloft. "Look at the wives he ran through," he finishes, taking a drag and tilting his head up to exhale before handing it to her.

"How'd he seem the last time you saw him?" she asks.

He shrugs. "The same." Moon watches him, wondering when this would have been but not wanting to ask for seeming to care. What she wants to know is if Dano will always love her more. If he will keep taking her side.

"Why didn't you go to the wedding?" she asks instead, taking a drag but not particularly wanting it.

"I should have made the effort," he says ruefully, reaching for the cigarette, but she makes him wait. Taking another drag, taking her time to exhale before handing it back. "But then I looked at the gift registry and was like, 'Who are these people?'"

"But you got them something?"

"Obviously," he says, smiling. "A very tasteful eight-hundred-dollar floor basket. They wanted a pair. I just kept hoping no one would get the other one."

She laughs. "Ruthless."

"I should've just gone," he says quietly.

Moon envisions the solitary basket on a cold, stone floor, missing its mate, and thinks of Stevie again. She swims over to her phone to check the time. Almost two. She calls Stevie, feeling lightheaded and sick with concern, but it goes straight to voicemail. She hangs up, then texts, *Where are you?* but the bubble remains green.

"This is weird, right?" she says, showing Dano her screen.

"Does she get reception at work?"

"But why would she still be at work?"

"Could be the new job," he says, turning to ash out of the pool onto the lawn.

"What new job?"

There's a subtle shift in his expression, a wince of regret.

She puts her phone down.

"What new job?"

Dano turns to put his cigarette out right on the pool edge. "She got a promotion."

"Why didn't she say anything?"

He sighs. "I told her to tell you."

"Why didn't *you* tell me?" It's the same thing as with the driving. "You can't keep secrets from me. I'm the mother."

"*The* mother?"

She splashes him in frustration. More angry than she cares to admit. She imagines them talking about her in the car, their condescension and their selective disclosures. It is the little black boxes of the Zoom call all over again. She sinks underwater and screams.

After a moment, Adam joins her and at first she's appalled that she can't even have this, a private moment to vent her rage. His trilling scream sits at a lower register, filling her water-blocked ears, but when her lungs begin to burn, bubbles exhausted, she rises to the top but only after he does. She glares at him but can admit to feeling better and swims close to hang off his wet shoulders like a remora attached to the underside of a shark.

"What?" he asks into her silence, face cast half in shadow.

She wants to make him tell her everything he knows about Stevie. If she's dating anyone, if she seems all right.

"You should settle down," she says instead.

He groans. "Bro, I'm so ready," he says, bobbing her up and down in the water. "I want a family so bad. A house in the woods."

Moon wonders if any of this is true. When he'd first arrived at her house, he'd spoken of nothing but directing. He'd claimed to have found his thing, the vérité of tight, run-and-gun crews, the fleet-footedness, the excitement and the immediacy. He'd had that annoying habit of camera people, talking about gear, lenses, rigs. The way he had been with F1, golf, fashion shows. And when he leaves, no matter how close she feels to him now, he'll forget. It's the worst, most reliable part of him.

STEVIE

Stevie glances up when a blond boy catches her eye. He is standing at the kitchen counter and she wills him to do it and he does. The boy picks up the can of Pringles. All evening at this ridiculous gathering, Stevie has had an unobstructed view of what has become her favorite aspect of the party. On the counter stands a tube of pizza-flavored Pringles and every so often someone will come in, shake it, pry the lid open to find it empty yet unfailingly restore it to exactly where they'd found it.

It is an allegory for Los Angeles. How everyone is a self-conscious, striving idiot with absolutely no thought for whoever comes after them. Plus, they were all starving and there was never any food. It was impressive how not a single person—there had been three—threw the can away. But when this boy opens it, he doesn't look around, reset it, or casually walk off pulling out his phone as subterfuge; he sticks his nose in the tube and inhales deeply, closing his eyes. He rears back as though to fill his lungs more completely, then replaces the lid and carries it, holding it against himself like a stuffed animal, and proceeds toward her.

He sits easily on the floor, leaning up against the couch the way she is, close enough that she feels his heat, and it happens so deterministically that she doesn't have time to react, only watch. He leans in toward her, still hugging the Pringles, tenting his legs to match hers, and she freezes, convinced he is mocking her, but she doesn't sense malice, only an uncomfortably candid curiosity. One of his nostrils is larger than the other with the nose ending in an appealing snub. His hair is cherub-curly with dark roots and light, almost white tips, and his eyes are teardrop shaped, like those unsettling porcelain figurines from the eighties that Moon used to collect, that evoke both pity and disdain, and his lips burst off his face like a sofa cushion with a seam down the middle. He is uncannily, breathtakingly beautiful.

He cocks his head to read her phone that hasn't returned to a locked screen. She has been reading *Call Me by Your Name*, a book she has read so many times that she mostly rereads her favorite passages.

"Kinda metal to be reading a book right now," he says, voice deeper than she'd expected and containing a laugh but not a mocking one. She recognizes the boy, but what she knows of his face and body are mostly from pictures. Video clips, tagged posts, countless shots of him mid-air, including a photo of him shirtless where Freddie had zoomed deep into his crotch to gauge from his dick outline to see if he was packing. Stevie can't reconcile any of it with the person sitting beside her. His hair seems blonder. He is also more attractive up close, which is not the case for most people. His folded leg exposes a brown thigh through the rip of his camel-colored corduroys, leg hair curled against his dark skin, and she wants to slip her finger in the hole to touch it.

"Yo, that part where they take a shit in front of each other at the hotel?" he says. "Incredible." She hugs herself, pleasure surging through her. She cannot believe it is him, that this is who he is, that Sage Castro is referring to a scene in her book that is omitted from the film adaptation.

For some reason in that instant she imagines him kissing someone else, a woman, or a man, it doesn't matter. It is so hot. But then she decides she wants to kiss him. In fact, she wants to have sex with him, and the fully formed impulse arrives so forcefully that she pinches her lip to prove that this is happening. She will make this happen.

"I only read at the really good parties," she says, and he laughs, nudging her leg as though they are friends already, and her insides warm to a painful degree. He blinks and she sees that he has twin smiley faces tattooed on his eyelids.

"Sage," he says, extending his hand, and the introduction is so unnecessary, but she tucks her hand in his.

"Stevie," she says, and this makes him laugh that they are being so formal, the pink wet inside of his mouth flashing, and Stevie's entire midline contracts. The eyes on his eyes appear again and she closes her own eyes in response, then opens them and exhales. She locks into him and he returns her look without embarrassment or discomfort, until he breaks into a grin and says, "Hold on, hold on," looking away to wipe his face clean of expression. He rejoins her in what becomes a staring match but he can't stop smiling and then laughing until she smiles and laughs until they are both laughing but fighting it, cheeks straining with the effort to still their mouths. She is devastated by his beauty. She imagines the sound and pressure of a vibrating gun against her eyeball and wonders if she could ever go through with doing it twice. She wants him and it is a revelation.

Over the course of a few hours, she does not leave his side and she can see the way other people at the party say hello to him, kneeling before him, transmitting warmth and curiosity toward her when he introduces her as his friend but does not get up to leave with them. He receives these interlopers with a presidential cordiality and she has to concentrate not to mimic the tilt of his head or the way he says *Hell yeah* while nodding. She knows that he is desirable and coveted but she is determined to win him, and when he pulls out a small amber vial with a dropper, telling her that it's LSD, she agrees to a microdose despite never having done it before, anything to enclose the veil of privacy around them.

He has clean, broad nails and pleasingly veined, large hands that are expressive and anguished like a Hellenistic sculpture, and she wants to put them in her mouth once he deposits the oily bitter drops onto her tongue, telling her with authority that it'll be chill, that it's *like a glass and a half of Tempranillo.*

They go upstairs, picking a room at random. For a moment they kiss in the dark, Sage tasting like her own mouth, an almost milky neutral humanness that is more about wet and warmth than flavor. Her hands travel to his broad, muscled shoulders, and the heat of him fills her palms and she is overcome. But then when they turn on the light, there are thirty pairs of multicolored sneakers all laid out in rows, facing the same direction on the carpeted floor of the modest-sized room that only otherwise houses a bed. Sage takes his shoes off, adding them to the formation. Stevie does the same. From the bed, the shoes seem like loyal soldiers awaiting orders in whatever undignified enterprise has brought their owner to L.A., and when Stevie feels moved by this, she wonders if she is high already.

The duvet gives off a pleasant detergent smell and Stevie licks her lips and checks her phone. It is almost two a.m. and she is concerned about her dwindling phone battery, so she turns it off and feels an alert peace, pleased with how smart and resourceful she is. The LSD dilates her scope of attention, her perception radiating beyond its regular purview. Her palms tingle, the pads of her fingers indescribably sensitive. And it is as though the eyes inside her eyes have clinked open and the mouth that has always lived in her chest cavity but has been dormant is now smiling. She is melancholy thinking how these sensations feel more like the remembrance of a forgotten skill than a wholly new experience.

"Do you think there's a camera in here?" he asks, and she couldn't be sure if he'd spoken out loud or it was a question that arose in her mind simultaneously. Her eyes snap open. There is definitely a camera in there. Creation in a content house never stopped. Privacy was irrelevant. Every modern utility and appliance would spy until humans had convenienced themselves to the point of extinction. Stevie pulls the bedcovers over their heads to conceal them completely. With the comforter and sheet hanging above them, they sit cross-legged on the bed.

"I'm hot," says Sage in the dark. Stevie nods. He asks to remove his shirt. Stevie nods again, unable to swallow the saliva in her mouth. He removes his shirt and she does too. In the wet heat of the dark, she keeps going, removing her bra, and then undoes her pants, catching a whiff of fried food as she struggles out of them and her underwear. She offers her nakedness as a gift to both of them. And he silently does the same and then when the heat is unbearable they take a vote on shoving the comforter to the floor with only the sheet on top.

She feels graceless in her movements, her heavy breasts pulling at her as she maneuvers, but when she's laid down on her back, she is relieved for the coolness and understands that this is the gift of her efforts and feels grateful to the unglamorous version of herself from moments before. Sage is keenly familiar to her already. When he blinks, the twin smiley faces flicker and this time, Stevie allows herself to reach out and touch the tremor of activity under the scrim.

"My mom says I have a face for background," she tells him.

He nods. "We all have a face for background."

He opens his arms to her and she rolls against him, pressing against his chest, and he squeezes. She inhales deeply. He has small, dark areolas, and she inches down to cover one with her cheek. She breathes him with her eyes closed until the contours separating them dissolve. She inches up and kisses his bare shoulder, intoxicated by his warmth and the smoothness of his skin.

He gets on top of her and, smelling the smells of him, the oils of his scalp, his skin, it's as though his closeness heightens the awareness of herself. Where his fingertips press against her is where she begins. His molecules seem to seep into her as though he is pouring himself from a silver gravy boat held high above them, filling her up as her naked thighs, ass, back, shoulders, and bare breasts become sensate, thawing. He looms overhead with impressive upper-body strength, and when she looks up, she reminds herself to remember this forever.

He dips his head to encircle her nipples leisurely, lazily, with a full, flat tongue, and a coiled, soaring sensation builds. He inches south, lapping at her wetness with startling, unhurried dedication, and when she comes, she bucks so hard she feels teeth. He grabs her ass with both hands then, still going, aftershocks rattling through her skull as fractals explode behind her eyes. She is openly crying now. The gratitude is immense, deafening, blotting out anything else, and he roughly pulls her down by the hips, closer to him, and licks his fingers, stirring her clit with insistent, patient circles with the pad of his thumb as he eases himself into her. He holds her there, unmoving, and the fullness is a marvel. He fucks her slowly, with tantalizing restraint, questioning, and when she moans again he picks up speed. She praises the buoyancy of the mattress, the way he pushes against the coiled bedsprings with his hands so she drives toward him, halving his efforts but redoubling each thrust, sliding into her so deep that the meat of her thighs are bludgeoned like saltimbocca cutlets against the mallet of his slender hips.

And when her engorgement builds to the point she has to pee, she shudders, bearing down, shattering, and he keeps fucking her as she convulses helplessly, thrashing, until finally he whimpers, his face contorting and he cries out, pretty mouth popping open as he shakes then slumps on top of her. Stevie stills. Their hearts hammer together and it's as if a light switch has been flipped. She feels instantly sober. He didn't pull out.

* * *

The next morning, Stevie wakes up naked in an empty bed with the covers kicked off. She is hot. Dirty. Tacky with what feels like oil that has congealed. There are no curtains in the room, the sour sunlight blaring at her, but when she gets up to open a window for air, she notices a curled, yellowed sign written in Sharpie on printer paper, taped to the warped Spanish-style window casements, that reads: *Does not open.*

She gets dressed, underwear crunchy with discharge, floor undulating beneath her sticky bare feet. Sage's shoes are missing from next to hers and she makes the bed, thoughts focused. She pulls on her mother's shirt, the mesh brushing against her skin, and reminds herself that she'd had an incredible night. She had wanted something and moved toward it and the outcome had been unpredictable but spectacular. In the bathroom it stings when she pees. When there is no toilet paper left on the roll is the only time she almost crumbles, but when she stares at the sunburst blue majolica tiles underfoot feeling penitent and humiliated, she shakes herself dry and tells herself to keep moving.

He didn't pull out.

She needs Plan B.

Stevie walks two miles to the nearest CVS, thirty-seven minutes away on foot, taking a photo of the map and otherwise keeping her phone on Airplane. Her throat is so dry that she cannot swallow without coughing, and a blister on her left heel has ripped open, wept, then bled, seeping into her sock. There is a stinging tightness on her cheeks and the back of her neck that suggests she might be sunburned, but as she stares into the distance at a palm tree with the top half of its leaves sawed off in a perfect horizontal line, the remaining fronds a deadened gray, she has a dignified sense of purpose.

A truck turns in front of her, the buckets and ladders jouncing in the bed, and just as she is about to cross, another car, a white SUV, hangs the left, wheels screeching, almost sideswiping her, but the glass is tinted too dark for Stevie's insults to land and then the car is gone.

As she continues, sun boring down as though to drill her into the ground, Stevie feels exiled. It is wrong to be on foot in Los Angeles. She senses it every time she walks. She is invisible to anyone fortunate enough not to have to look, indistinguishable from any other vagary of human misfortune on the landscape. She stops for a moment to turn away from the street, to take off her shirt and change into her work polo from her backpack, hoping to add another layer of anonymity. To insulate herself.

She smells disgusting in a private way that she also finds enticing. As though something deep and far within her has surfaced and become exposed to the atmosphere when it shouldn't be. Skunks and sesame oil. The hairsbreadth between hamburger and shit. It reminds her of certain kinds of savory potato chips, imported ones that purport to emulate exotic, expensive ingredients, prosciutto or truffles. It is all over her hands, this aroma. She stinks of sex. Each dull throb in her pelvis is proof of this. That Stevie fucks.

She tries to feel like a new person. In a few short weeks everything will be different. Her solemn face in a new state ID, a blank slate. She almost cries thinking of how badly she wants her mother.

Entering into the refuge of the air-conditioned CVS, the air redolent with the ammonia-tang of industrial cleaning products that also smell exactly like cat pee, she makes a beeline for the aisle full of female shame products. She passes the pastel-colored tampon boxes advertising pearls, wipes, sprays, the pregnancy tests that are kept under lock and key, and then finally to the emergency contraceptives.

She feels adult and capable. Like a woman who is making powerful choices for her future, but when she stoops to peer behind the locked plastic partition, she sees the shelf is empty. She coughs from the shock, her arid throat seeming to close as her vision swims. She rises unsteadily, searching for help, and slowly she realizes that there's no one else in the bright store. It is uncannily absent of both customers and workers. The registers are vacant. There is a dream-like serenity to the scene and as Stevie returns to her aisle, she presses the plastic buzzer to summon assistance, but as she pushes it, she cannot observe any relationship between the button and any kind of outward alert, no sound or visible signal.

She presses the buzzer repeatedly, unable to detect whether the button is actually depressing or if the resistance is her hands pushing back against her. She rubs her fingers, willing herself to understand what is happening, and then finally a small form in a blue polo exits from a swinging door in the far back of the store, moving toward Stevie without any sense of haste.

"I see you," says the woman without blinking, radiating hostility. And despite both of them wearing polos indicating service positions, Stevie understands there is no collegial mutuality to be had here. She tells the woman she needs Plan B, hoping to elicit some rueful recognition for her predicament, but the woman stops short and sighs.

"They're behind the register," she says, her weariness increasing. "But we're out."

A high-pitched whine burrows into Stevie's ear. The woman glares back, as though Stevie is leveling a private campaign of pain-in-the-assness at her. Stevie does not belabor the whole purpose of emergency contraceptive, how it is contingent on availability in extremis, instead she swallows hard and wordlessly strides back out into the explosive sunlight, eyes streaming.

Stevie's entire body throbs as she goes. Her feet hurt and she's dangerously overheating. She scans the parking lot, then proceeds toward traffic, urgently swallowing against the tide of cloying warning saliva before vomiting into a trash can. Even in her diminished state, she's impressed by the propulsive force of the liquid that springs out of her, plashing the colorful detritus below, the plastic drink cups, food wrappers, a bulb of bright plasticky white, a balloon or ball, she thinks, until it reveals itself to be a diaper, parceled nice and tight.

Staring out at the cars stopped at the light, she pants, squinting to make out the faces behind the wheels of the cars, but she can't, the glass too thick and polarized, protecting the precious meat inside as Stevie bakes on the hot street. She glances unseeing at yet another white SUV, feeling disgusting but also strangely invincible. She spits a soft lump out into the trash, convinced that the SUV had seen her puke. She smiles, picturing the wan, glossy-haired figure behind the wheel, praying that whoever is inside had glanced up from their low-fat spinach feta breakfast wrap right at the critical moment Stevie's throat opened.

She hopes the sharp aroma of the goat cheese gives off the precise whiff of vomit and that the driver will smell it all day, in her hair, the cuff of her shirt, the interior of the car, that she will be besieged by images of the sick evicted from Stevie's guts whenever she does.

Newly voided, Stevie feels even more victorious, the way she imagines dogs do when they stare you dead in the eye, and turn to present their dilating assholes at exactly the instant shit appears right out of the wink.

And just as she contemplates passing out, she calls her mother.

SUN AND MOON AND MOON MOON

Known as a mini moon, the earth's gravitational pull occasionally, temporarily, captures an asteroid or a comet around the size of a school bus but undetectable to the naked eye. These bodies are trapped for stints of varying length, orbiting the planet, and those bits of debris are usually named by the year of discovery, the month, and how many other objects are detected within that month.

Collectively they are referred to as a subsatellite, submoon, or mini moon, and there is a hypothetical situation in which The Moon, as in, our moon, would also have such a companion. In this case, it would be referred to as a moon moon. To qualify as a moon moon, the object would have to remain in what is referred to as an orbital Goldilocks Zone. Close enough to be gravitationally bound to the moon but far enough out that it won't be destroyed by tidal forces.

No moon moons have been observed in our solar system, but there are multiple theoretical candidates.

Moon's mother was also a Moon. Sun-ha Moon. She'd have gone by Sunny Moon-Trees had she been the sort to hyphenate, or been a yellow-haired hippie type who closed her eyes when she danced, but Sunny, who'd moved to America at twenty-three on the arm of Major Jerry Trees, was instead stunningly susceptible to GOP ideals. She'd been pregnant in her passport photo, in fact, she'd already been up the duff by the time she and Jerry made eyes at each other at the jazz club near Hamilton Hotel, and the guilt of it almost destroyed her.

When Moon was born two months early but fully grown at nine pounds, hair thick and black, with dark knowing eyes, Jerry had been shocked to find his daughter, the girl he'd named Theresa after his Irish-German mother, to be 100 percent, full-on Korean. Not even the Czech and allegedly Cherokee alleles from his father's side could answer for the girl's coloring, her flat nose, the epicanthal folds in her eyes, her broad shrieking face.

Cuckolded but too devout for divorce, Jerry never forgave Sunny and to her credit, Sunny couldn't either. Miscarrying six times over the next nine years, each recurrent loss ensuring the likelihood of the next; after a while, both Jerry and Sunny couldn't forgive Moon for what she symbolized. Sunny tried her best. She tried so hard it gripped her fists, split her teeth, and calcified her heart. She was a dedicated member of the church's flock. She wore her hair sprayed high and close to God. She drove a big truck, made sweet tea, fund-raised for local charities, and swallowed her mother-in-law, Theresa Senior's, abuses every Sunday night dinner, but after each dead baby, when Jerry would leave for long weekends, sometimes bringing his fishing gear, other times not bothering, Moon Sun-ha returned to herself.

Moon Sun-ha would roast dried cuttlefish over the open flame of her gas burner and make steaming vats of kimchi jjigae that her husband couldn't stand the smell of. Sun-ha and Moon pushed all the chairs under the dining room table and ate on the floor, off a small lacquered fold-out table, and Sun-ha would answer to 엄마 while she and Moon ate, bellies gurgling from the influx of millions of probiotic microorganisms flooding their guts, watching dramas until four in the morning from the VHS tapes borrowed from the Korean grocer off Veteran's Memorial.

They would sleep on the floor of the living room, rolling out thick furry blankets, blasting the central air to sixty-eight, her mother extracting the wax from Moon's ear with a long ear spoon, stroking her hair until she fell asleep, and Moon had loved this closeness, being close enough to smell her smells. But when the veil thinned, it also meant that Sun-ha's rage, her frustration, and her grief would leach out. Her mother would drink and scream, eyes at half-mast, transforming into a swaying hailstorm of closed small fists. And Moon knew it had nothing much to do with her and everything to do with who she should have been.

And when Jerry returned with soft pralines from the truck stop, unspoken penance for his absence, their faces would be bloated from sodium, the house aired out, the fridge cleaned, and once again the sun would be eclipsed for the trees.

DAY EIGHTEEN

MOON

ELEVEN DAYS UNTIL THE NEW TENANTS

Moon watches Stevie through the hazy fug of morning, perched awkwardly on the low cement slab of a parking partition with her oily head sunk forward on her knees. Her daughter looks exposed. Discarded. A target in her bright purple uniform, so far outside of whatever institution lays claim to her. The girl looks criminally uncared for, like an unhoused person nodded out on fentanyl or cheap grain alcohol. Even with her backpack sitting an arm's length from her feet, Stevie doesn't so much resemble a victim of a fresh crime as a girl with nothing of value.

It's clear that Stevie has failed to prevail in whatever group has ditched her, her friends, colleagues, possibly a lone, asshole date. And Moon's baffled by how she's reared such an obvious runt. Stevie's miles away from home, work, any kind of safe harbor, and instead of working it out, she's called her mother.

Moon looks around, at the hardscrabble landscape, at a stubborn tree root tunneling out from the ground, lifting up the concrete pavement. All night, ruminating about Stevie, she'd imagined all manner of cold grim terror. Predators and accidents, drunk drivers and acts of God. But just before sunrise, long after Dano went to bed, Moon checked the Pool House again, crossing the lawn, barefoot on the wet grass and then, standing alone in the bug-infested room still reeking of vinegar, she'd opened the closet door, and looking down at the sheets, rumpled and unslept in, a strange calm washed over her. She didn't know how to explain it, but just for a moment, she'd had the sense that she was witnessing a moment whose special significance wouldn't be revealed until later. She'd wondered if Stevie had left. If she'd packed a bag and gone.

For a delirious instant, Moon allowed herself to imagine that Stevie had cooked up a plan and carried it out. And even as Moon's heart ached at the loss, the thought that Stevie was capable of escape filled her with thrilling exultation. In the same way Moon left Sunny and Sunny had left her mother before her, Stevie leaving meant that her daughter was restored. That Stevie could still impress and surprise her.

But now Stevie stirs, shifting her head to scratch it against the forearm wedged across her knees, and her slumped posture screams defeat, and this transports Moon, inversing the roles. She's overtaken by a disorienting sense of displacement that she is somehow simultaneously looking at Stevie in the future as well as herself in the past. Her palms sweat, heart thudding in her head, and in her distress, she turns the car in her daughter's direction and hits something hard. The curb crunches noisily against the chassis and Moon's anxiety transmutes into alarm, the absurd terror that she's hit her daughter, the surreal and ghastly idea that she's killed her, and she wrenches again to right herself. And across the parking lot, Stevie's head lifts.

Mother and daughter's eyes meet. Moon is rapturous with relief and her love for Stevie is transmitted as white light, the confluence of all the colors, every moment of their complicated history. Stevie's face is blank and pale with alarm, the innocence of a child, but then—a cleaving—instead of mirroring relief and love, Stevie's expression curdles to regard her mother with open condescension. She shakes her head scornfully, mouth curling in disgust, and sets her forehead back down on her knees.

In an instant Moon sees Stevie at every age at once even as she's confronted by the unbearable reality of her daughter, the lumbering, dead-eyed outer husk that must be covering her child in some deimatic behavior like a blowfish inflating into a spiky poisonous ball. Moon realizes that who she yearns for, who she'd wanted as she drove over, is Stevie at thirteen. When she had dyed pink hair with star-shaped pimple patches on her cheeks. She misses the closeness of her daughter's sweet, pliant body, the weight of Stevie in her lap, skinny, febrile arm looped around Moon's neck. She grieves for Stevie. The Stevies who are now dead. Overwritten and engulfed. Even the one at her sober anniversary. The one that felt promising, accessible, earned. They've all been eaten by this other shambling parasitic version who inspires neither sympathy nor love.

Stevie finally rises, dusting off the seat of her pants in large, ungainly swipes, her movements viscid and lurching, the obvious markers of a hangover. And anger wells in Moon with ever more judgment, and then the words she'd said to Dano return to her. That she'd called herself *The* Mother. Reminding her that she does not always know where she ends and Stevie begins and that her scorn and shame must be a product of her own self-loathing.

The car door pops open and hot air rushes in. There is a smell. Of sour socks. Communal yoga mats. Pressure builds inside Moon as Stevie tosses her bag in, barely nodding hello. She stumbles into the seat and sighs, fumbling for her seat belt. Once she's done, Stevie leans back, eyes closed in a clear indication that she is not to be spoken to.

"Are you OK?" Moon makes herself ask.

Stevie sighs. "I'm fine," she says in a tight voice. "Just tired obviously."

Moon forces herself to count down from five. "Did you at least have a good night?" she asks. "Was it fun?"

"Can we not," responds Stevie, barely bridling a rage Moon cannot understand. Eyes still closed.

She battles the horrible sense that something has become catastrophically derailed. The track is snarled and now this Stevie is wrong and there's nothing Moon can do. They drive in silence and as Moon downshifts, she wants to inch her forearm closer to graze Stevie's leg but doesn't. Her daughter's eyes remain obstinately shut. She imagines smacking her to attention, spoiling for the roaring fight they could have, but then she has the thought to recite her favorite prayer: *Help me.*

At the light, Moon imagines an orb of bright white spreading from inside her, and for a moment she calms, but then, Stevie shifts her feet, kicking her backpack gracelessly, so Moon reaches for it to stow behind them when Stevie opens her eyes. "Stop," she snaps, pulling the bag back.

In an instant, Moon thinks drugs. She has practiced for this occasion, what she would say without veering into hypocrisy. But when Stevie unzips the bag, Moon sees a scrap of fabric caught in the zipper, sticking out like a tongue, and she recognizes the print. Even as cars honk behind them, Moon fingers the delicate webbing of snagged textile, her mesh top with butterflies, one of her favorites, one that had made best-dressed lists. Heat builds in her cheeks. She blinks rapidly, then crosses two lanes of traffic and pulls into a parking lot.

Stevie sits up, holding the shirt limply in her hands, expectant, penitent, and again Moon thinks of Sunny, not wanting to be like her. She thinks of how her mother would scream so close that she could feel the flecks of spit on her cheeks. *I hope you have a daughter*, Sunny had once said with so much vitriol it sounded like a hex. *I hope you have a daughter exactly like you.*

Stevie is nothing like her. Moon had feared Sunny, respected her, longed for her. Nobody takes Moon seriously, least of all Stevie. Heart clenched in her chest, she tries to regulate her breathing. Reminding herself that at least her child is safe.

"Moon?" Even that Stevie still only ever refers to her by her last name is infuriating. "Moon? Can we get it fixed? Maybe we can take it to a really good tailor."

Moon's throat strains, wanting to screech. Even if they could mend the hole, the pattern would be off. The tear would always be there, the thick unsightly seam, an ugly little grub testifying to a lack of care.

"You know where I wore this?" Moon says, remembering suddenly the animated film that she'd voiced. "You were three. I only did it so you could watch something I was in, and the second you heard my voice, you freaked out. You didn't like that at all."

Stevie regards her warily, then nods, whispering the name of the movie.

"You were a dragon," Stevie recalls. "They gave you boobs."

Moon laughs and Stevie does too, but then her face scrunches and large tears begin sliding down her cheeks. "I'm so sorry," she says.

Moon shrugs. "It's just stuff. It's all gonna be your stuff anyway."

Stevie covers her face with her hands and begins properly sobbing like a child. Moon gives her a minute, looking out past the dashboard to see that she's parked in front of a dry cleaners. She'd once left Stevie with her dry cleaner but she can't believe it now.

"Are you sure you're OK? Was it a terrible night?"

Stevie nods, crying harder, and Moon's heart seizes. She wants to inspect Stevie's entire body for injuries.

Instead she waits.

"I went to a party," Stevie wails. "It was whatever, but then it was amazing. Part of it was amazing," she sobs raggedly through her hands, overtired but unharmed, her tone suggesting the same friend or boy drama that has beleaguered daughters since time immemorial, and Moon stifles a smile.

"Worth scaring the shit out of your mother and ruining archival Gaultier *amazing*?"

Stevie removes her hands and gathers them in her lap, and with this one gesture, she seems to visibly shrink in size. "Mom, I don't know what to do with my life," she says, and they both go very still, equally startled by the word.

There'd been a fight about this once. The Mom thing. But only once. Stevie was still in high school and their money troubles were beginning. They'd been in a vintage boutique reselling one of Moon's Fendi baguettes and Stevie was whining about the wait and Moon had snapped, humiliated about the situation already, telling Stevie she was sick of this "Moon" shit. *I'm not your little buddy*, she'd hissed. *We are not fucking colleagues. I don't work with you.*

Stevie had screamed right back.

You're the one who started it. You're the one who wanted to be my bestie, my best friend, she'd said in a mocking singsong. *Admit it, you never wanted to be a mother.*

According to Stevie, Moon had demanded, out of vanity, not to be called Mom on set because it was humiliating, because she *didn't want to seem old*. And it was *literally pathetic*.

To Moon, who has an almost photographic memory for dialogue, who often loses sight of the *fight beneath the fight*, as a therapist once said, shot back that this didn't make sense. *Of course they know I'm your mother. Why else would a girl like you be on set?*

It was the *girl like you* that even as she said it, she'd known would be a problem, the way any misspoken word could destroy a teen girl. What she'd meant was that they obviously belonged to each other. But sure enough this had devolved into an awful, full-on bawling meltdown about Stevie not being good enough for the show. The Mom thing had been tabled.

But the truth is, Moon had been utterly devastated to stop hearing the word. Mom. Mommy. Even 엄마, which Stevie would only ever whisper, in private, behind her hand, making Moon press her ear up real close because Stevie was shy when speaking Korean.

The bruise of it lingered. Further, there was something distancing and impertinent about the way Stevie said her name. Once, she'd even gone, *Oh, that's so Moon*, when she heard Moon mispronounce a word. And even the way Stevie would smile over her shoulder at school drop-off, barely waving, saying, *Bye, Moon*, and disappearing into the building, crushed Moon. She'd been mortified in front of all the other moms but played along, saying, *Bye, babe*, just as coolly, as if this was their thing, since she didn't want to embarrass Stevie even as her cheeks burned, even when she knew how the other women talked about her behind her back.

So instead of making it a big deal now, Moon smooths over the word that hangs between them in the stale air of the car. "Well, what do you want to do with your life, honey?"

Stevie looks up at her, chin quivering, face red and gleaming. "How do you decide? How do you ever know if you're doing the right thing?"

It is so melodramatic and earnest. And Moon thinks about how to phrase exactly what she wants to say without obvious pleasure.

"You take all the information you have about the situation. And then you take everything you know about yourself and all the people involved and then you make a choice. And then you let go of the results and just see what happens. And if on the off chance you got it wrong, you forgive yourself because you didn't have the information but maybe next time you will."

This is what Moon wants to say. Instead she says:

"Nobody knows shit about shit, baby. You know that."

Stevie nods solemnly and then covers her face again.

Moon reaches for her shoulders and Stevie collapses against her.

"Let's go home," she says, feeling Stevie's hot little head against her neck.

Stevie takes a halting breath and nods. "OK," she says. "Thanks, Mom."

And inwardly, Moon beams.

ADAM

When Adam opens his eyes from a nap on the sofa, he startles, his cold laptop almost sliding off his chest before he catches it. His screen animates, revealing real estate listings before he snaps it shut.

Stevie jumps back laughing. "Jesus," she says. "What kind of depraved shit were you looking at?"

"What happened to you?" he asks, checking the time.

"Nothing," she says with a wave of her hand and an eye roll, hair dripping wet from the shower.

"Moon was super worried," he says.

"Just Moon?" she asks, feigning injury.

"Where'd you even go?" He sits up.

"It was dumb. I was dumb. I was with friends," she says. "Then my phone died and I passed out."

It's the first time Stevie has ever mentioned a social life and he doesn't even know what to imagine. He doesn't know if *friends* implies two or twelve. She doesn't hang out with her high-school friends, that much he knows. And he wonders if she's fallen in with sad, random work-people and he feels strange about never having asked.

"You couldn't borrow a charger?"

"I was in a four-million-dollar house, what's the worst that could happen?"

He stares at her, scanning her face, understanding that she's not shitting him, understanding that she cannot fathom being harmed so long as she's indoors. As if unspeakable acts don't mostly happen in the privacy of a home.

"Me and Moon already talked about it," she says, sensing his lecture. "I promise to be more responsible."

Stevie smiles sweetly at him then. She wants something.

"What?"

"Can I borrow your car?"

In the car, at a light, she yawns. The afternoon sun is falling in a wide, harsh beam across her face and her eyes are rimmed red, giving her a wan brittle aspect. Like a very old small dog. He wonders again about her evening. *A friend's house* could mean anything and he thinks how L.A. is a town for some of the most depressing house parties, recalling all the glittering nights he's spent in cantilevered glass homes perched at high altitudes, shimmering pools, corporate holiday parties hosted by executives at their private estates, attended by A-list stars who you might never see, discreetly tucked away in cordoned-off areas of the house. He's always found it odd, the relationship of L.A. people and their compounds. How the brutal climate and varying nexuses of power forced third spaces to be built straight into their homes with all the trafficked, impersonal air of a hotel lobby or the bar at a membership club. No matter how distinctive the art or individualized the collection of books, he always felt like he was on a set. Or possibly at the scene of a crime, unwittingly implicated in a trafficking ring because there was a sex dungeon in a padded room off the kitchen.

He hates L.A., he reminds himself. Even as he's spent an hour thinking about buying Kip's house, which is newly on the market. He'd met Kip at exactly such a weird gathering, at the house of a Malaysian business tycoon who would give away priceless pieces of artwork whenever he did enough ketamine.

"Have you ever done LSD?" Stevie asks suddenly, voice low and serious, hands at ten and two.

He glances at her. So this is how her *phone died.*

"Sure," he says. "I don't love hallucinogens, though. They're too time consuming."

"You could microdose," she says. "Like to where it's a glass and a half of Tempranillo."

He laughs and wonders what kind of idiots she's been hanging out with. She glares at him for an unnerving duration as Waze tells her to cross three lanes to shave forty-six seconds off her commute, making Adam wish he were driving.

"When have you had Tempranillo?" he asks mildly, and she ignores this.

"But it's not, like, permanently damaging, though, is it?" she asks after a while.

"It's one of the less harmful ones," he says, wondering if this is strictly true. "But please tell me you know better than to do drugs from strangers."

"Obviously," she says, and he feels as though he has passed a test not to have visibly freaked about her recreational drug use. "What did you and Moon do last night?" she asks, and he swears he can hear a note of derision, as though she is asking only to be polite.

"We went swimming."

"Swimming? Just the two of you? So wholesome. Guess it's my turn to get a DUI and go to rehab."

"That's not even funny," he says as a deafening chorus of sirens sail by.

She signals, then glances over at him. "It's a little funny."

He loves Moon and it's not his place but she's definitely too permissive. Stevie has only ever lived in L.A., in a bubble, and twenty is such an absurd age. There are times when Stevie seems precocious, well-read, and others where she is obviously lying about her glaring knowledge gaps. He can see instantly from her vague expression and her eagerness to move on when Stevie hasn't caught a reference but she always pretends she has. It's behavior a real older brother would mercilessly stamp out but it's unsettling to think how easily she's swayed or carried away by circumstance.

It seems related to how she can also be exaggeratedly floppy at times in her movements, melodramatic in the way her generation is always performing. At the smallest provocation, she'll gasp or throw her head back to laugh as though being filmed. And in this way Stevie is much younger than him and possibly even younger than he'd been at her age. They're not outright character flaws, but they're small tells that signal unreliability and immaturity, and if Adam intervened she'd be better off. She'd know how to park, for one. She'd also know how to borrow a charger, cover her tracks, and get herself home no matter how many *glasses of Tempranillo* she'd had.

Stevie needs to spend time in New York, he decides. To know her way around a real town. Take the subway. Interact with people other than her mother and the tourists at work. Considering New York, he briefly worries that his body will be in shambles again once he returns. At the light, he nudges himself. There's still a persistent sense of distance. He tries to sneak up on his penis a few times a day, touching it impulsively or trying to raise it from the inside. There is such a metric as "erection quality," and he resents knowing about it from reading about the erection data of an anti-aging tech billionaire who'd monitored the duration, frequency, and rigidity of his erections and compared them to his son's.

"You know how many times Moon's stayed out without saying when she'll be back? I'm talking days. Weeks." She edges behind a row of cars to enter into the parking lot of the CVS next to the Whole Foods. "I'm not saying last night was on purpose, my phone did die. Just that, she can't really say shit. What is she going to do? Ground me?"

"She could," he says, watching the large vehicles nose toward them like giant sea creatures. He doesn't know why everyone still insists on such enormous cars. "Her house, her rules," he finishes.

She slides into an empty spot, well over the demarcation line for the spot beside it. "Dano," she says patiently, switching off the car. "You know we don't live in that house, right? That we live in the Pool House? Both of us?" She gives him a meaningful look, as if it's not possible that he's this stupid. "We've been renting the Big House, the one you've been staying in, to rich assholes for years. You have to know this. You keep asking where her books are and why the food is so mental. Tell me you knew."

There's a mild tingling in his hands and it dawns on him that he must have known. He has a strange sudden lurching feeling then, the sense of faltering when you misjudge the distance of a step, and he's embarrassed. It is the feeling of the lights being switched on all at once at a party. Exposing the convivial collective ambiance for the murderously depressing rec center that it is. It's always been there, the impersonality of the guest room, the collection of ketchups (what normal person buys Hunt's?), the random pineapple-themed serving trays left over from an event. He feels like an idiot but he's also indignant that this has been kept from him, he hates feeling this way, stupid, excluded, without a valid reason to warrant the lies.

She gives him a funny smile. "That's how much she loves you," she says. "She'd rather die than have her precious baby boy stay in a hotel. Meanwhile me and the fucking fruit flies can go choke in the Pool House." She turns the car back on again, looking at her side mirror. "Do you think I should move over?"

When they exit the car, he peels off for Whole Foods as she heads into CVS. He walks through the freezing aisles, bewildered and injured. For all his efforts around the house, all that cooking and laundry, he's still found himself on the outside. He's trusted enough to use the mesh bag to wash their bras and underwear, he's spent hundreds on prebiotic sodas and cottage cheese, they go through an absurd amount of cottage cheese, but he will only ever be a guest.

He grabs a basket, making space for a young mother to push past with a baby and a toddler. He respects Moon's privacy as well as her pride, but he can't fathom how she could lie to him for so long. Or what it says about him that Stevie had been complicit in coddling Moon's *precious baby boy*.

He picks up some obscenely expensive steak, a good loaf of sourdough, corn and butter, and because he's forgotten his tote again, he carries his purchases loose in his hands, and by the time he makes his way to the drugstore, Stevie's still in the serpentine line of the single open cashier. She seems out of it, not immediately spotting him, blinking slowly with a haziness to her gaze. He wonders if she's still tripping, and cradling his groceries in one arm, he goes to the refrigerated section for a coconut Bai for himself and a coconut water for Stevie and joins her.

It's been a fortnight since his mother's birthday. She's even stopped calling, which is never good. But with this new information, that Moon and Stevie live in the Pool House, sharing that unspeakable dingy mattress with its depressing floral sheets, he can't just leave. He opens his drink and throws some back, the metallic taste of electrolytes and monk fruit and tropical flavorings rushing into his long-empty stomach that contracts acidly at the assault. He feels bilious and queasy.

The meat in the waxed paper is cold and limp against his forearm, and he wonders if his body heat will cause it to spoil in the same instant he is strangely repulsed by the heft and unmistakable deadness of the fleshy apportioned clump. He imagines blood leaching from it, pooling onto the butcher paper, envisioning the way meat cleaves, revealing fibers, sinew sliding and shifting, and there is a disintegrating, fading feeling that comes over him to where he can no longer sense his hands. He has to do something. He doesn't know what but they need him.

He brushes the back of his hand to his penis reflexively and when he sets their drinks down on the counter, it occurs to him that Stevie is not holding anything, nothing in her arms, and just as he's about to mention it, she asks the salesclerk behind the counter, a man with a greasy fringe that splits into oily sections, for Plan B, and Adam freezes.

The man looks at Adam, then Stevie, then back at Adam.

"Together?" he asks, and Adam, with his wallet out, credit card poised, can't speak. Instead, he rams the card blindly into the slot but nothing happens. He pulls out and tries again, which is when Stevie takes it from him to hold over the reader until it beeps and gives it back to him.

A FUTURE AT PEE WEE'S

[1993–PRESENT]

In 1993, a St. Louis woman won a $78 million lawsuit against Domino's for their "thirty minutes or less" delivery pledge. She'd sustained a spinal injury when a delivery driver ran a red light, slamming into her. Everything in the industry since, long before Stevie was born, has trended toward speed and exceeding the limitations of human capability. Even now at a multibillion-dollar nationwide delivery company, drivers are told by their dispatchers to turn off the third-party surveillance system that monitors safety and the speeds at which they are driving. The app, for the record, is called Confidante.

At Pee Wee's, the namesake of Harold Peter Henry "Pee Wee" Reese, pal to Jackie Robinson and shortstop for the Brooklyn/Los Angeles Dodgers in the forties, there were multiple software systems ensuring the most efficient and safest conduct from their employees. Every moment was accounted for, with every employee accorded a unique number, and the value of each employee was dictated by the speed of their transactions, for every second of every day. A customer amounted to a point, as did every order. Processing more orders accrued more points and units sold, which equated to a number called a throughput. A throughput determined every aspect of your standing within the Pee Wee's organization. Whether you'd get a raise. Whether you'd get shifts cut. Whether preferential shifts were available to you. Everything boiled down to this number but ultimately it was directed by chance.

Cash transactions, customers changing their mind, anyone ordering a quesadilla—fucking quesadillas—a menu item that required physically leaving the line, moving to a second machine, having your soul leave your body as you stood there waiting until the cheese melted because of liability issues; all these randomized events bungled the flow of the line, chewing through seconds to ruin efficiency metrics all through no fault of the employee.

Even still, that employee's throughput suffers, which compromises the team, the store, and then the entire regional patch. Pee Wee's locations where crews consistently hit their throughput quarterly goals were given cash bonuses or opportunities to win vacations. Several years ago there had been a speedboat, but possibly this was only a rumor. By 2028, almost half of Pee Wee's locations will be reconfigured to service only in-app orders. There will no longer be a dine-in area and the kitchens will be fully automated.

DAY TWENTY

STEVIE

"She's alive!" Stevie says with a smirk to Freddie. They're back at work and of course Freddie hadn't texted when she'd gotten home from the party, an event that is already unfathomably long ago. But Freddie doesn't meet her eye, ignoring her so pointedly that Alvin who's stationed between them clears his throat into the awkwardness. "Hey Stevie," he says, but Freddie doesn't respond. Stevie's heart drops. "We haven't been makeline buddies in a while," he adds with such compassion that Stevie can't look at him either.

She returns to her order, the words blurring on the ticket, and she wonders what Freddie knows, worried that word got back to her of Stevie disappearing into a room with Sage. But as her hands robotically compile the ingredients, annoyance wins out. Freddie's the one who'd ditched her first, who'd left her without a ride. Freddie was disloyal. Besides which Sage was an asshole.

As the lunch rush picks up, Stevie keeps making small, stupid mistakes. Forgetting substitutions, adding the wrong chicken. She is sick from fatigue, closing her eyes for longer and longer intervals. It recalls the early days of her job. How she'd never worked harder, never been on her feet for so long. Adjusting to the commute had been rough, the stress of arriving to a location so far from home, taking the bus and metro in, a six-mile commute that sometimes took almost two hours.

Nothing had prepared her for the rigors of real, manual labor. Even on thick, rubber nonslip mats, by the end of the day, her calves cramped, the cartilage in her knees and the complicated bones in her feet felt brutalized. The bolts of her joints, the cords of her muscles, everything throbbed. The particular collision of repeated ladlings from deep thirds, sixes, rattling round-edged hotel pans for protein dregs were felt in the knuckles, elbows, shoulders, lumbar, even the jaw, and when she got home and lay down, the entirety of her skeleton sang with pain. Humming like a struck chord.

Freddie's lunch is scheduled before hers and she leaves with Arrow, one of the new hires. By her own lunch, Stevie can't take it. She corners Freddie at her locker.

"What's up?" Stevie asks, cheeks tingling. She doesn't want to say the words, the juvenile, sniveling question, *Are you mad at me*, but it's burning her throat, she will cry if she says them, she knows this about herself. "You're being weird."

Freddie gazes at her, lids raised halfway, as though she cannot endure how dull the inquisition is already. "I'm fine," Freddie says in a monotone. "Just tired."

"Was your dad mad?"

Freddie stares at her, unblinking. "Why would he be mad?"

Stevie doesn't know what to say. She retreats, all courage for confrontation exhausted. She busies herself with her phone, faint with adrenaline, when she sees an email from corporate. There is a link to another link, an encrypted message, followed by a large block of legal text about privacy. The note itself is short. They are pleased to inform her that she has gotten the job. Her start date is in two weeks. She will report to the training kitchen in Boston. Facing into her locker, breathing in the familiar musty, metallic scent, she buries her phone deep into her backpack as though hiding it will somehow make the message disappear.

It's the acceptance letter from NYU all over again, none of the soaring happiness she'd anticipated, only free-falling dread. And Stevie wonders if she's ever felt pure joy. Or any feeling that wasn't dominated by terror. Forgoing her staff meal, usually her favorite part of the day, she walks outside. It is bright and warm in the midafternoon with a breeze. She crosses the street, toward Beverly, wondering if it's already cold in Yarmouth, and thinks how wild it is that she'll be on the East Coast by Thanksgiving. She feels an uncontrollable propulsion in her body, like her blood is moving too fast or she's over-caffeinated, and she thinks back to how a secret, ugly, black-hearted part of her had been happy when she couldn't go to NYU.

What she'll never admit to anyone is that when they hadn't had enough money, she'd been relieved. She still isn't sure she could have ever gone through with it. The prospect of making new friends, or worse, keeping the ones she had distressed her immeasurably. New routines, neighborhoods, learning the subway system, it was too much. Faced now with finding an apartment, a car, and all the requisite paperwork to recoup relocation expenses, she wants to climb into bed and stay there until she's thirty. It feels insurmountable to tell Moon about any of it now, and she cringes to think how she'd called Moon Mom in the car. Something about it reminded her of the time she said *I love you* to her first boyfriend. Boyfriend and mother had gotten the same look. A pleased, clamped-down grin that attempts to squelch laughter. Not that Moon was making fun of her, more that while Stevie never wants to upset her mother she also can't stand the thought of making her happy.

She wonders if it's possible that she's forgiven Moon. And if the worst is behind them whether it even makes sense now to leave. Walking toward Seels, toward the crew of boys posted up, lingering on the tall, wide curb, a few more with their legs looped over the sun-bleached blue railings of the Chase Bank next door, Stevie tells herself that she is not looking for Sage. She scans the skater boys' faces, their long limbs dangling attractively like vines, legs swimming in baggy jeans with filthy frayed hems. She is desperate to change the channel in her head. She doesn't want to think about Pee Wee's anymore and she doesn't want to think about Moon. She passes the boys, keeping her eyes ahead, their attention and loud voices making her cheeks tingle, and she shamelessly removes her scrunchie as she walks, loosening her hair, breaking her own heart when none of them are Sage. Sage who she will never see again.

She heads back toward work, thinking of the line, the gloves, Freddie's silence, making burritos for at least the next three to five years someplace else, and finds herself bypassing the store to cross the street again and enter the cupcake boutique. She's stunned by the blast of cloying, chemically sweetened air and the K-pop played at a volume that immediately gives everyone inside a frenzied sense of urgency. It is packed as if the cupcakes were being distributed to customers for free and Stevie almost collides into a young girl with a cupcake and a tiny furry mic, but scanning the room, she spots Mel beside a plinth where ever more cupcakes are displayed like jewels, helping an older couple make their selection.

Mel this time wears a pink satin chinoiserie minidress and hugs her warmly.

"I had so much fun the other night," she says. "I didn't get home until literally two p.m."

"Amazing," says Stevie. "Hey, so you know Sage, right? Sage Castro?"

Mel laughs, instructs her customers toward the register, then shoots Stevie a wide, knowing smile. "Look, I'm all about that 'yes-and' energy, but he's not called Sage for nothing." Then, dropping her voice to a whisper, she adds, "You'll have to smudge that pussy when you're done with him. I swear, he could be called Palo Santo. He dickmatizes everybody."

But Mel gives her the number anyway, hugging her again to say, "Go with God," in her ear before she leaves.

Stevie's ten minutes late when she clangs into the back metal door, and when she arrives, Xan exclaims, "Speak of the devil." Her boss is surrounded by most of the staff, including line cooks. And it takes Stevie a long, dreadful moment to realize that Xan is talking about her, her exemplary record of service, her multiple achievements, and when Stevie glances at Freddie, Freddie and Arrow snigger right in her face.

When Stevie's promotion is announced in front of the entire team,

Xan begins to clap and not a single other person joins her. So Xan claps louder and slower, radiating outward, clapping into people's faces with increasing insistence, until one by one they join in but with big, exaggerated, jeering motions and stifled laughter, the twitchy smiles of even the kitchen crew sailing back and forth across the room. The extravagance is mortifying and Stevie, struck mute and frozen in place, is wholly unprepared when Xan stretches her arms out for a hug. The hug is like colliding into furniture. Hard, cornered, abrupt. And when it is over Stevie pulls away shuddering with regret, backing into Freddie, who shoves her, before turning to walk away.

* * *

Sage is standing on the other side of the screen door, shirtless. He is wearing jeans and holding his laptop in one hand. "That was fast," he says. He opens the door and she covers his mouth with hers, pushing him back into the warm, dark room. His breath is hot, sweet, as if he has been drinking Sprite, and he whispers, "Wait," and pulls away.

She sobers briefly, allowing that he might tell her to leave.

When she'd called, he'd been happy to hear from her, wanting to explain why he'd left her at the party. Something about a car but she'd cut him off.

Can I come over? she'd asked instead.

Yeah, OK. Sure.

He sets his computer down on the coffee table then returns to her. On the screen she sees, frozen, a skate video mid-trick, and it occurs to her that he might have been watching himself, which she finds both distasteful and arousing. The apartment is small, tidy, and dark. The curtains are drawn and the furniture is nondescript with shadowy shapes of plants, but Stevie acknowledges little of this, confronted by Sage's bare torso.

She does not care what happens tomorrow or the day after. She wants to be used. She wants to use him. She stares openly at the dark hair curling below his belly button and his eyes glint, alert, in the low light. Again, she rushes him, fusing her mouth to his. He kisses her back, pulling her closer as a now familiar tinny whine of frequency drills into her ear. Her head is pounding, the persistent force numbing her from herself, absolving her of her actions. Crushing his lips against his teeth, she almost smiles, thinking of how he was watching a video of himself, wanting to laugh, incredulous that she can make this happen again.

There is a pressure building inside her, a snarled, felted mass of contempt forcing itself up through her, crushing the basket of her rib cage, but she kicks her shoes off, moving forward. She kisses him harder before the hopelessness closes in too tight. Squeezing her eyes shut, she makes her fingers grapple into his waistband. The metal of his belt buckle is cold against her stomach. And she moans when his erection digs into her as they collide into the wall of his narrow hallway, popcorn stucco scraping her elbow as their teeth clink together.

He pushes her down onto his bed in the dark. Her shirt is pulled up along with her cotton bra. A hard edge digs into her ribs, a book, and she shoves it to the floor as his tongue slides up her neck and into her ear. The wet heat blots out sound and thought. He knuckles into her panties, moaning into her hair when he feels how wet she is. He pulls away then. He is on top, knees straddling her, the ripple of his lean stomach, the hard V of his hips stretching out from his undone pants, the band of underwear exposed. His lips are swollen, hair falling into his eyes. His eyes are almost black like a shark's and he grabs the waist of her work khakis with both hands, lifting her up by the hips to center her on the mattress below the tent of his legs, forearms bulging.

The deft movement makes her arch up, kissing his neck when she falls short of his mouth, pushing his hands away to undo her own pants, shove them over her hips, hitching her heel in the crotch to free one leg and spread them apart, wide, reaching into his boxers to grab the thick length of his penis, his jeans still scrunched down at his knees, and buries him straight into herself with one urgent motion.

She sighs raggedly. The high-pitched ringing in her head growing louder. The pressure in her face, her jaw, builds as he fucks her. Her moans are ugly. And when he drives into her, she looks down at the slick place they are joined instead of looking at his face.

"Don't finish in me," she says, his temple salty against her lips. For a moment, she resents him, disgusted by the things she is letting him do to her, the way she looks, the smell they are making. A distant part of her remembers herself, feeling foolish, embarrassed to have forced her way in, the eagerness, her obvious hunger. She may have remorse for how she will remember this in the future. And longing. But she'll also be left with the hard-edged knowledge that she can get things if she is mercenary. If she refuses to care about consequences.

His hips slam against her and she cries out, grinding circles into her pussy with her hand. He burrows his face into her neck, his fingers brushing hers as he reaches down, slick, wet fingers that grope inside her ass until the mounting pressure shatters. She comes so hard she sits up, her open mouth hitting his chest as she convulses violently, helplessly, until he cries out, the perfect line of him from his pelvis to his corded neck, wrenching away from her as he grabs his cock in his fist and pumps hot, jellied streaks onto her belly.

He slumps beside her. Her teeth begin to chatter, their sweat, their mess cooling on her skin. Only now he frees himself completely from his jeans, kicking them off, but then rises to his feet to shake them out and drape them carefully on the back of a chair. He crosses the room, opens a drawer, pulls out a pair of clean boxers and puts them on, and observing this small domestic act, the disclosure that he is tidy, possibly fastidious, gives her a sense of unwelcome context. Of domesticity. Of reality. She is not interested beyond her flattened perception of him. She wants to learn nothing more. Her own pant leg is flipped inside out, the white lining of her pocket exposed like a flag, her sodden underwear tangled at the crotch. He returns to her with a box of Kleenex from his desk and when she doesn't move, he wordlessly wipes her belly, then tosses the tissue in a slim silver trash can. She shucks off her clothes and gets back into his bed, naked. He joins her, pulling the comforter close, and then folds his tanned arms over her.

Neither of them speaks, his chest is warm against her back, and she allows her eyes to adjust to the dark. She registers the orderliness of the room. She will never see him again and her heart splinters, sorrow humming in her belly. She welcomes the sadness. Deserves it. And when she opens her eyes again, she notices that on his bedside table is a small alarm clock. It is white with hands, old-fashioned, and she thinks of Sage as a boy. His face. There are also books but she does not want to read the spines or recognize them. Beside the small stack is an oblong plastic case with a sticker that reads: *mouth guard*. Stevie can't bear it. Her eyes threaten to fill with tears so she closes them, quieting her breathing. Then her stomach grumbles audibly and she clamps both hands over it and he laughs.

It's time to go. She slides half off the bed, hanging almost upside down to reach for her pants, and she sees the cover of the book that she'd knocked off the bed and it is a library book on nonaggression. Blood rushes into her head, her jaw throbs powerfully. She is almost sick with hunger.

"Thanks for this," she says as she hears someone call out his name in the living room.

Sage gets up, putting on his pants.

"Hang on a second," he says, leaving her, shutting the door behind him.

She hears the rise and fall of questions and answers and by the time he returns she is fully dressed and he's put on a navy sweatshirt with a strip of plastic sticker that indicates that it's new.

"You out?" the woman asks when Stevie reaches for her backpack in the living room where she'd left it. The woman is standing with the fridge door open, with pale gray hair, wearing jeans and a crop top, and even from across the room, Stevie sees the resemblance.

"Yeah, I have to . . ."

"Wren," she says. "Sage's sister."

"Stevie."

"You sure you can't eat with us?" asks Wren. Her hair is shaved to the scalp on the left, and where Sage is slight, Wren is sturdy, her arms and abs muscled. She looks like someone who can take a fall. Sage pours Stevie a glass of water from a Brita pitcher and she takes a sip, then drinks it all.

"I'm good," she says, setting down her glass on the counter.

"Nah, you should eat," says Sage, and she feels exposed, knowing he's referring to her growling stomach. He picks up her glass, fills it again, and gives it to her.

As Wren and Sage cook, pan-frying dumplings and pancit, Stevie furtively looks around. The apartment features trippy sixties art deco flourishes like stacked, square wooden frames that form a room divider separating the kitchen from the dining area. There are books all over, in orderly piles on the floor, but otherwise no clutter. She could have this when she moves out, Stevie thinks. A plain white box she will make nice. A person can get used to anything. Even Massachusetts. Maybe Moon and Adam would visit her and she would cook for them.

But why couldn't they have it now? They could move into an apartment just like this, in a building down the block. How expensive could it be? She could pay for the deposit, manage half the rent. And when Sage and Wren lay out placemats and set the table, putting out two small porcelain chopstick rests in the shape of Dachshunds and a regular wood one for Stevie, she pictures the siblings picking them out at a store, just two, just enough, and finally, she catches herself and remembers who Moon is. That enough is never enough. That she'd never sell her house, no matter the cost.

Brother and sister add chili crisp from a jar to their bowls, so Stevie copies them. Wren tells them about her day, minor dramas involving the women at the salon where she works, and Stevie figures her to be in her late twenties. And when she asks Stevie what she does for a living and Stevie says fast food, Wren says, "Now that's a real job," and seems to mean it.

Her neck is stiff so she takes down her too-tight ponytail to gather it into a low bun.

"People would kill for that hair," Wren remarks, and Stevie makes a noncommittal sound, hating to be observed.

"Bet it gets heavy, though."

"I get a lot of headaches," says Stevie.

Wren appraises her, still chewing. "Want me to take some volume out?"

* * *

There is something awful in the sound and sensation of the slicing. Stevie's scalp prickles as Wren saws across her ponytail. She recalls the sulfurous smell of the salon Moon used to visit. The tuberose, citrus, and espresso wafting beneath the scent of dye and chemicals. In the years before the show, Moon would get her hair stripped, then bleached. Strands parceled into tin packets like shingles on a roof and they'd wait for hours. Stevie had enjoyed the attention from the employees, the magazines they would bring her, bottles of sparkling water, even the smallest glasses of champagne.

Stevie has had the photo saved for a while. She doesn't know what convinces her of it in the moment, the haircut is so drastic, so new. But she likes the careening, dazzling sense of doing a thing she can't take back. As Wren cuts her hair on the balcony that is suspended above a covered courtyard, no sky above, no breeze, the floor that Sage had covered with newspapers as though lining a birdcage, Stevie leaves her body.

When Wren hands her the severed ponytail with a hair-tie still attached, it evokes a dismembered leg with a shoe on its foot. Stevie's mutely horrified. She feels maimed, but forces herself to smile, not wanting to seem ungrateful. Warm air flicks her hair in various directions as Wren tugs at it with a rounded brush, and when Stevie is handed a mirror, her hair hangs at exactly chin length. Blunt, simple, precise, with a middle part, and pitched at an angle, longer in front. The ends are tousled and her neck, distanced from the rest of her body, goes on for miles. Her head appears huge, disproportionately, freakishly large and tears spring to her eyes as she whispers, "Thank you."

It is exactly as it is in the photo. She has done this to herself. This will be the person she is now. Wren gives Stevie a Ziploc bag for her hair, and the way it coils heavily at the bottom of a plastic pouch reminds her of a very dead animal, and uncannily it is cold to the touch with a bead of moisture, as though it had been breathing.

THE WOMAN

[A YEAR AGO]

The bus from the Big House to Pee Wee's was often late, and whenever this happened, there was little indication given to how late it would be. Instead of making attempts to guess its arrival time, it was the habit of maps apps to declare that the bus had *not* arrived fourteen minutes ago if the bus was fourteen minutes late.

On the bus, a pre-recording announced each stop, but with unequal enthusiasm applied to the reading of the street names. Stevie had always found it hysterical the way the voice actor would mumble *Las Palmas* but scream *Hollywood Boulevard!* with such vigor as though they were in the recording booth reflecting on the grim state of their career but then managing to rally, remembering their dream of bright lights.

Along the route was a storefront for Ripley's Believe It or Not, and one morning, Stevie looked up from her book at a strange, bellowing sound. It was reminiscent of a sea lion or some other exotic animal the way it lowed mournfully, and as she attempted to spot its location, her attention landed on a gray-haired woman in front of the still-closed tourist trap. The woman wailed insistently. Loudly but generally. No accusation or target. She opened her thin-lipped mouth, leaning back to expand her chest every few moments as her hands roved busily around her. It was as though the trunk of the woman and her arms belonged to separate entities. Her industrious fingers removed a navy beanie from her head to clutch between her legs, in the folds of her long, faded red skirt that was sooty at the hem. She yelled as she elbowed out of a hooded sweatshirt. It was a shock, the milk-white flank of her, a body that was so markedly younger than her face. Her breasts swung freely in the morning air before she pulled on a different sweatshirt from her sun-bleached blue and yellow IKEA bag.

The woman then unhooked her skirt and stepped out of it,

again, completely naked without underwear—full-bushed vulva—and despite the spectacle, no one was laughing. It was astounding. No one seemed to notice. It wasn't that they looked, then looked away. The screaming protected the woman. The torrent of unintelligible glossolalia amounting to a physical shield. Through her repugnance, the woman could distort and alter the tide of attention. A feat of unimaginable power. The woman's repellence was so mighty that she could manipulate reality. All by screaming. All by being someone no one wanted to be caught looking at.

DAY TWENTY-TWO

MOON

ONE WEEK UNTIL THE NEW TENANTS

"Humor me," says Dano, pulling into an A-frame with a cluster of balloons tied to the mailbox. "I just want a peek," he says of the open house. The three of them have just had lunch at Little Dom's, with Stevie's altered appearance shocking Moon from across the table each time she spoke. She has no idea what prompted the change. Stevie had left for work looking one way, returning another, absented of all that precious hair.

Did you at least keep it? she'd asked, wanting to lay eyes on the missing part of her daughter so she could at least account for it.

It's just hair, Stevie had said impatiently, and Moon understands now, how when she'd dyed her hair with mustache bleach in eighth grade, why Sunny had shrieked as though she'd tipped a priceless family heirloom onto the floor.

Moon trails Adam and Stevie into the house, eyeing her daughter's bare calves, thinking how at lunch, the two men at the outside table beside them had openly stared at Stevie, timing the pauses in their conversation to her crossing and uncrossing her long legs. They'd easily been in their fifties, the one with a slender, fluted nose facing Moon, possibly even in his early sixties. And when he'd spotted Moon looking, he'd smiled and raised a glass with sheepish good humor, as though Moon were some shrewish governess.

It's not just the hair. Seemingly overnight, every aspect of Stevie has undergone dramatic transformation. Even her checkered minidress that displays her cleavage and flatters her waist is an abrupt departure from her usual leggings and hoodies. And Moon can't help but wonder what it means. She knows it has to do with Stevie staying out all night. The lurid, neon underwear. Even how she'd called her Mom in the car. It might be a positive development. Possibly, they're being restored to their rightful places. And isn't this what she'd been working toward for so long? The timing would make sense. Moon is on solid footing now. And while she hasn't been to meetings, she's nowhere near wanting a drink. And soon, she'll even be working again.

Gazing around the open house, she struggles to see the appeal. She hates the house immediately, with its predictably Zen themes and stone furniture. Open format. Glass walls. Windows opened for a cross breeze, an uninterrupted line from the front door to the dining area, and the kitchen and living room beyond. All that luck and good fortune shooting straight through. Pouring out into the panoramic view with the overhanging steel roof that leads the eye directly outside. It's a meager stab at a Case Study House #22 motif, the roof lacking everything of the scale and precarity of the original, and it occurs to Moon that a person sitting inside would forever be gazing out. That this is a home of someone who is seeking. It's a monument to dissatisfaction.

Still, there are several other prospective buyers, all couples from the look of it, a few pregnant or accompanied by small children, dead set on ignoring the reality of soft, yielding skulls against hard, brutalist surfaces. Moon can't imagine what they're thinking, what Dano is thinking. In some ways, she supposes it makes sense. He is a striver. A collector. Especially of other people's tastes. And here is a house, perfectly staged, ready to go. It's not an indictment, rather an observation. It's just who he is.

He's always admired and borrowed Moon's preferences, for example, in clothes, books, music, movies. When they first met, he'd confided in her that he hated everything in his closet, wearing the same patterned board shorts that he admitted were a bathing suit. She'd had things sent to him from designers and labels, until months later, he was sitting at those same designers' shows and presentations, never once giving her credit. Which was fine, perhaps a little graceless.

"Are you working with someone?" the real estate agent asks. She has small features and thick wrists and is unveiled in her curiosity about the configuration of their family. Moon can't tell if the woman presumes Dano is Stevie's partner or Moon's, but as her attention continues to linger on Dano, swiping through her iPad, mentioning the Tesla charging station, it occurs to Moon that both she and Stevie have been discredited as contenders and that the agent is hitting on him. Moon removes a glossy copy of the floor plan fanned out on the dining table, insulted and annoyed about feeling insulted. And as she adjusts the collar of her sweater, a cashmere zip-up that could be Cos but could also be Lemaire, she thinks how she could easily still pass for thirty-eight.

She walks up to Dano, interrupting the agent, and asks in a stage whisper, "Babe, what's this all about? You hate L.A."

"I don't hate L.A.," he says, flashing a broad smile, not at the agent but at Stevie. And Stevie, curiously, returns the smile with a satisfied look. A look that suggests intrigue, that intimates that they've discussed this before. That they've talked about him moving back.

Moon is astounded. "You absolutely hate L.A.," she attests, wondering with mounting incredulity if he's already done it. If he's put in an offer. And the thought of him living so close, of dropping by unannounced while the Brooklyn people are still in the Big House, of him somehow knowing them and the confused conversation that would follow, all of it sends Moon into a tailspin. "What about the fires? Earthquakes?" she stammers.

Again, he gives her a bemused look and she knows what he's doing, daydreaming about how it will be once he's back in Silver Lake, or maybe one of the Bird Streets up in the hills. How he'll go to Maru for a matcha. Stop to greet another actor at All Time, both of them casual yet sheepish but oh so normal, just stupendously, disproportionately lucky and wealthy and good-looking. All a full flight from reality.

She rolls her eyes. "How many times have you referred to L.A. as a dystopic hellscape that's going to run out of water in a week?"

"Moon," says Stevie, laying her hand on Moon's arm. "He likes it now, OK?"

She takes a step back. This confirms it. Not only have they talked about it, they've apparently workshopped Moon's probable reactions. And between the driving and Stevie's promotion, news that she's still yet to directly share with Moon, Moon can't understand what more she can do to earn a seat at the table. It's her fucking table and it's her house. Her family.

It's one thing to pass off a love of Lucrecia Martel, Banana Yoshimoto, and Chantal Akerman as his own. Dano can even fail to recall that his love for Hong Kong was hers first, that she was the one to introduce him to Wong Kar-wai in her trailer, the Technicolor smear of neon lights, the writhing boredom of nocturnal yearning. He's now closing in on Stevie in a way that isn't only inconsiderate, it's unprincipled.

Instantly, she's reminded of how Stevie had been with him when she was younger. The way she'd follow him around, absolutely heart-eyed. It's unconscionable for him to be raising her hopes in this way. Not to mention that Stevie, credulous Stevie, should by now know better. That despite everything, the matcha, sunshine, the days spent together, it's all one more way for Dano to avoid whatever he'd run away from in New York in the first place.

"Besides, how can he hate it here?" says Stevie, grinning at him now. "*We're* here." Sometimes Moon could kill her for her guilelessness, her eagerness to be duped. Stevie has to know that once Dano leaves it will be years before they see each other again. This, she decides, is exactly what Mac had been talking about. Dano does seem abused. His constant, competitive campaign to be liked, to be liked at the expense of others. That quick gratification will be his first and keenest instinct no matter the collateral damage.

But now, standing in the kitchen, staring at a giant Buddha head on a pedestal beyond Dano and Stevie, she wonders if this is all her fault. She is the one who'd invited Dano to stay with them. Who'd wanted Stevie to move in from the Pool House. Who'd ultimately set Stevie up to be disappointed from an already vulnerable position. And then, her view of the Buddha is obstructed by the figure of a striking blonde who, for a split second, Moon mistakes for being naked, the cream of her leggings and workout top so closely resembling her skin. She has a yoga mat over her shoulder, as well as a canvas bag filled with sunflowers, and she's eating something from a small tub with her hands, and all of a sudden Moon sees that it is Corinna.

They stare, both suspended in that moment of indecision of whether they'll acknowledge the other, but Stevie turns, then Dano. And Moon, on instinct, removes the sunglasses hooked on her sweater and puts them in her purse as though she and Corinna will come to blows. Corinna pops the rest of whatever she is eating into her mouth, sucks her finger and thumb, then snaps the container shut. She is tall and bronzed, with a smattering of freckles at the bridge of her nose, radiating health, vitality, and total composure.

She greets Stevie first, touching the ends of her hair, telling her how good it looks, and Moon's breath catches at their familiarity, at the shy, adoring expression on Stevie's face. Then Corinna greets Dano, kissing both cheeks, remarking that she hadn't known he would still be in town, that she'd texted, and again Moon wonders how close they all are as Corinna steps forward for a hug in the same instant Moon extends a hand, resulting in a jumble of glancing arms before they settle into a small, awkward circle.

"Two million dollars and you can't get a tub in the en suite?" Corinna says, raising her copy of the floor plan.

"At least they have a Tesla charger," Moon responds. And when Corinna smiles there is food in her teeth.

"I'm sorry we barely got to talk," says Corinna of the funeral. More specifically to Moon she says, "It's nice to formally meet." She has a truly unsightly amount of dark raw seed and mashed drupe from the vegan macro balls she's been eating, a food that unfailingly reminds Moon of dung beetle turds rolled in coconut. The imperfection makes her seem even more young. Achingly callow. Moon had seen it at the funeral even from afar, the doe-eyed confusion, face like a window flung open.

She's overcome with complicated sadness. All the enmity she'd ever felt toward Corinna evaporates. Shame crackles through her instead, regret detonating in small explosions throughout her body. It is like meeting the niece of a friend. She can't believe she'd slept with the young girl's husband, and her thoughts are overcome by a sense of obligation. That Moon is responsible for Corinna now in some way, that she is partly to blame for their ill-fated marriage.

Helplessly, she finds herself slipping into Mac's thinking, the contours of his selfish calculus that is so familiar to her. He would have seen Corinna on set, radiating light, youth rising off her like steam. His eyes would have dilated, serotonin exploding in his limbic system, hands twitchy with the promise of future happiness. There would have been dinners, gifts, a watch rather than a bracelet, first-edition books that she may have mentioned once from childhood. He would have wooed her completely, swaying her parents with his relentless, driving attention, post-prandial coffees with her father, inviting them all on vacation to northern Italy, then Switzerland.

She'd always felt that Corinna had stolen Mac from Stevie, not her. Moon had never doubted that she could summon him back if she wanted, but she was convinced that Stevie would have been considered in his will before Corinna's arrival. Now, looking at the two girls, what she feels most sharply is that she and Mac owe them both. She pulls her compact from her bag and hands it to Corinna, opening the mirror. "Here," she says, confused by the tide of maternal feelings rising in her. "You've got something . . ." Moon points. Corinna's eyes are saucers. "Thank you," she mumbles, touching her fingers to her mouth in a gesture identical to the one of Stevie hiding her braces in seventh grade.

Stevie turns away with Corinna, their sloping backs huddled together, seeming like sisters then, as an absolute riot of emotion crashes through Moon. And when Stevie takes the mirror from Corinna to deliver back to Moon—their emissary, their intermediary—all at once Moon knows why Stevie didn't go to Mac's wedding. The cold shock of remembrance: Stevie in the living room moments after he'd left. She had been home that day. She had to have seen.

"I thought your dress at the funeral was amazing," says Corinna, clearing her throat. "But you always look amazing. I probably should have worn black but . . ." She shakes her head. "I don't know what I was thinking."

"The contrast was good for photos," says Moon.

Corinna pushes a strand of hair behind her ear. "My mom says it washed me out but Arthur bought it for me. It arrived a few days after he . . ." Her eyes fill with fat glistening tears. "He was always telling me what to wear," she says with a croaking laugh, wet sliding down her face.

Arthur. Now Moon sees the rest of it. How eventually Mac would have caught his own reflection beside his young bride. One too many barbs from friends. Exasperated remarks from their wives across fire pits. How the conversation hopscotched over Corinna's tender head, inside jokes, cultural references made to deliberately exclude her, reindeer games from his old school chums, keep-away, his girl polite but vacant, and it would be obvious and unavoidable, the complete trope he had made of himself. Moon knows how he had always loathed his enduring potatoey Scottishness, the frowzy coarseness of his family, the cheap lace curtains and meat teas no matter how much money he'd paid for capped teeth, his cars, the Malibu house with the beach frontage. He'd kept up his Titian hair, the Marvel villain three-piece suits, the timepieces, the shoes, but he would have caught himself in the end. The lampoon of him. The broad, predictable punchline.

Corinna sniffs, her blue eyes radiant now, her lashes darkened with damp. "You know, me and Arthur were watching *The Hermitage Volumes*. You were so pretty, I mean, obviously you still are. I hope the remake happens," she says, naming the filmmakers with familiarity, they are apparently friends, a part of the same generational cohort of influencers that all have podcasts and zines.

Moon's stunned by the brusque mention of *The Volumes*, by the blistering discomfort of imagining Mac watching the most tender private moments of her youth with his young wife in a way that feels wrong, almost criminal. She pictures his meaty hand in the girl's fine blond hair, on her thin thigh, in bed, in some halfway state of dishabille, lolling while spying on Moon, and she is so repulsed by the unctuous sense of violation that she barely notices the shift in mood when Corinna retrieves a Kleenex from her bag, blots her tears, and turns to Dano. "Look, I'm not accusing you of anything, but since you're here I need to know," she begins. "What happened with you and Mac in Hong Kong?"

ADAM

Adam can barely register where he is. Or why Corinna is there. It is absurd that she'd be cruising open houses now. Apparently after yoga, given her clothes and the mat she's carrying. She seems sanguine. Utterly unperturbed. Nothing like a woman who has buried a husband inside of the month.

He looks at Moon. Then Stevie. And Moon again. He has a stupid smile frozen in place. His idiot placeholder smile. His brain doesn't know what to make of this spectacular glitch in the simulation that the four of them would be convened in this way. His plane to New York is in less than a day.

Moon turns to him, eyes soft, full of genuine confusion, and he sees that she is still on his side, unsettled by the intrusion of Corinna.

"Wait, what is she talking about?"

He wonders if he is being punished. Again, he imagines Mac shaking with laughter.

"Mac went to see him," supplies Corinna, and Adam experiences a rolling wave of nausea, the kind of physical shame that he recalls from childhood. "In Hong Kong. Right before everything."

"I barely saw him," he tells them.

"But you did see him," says Moon, the hurt and shock plain on her face. Nothing is going as planned. He'd had the vague idea that they'd like Kip's house so much they could at least talk about moving. It was true that he didn't have the liquidity to make a formal offer now but it was intended to be a starting point. A conversation. Moon would downsize and Adam would help. All he knows for certain is that when he told Stevie he'd booked his tickets she'd thrown her arms around him and whispered, *Fuck*, so dolefully in his ear that he couldn't breathe. It had been so long since he'd felt the pressure of a hug. Ages since he's been touched with pure unprompted affection that he felt a leaching sensation in his chest. He glares at Corinna, hating her.

"You lied to me," says Moon, voice steely now. Against him.

"I didn't . . ."

"You said you hadn't seen him since before the wedding," says Moon, and this is not strictly true. She'd never explicitly asked.

"He saw him a week before he died," Corinna says, and Adam has trouble swallowing. It's all coming out wrong. It's so damning the way she puts it.

"He didn't tell me he was coming," he says weakly.

"You asked him to come. You called and said you needed him," says Corinna accusingly. Her face is flushed, a hale pink glow. "It's why he wouldn't let me go with him." Corinna says.

"He told me you needed him. That you needed his help," she insists.

This at least he knows is untrue. He hadn't talked to Mac in months. But the way he comes off as a feeble, fussing infant is so in keeping with what Mac has always thought of him that Adam takes a step back with genuine hurt.

"I don't know what to tell you, Corinna," he says in as even a voice as he can manage. "But I didn't call him. Check his phone."

"I can't check his phone," she says, and he can see now that she's desperate. That she's less accusing than beseeching. He feels sorry for her then.

"Why wouldn't he let me come?" she asks again, eyes so rheumy they appear unseeing.

"I don't know, but I don't think it had anything to do with me."

He can't breathe thinking how upset he'd been when Mac came. How invaded. Mac had asked for his address under the guise of sending him something, *supplements*, he'd said, but he'd shown up instead, leaning against the buzzer, grainy and grinning, fish-eye lens distorted in the camera view with the maximum number of duty-free whiskey bottles in a plastic bag.

He scans his memory. Mac at the restaurant. At the bar. He's been nursing his guilt for weeks. But now that he's spoken it all out loud, he's reminded that with Mac every joke had been about suicide. Walking into the ocean. Swinging from the rafters. Holes in heads. And for what it's worth, Mac hadn't died in Hong Kong. He'd returned to L.A. He'd been back at home with Corinna before he'd made his choice.

"I saw him, he got drunk. Then weepy. I went home. If he didn't want you to come for a reason, I don't know it."

"I can't believe you didn't tell me any of this," Moon says, voice barely above a whisper. And he knows there is something about the situation that is quintessentially him. Not the individual factors themselves, Hong Kong, the open house, L.A., but that once again he finds himself surrounded by confused, furious women whose rage only seems to intensify even though none of this is his fault.

Moon doesn't trust him at all now, he can see it. He turns to Stevie but her expression is unreadable. He hears the distant tinkle of wind chimes.

Finally, Corinna gives a dry laugh. "I don't know what I thought you'd say," she says, shaking her head. "None of it makes any fucking sense." She stares dully into the middle of the room. "I've run through that morning a million times. He had a meeting that day. He gave me a kiss. The little smoothie container I gave him was still in the car." Her bottom lip is red from where she's been biting it. "We had dinner reservations."

STEVIE

They return to the sweltering car in silence, the AC roaring still-hot air at them as the vehicle beeps to indicate that their seat belts are unfastened. Mostly, Stevie can't stop thinking about the sad little smoothie cup in the drink holder of Mac's car. She'd always figured Corinna knew more. That they'd fought. Or possibly Corinna had found out about him and Moon and retaliated with someone beautiful, another actor, someone golden and young, and that Mac had discovered them.

"Moon," says Adam, and Stevie flinches, wishing he knew to shut up. Moon is furious. Engaging with her now only shows weakness and she'll be spoiling for any reason to eviscerate him. She doesn't even need to look at Moon to know that her eyes are closed. That it's all about to be so dramatic. Her mother might be sober but she's still the same person. In fact, she might be more like herself. A distillation. Rather a crystallization. Solid Moon.

He puts on his seat belt, clearly agitated, and Stevie does hers up in solidarity, but the car keeps beeping at Moon, for the undone seat belt in the shotgun side, and when he says, "Moon," fear threaded all through his voice, the car crash is already happening—the slowest, stupidest collision—because the next thing he does is so predictable and so avoidable. He reaches over to tug Moon's seat belt, to help her with it.

"Don't," shouts Moon, hand in the air, and Stevie wonders if she'll do it, actually hit him but then she lowers it. "I can't believe you saw him. You saw him and you kept it from me."

Adam doesn't respond.

"There's something wrong with you," says Moon. It's a statement. A verdict. "Who lies about something like that?"

"I didn't lie. You asked how he seemed and I told you."

Moon scoffs. "Listen to yourself," she says. "A week before he jumps off a bridge, a man gets on a twelve-hour flight for an unannounced visit and you don't think that's significant? In fact, you know it's significant. It's why you hid it from me. How am I supposed to believe anything you say when you're foundationally dishonest? Lies of omission are lies, Dano. Keeping things from me is a lie. You're a liar."

"I didn't lie," he says. They both sound like children.

"What about the movie?" says Moon, and Stevie cringes. It's a low blow. An obvious sore spot. "Where's the footage? What's it even about? I talked to Rory at the funeral and your agent doesn't know anything about it. Is it real? Everything about you is suspect. Even this." Moon gestures at the open house. "You're never moving back to L.A. I can't believe you'd get Stevie's hopes up."

"Leave me out of this," says Stevie from the back. She's had enough. She's tired of Moon's bullying and Adam's submission. She's sick of all these fucking moments in cars. Moon turns to her, the vein in her forehead ticking.

"Did you know he saw Mac?" Moon asks her.

"No," she responds. "And it doesn't matter."

And then, suddenly, something in Moon's eyes shift. Softens.

"When's the last time *you* saw Mac?" she asks, and Stevie pictures him the way she has a million times since he died, through the window, holding his shoes, walking straight past her and into his car.

"I don't remember," says Stevie, but her voice breaks.

"You were there. Why didn't I remember you were there?" Moon asks.

And it's only now that Stevie puts together the pieces of that day. They'd talked once Mac left. Moon had been wearing her robe, the white, fluffy one. She'd been wasted, giggly, wanting to order dessert but when she sat on the couch, she'd curled into a ball and started crying so hard she began hyperventilating.

It was the last time Moon drank. The day she'd found out Sunny had died. Stevie had only cataloged it beforc as the final time she saw Mac, but now everything shifts and contorts in her mind. All the half-truths and evasions rising to the surface.

"You lied too," says Stevie. "He knows we live in the Pool House. I told him. And you know what else? He was in L.A. already when you called. He didn't tell you because it would have spoiled the story. You both didn't want to spoil the story."

She watches the flush deepen on her mother's face. Lies of omissions are lies but sometimes they're acts of service. Acts of love.

She'd kept so much from Moon and not always because she'd had the capacity for it. When Moon returned from rehab, she'd spread her arms and gone, *Look how fat I am! I've never eaten so many carbs in my life!* Meanwhile for two weeks Stevie hadn't had a car. Cash. Or access to Moon's credit cards. She hadn't even known when Moon would come home. Even before the tenants, they'd never kept much food in the house. The packets of microwavable rice and frozen foods were dispatched first. Quinoa, soup, popcorn. Sweet potatoes, then sardines. The beans, Stevie had to learn how to cook from a video. And, then, finally, when Stevie went to sleep hungry for the first time in her life, when she let herself wonder if Moon was gone for good, she'd gotten up in the morning and traveled by bus for a job where her number one priority was that she could start immediately and eat for free. A staff meal she still half saves in case she needs it the next day, no matter how grim and slimy it gets.

And when a puffy, pale Moon had asked her, *Was it hard?*, looking contrite but with the same hopeful expression Mac had on his face, Stevie shook her head and said no. It was the only trip Moon had returned from without a box of chocolates.

"It's about the intention," says Moon. "And I didn't lie. That house is still my house."

"Moon," says Stevie, wanting her to relent. For once. Just once.

"Oh, so it's *Moon* again. I guess I've been demoted," she mutters to an unseen audience, and it reminds Stevie of the night Moon had told her about Mac. *Our* Mac.

"Stop it," she tells Moon. "Stop acting."

"Who's acting?" Moon scoffs. "Dano's the one putting on a big show." She turns to him. "Tell me, if you knew we couldn't afford the Big House this whole time, why the hell didn't you go home?"

Adam looks stricken.

"He was trying to help."

"Help?" Moon jeers. "Help how? By lazing in my heated pool? Ashing all over the lawn?"

Adam says nothing.

"Why can't you work this hard defending me? Even once?" says Moon. "And why wouldn't you tell me about your promotion? Or ask me to take you driving?"

Stevie shakes her head. She can't even be angry at Adam for telling Moon. She just hadn't wanted her to know she was leaving but now it doesn't matter. Still, it's incredible how quickly everything becomes about her mother. Even the last time Adam had betrayed her confidence. *Yours cordially, Delilah Moon.*

She thinks of that *Anna Karenina* quote about unhappy families, and the truth is, the only happy family she knows was on TV. And for some reason, she thinks about the very last episode of *Wabi-Sabi* but can't recall it. She has absolutely no memory if it had a happy ending.

She looks at Adam in the mirror. "Dano?"

He glances up.

"What time's your flight tomorrow?" she asks.

"One," he says.

"Can I come?"

BONUS FEATURES

To many viewers, the best part of the *Wabi-Sabi* DVD box set was the bonus features. There was a director's commentary. As well as a cast commentary. But the prize, at least to the most ardent fans, was the blooper reel. It was an impressive thirty-eight-minute supercut of flubs, blunders, yips, and retakes, and right smack in the middle was an almost six-minute run of the same scene in which Dano, Moon, and Mac can't stop breaking.

Taped during the second season, the Halloween episode, it is the only segment where the editor let the sound play out. The premise was dumb and cozily predictable. The Sato-Connors were throwing a Halloween party. Moon was dressed like Elvira, Mac was in a toga, and Dano was covered head to toe in dark green paint, the whites of his eyes strange and menacing in the close shots. And at that point in his life he had no way of knowing that the footage would sometimes resurface later as an example of him doing blackface in his "shameful racist past." He was supposed to be Michelangelo, a Ninja Turtle.

Shot during a glorious honeymoon phase when the cast had only just fallen in love with each other, before any of the rancor had set in, the line had been Moon's. She was supposed to shove Mac away from the table, dump snacks into a bowl, and tell Dano, "Forget Cowabunga, I'll Cowabung you."

It was a stupid rejoinder but there was something in the way she pushed Mac, palms sliding off his oiled belly that spun her around with enough force to land in Dano's lap. Ever the improv professional, she went with it, turning to scream at her stepson's matte green face but then she absolutely crumbled. She does it a half dozen times, at first getting frustrated, apologizing and getting angry, shaking her head as she rubs her fingers together, chanting, *OK, OK, OK, come on guys,* as if they were throwing her off, and by the time she finally gets it, the white bedsheet is trembling so violently from Mac's stifled giggling that they set each other off again, the three of them absolutely corpsing, laughing so hard they're hanging on each other, crying.

On the track you could even hear the laughter off-camera in that strange disembodied lower register away from the hot zones of the mics. You can tell that the people gathered around, the unseen crew holding all that heavy gear, are losing their minds cackling, and it was these people Stevie was most jealous of. Not the depicted family, but the family they all comprised when the cameras stopped rolling. A real-life family that still wasn't her real-life family.

PART III

DAY TWENTY-THREE

NEW YORK

STEVIE

When Stevie and Adam land at JFK, it is shortly before midnight. It is loud, cold, and bright in the airport. Stevie is disoriented. She is appalled by how cold she is; it seems impossible that they're even indoors. She can see her breath. And when a dark shape darts low in the corner of her vision, startling her, then swoops up before settling in the rafters, she can see that, improbably, it's a pigeon.

She is really not in L.A. anymore. A New York pigeon, a sight as iconic as a steaming manhole cover or the rushing subway. Adam is as distinguished to her. He's striding ahead, moving with purpose. And she does not know why he is walking so fast, as far as she knows they have no place else to be, but she also gets the sense that this might be how he moves here. As though he is already late.

Last night, he and Moon had argued about Stevie's flight, about who'd pay for it. And at first Stevie had felt guilty but as it progressed, it struck her that they were using her as a meeting place for the fight they weren't having. That they'd lied to each other. That they weren't as close as they'd previously thought and how it pained them.

Stevie had stayed upstairs, praying Adam wouldn't cave, hoping that if she avoided him, he wouldn't have the heart to disappoint her in the morning. But this was before she'd learned they were flying business and that her ticket alone cost $2,869 since it was bought last minute. It's a staggering figure that she doesn't know what to do with. A coach ticket was six hundred dollars, as long as she didn't bring luggage or pick her seat, and still, this had felt like a reach. She intends to pay him back, but $2,869 is an unfathomable figure. And one she would have never agreed to and the debt fills her with intense disorientation. No one has spent that kind of money on her other than Moon, and even then only with seeming resentment, and housing or food is one thing, the luxury of a last-minute trip is entirely another. It makes her wild-eyed to think about.

Throughout the flight, as she reclined her wide seat to watch her personal TV, extracting the leather headphones from their zippered case, even as she sipped champagne and ate her tiny steak with real silverware, she'd been mystified as to what it was exactly that cost so much. It felt scandalous and wasteful, as though someone had given her a gift she didn't have the taste to properly appreciate. But whenever she glanced behind her where Adam sat, she was stunned to discover that he mostly slept, refusing his meals, occasionally drinking from a long bottle of Smartwater that he'd paid for before he'd even boarded. That he would fritter away all that money, in fact seeming to work hard not to notice it, unsettles her completely. And that was before his costume change.

After they'd landed, he'd stepped into the aisle and put on a long, dark coat. And when she'd turned she'd been startled by the unfamiliar figure who opened Adam's overhead bin and pulled out his luggage. That he looks like New York is what makes him so unrecognizable. There is no other way to describe it, and with his transformation she feels tricked, as though he'd deliberately kept this part of him secret, but also covetous, desperate to undergo a similar improvement of her own.

In her puffy coat, one that she sees now is obviously childish and makes cheap plasticky swishing noises as she moves, she doesn't resemble anyone that Adam would know. And as he walks ahead of her, the lining of his charcoal jacket flicks out, revealing a startling purple, giving his smooth strides an attractive, impish cast.

The pigeon glides from the rafter to another and this time Stevie reaches for her phone. There are two other pigeons awaiting it, watching. And as she takes a picture of the three birds, Stevie thinks of Moon by herself in the Big House.

She looks down and stops short. He's gone. She can't see him.

And now she's lost.

More than ever she feels as though she is outside. At a town square or a marketplace where thousands convene, then scatter to far-flung places. No longer tethered to anyone meaningful in the crowd, she cannot tell if staying put is the best course of action or moving to a recognizable landmark like an information desk. She sways on her feet, seized by multiple competing urgencies. Hunger. Fatigue. Cold. She also needs to pee. Scanning every face in the sea of people, all the heads blending together, the galloping panic puffing her breath out in visible gasps, she roots in her pockets for the phone she just had but now can't find.

A man collides into her, hard. He turns to raise his hand, apologizing, but then breaks into a radiant smile, advancing to embrace a girl Stevie's age who throws her arms around him and calls out, "Dad!"

Another man rushes Stevie, looking straight at her this time. He's wearing a blazer, smiling, nodding as if he knows her, and Stevie smiles in response but steps back, prompting him to reach for her suitcase handle. "Taxi," he commands, nodding more emphatically, and she releases her luggage, too swept up in his conviction to be rude, but when he takes her by the elbow guiding her away, it's wrong. She wrenches away, *sorry, sorry*, feeling like an idiot, feeling disagreeable, and casts around for help, throat tight, heart pounding, and that's when she finds him again.

Adam is looking for her. The distress plain on his face. He'd stopped, turned, and it occurs to her that he is attuned to her absence in a way Moon never had been. Moon who's lost her in parking lots, grocery stores, or outright left Stevie more times than she can count. But here Adam is, not twenty feet away with his phone pressed to his cheek. She could wave and he would see her but instead she watches, feeling the phone vibrate now against her from somewhere in her bag. He drags his free hand through his hair and she has the distinct, intense thrill to know that she is the subject of his concern. She finds him shimmering and sympathetic, this man in his coat, and finally, when she lifts her hand and waves, moving toward him, she's elated by the sense of rescue.

"You found me," she says.

"You scared me," he tells her, touching her shoulder gently as though to verify that she's unharmed. It is a wonderful, comforting feeling, so different from Moon, who always seemed crazed at the moment of discovery, as though liable to slap Stevie for having scared her. Adam seems only relieved.

The car ride is like nothing Stevie had imagined. It is not a yellow taxi but an unmarked black sedan. There are no gleaming towers, Times Square. And the World Trade building is not visible from the Queens highways near the airport. The streets are unremarkable and suburban, they could as easily be in Sherman Oaks. And they don't go into Manhattan but rather Brooklyn where he lives. They drive for a while on the small, dark highways, but as they approach the bridge, she sees it all, the steel turrets, the testaments to human ingenuity, the twinkling cables on the soaring towers. She is captivated, bowled over by the sight, and when she turns to him beaming, he smiles at her and squeezes her thigh, his palm warm through the cotton of her leggings.

The car winds down tree-lined roads, foreboding stone buildings huddled together, and then the magnificent view again, doubled in a black pool of water, and in her excitement, she can't comprehend where they're going, the driver seems intent on heading straight into the mirrored tide full of skyscrapers, but then the car slows and turns at a dead end, finally parking.

Adam yawns, then looks around.

"Home sweet home," he says.

Weeks ago, in passing, she'd asked him what his apartment was like.

Old, he'd told her, peering over his laptop in the kitchen.

But now as she follows him up the wide exterior stairs of a grand stoop, she notices the stately double doors, their gold handles, the carved stone posts with Italianate flourishes that flank the entryway of his three-story town house in his tree-lined neighborhood. As he fiddles with his keys, she reaches out to touch the rough sandstone facade, wondering how old it is, wondering who else has touched it, mystified by its seeming permanence the way it is with large trees or great rocks, knowing it will be there long after she's dead.

He is rich. She understands this now, and that he'd been evasive about it. Still, when he pushes open the outer door, leaning into it with his shoulder, she braces for neglect. For possible hoarding, ancestral dissatisfaction calcified into the walls, and for the moment she's wedged up against him in a strange chamber, an anteroom, smaller than the smallest elevator that smells of dust, old books, piles of newspaper, awash in swimming amber light, and she wonders if he dreads being home until the second door swings open and she sees that he is a kind of wealthy that instantly alters her understanding of her business-class ticket. And who Adam Dano is.

The interior is breathtaking. The house is narrow with high ceilings, wood floors, and stairs that lead up and down, with small explosions of color in the furniture gathered in the sitting area to her left that also features a fireplace. It is nothing like the Adam she'd been living with, indolent and easygoing. Like the lining of his coat, the space reveals forethought, calculation. There are a surprising number of plants, real upon touching, and the air is not stale for his absence.

"This is it," he says, removing his boots, unlooping his scarf and hanging it on a peg, along with his jacket.

"It's nice," she says weakly. She has no exacting design language to communicate her thoughts. Only that she notices the red of the circular armchairs is echoed in the red of a large framed canvas that resembles hand-painted supermarket signs. *Grapes $2.99!* He takes her jacket and her eyes travel to the blocky heathered sofa, the leather-covered chair recognizable even to Stevie as an Eames, and a dining table with worn wooden seats that remind her of French schools from old movies. Running alongside the left wall is a floating shelving system full of books of all sizes, and on the facing wall, a trio of canvases, all women, hyperrealistic paintings where the subjects face away.

She thinks to ask about the pictures, but when she turns, Adam is busy sifting through his mail, the large piles collected in white postal boxes on a bright yellow metal sideboard. He opens a large envelope savagely, hooking his finger in the flap to tear it, and again she's filled with doubt. She does not know this Adam. The one who owns this house, who dresses this way, an Adam with mail and responsibilities.

"Don't worry about babysitting me," she says, nervous about imposing. "I'm sure you have better things to do." She steps further into his house, recalling that he has been gone over a year, wondering how anyone could leave a home like this, their own home for so long, then thinks for the first time who else might have lived there. She continues toward the kitchen, marveling at the canary-yellow refrigerator. Adam still hasn't responded, making a vague murmur, and her heart sinks at his obvious regret in allowing her to come.

As they'd left, he'd asked about her return flight. She'd told him she'd stay four nights. A stupidly short trip but she only has three personal days and one day off. She'll have to work on her birthday, the day after her flight back. She will be twenty-one then, an adult by every measure. But what she hasn't told anyone is that there's a bus leaving Chinatown directly for Boston, and in her fantasy she'd go straight to management training and not face Moon at all.

"You hungry?" he asks, apologizing for his distraction and hurrying toward her. He washes his hands and opens his fridge, which is suspiciously well stocked.

"Is it just you in here?" she asks.

"What do you mean?" he says, twisting open a sparkling water.

"Well, how long has *that* been in there?" she asks.

"I had someone come in," he tells her impassively, and it dawns on her that whoever it is also cleans, brings in the mail, and cares for his plants. He pours the water into glasses so thin that when she raises it to her lips she can imagine biting into it and slashing her mouth. And then he gives her a tour, pointing out what she's seen already, the sitting room, and the working fireplace. "There's also a downstairs but we'll do that later," he says. He leads her up to the second floor, running up the stairs two at a time as he had in the Big House, and shows her a white, tiled bathroom with a tub. "That one's yours," he says, and then opens the door to a guest room with a blobby multicolored rug, a swooping wood chair made of oversized, interlocking puzzle pieces, and a round canvas with cartoon daisies hanging above the bed.

He points out the laundry room and then his own room, which contains a gleaming black piano beside his bed. "I didn't know you played," she says, wondering what else she doesn't know. He chuckles. "*Playing* is a generous assessment," he says, touching the lamp on his nightstand to fill the room with warm light, and that's when Stevie looks up and sees her mother, a giant looming poster of her framed on the wall.

"Oh," she says, the word seeming to echo in her head, her shock is so complete.

It's the movie poster of *The Hermitage Volumes*, and Stevie is astonished by its presence but also the belated realization of what's happened. What she's done. She turns to Adam to see if he sees it but his face is unreadable, and she wonders, with a confounded sick feeling, whether or not she'd known when she'd shown Wren the reference that she can see now is exactly Moon's haircut from her first film.

She's never seen *The Volumes*, only parts, some photos, but she knows she's seen this poster somewhere before. It is familiar as a ghostly impression in her memories, the way it can be with déjà vu, a vivid, highly specific suspicion. And now, confronted with the source of her inception, she wonders if she'd asked to be made into Moon. To emulate her mother at her age because Stevie is so empty of any other inspiration of her own.

"Did you take lessons?" she asks Adam, keeping her arms stiff by her sides, her head dazzlingly hot.

"For a long time when I was younger and again more recently, but it's hard with traveling," he says, keeping his eyes on her, seeming intent on ignoring the poster right along with her.

"That makes sense," she says. "I guess you could pick it back up now."

"I guess I could," he says, then gives her a strange, stiff look. "It's just that I never got any better," he finishes. And Stevie gets the distinct sense that they might be talking about something else.

MOTHERBOYS

There are certain boys in New York that will always reek of a mother's influence. Motherboys. Usually an only child. Slow and soft with wet lips. Tender. As though they have been chemically castrated. They are different from the Italians who are devoted to their mothers but are roughnecks; quick-tempered, pugilistic usually, kissing their mothers proudly on the mouth, having them wash their skid-marked drawers even once they are married, eating their food with beatific pleasure, moaning, eyes closed, enamored but pious. Catholic, so Catholic. Mary. Holy Mother. The Virgin. Their mothers are the most beautiful women in the world but they are not attractive.

Rich WASP boys are different. And while the Danos did just fine, it is the Fishers with the real estate holdings and the serious money. As well as the New York pedigree that the Czech side of Adam's family were diffident about. It is why his mother, Katherine, has dragged Adam to various fundraisers all his life. It is why he has owned his own tux since he was six. And why, whenever he sees Tony Hale at industry events, the actor who'd played Buster Bluth on the show *Arrested Development*, he feels uneasy and tends to avoid him. He is aware of the optics of what it means to squire his mother. He only obliges when he is indebted to her in some way or when she is of particularly ill humor.

Once, at a gala in support of the Noguchi Museum, he'd been assigned the seat beside the sales director of an esteemed gallery, an obvious setup by Katherine since they'd both gone to Choate. He'd been idly attracted to her, but later, tucked behind a stone sculpture getting a drink, he'd overheard her tell someone that she found him *eminently fuckable.* But that ultimately she couldn't go home with him because *Adam Dano is such a son.*

Adam knew this. It was the quality he hated most about himself. At Fisheries, the residents and workers called him *Fingerling* behind his back, as well as to his face, insisting it was a sign of affection. A newly hatched fish is a fry. Once it has developed working fins and scales, it is known as a fingerling. He knew there was something in his face that compelled ridicule. A quality that everyone seemed to agree on.

There is a German word for it. *Backpfeifengesicht*. A face that's begging to be hit. This is Adam's greatest fear, that he will remain a fingerling forever.

DAY TWENTY-FOUR

ADAM

It's been almost two years since he'd visited his parents' on West Seventy-Second, and in the cab uptown, he tries to feel calm and self-possessed. He wonders if he can think of this time in the city as a bloodletting. A necessary tactic to restore balance to the humors. He cannot think of it as a permanent arrangement. It would make him feel like the room is filling with an odorless, poisonous gas, but for now at least he can go see his mother and dress according to her tastes. Somber. Contrite. In a dark sweater and wool trousers, sober charcoal socks and monk straps. Like some Oxbridge-educated banking scion at their arraignment.

He'd called her from arrivals. *I made it*, he'd said. *Finally at the correct airport*, he'd joked. He'd wondered if she'd insist on seeing him immediately, what he'd do with Stevie if that were the case, but she'd said, *Welcome home*, in a bright mannered voice, her public voice, with a bustling din behind her, a restaurant, or lobby, indicating that she was out, that there would be people waiting for her. *I wanted to at least say hello*, she'd said, and he pictured her quick eye roll, her falsely chastened expression at her rudeness for picking up, and he couldn't fight the sense that she'd arranged to be out. To imply that she'd been busy. That she hadn't waited for him.

He'd endured months of complaints for not calling. That outside of his constant spending, she wouldn't know if he was dead or alive. And now that he's back in New York, he feels as he so often does, which is that his mother only wants to keep track of him. That she only wants him under her thumb while entertaining no real interest in spending time with him.

To be fair, Katherine is very active. She serves on the board of trustees for several museums and runs her own nonprofit for literacy and arts education. She has fantastic taste and loves art, it just happens she doesn't believe the TV shows or the kinds of movies he makes necessarily qualify.

Presently, he is stuck in traffic, having hailed a yellow cab on Montague instead of Ubering in a flash of misguided civic virtue, and if he's late, he'll have to add it to his mother's growing list of his shortcomings. Even still, if he can get her into the spirit of beneficence, if she believes it was her idea and that it will be good for him, she may be swayed into discussing a future for him at Fisheries.

It will be a matter of mood. And if she is drinking. She's wanted to hire him for her foundation before. And this could be perfect. Once the new incoming executive director is established, changes will be expected and he doesn't at all worry about Katherine's talent for diplomacy.

He rolls the windows down, letting the cold air toss his hair as they finally make their way through the park. He feels uneasy about how he'd left things with Moon. He wishes she were there and he hasn't been able to sleep for the lingering bad feelings from their fight. It's not the first time they've argued. They've often had to take breaks but usually they were unspoken reprieves during hiatuses in which they still texted as though to make sure they were still friends. He knows better than to contact her now, but he'd hoped that she'd change her mind and come with them at the last minute. As they were leaving, she'd said what they always say, *I'll see you soon*, and he'd been so relieved by the small sign of détente that tears sprang to his eyes.

He wants to show Fisheries to them both. He harbors a stupid fantasy of all three of them living and working there. Time at Fisheries surrounded by creative people would inspire Stevie to figure out what she wants to do for herself. Distanced from the doldrums of her life, she could envision herself completely anew. He knows that closeness to nature, the seasons, feeling insignificant in the middle of the forest, to be as far away from the internet or the endless competition would be fruitful for all of them. He just knows it.

He takes another intake of air from the park and feels bittersweet relief, wondering why he's fought it so long. This could be what he does for the rest of his life.

But when the doors to his parents' elevator slide open into their apartment, his chest tightens. He is immediately delivered to the claustrophobic, throttling sense of childhood. It is the smell. The dark deep scent of the wood polish, the fusty pulp of first editions with a ghostly hint of the bergamot in his mother's perfume. Katherine considers the receiving area to be the domain of the staff, the way anything from outside is relegated to the help, like mail and other deliveries, and usually there is someone to greet him once Hector the doorman calls up, but today there is no one. He checks the time, he is nine minutes late, less than the fifteen beyond which Katherine deems contemptible.

Sometimes when he visits, Katherine herself is there. Not to greet him but to startle, mid-sentence in her instructions to the help, flustered and seemingly annoyed by his sudden intrusion. He feels as though he has mistakenly entered the house of a stranger holding a bottle of his mother's perfume in a gift bag for her birthday. He scans the room. There's a cream-colored runner extending from the elevator doors that reminds him of a drawbridge, or a gangplank, the dark wood floors on either side like water or lava, stopping well before the circular table with a large bouquet of fresh flowers. Above it hangs a chandelier, and while he knows he's seen it all a thousand times, he also has a disjointing sense of agnosia that he can't remember if the runner was cream or if it has been replaced and was once a more mushroomy taupe. Or if he's misremembering the carpeting altogether, convinced now that it might have been a large square before.

Finally, a short figure enters from a door behind him, swinging in from the chef's kitchen. He does not recognize her and suspects she is Asian, possibly Pinay, and she wears a navy shirt and slacks and her hands are clasped together as if arriving with the terrible news that the Chateaubriand special has run out for the night or that the opening act for the show has changed. She has an unhurried manner and wears low sensible shoes that miraculously make no sound even as Adam listens for it as she approaches.

"Mr. Adam, hello," she says, offering to take his coat, introducing herself as Feli, *Ms. Katherine's helper.* She tells him they are serving lunch in the dining room, and from this, Adam can't tell if his father will be joining him, but he doubts it. He's led through the gallery and the adjoining living room with the hushed seriousness of a museum tour, lifting his heels slightly, his hard shoes making a noise that seems effete to him, too reminiscent of a woman's high heels. He is glad Stevie hasn't joined him to witness his family's ridiculous, mercenary wealth, the marble fireplaces and the meticulously replicated molding. Plenty of his friends were rich, some with grander homes, but in high school Adam never had them over. Even girlfriends he'd insisted on meeting elsewhere. Especially the women he met out in the world, often older, college-aged daughters who still lived with their families out in East New York or Bushwick, who'd smoke his weed on their poured tar rooftops and sneak him into their bedrooms from the window.

At his parents' house, on the fifteenth floor of a duplex that includes the penthouse, almost four hundred feet up with panoramic park views and a wraparound terrace, he wonders how it can feel so stifling. He'd only ever felt like he was waiting in this house. Or somehow in the way. And when they cross the threshold into the library, everything a dark walnut, with floor-to-ceiling books, many of them priceless, burnished leather chesterfields, an almost cartoonish rendition of a library in a murder whodunit, he wonders if he can actually go through with it, endure the way everyone will talk about him if he goes to work for his mother. The way his father will refer to Adam as *her* son, even when Adam is right there.

Booking his first commercial at thirteen, a national spot, he'd been naive to think that getting a job, going to work, earning money would shift his father's esteem, instead the man had been mortified by the idea that any of his colleagues would recognize him. And even when the show had been a success, whenever it came up in polite conversation, *Oh, you and Katherine must be so proud*, he had the tendency of laughing too loud, a bark of embarrassment, invariably shifting the subject to golf, investments, gossip from the various Ivies they'd attended.

And when they came to his first big play on opening night, Adam waited afterward for them, distracted as he chatted with his friends who'd gone back, writhing with self-consciousness about the subject matter, but still, giddy and flushed from the compliments and the taut athletic thrill of hard work. He'd kept his eye on the door, wanting his parents to meet Rana, to see if they'd been impressed, only to discover later that they'd left at some point despite there not even being an intermission in the hundred-minute show.

The bar cart from the main library's been rolled in, which satisfies the question of whether his father will join them since he hates entertaining in his office. And he gets the sense that his mother does this on purpose, goes around scenting his father's personal spaces and flouting his rules whenever he stays out in Palm Beach too long since his mother loathes Florida. He wonders how much time his parents even spend together at this point and then, as if summoned by his prying thoughts, his mother comes in, holding her wrist as if she's been injured.

"What are you doing in here," she asks, giving a breathy, flummoxed laugh, as though he has wandered into a cocktail party wearing footie pajamas. His mother is a beautiful woman, red-haired and pale, moving with the alert elegance of a dancer, and even now, at sixty, wearing heels. She is dressed in an ivory silk blouse, narrow gray skirt with large wire-rimmed glasses hanging from a chain around her neck, and he can still clock the subtle differences in her face, even her frame, as though she has been ever so slightly deflated in the past year.

"What's wrong with your wrist?" he responds, sounding peevish to himself, but she kisses her teeth, dismissing him with a shake of her head.

"Nothing," she says, setting her bracelet down on the table, its slithery length clicking on the surface. He looks down at it and, knowing she will never ask for his help, proceeds toward her.

"Happy birthday." He holds the bag out by its ribboned handles.

She takes it, then immediately sets it down on a side table. "Thank you," she says, without making a move to open it.

He gives her a look but then softens, picking up the chain to string between his fingers, calling her forth with a nod, and she relents with a small eye roll, exposing the pale blue inside of her wrist.

"That clasp's so fiddly," she says, and he slows his breath, praying his hands won't shake. By luck, the tiny lobster claw fastening stays upright under his thumbnail as he loops it, and she looks up at him, detached still but as though her regard for him has improved. She pushes the bracelet up when he's finished and she retreats back to her corner but with a fond look on her face.

"No more of those," she says, nodding toward the shopping bag containing $630 perfume. "They've changed the formulation and it doesn't last at all anymore."

"Next time, I'll just take a stab at something I think you'll like," he says dryly, knowing what a disaster it would be, and finally this makes her laugh, throwing her head back, teeth flashing.

They have a drink, blisteringly potent gin Gibsons, dry and with three onions the way she likes them, to discuss his mother's new venture, financing a play written by a *brilliant young woman, a true visionary.* And in his hazy tipsiness, he remembers again how they'd never once talked about her leaving that night at his play. He'd gotten decent reviews, it had always meant to be a limited engagement, selling out for the entirety of its run Off-Broadway during the holidays. And whether she acknowledges it or not, it's her love of theater, all the productions she'd taken him to when he was younger, even the more experimental stuff mounted at La MaMa, that formed his desire to be an actor. He eases into his languor, enjoying the way his mother's face animates, the pale opal gleam of her nails as she speaks, and he tells himself that she isn't so unknowable, that the more time they spend together, actually working together, the more compatible they'll become.

"You've always had such a prescient eye for talent," he tells her over their meal of cold roast beef, a wet mass of trembling gristle, fat and blood served alongside vegetables blanched so long they appear exsanguinated. At the comment, Katherine glows as if lit from inside.

"I really think I can help her," she enthuses about the playwright. "If she just gets out of her own way, if she doesn't let herself get so didactic about personal politics, sky's the limit. I keep telling her how crucial she is for women. But who knows if she'll shoot herself in the foot."

He is well on his way to getting drunk and he can see that she is too by the softening focus of her eyes and he wonders if it's a bad time to bring up Fisheries. Whether this particular visit wouldn't be better off as purely a reunion, rather than summoning conversations around a job. But there are too many natural openings.

"I love everything I'm working on at the moment," she says, picking up her wineglass and looking around the table when she finds it empty. "You wouldn't believe how fast the days fly." He tops her up and she raises her glass. "I'd worried about sixty," she says about her age. "I still can't believe it as a number that has anything to do with me. I think I'll always feel about thirty-two. But generally, I do think I'm wiser. At least about how to spend my time. I have far more energy than I did at forty, it's spectacular. The true secret is to be of service. It's incredibly diverting to devote yourself to good works." She picks up the napkin she'd used to cover her uneaten food ages ago and dabs at her mouth. "I hope you'll find something to love as much," she says, smiling creamily. She extends her hand to touch his on the table and it delivers a warm spread of electricity up his arm. "You know I've only ever wanted you to be happy," she adds.

He loves her then. Truly loves her. And he thinks about how all of the untroubled moments in the house revolve around her. How the only times he'd ever felt safe or beloved was when she would allow him to sit beside her in bed, the two of them reading companionably until she switched off her lamp, signaling for him to leave, or he switched off his, indicating that he would return to his room. They both had insomnia and one night as he was getting water, he'd run into her doing the same and they'd started reading parts of the paper standing at the kitchen counter, discussing a review of the Judd retrospective, and then both retired to her room since his father was in his on the other side of the house.

Sitting beside her, he would read the same passage multiple times, distracted by her closeness, the way her hair fell on her shoulders, hair he never saw down otherwise, and how in the lambent lamplight, she would seem mythic yet strangely accessible, like watching a queen from a fairy tale buttering toast. They never spoke and he loved this. He could forget the steely timbre of her voice, allowing intense possessiveness to course through him.

"I think I'd like to come work for you," he says, and his mother's smile goes thick and frozen as she sits straighter in her chair.

"In what capacity?"

"Fisheries, I know you're looking for an executive director."

"Darling," she says, and the forbearance in the single word slices through him. "I know in your work, all those producers and vanity titles are meaningless, but in my world, an executive director is a real job. It's managing teams of teams, it's interminable meetings, it's someone with decades of experience, minimally, doing exactly that. It's very public. Moreover, you have to know it's not my decision. I can't just hand it over to you like the country seat of a kingdom. I wouldn't even know where to begin putting your name forth for something like that."

She gives him a look of grave concern, as though in the next moment she will press the back of her hand on his forehead to check for fever.

"Hang on," he scoffs, bristling about the abject lack of faith that he'd only known to expect from his father. He doesn't spend any time clearing up the confusion, that he hadn't exactly intended to go after the position, because his mother's undiluted apprehension is a rude shock, not to mention an insult. Whether or not she respects his work or acknowledges his accomplishments, he is not an unsuccessful or incapable person. "I love Fisheries but it doesn't mean I want to make it my full-time job," he says coldly.

She withdraws her hand from the table and frowns.

He shakes his head. “You’re the one who complains every year about increasing visibility for the foundation,” he says. “And I just wanted to help. Honestly, I swear it’s like the moment something is my idea even if I’m agreeing with you, you hate it. You never support anything I do.” He thinks bitterly about the play, the show, even the film in Hong Kong, which could eventually become a success despite everyone’s doubt.

She shuts her eyes for a long beat. “Darling,” she says indulgently. “I know you must be exhausted after all the traveling and the funeral business. If it’s about getting out of town, you can go anytime. There’s a new groundskeeper. Phillip retired last winter after forty years, but I can give you our new man’s number, Jessup, and he’ll set up Windcrest Cottage for as long as you like, just give him a day’s notice.” She picks up her phone, then puts on her glasses to type into it. “And I don’t honestly think you can say that we don’t support you. You’ve never gone unsupported a day in your life.”

DAY TWENTY-FOUR

STEVIE

She's in a car headed uptown to meet Adam. Her hair is doing an odd thing. She's slept on it strangely and no matter how hard she's tried to tame it, it fails to resemble anything but a child's craft project, a piece of felt cut into a random shape and fastened in place with glue. She has a splitting headache, an awful tightness from temple to temple. And her jaw aches as though she's been grinding her teeth. It was noon when she woke up, feeling abandoned and despondent like a child rousing from a nap to an empty house. She's hurt that he didn't invite her, even as she hadn't wanted to go, remembering Katherine from the one time they'd met during a wrap party for the first season of the show as a frightening woman with assessing, unkind eyes, who Mac had called a spitfire and Moon had referred to as *Munchausen by proxy*, a term Stevie later had to look up. But Katharine had been odd, shaking Stevie's hand with such a competitively firm grip that even as a child, she'd had the sense that there was something wrong with her.

He'd left her a foil-wrapped egg sandwich in the oven and she'd walked around the empty house eating it off a small plate with a sense of danger since she'd doused it liberally with hot sauce and could easily imagine staining some priceless surface. Then she'd gone up to his room to sit on his bed and stare at the picture of her mother. It is just so bizarre.

I don't think of her as Moon, he'd said later when she'd called up the courage to ask about it. He seemed embarrassed without being able to admit it. And while on some level the abstraction makes sense, she still can't imagine having a such a large depiction of anyone she remotely knows hanging in her house at all, let alone someone else's mother so close to where she sleeps.

She walks into his adjoining bathroom, opening the medicine cabinet to reveal a shocking number of products, cleansers, sunblock, face masks, various glass bottles of serum with dropper tops, hair stuff, and six different colognes, only one that she recognizes when she uncaps them to spray into the air. It smells exactly like Mac.

And when she turns on the light to his walk-in closet, she laughs. It's huge. Cavernous, almost the size of his bedroom, much larger than Moon's, with an intentionality not only to the way it is organized but how it is displayed. It is wood paneled, all the hangers pointing in the same direction, multiple magnificent coats, sweaters folded on angled shelves, pants, suits, another area dedicated to jeans, at least twenty pairs, and a wall of shoes, each shelf with its own recessed light. It is the closet of someone who takes comfort in possession, who is reassured by the control of ownership, and she thinks how alike Adam and Moon are and how unlikely it is that she will ever get to create such a collection of her own.

Back downstairs, she sets her plate down on the floor, licks her fingers, wipes them on her boxer shorts, and sifts through his mail. A year's worth but disappointingly free of bank statements. There are also no utility bills, no mail addressed to him directly, all of it made out to ADO LLC sent to a P.O. box, a huge stack of magazines—*New Yorker*, *New York*, *GQ*, *Vogue*, *Vanity Fair*, *Bon Appétit*, the first issue of something called *Vittles*, as well as an entire magazine dedicated to cake. There are also an astonishing number of invitations, *A.D. and Guest*, various postcard-sized save-the-dates, fundraising notices from museums, theaters, local politicians, but among the mail he'd opened last night is a Visa bill, lying there, practically pulsing, and she tells herself she'll glance at it just for a moment, but when she sees the balance, she feels sick with fear. As though she'd happened upon positive test results for an aggressively fast terminal disease.

She sits on the floor, then enters his address into Zillow, but there's no information. A Google Earth image of a cluster of squares tufted with green bits of tree with the highway and the water to the left. There is not even an estimated price, just two dashes beside the dollar sign, no number of rooms, or square footage, all the information deliberately expunged. But there is a gallery of comparable homes featured below so she clicks on those, all within the seven- to eight-million-dollar range, but she suspects Adam's is worth far more. She's looked up her mother's house before, there was a time when she checked it obsessively as though she were weighing herself, and while she's never known the exacts of Moon's finances, she did once open a residuals check for $18.68, only to find it again a year later, uncashed and expired.

She'd been inspecting his cupboards when he texted for her to come meet him uptown, that he'll send a car. And now in the ride over, her idea of Adam has shifted again. She doesn't know where she's going, he hasn't told her. And while her headache has settled right between her eyes, she hadn't wanted to ask Adam for a painkiller, not wanting to plant the idea in his mind that she'd been rooting through all his things in search of one.

She's dressed in all black. In her nicest, least-disgusting leggings, boots, and a fuzzy sweater, leaving her coat behind because she's embarrassed of it, but now she feels uncertain as though her outfit is contrived and unsophisticated. New York–coded in an uninitiated, meme-based way. And her feet hurt already despite having done nothing but stepped into the car.

They're on the highway, the city glittering over the water beside her, staunchly refusing to be photographed well. And then she is on a bridge, and then, *bang*, she's in a part of town where the buildings are so tall she can't see their tops even with her nose pressed up to the cab windows. And all the while, she thinks, *This is New York. Actual New York.* She imagines living there, taking the view for granted, tapping away on her phone with a sense of importance, having drinks, making clever, droll friends, leading a life. She gazes out at all the pedestrians, all on their phones, holding coffee cups, listening to AirPods, lost completely in their thoughts, their long, determined strides, not having to drive, not having to be stuck in traffic, and she thinks, *That. I want that.*

The car stops and the driver gives her a pointed look. Finally announcing, "We're here," to indicate for her to get out. On the street, she tilts her head back, taking in the whole building soaring above. From where she stands she can make out the edge of Central Park, hotdog vendors, the exhaust and perfume of the street, human musk, food swirling around her, and when she peers down Fifth Avenue, the view is spectacular, yellow cabs, pedestrians, it's every movie she's ever seen, it is the New York of *Home Alone*, *Breakfast at Tiffany's*, resplendent with designer boutiques, jewelry stores that take up the entire city block, and then she hears her name and turns, and standing beside a department store window is Adam, and Stevie's heart explodes from having someone to know in New York.

"I love it here," she announces, meaning it. All the noise filling her ears, quieting the chaos in her head, the layered chatter, so many conversations, the people, their shoes, their expressions, their hair. She turns around and almost applauds, the manhole behind her actually emitting steam, dramatic plumes gusting around a gleaming white building, and when the fog shifts, she sees that of all things, the monument is an Apple store.

"Where are we going?" she asks.

"Bergdorf's," he tells her.

Through the metal doors, they're met by walls of leather goods, deep, warm scents of cologne, and a docent whose real title on his badge reads *docent*, as though they are in a museum. On the third floor, a man with thick lashes and a gleaming bald head, Malcolm, hugs Adam and ushers them into an enclosed fitting room with leather seats and a cowhide carpet. Inside, there are two racks of clothes and Stevie sits while Adam sifts through them without ceremony, requesting a cold brew, ordering one for her too without asking, and as he surveys the clothes, eyes flicking back and forth, hangers shushing against metal, he sorts, eventually creating one rack of discards and another of things he will try on.

There's a shrewd efficiency to his choices but no way Stevie could have predicted them. An enormous olive coat that swallows him, a powder pink cardigan bright with flowers. Despite the cold weather, there's several pairs of tailored shorts and Stevie wonders if perhaps he really will move to L.A. He tries on a bright woolen suit. And each time he strips down to his boxer briefs without embarrassment, Stevie and Malcolm find somewhere benign to affix their attentions. He puts on a spectacular cable-knit sweater, chocolate brown, his head emerging from the turtleneck with tousled hair. He is shockingly beautiful and as he tucks his hands into the pockets of the loden flannel trousers, laughing when they're still sewn shut, he turns to the mirror, first pursing his lips and then letting his mouth hang open slightly, and she sees Malcolm staring at him, unblinking, lips parted; in the same instant, she catches her own reflection in the three-way mirror and shuts her mouth.

All at once, she understands that he is hotter in New York. Or else that he can make himself substantially more attractive through sheer force of will. She is astonished. Jealous. Even as she enjoys watching him preen, even as her headache is edging into a state of priority. She's glad to be sitting, swiping through her phone for Brooklyn apartment shares in neighborhoods she knows nothing about, aware she should be looking for housing in Massachusetts, a state she misspells every time. Mostly, she steals glances at the expanse of Adam's bare, muscled back.

After a while, she feels his hand on her shoulder and he thanks her for her patience and then, absently, says, "It was actually really good to see my mother," as though they are midway through a conversation about her, before deciding on yet one more cable-knit sweater but in green.

When they leave, they leave with nothing. She knows he's bought something, just not what or how much. No money has changed hands and she can't account for the mounting strangeness of his mood, not quite anxious, twitchy, almost euphoric. And she wonders briefly if he's high. If he'd somehow taken something without her noticing.

He insists on taking her to the women's department, apparently a whole separate, larger building across the street. And on the sixth floor, they are greeted by another salesperson, Marjorie, a compact woman in a black skirt suit and fishnets, who tiptoes to kiss his cheek when they hug. She asks about his travels as they walk through a wide, bright hallway, and Stevie is subdued, overwhelmed by the clothes, the lights, intimidated as she passes a woman in the middle of the sales floor, head and shoulders sprouting out of a voluminous rose-colored dress that two others have to help her out of.

They pass different sections, each space smelling distinct from the last, the furniture altered to complement the clothes, even the mannequins posed as if they are entirely different sorts of people, people who would not share a meal with the mannequins next door, some in dark, paneled jeans, others in ragged black shrouds that partially cover their faces. Stevie is flustered, worried that she will be expected to know what section she belongs to. Her left heel stings painfully as they walk, and she recalls how in her last year of high school, she'd worn the same handful of tank tops and sweats. Marjorie, noticing her limp, parks her on a high-backed leather chair and clucks at her shoes.

"Stay right here," she instructs, and Stevie is exhausted yet buzzing, relieved to be off her feet as she watches Marjorie walk away. She's had two cold brews to Adam's three and feels insane.

"So your mom was good? She wasn't mad?" she asks, studying his expression. From where he stands she can't check his pupils. He looks up from his phone, confused. "About her birthday?" Stevie adds.

"She's not like that," he says, waving off the notion. "She's really excited about her work. This new play she's producing."

Stevie had no idea his mother was also in the business but it seems like a plausible source of tension. He says it defensively and seems to vibrate with a glittering recklessness that she definitely doesn't like. And while he could be a little drunk, she decides that he isn't high. She longs for the Adam who had been unhurried and easy in L.A. Splayed out on the couch or a lawn chair, sometimes the floor, not even napping or reading, just lying there like a phone on a charging pad, almost dull in his lack of affect.

Marjorie returns with a pair of shearling slippers, and when she holds them out for Stevie to step into, Adam says, "It's for her birthday." And Marjorie chuckles, "Yes, so you've mentioned." And then it begins.

Marjorie leads Stevie around the floor, asking how she likes to dress, the climate she lives in, the colors and fabrics she is partial to, and with each new inquiry, Stevie can only think of her Pee Wee's shirt and her two pairs of tan Kirkland pants. Everything else is a mystery. She doesn't mean to be uncooperative so she gives Adam a hopeful look and he says, "Something classic," naming a few designers as Stevie holds her breath, not wanting to break the spell. She doesn't know what he intends but she has the sense not to interrupt. She looks down at the Ugg mules on her feet, rather than make eye contact with him, wondering how Marjorie knew her size.

Marjorie holds a cardigan up against her, then blouses, dresses, she tells her about how certain cashmere sweaters are impossibly soft, sumptuous and pillowy, three-ply, but how other sweaters are featherlight, warm but not overwarm, holding out various different ones for both her and Adam's inspection. But as they pass a luminous blue suit with heavy shoulders and billowy pants, Stevie wonders if this isn't her secret heart. If she's not the sort to wear an orange dress made up of millions of mesh folds or a green so vibrant it makes her teeth throb. But Marjorie and Adam lead her through a hall of framed photographs and illustrations until they are in a quiet room with a three-way mirror where they're met by another woman who wheels in a rack of coats. In deft, smooth movements, Marjorie selects one and holds it out for her. She puts it on, a navy peacoat that swings out at an angle from her body, and Marjorie glances at Adam and mutters, "Too much," helping her out of it.

"This one," says Marjorie, selecting a longer cut, and Stevie slides it on. "Oh, this is it," enthuses Marjorie, stepping away from the mirror so Stevie can see.

Adam smiles.

"Is it?" he asks, but she can see that he already knows.

She can't stop grinning. The coat is narrow and skims her body almost to her ankles in thick gray fabric so dark it appears black. It has a dramatic notched collar that is layered somehow, an exaggerated trench coat, belted with deep pockets and lined in dove gray silk. She feels criminally unworthy of it, and as she looks at herself in the mirror, she has the unwelcome premonition of the coat over time, its dinginess, missing the belt eventually, thrown over a Pee Wee's polo, reeking of cooking grease, but she evicts the image from her mind to turn her body slightly and lift the collar. She pouts, then catching herself, smiles, just as she sees Adam in the reflection looking at her.

"That's very good," says Marjorie, and stepping behind her, between them, she tugs at the sleeve, indicating that the cuffs are too long.

"We could have it tailored no later than Thursday," she says.

"Thursday?" he asks, and Marjorie, reading his expression, responds, "I'll see what we can do." It is only Tuesday.

Again, there is no way to know what he plans to buy for her and no way to tactfully ask. She can barely keep track of what she's tried on: shoes, shirts, pants, skirts—a unit of clothing so foreign that she cannot imagine herself ever reaching for it—but her overwhelming sense is one of disappointment. She has been given a chance to make herself over completely. To become the version she needs to be, but everything about her future feels mysterious and impenetrable. Her attention is flagging but still they make their way across loungewear and intimates, a sea of white cotton nightgowns, and she's stricken by the sick deceitful sense that Moon would not approve of what she and Adam are doing together.

Afterward, they're both famished. Lightheaded and dazed. They forgo the restaurant on the seventh floor, Adam doesn't want to see anyone his mother knows, and they head to a small French bistro a few blocks away. It's cold on the street and Adam gives her his coat a second time, sliding it over her shoulders like a slippery, heavy cape, and when she follows him into the restaurant and the coat check girl takes it, Stevie catches her glance at Adam with appreciation. They're led across a black and red checkerboard linoleum floor to the bar with red leather stools. He orders for them both from a prix-fixe menu. "There's a strategy," he insists, ordering duck for himself, a steak for her, fries and salads and soufflé potatoes and snails to start. He orders wine for both of them and suddenly she is on a date. But despite his smile, he twists one corner of his napkin frantically between his fingers. She wants to ask him what's going on, what she can do, but breaking character now might damage him somehow, akin to waking up a sleepwalker. He seems so brittle. So much like Moon in the moments before a crash.

DAY TWENTY-FOUR

MOON

FIVE DAYS UNTIL THE NEW TENANTS

It is strange to watch herself onscreen. Partly it is her considerable youth. She is so young, younger even than Stevie, so young that she can't reconcile it with the way things had felt when she'd first left home, the story made vivid by her retellings but the lived experience of it dimmed in her body. Moon now, in the present, yawns. The yawn grows deeper, she hasn't slept well. Last night, after tossing for hours, her eyes had flickered open in the dark and inexplicably she'd wanted to go outside, desperate for air.

When she stepped out, the yard lights clicked on, the bright white blinding her. Uncertain and half asleep, mute with fear, she'd been pinned in place by the spotlight, and in the moment of horrible, paralyzing terror, she'd heard the doleful howl of a coyote from somewhere behind her. She'd whipped around, frightened as a child, and heard another, then another, yet another, until the entire landscape pulsed sickeningly with the call of prairie wolves going off like car alarms. She'd run back into the house, sank down to her haunches, the hammering brightness still alive behind her eyes, and held herself, shrinking as small as she'd go, crying audibly, crying for her mother.

Afterward, she couldn't sleep, thinking instead of the dream she had after Sunny died. The one where she followed a woman in a thickly carpeted hallway of a house, a woman who she only knew to be her mother from the steadfast logic of dreams, calling her name, wanting her to turn, even as she was terrified that she would, convinced her mother's face would be ghoulish or rotted or worse, a Sunny who didn't recognize her.

She yawns again, focusing on the screen, on the grainy black-and-white version of herself at eighteen years old, wearing a white nightgown, putting a jigsaw together in real time with no sound. She cannot remember what the puzzle was, the picture it made. There is no sense memory in her almost fifty-year-old body to accompany the visual. Mostly she marvels at the dexterity of the hunched position, one foot hooked onto the chair, knee by her ear, neck craned forward. It is a posture that can only be maintained by children, and Moon now reaches for the knot at the base of her neck with one hand. She is stiff just looking at it.

She hugs herself tight, grateful to be alone in her room, in her robe, her good robe, on her bed. She never watches herself, unless she absolutely has to, she doesn't know many who do, who don't find it excruciating, though there are some, the rare sociopath or the rarer, well-adjusted person who can watch with the steely dispassion of an athlete watching game tape. *The Hermitage Volumes* have been in a box with a drive in the back of her closet for decades, but it was the run-in with Corinna, Stevie leaving, and the reminder that some naif actress will be playing her in the retelling that prompts her to skim through it all again. Just to see. To check.

But a remake could never capture the intention of the original. It would not be real. This had been Moon's life. She'd only allowed herself to be filmed because she'd had nowhere else to go. She'd told herself she was in love with the director, her life molding around the contours of necessity, Moon's own will and desire so malleable and yielding but also mercenary. At the end, she'd needed to want it for what it would give her in return. And now she has the sense that she is peering inside a very old box, menacing holes drilled into the lid for light, for breath, reaching inside to inspect her own suitability for market, checking her hands, feet, eyes, teeth. And she knows she would sell the girl again for what she wants. That it is a gift that she can sell her twice at all.

Watching herself calls up a strange familiar scorn. Frustration. The same choking exasperation she feels watching Stevie move around in the world. Partly it's their embarrassing lack of pretense. The Moon onscreen is not obfuscated by a role. She is defenseless. It's her. Purest her. Not yet even playing Delilah. Here is Theresa Moon pure and unfettered, blundering and vulnerable. Theresa is bawdy and fun. Cool. A good hang. But as a disguise. In truth, she is skittish, studied, her own perceptivity functioning as a clever little tool. A pernicious, dogged handicap. There is a price in knowing exactly what everyone expects her to do, wants her to do, well before needing to be told. Not yet knowing that it works less effectively over time, that it becomes a less charming quality in middle age and that it's lonely. It is acting, which differs from living, and is isolating in a distinctive way. But there'd been such ambition in it too. Wanting everybody to be so wretchedly in love with her that it ruined their lives.

On-screen with her head down, attention fixed on the puzzle, long hair falling into her face, concealing it completely, Moon wants to reach into the screen and draw back the black curtain. But then, all of a sudden, the girl rears back, face alive, beaming, laughing, and talking soundlessly to someone on the other side of the room, and she is beautiful the way children are beautiful, cheeks cherubic and a full, blossoming mouth. The adoration radiates off her, the way she pitches herself forward to whoever is speaking, the director, away from the audience, and it is love but love born from need, and Moon feels as though she is watching someone falling, aware of the collision to come but indifferent to it.

That she is younger than Stevie here is unthinkable. Stevie is still so breathtakingly, destructively young, and Moon remembers how her daughter had looked in the morning on the way to the airport, how they'd embraced, and how helpless she felt releasing her. They have not spoken. She only knows that they'd arrived safely from Dano's update in the group chat. She'd known better than to try and stop her. The same way she won't hound Stevie now. Stevie will have to come to her. And she will. She has to.

An inelegant jump cut judders into the next scene. Suddenly her hair is falling raggedly around her ears. The long thick ponytail hacked off. They'd all gotten lice. She'd shaved their heads but chickened out before they could do her. Instead they'd used a pair of children's craft scissors, dull and snub-nosed, that splintered the hair where it was cut. A tall, skin-headed boy steps into the frame, stooping over the coffee table, scalp as pale as the soles of his feet, and begins rolling a cigarette, pinching tobacco laid out on a book. The other boy joins him to sit on the armchair. The boys were brooding and beautiful. Resembling each other. Square-headed with Roman noses and brutish overlarge features that gave them an animal keenness, alert, primed to fight or give chase. They were speed freaks, wounded and abandoned, but at six foot five with shoulders as wide as doorframes, to Moon they seemed otherworldly, like fallen angels. When they weren't tweaking, there was a languor about them. Curled in on themselves as though in penance for taking up so much space. She loved climbing on them, nudging her way between their long bodies, watching them smoke. An early review misrepresented them as father and son, a rumor the director maintained, but Moon knew the true story. Mainly, the boys had been lovers.

Most of the footage is them bonily clanging around in the house, killing time, but the inevitable end, the tension that served as the driving force of the entire enterprise, was the implied conclusion of sex. In the clip of the scene that circulates the internet, she wears her white nightgown like a bride, rendered younger by the inexpert haircut. Moon knows now that a child who swears they are grown is never to be believed. It is always an act of ventriloquism, an act of survival, false consent performed under coercion for adult absolution. Forgiveness by name. And that there is a difference between pretense and pleasure and it can only be learned by experience. And time.

It is peculiar even now. The blurred lines between arousal and fear. She hadn't felt the harm in the asymmetry until years later. The shame of her exploitation contextualized by reviews, think pieces, legalities, until the excitement became unease and her disquiet became legible. It's astounding how much she'd loved the director in that house. Would have done anything for his approval. And how the spell had broken so cleanly when she left. It's why she'd never moved in with Mac. She told him she wouldn't go west of the 405, but it was that she knew better than to trust herself in yet another man's house. All she knows is that you won't know. You won't know that they're not the one. She hadn't known.

Moon hadn't been a virgin. Nor had the sex between them always felt shameful. And there were times when she'd loved how the boys' bodies felt against hers, how she would snuggle up beside one and the other would follow, pressing along her back so she would close her eyes to guess whose hand was on her, inside her, never peeking to even find out who it was. The boys smelled different, one with taut, striated muscles, the other with a shockingly large penis, the way she would later learn it could be with narrow, mute men. But it was the director they all performed for. The director whose house it was. And the director from whom they kept the boys' secret.

She hits pause.

All at once she is plunged back into memory. Sucked into the TV like the little girl from *Poltergeist*. She recalls the wood grain of the coffee table, the hot, cracked pleather of the couch, the torment and the scratching from the lice. She'd bloodied her scalp with her fingernails, unable to sleep for days, the sense of crawling so alive on her body. Fevered with despair when their water got shut off that same week. How they would stink in the dark, unable to sleep in the thick, still air, and she would dream of her mother's plastic bathtub that she'd mocked for being tacky, pink, and fabulous, with gold Jacuzzi jets, not knowing how desperately she'd miss them one day.

Moon doesn't know why but when she tries to recall anything else of the eight years in L.A. before Stevie, there's nothing. There is Texas. Then *The Volumes*. Then Stevie. No in-between. She'd met Mac at some point but the rest of the footage is missing. She was Stevie's age and then there was Stevie. Everything else is redacted. Blacked out. Then there's the show.

And now is now. Moon pictures her mother's swirled, injection-molded Jacuzzi tub again. How the hard water would form a crust of lime on the gilded faucet that was shaped like a swan's neck, water pouring out of its open beak. Those times Jerry left, Sunny would run the tub for them, sitting behind Moon, scrubbing her back with a neon green nylon cloth with thin black stripes. Her mother holding her shoulder steady with one hand scouring for dear life, Moon's mind going still. And afterward Moon would feel soft, almost slimy to the touch, slick, like a porpoise. Clean.

They were both so happy with Jerry gone. Even as Moon knew why. Even when they never talked about all those dead babies, Sunny's pallor, her grief. And now Moon misses her mother with disbelieving intensity. Instead of forcing it back, wrenching the portal shut with both hands, she lets the tide take her. She longs for her mother, awash in indescribable pain. She cannot understand how she is still alive with this agony inside her, and it reminds her of that old joke about women, *Don't trust anything that bleeds for a week and doesn't die.*

She doesn't remember where she'd heard this joke, or the one that goes, *What do you call a sixteen-year-old virgin in the South? A fast runner.* She does remember being told by a man that most female animals die after menopause but that women don't. Another man had corroborated this at the dinner table, at the same event. They'd been talking about fatherhood, about how rewarding it was, how everyone should do it, attempting to convince another actor, a woman, to have a child, as though she would have the same experience they would. As though their wives weren't at home with their children in that moment.

Moon sets the remote on the kitchen counter before she even registers that she's come downstairs. She opens the refrigerator door for the bottle of beer that she's never forgotten. It is just beer. There are only two. Hardly anything. The cold heft of glass is pleasing in her palm, the condensation a thrill. She twists off the top, the rich yeast detonating around her, the sharp tang of thirst flooding her mouth. Sunny loved beer. Shiner bock. Texas beer. The one with a ram on the label.

She holds the bottle under her nose, gripping it by its shoulders. Enzymes clamoring on her tongue. She leans hard against the counter, knowing she should call her sponsor, knowing she should pray. She remembers that prayer isn't always talking to God. It is abjuring faith in yourself. It is admitting defeat. Anguish. She thinks about the St. Francis prayer card still in her wallet and she doesn't recall all the words but she remembers the sentiment. She drops to her knees.

Lord, make me an instrument.
Where there is error, truth.
Where there is doubt, faith.
Despair, hope.
Let me not so much seek to be consoled as to console.
To be understood as to understand.
To love rather than be loved.
For it is in giving that we receive and it is in dying that we are born to eternal life.

ALL THE WAYS TO DIE

Fratricide is killing your brother.

Sororicide is killing your sister, but fratricide means the same thing.

Patricide is killing your father.

Parricide is killing any relative, including your father.

Matricide is killing your mother.

Mariticide is killing your husband. These two words are strangely close.

Neonaticide is killing an infant within the first twenty-four hours or month of their life.

Infanticide is killing a child within the first year of its life.

Pedicide is killing a child.

Prolicide is killing your own child.

Geronticide is the abandonment of the elderly to die.

DAY TWENTY-FIVE

STEVIE

It is agonizingly bright in the room, lightning splitting her head wide open, and Stevie gropes around the bed, shoving pillows to the floor to locate her phone. She isn't home. That much she knows. Not in the Big House where the windows face away from the sun or even the Pool House where the light isn't as thin. This light is white. Sharp. Clinical. Something is wrong. She can't lift herself up. And she's wet, covered in a film of sweat, and when she tilts her head she sees a shock of absolute blue, which she understands to be sky.

She hears herself making plaintive noises and carefully touches her eyes to maintain that they are still there, that she hasn't sustained a dramatic physical injury that has structurally altered her face. Her cold, dry touch barely registers, the agony is so piercing, so total and impressive, so unlike anything she's experienced that a fantastic wave of nausea sweeps through her and she moans, a whole mouthful of saliva spilling out. She pants, dazed by the colors of the hooked rug, the upside-down vision of all the shopping bags delivered from the day before, and only then does she remember that she is with Adam.

She calls out, begging Siri to find him. And when he rushes in, holding his phone, she is so relieved that she immediately begins sobbing, feeling the mattress dip when he sits. He is fully dressed and showered, smelling beautiful, clean. "It's my head," she tells him. "There's something wrong with my head."

In the car, he leans over to fasten her seat belt, her head lolling back. The scent of air freshener is too powerful, she feels like she might throw up, and she has the sudden recollection of the night before when she'd gone to the bathroom, of all the lights being on downstairs and the voices she'd heard. But then, the car rumbles over a pothole and her tender, pulped skull bashes against her window and the pain is blinding and he wraps his large arm around her shoulders, guiding her toward him, cradling her.

At the emergency clinic, a young blond doctor in a long-sleeved skeleton shirt takes her medical history. The receptionist is wearing cat's ears, short whiskers eyelinered onto her cheeks. Stevie's forgotten that it's Halloween and the desultory costumes inspire no confidence even as they tell her she's fine. She isn't hemorrhaging to death. She needs emergency oral surgery.

"You had to have seen this coming," the doctor scolds about her wisdom teeth. There had been headaches, the pressure in her sinuses, but nothing that indicated it was originating from inside her mouth. And in a second car, she hears Adam speak to his mother, voice tight, the call short, asking after her dentist and Stevie cringes, knowing she's making more trouble than she's worth. And then they are in a Midtown office where the dentist, *Drew*, a wiry, gray-haired man, is surrounded by framed Broadway playbills and is wearing the leather jacket costume of the sadist dentist from *Little Shop of Horrors*, complete with a gas mask.

All four of her teeth are impacted, he informs them, blessedly removing the mask when he speaks. They're coming in sideways, ghostly battering rams, slicing through her gums in the X-rays, shredding the soft padding of her cheeks from the inside, the right one exposing a nerve. A woman enters, seeming competent for being the only one not in costume. She is young and small with kind eyes, corn-colored hair, and a large mole on her cheek, and it is while wondering why she doesn't have it removed that the anesthesia takes hold and Stevie passes out.

In the next moment, her shoulders are stiff and her mouth is full of gauze. Her throat is unpleasantly dry and the radiating pain in her head has dulled to a thudding, more general ache akin to an old bruise. When she touches her lips tenderly they are cracked and dry.

It's dark when she wakes again. There is a terrible leeching sensation in her head. All the moisture is being pulled out beyond what a human person can survive. Her bones feel fragile, as though she's risen from the depths of a medically induced coma. She doesn't remember going to sleep and she's stricken that she's missed the day. She feels cheated, unbelievably disappointed. Fully awake now, at midnight, the entirely wrong time, she wonders what she'll do, already bored by her prospects, but then the events from the night before return to her whole cloth. Between Adam and the woman who had come to the house. Upon hearing voices, Stevie had peeked over the banister on her way to the bathroom, down at the wedge of living room at a figure on the couch. The top of a woman's head, small, blond.

You don't even tell each other where you're going anymore? Adam had asked from the armchair where Stevie could see his knees.

He's sleeping, responded the woman in a low tone. Her voice was sexy, husky.

So he just lets you leave the house at three in the morning?

What do you mean, "lets"? she'd asked with a laugh. *I left him a note.*

Saying what?

That I went for a walk.

This makes both of them laugh.

They were both quiet after that until Adam joined the woman, positioning himself in front of her and taking her wineglass to set it on the end table.

I'm mad at you, she'd said, and even though Stevie still needed to pee, she'd edged her hand into her panties at the drop of the woman's voice. Stevie imagined the woman's face, deciding on brown eyes for her, the way the woman in the crypt had dark eyes. Definitely a smoker with that voice. She was slight, too short to be a model, but she could have been stunning, an actress but also in New York the possibilities are endless, a viola player for the Philharmonic or a principal dancer in the ballet. Stevie imagined her to be young, in her twenties. Physically strong, wearing long scarves on her subway rides to Lincoln Center.

The woman took off her shirt, exposing her small braless breasts, and Adam pulled off his T-shirt from the scruff of the neck and then for a split second, as if detecting Stevie's presence, he'd looked toward the stairs and Stevie's breath caught, but then the woman pulled him closer and they'd kissed. When the woman unbuckled his belt, Stevie knew she should leave, that what she was doing was wrong, but more than anything, she'd been frustrated that she couldn't lie down without losing sight of them. Instead of getting on top, the woman said, *Here, let me,* directing him to the sofa, blond head over his lap, but after several more moments, she'd sighed, pushed her hair off her face, then sat beside him.

Well, this is suboptimal.

She was still shirtless when she got up for the kitchen.

You know we do Viagra now? she'd said, and Stevie heard the fridge door open then shut. *It's literally on our shared cal for sex nights. A big "V." I could bring you some.*

But Adam demurred, then apologized, and Stevie felt his mortification so forcefully that her heart ached.

We're all sorry, she said. *We're all so fucking sorry*. Stevie hated her then, the bitter hardness of her hurt feelings. She left them, creeping back into her room, and sat on the floor, waiting for the woman to leave. She calmly closed her eyes in the dark, still wide awake, opening her eyes behind her eyes, then walked backward from her consciousness as though retreating from the slit of light under a door. She receded into herself where things were quiet and calm but ultimately lonely, but this time she'd felt herself stumble and rear into the softness of another body. Adam. As a boy. It was a delight to find him and she'd remembered how pained he'd been when they left L.A. How upset he'd been to disappoint Moon. She recalls his misery, the grim expression on his face, his physiognomy resembling a child right at the brink of dissolving into tears. He'd been desperate to mollify Moon, desperate to connect with her but failing and Stevie understands that finally he has occupied her role, giving her a reprieve, playing the position for her, and taking the body blows. And remembering this now, she is so full of adoration that she smiles in the dark, the smile in her chest smiling too. They are two of a kind. She is more than one. So this is love. Her love for Adam is a snake swallowing a chicken whole. They really are siblings. They will take care of each other.

KOREA

[GOJOSEON KINGDOM FOUNDED 2333 BC ACCORDING TO KOREAN MYTHOLOGY; AKA NOT AUGUST 15, 1948, ACCORDING TO SOME OTHER PEOPLE]

In Korea people were constantly throwing themselves off bridges. And for some reason, ever since she was a kid, Moon would tell Stevie stories of how intense Koreans were. *How metal*, was how Moon put it, as though she were impressed but also horrified. Moon rarely talked about her family and Stevie had never been to Korea, so while all of this felt like an education, it also felt like a warning. As though some essential Korean spore inside of Stevie would detonate and that she shouldn't be surprised when it happened and that it would be wild and irrepressible.

고려장 referred to escorting your elders to a mountain or plain and leaving them to die, Moon had told her once. It's an honorable way to go, she maintained, but then again Moon had a thing about old people. Especially old women. She would visibly flinch when she saw them. In any case, she'd also told Stevie about how with all the suicides, there'd been a campaign to deter jumpers. *Americans will just put in a net*, said Moon, but Koreans tried to discourage jumping before it happened. At first, they'd added affirmations and rails that lit up as you walked, to acknowledge your presence, your existence, a physical indication to signal that you mattered. But when that hadn't worked, they tried pictures of food, and apparently remembering how great eating was worked better. That was Koreans for you.

DAY TWENTY-FIVE

MOON

FOUR DAYS UNTIL THE NEW TENANTS

The location for Moon's callback for the kidnapping sequel is a squat mirrored building on Sunset, fairly close to another building where Moon once had to pick up her pass for the MTV Movie Awards twenty-some-odd years ago. The entire cluster of buildings feels familiar but scaled down, shrunken, the way it is in a dream or a movie lot. Her vision swims, her sleep has not improved. She has the sense when she pulls her car into the garage that she has stepped into a different life.

When the elevator doors open, the office is large, just one big room with giant potted plants, crawling with young, stylish workers of varying races and gender presentations, tapping at their computers on tables, wearing headphones. And the sense of industry is such that it would not surprise Moon a bit if they were typing strings of meaningless letters onto their monitors, not listening to music at all. The space is pleasant, anodyne, like a bookstore with a lifestyle component or the lobby of a nice hotel that also functions as a coworking space, nothing like the low-ceilinged corridors she'd frequented starting out, with rows of chairs filled with actors muttering their lines in some hallway.

They are running late, they tell her, offering her water, and she takes a seat on a green foam sectional that resembles an L-shaped Tetris piece laid on its side. And she recalls the days when she'd have to crisscross all over town, consulting a Thomas Guide, flipping to J-5 or whatever it was, needing to get from Burbank to some ratfuck office in Manhattan Beach in less than an hour despite all that traffic, trying not to ruin her hair for having her windows down as she drove.

Moon thanks the office manager as she brings her water, a tepid glass with small bubbles, no plastic bottles anymore, not ever, and takes a sip, anticipating the metallic taste. In the end she hadn't drunk the beer. Instead, she drained it into the sink and then, knowing she would not sleep considering the other one, cracked the second open and did the same, keeping her head turned so she wouldn't smell it.

She takes another sip of water, setting the glass down on the coffee table, casting around for a coaster but not finding one. Auditions had always felt like a stacked gamble, a waste of gas, she never looked like the others reading for Britneys, Laceys, once even a Sloane—not just hot, but rich-hot. She was not the Becky of their dreams. Nor a Nikki or a Tiffany, but she could pretend to be learning everyone's names, the receptionist, the assistants, elbowing her way into the rooms, keeping her head high even when all the character descriptions were implicitly white unless there were other cues: nail salon, masseuse, liquor store, gangbanger girlfriend.

She could have dated Quentin Tarantino or Nicolas Cage. Gotten a leg over and a leg up. But then she would have been dating Quentin Tarantino or Nicolas Cage.

She really could have had anyone.

Been anyone.

She'd been so beautiful then.

Desirable.

Her breasts high and succulent.

The way they'd all looked at her with open vulpine want.

How they'd fucked her with a hand around her throat, *mine mine mine.*

How it seemed they wanted her more when they discovered she was a mother, not to keep but to borrow, knowing she would always return to her daughter at the end of the night.

She checks the time. Fifteen minutes late. Then twenty. She tries not to read into this, and then for no reason at all Stevie as a baby pops into her head. Shirtless, her little blinking innie nipples, and how she'd looked in her diapers, crawling purposefully. The funniest kid. The weirdest kid. So set in her ways the moment she showed up. She specifically envisions Stevie in their old apartment, she couldn't have been more than one, unfailingly returning to the same corner of the carpet on the living room floor whenever she took a shit in her diaper, crouched low, consternation pruning her little red face, bashful and evasive whenever anyone noticed or talked to her. How she would turn away in protest, furious if Moon ever watched. Crying if Moon laughed. That had just been her place. Her little private area that she liked best. The Japanese have a term for the need to take a shit when entering a bookstore. There are places that are more welcoming, disarming. That felt like home.

The apartment had been in Koreatown. With a roommate who became a flight attendant last she heard. A former Mormon who'd broken the lease when she'd met a man on a cruise ship. Stevie had loved that apartment. There's a weight lodged beneath Moon's sternum now. She's leveled by how much she misses Stevie. She doesn't want to stare directly at it or name it, fearing she will alter its behavior like a subatomic particle being observed, but it's the rediscovery of a feeling that she'd believed was lost to her forever. It is such a relief. The crush, the sensation of it, the physical pressure of ache that spreads out from her chest. She fights back tears, not wanting to ruin her makeup, but it has never been Stevie who has left.

She recalls now how much she'd loved being pregnant. Filled with Stevie. She'd never had less anxiety in her life with Stevie inside her. She'd loved her body desperately. The new heft of her breasts. The full juiciness of her thighs and the hardened roundness of her belly. She hadn't known that her crotch would darken and her armpits too, resembling the just-plucked skin of black chickens. She'd been sick almost every day for the first seven weeks, but when it passed a powerful calm cocooned her. She'd read no child-rearing books. She didn't need an app comparing the size of her baby to fruit, she felt she could sense it all. Maybe it would have been different with a boy, but with Stevie, she'd experienced tranquility, or altitude, as though nothing else mattered or could touch them. She'd felt like a mother.

She'd attended the New York premiere of her first serious film at Lincoln Center, buoyed by rave reviews at TIFF, she'd done the red carpet in a skintight Alaïa gown with the midsection cut out, her thirty-one-week stomach oiled, strewn with Van Cleef & Arpels belly chains like half a million dollars of Christmas tinsel, and the paps had gone ballistic. She'd felt regal as she stood there, blinded by the lights, turning in profile, talons clutching the base of her belly that jutted out like the nose of Norma Desmond's Isotta Fraschini, scarlet pustule of a belly button glistening like a hood ornament. She'd felt triumphant and self-possessed. Finally, a role she didn't have to audition for. A role she would die in.

But when Stevie was born forty-eight hours later, at thirty-two weeks and one day, at 3.8 pounds by emergency C-section on the night of Moon's birthday dinner, to be held in a clear box for twenty-six days, wrinkly, ashen legs kicking in fury, fists tight, hair dark and full despite the premature lungs that needed a respirator to breathe, every fear Moon had ever known attacked her at once. Her hair fell out in clumps, she was told to catch up on sleep but couldn't, and with streaming eyes she watched all the capable NICU nurses attending to all the miniature babies suspended individually in their plastic isolettes, knowing they could smell her unfitness as a mother wafting off her in offensive waves, like a disgusting perfume.

Stevie had never been an easy child. From the time she was tiny and writhing in her plastic box, Stevie had been outraged by the unsolicited imposition of existence. Moon knew from the moment they met that Stevie would suffer more than most. Raising a newborn alone had been gruesome. Everything made Stevie cry. Buttons, overhead lighting, wind chimes, mobiles, tinny sounds in melodic arrangements.

Wooden toys. Flowers. Cats. Most male faces. The first few years of their lives had seemed remote. A reel comprised of the same four or five moments of bludgeoning emotional and physical turmoil.

She remembers when they were both so much younger, babies truly, how she would wait until Stevie's head was turned to sneak away. In the hall Moon would unfailingly weep, Stevie wailing when she noticed, the sitter's sonorous voice rising and falling, as Moon's breasts ached then leaked. The anguish and the precarity, the logistics, all of it had been untenable. Once, she'd left Stevie for three hours with her dry cleaner. She'd begged the woman, whose six-year-old did homework at the counter, to watch her, and the woman eyed her, alarmed and suspicious, but then looked at Stevie sleeping sweetly in her bassinet and relented.

They'd always been kind to her, the woman and her mother. They gave her 송편 for 추석, chewy and slick with sesame oil. During the audition, she couldn't get Stevie out of her mind. They'd told her to improvise, *Do a fun run*, but she'd gone wooden and vacant instead. It was a show, a job that would've been local, that would have afforded her stability, but she could hear in the briskness in their thanks and the deadness of the air that she wouldn't advance.

On her way back, stopped at a light, she was seized by a sudden paralyzing certainty that she would never see Stevie again. Not that the women would do anything reprehensible or harmful to her baby. More that when Moon returned, they wouldn't know who she was or what she was talking about. That Stevie would simply cease to exist, trapped in another timeline. Moon's life would be violently and irrevocably altered and no one would pity or believe her. What kind of mother left a child without the intention of abandoning her? Stevie was a baby. She had no ID. She hadn't even had her chickenpox vaccine yet, only MMR. Not to mention that Stevie didn't even resemble her, she'd had the good sense to take after Moon's three-night-stand, the way babies know to mimic the man, baiting the hook.

She'd rushed back to West Olympic, numb, blazing through changing lights, disbelieving that she'd left her baby with strangers. And by the time she'd pulled into the strip mall and parked outside the doughnut shop next door to the cleaners, she knew she'd kill herself if Stevie was gone. The certainty was reassuring. The choice deep and ancestral. But after locking her car, instead of running into the dry cleaners, she'd calmly walked to the liquor store catty-corner to it. And in her car she drank the small Smirnoff bottle, the kind from mini bars, then drank the second. Then she put a piece of gum in her mouth.

Stevie had been fine. She'd been in the back with the grandmother who was eating dried anchovies dipped in gochujang, chanting a nursery rhyme, bobbing Stevie's fat fist up and down to keep time, and when she saw Moon the woman declared, 엄마 왔다! 엄마 왔다! And until that moment, Moon had not heard herself be called the term she sparingly called her own mother, and the alcohol glittered pleasantly in her vision as she realized that she was an 엄마 and she thanked them, bowing deep, hands shaking, eyes misting. And when she lifted Stevie's car seat, her daughter was heavy. So incredibly heavy and she missed her own 엄마 so desperately that once in the car, she sobbed. Stevie startled and began crying behind her. The two of them wailed, strapped into their respective seats, Moon too exhausted to get up to get her even if she'd wanted to.

Moon checks the time again. Twenty-nine minutes. The feeling rising in her isn't impatience or anger but capitulation. She leans toward the low wooden coffee table to pick up a large photography book. She flips to a page at random, a blue and white spread, and it takes a while for meaning to rise up from the pages, from what first appears to be damp, matted terry cloth. It is a polar bear, emaciated. Sopping, grayed fur hanging off its bones like a dingy wet towel set against a bright blue sky. Shocked, she turns the page. A beached whale. Eye open, vision occluded. Dead. She turns again to a series of pigeons flattened into downy pancakes on asphalt. She flips to the cover.

The image is an innocuous cluster of trees in some altogether pleasant vista with the title *HOME* in large white letters. According to the back flap, the book is a collection of habitats that have been destroyed due to climate crisis. Homes that cannot be returned to. She smiles without meaning to, but it's just so manipulative. Hilariously heavy-handed. Designed for guilt and virtue signaling. She wonders if it works, this book. She imagines whoever bought it feeling terrific, perfectly absolved, having it sent to themselves overnight on a plane, carbon emissions flying all over the place just to make whoever happens upon it feel implicated and morose.

The elevator doors open, disgorging three people all wearing the drab office gear of start-up drones, two in fleece vests. She returns the book to the table.

HOME.

The word snaps her out of some reverie. She thinks about how she can go outside. That she doesn't have to sit in the freezing air-conditioning anymore, listening to other people work. But instead, she thinks of *paradise*, her stepfather's brown leg against the red plastic chair in the photo. How he'd moved to Vietnam, *to paradise*, as he'd called it. And how for so long she'd imagined bringing Stevie to her mother's house. To the address where they no longer lived. Where nobody knew them. And she thinks of place. Of Stevie's spot on the carpet. The way she looks beside her in the car. At all those different ages.

And when finally two men, also dressed in fleece vests, come to her in the waiting area to introduce themselves, different producers of the kidnapping movie than the original, Moon rises to her feet.

"We don't usually dress like twins," the taller one says sheepishly, holding out both hands to shake hers.

But their clothes don't matter. Their youthful age. The generic, brown-haired, middling comportments.

Moon knows she will campaign for this job. She will get it. She will show up. She will do solid, irreproachable work. She follows them past the framed movie posters, chatting amiably about traffic, her soul nowhere near her body, floating around and musing of how home is not a location. Stevie is home. All Moon has to do is be a home too. So Stevie always knows how to come back.

ARTHUR GARETH MACLEAN

[1965–2025]

Mac was not one to bungle an exit. He'd dressed with care that evening, knowing that sneakers, no matter how expensive, would be inappropriate. Thinking of his mother, he also felt the occasion called for proper socks. Red Falke wool with burnished brown lace-up Berlutis. A bright blue, summer-weight Henry Herbert suit. No tie. He was an artist, not a banker.

He'd pulled his G-Wagon over at 6:11 p.m., in the thick of rush hour, amazed that the salt water on the air smelled more metallic there, exhilarated that he wouldn't have to find parking. There was no shoulder on the road and that didn't matter, the traffic gridlocked, his GPS given up, tracking him over blue, baffled by the destination address as he opened his door and left it jawing wide, keys dangling in the ignition, not a single valet in sight.

The wind! Oh, it was the wind that made it frightening. Rushing in his ears, whipping his hair, lifting the back of his jacket. He was glad there wasn't a tie flapping in his face. It would have made him appear foolish. The extreme close-up giving him the fatuous air of middle management. He was proud of his upper-body strength, the way he could even now pull himself up, aware of the figure he cut backlit by the honeyed light of Magic Hour.

He sensed the attention of cars slowing somewhere below, the audience, the timorous quavering of a far-flung news-copter rotating toward him, the freakish way all Los Angeles natives can portend some incoming traffic fuckshit, the way animals sense storms. Once over the ten-foot-high security fence, hoisting himself up the way he'd practiced on the pull-up bar that hung from the beams of his house, where he would have swung from had he been a less considerate man, he kept his gaze ahead, into the grainy cerulean atmosphere. He could just make out the lump of Catalina Island, dotted with white buildings, the ships beside it, all dissolving into the horizon as his eyes watered.

As flinging bridges go, the Vincent Thomas Bridge is about as good as you'd get in Los Angeles. It's a 185-foot drop. And according to the Federal Aviation Administration, the upper survival limit of human tolerance to impact velocity in water is close to 100 feet per second or else 68 miles per hour, or the equivalent of a 186-foot drop, but Mac felt that God would help him that last foot. The only suspension bridge in the area, and connecting San Pedro to Terminal Island, the 1,500-foot bridge eliminated the need for a ferry, but that day, Arthur Gareth MacLean only narrowly missed a sunset whaling charter when he hit, pounding the surface with his soft Scottish body as though it were concrete.

He had remembered to stretch out his arms as he soared.

There'd been two eyewitnesses. A man and a woman. The man happened to be facing the right direction. Or the wrong one, seeing as the raft of sea lions was on the starboard side and the man, in a fit of pique, having been promised a gray whale migration, refused to look, opting instead for the bridge view as Mac dropped out of the sky. The witness, an out-of-work screenwriter who had recently begun driving Lyft, only later discovered that the death he'd witnessed was someone "in the business," and duly his descriptions became more florid. In the final write-up, he'd described Mac as *a flame-tressed figure who'd leapt as if in pursuit, arms outstretched like Christ on a cross.*

The other eyewitness also remarked on Mac's hair. She'd privately thought the man on the bridge resembled a flying squirrel. It was the jutting head and the belly in his bright white shirt, his comically spindly legs trailing uselessly as he fell, but comparing a dead man to a rodent felt disrespectful. People had their reasons. The reasons usually being debt, as it had been for an uncle, her mother's brother, who'd hung himself with his belt. She thinks about this sometimes. How her uncle had been waiting for a doctor's appointment. She'd always thought that whatever had prompted the man to remove his belt, loop it on the metal window frame, tug with both hands to test it, and proceed to leave the world may have been an impulse. One he might have gotten over by midafternoon. It could have been that they'd left him alone too long. They always left you alone for too long. She hadn't given her name to the reporter and didn't want to. She didn't want her name associated with the event. She's not superstitious, her relationship with God is too secure for that, but she doesn't even like looking at the backs of ambulances in traffic for fear that the doors will swing open and she will see someone slide out. Her report differed from the erstwhile writer's.

She was parked in the cruise terminal and saw the whole thing. She'd seen a man who was afraid. He'd hesitated. Alone in her car she didn't make a sound. Only sat up straighter as though her attention might pin him back. She thought he would stay put. Wait until the cops came. He was white. He would be safe. But then he went, arms and legs starfishing out. Her uncle hadn't left a note. And later when she found out who it was that she'd seen, she learned he hadn't left a note either. This made sense to her. What was there really to say?

DAY TWENTY-SIX

STEVIE

Pudding. Mashed potatoes. A roasted tomato bisque that looks and tastes grisly. Everything is eaten with a spoon, even milkshakes, not wanting to disturb the precious blood clots that protect the raw gore and nerves beneath the dissolvable stitches. She takes antibiotics that curdle her insides and make food taste metallic on her tongue, of old spoons, blood, everything smelling of batteries. After eating, she angles a needleless syringe to carefully rinse out food particles from her gums, gargling with salt water.

She is supposed to go home tomorrow but can't imagine how. Instead she sleeps all day, dreaming of Pee Wee's, strangely vivid nightmares of filling orders incorrectly, being called in to corporate for being caught on camera sneaking her own pee into the hotel pans of beans. They are dreams that make no sense, things she wouldn't do, and every time she is called to defend herself, she is belligerent and furious, nothing like she is in life because in her dreams she has conviction.

Adam returns to her bedside, bringing water, coming in whenever she calls for him, giving her a painkiller.

I'm bored, will you lie with me? she murmurs, embarrassed to ask, making her voice low and soft, sounding practically asleep, and he does, feet cold, body long and soft in his white T-shirt. They talk until she falls asleep, and she feels closer to him but without effort or responsibility as though her nighttime self is working toward intimacy independently of her, like elves cobbling shoes overnight or toys that dance in the dark.

Why do you think he did it? she asks him.

He's quiet for a while.

I think he was just called to it.

She senses him look at her, only the gleam of his eyes visible.

It can happen to anyone. And the way he says it is comforting. As though it's happened to him. As though he suspects it has happened to her.

You're not pissed at him? At all?

No. I get it.

Do you feel sorry for him?

She hears him shake his head then make a low noise in his throat.

He got to do what he wanted in the end.

Why didn't you tell us you'd seen him? she asks.

I don't know. Maybe because I didn't want to see him.

She feels the same way about Moon. She wishes she could call her, to tell her about her teeth, the city, Adam's apartment, but she doesn't want their fight to end. For her mother to think she's off the hook. Stevie's sick of mollifying, placating, bending.

I get it, Stevie says. *You don't want it to count. Mac coming to see you shouldn't count.*

I should have told him to go.

You were never going to tell him to go.

I was never going to tell him to go, he admits.

He feels like a part of her then. Not older or younger. Just the same.

Remember that promotion?

He clears his throat and says, *Yeah?*

I have to move to Massachusetts.

Massachusetts. He says it dubiously as though she has pronounced the word incorrectly.

I don't want to go.

He doesn't say anything, she can feel him waiting for her to continue.

I wish I could just live here, she says, thinking about Sage and Wren.

How Wren cooked and Sage gathered the dishes, the companionable peaceful way they lived.

But what about Moon? he asks, and when he does, Stevie's grateful for the dark.

DAY TWENTY-SIX

MOON

THREE DAYS UNTIL THE NEW TENANTS

So she has a job. She will be working again. Her deal is incoming. She knows from the tightness of the schedule that something has gone awry, that she hadn't been their first choice, but she doesn't care. And when Tali calls to congratulate her, she basks in the warmth of accomplishment. Mostly, she wants to call Mac. She tells him in her mind, conjuring the version of him that she finds herself talking to.

She's in the Pool House, cleaning, readying for the tenants' arrival. The sun is setting, giving the sense that the entire enclosure is being slowly submerged into water. She has yet to eat a meal but enjoys the calm lightness that takes hold, thoughts sharp and focused. The hours glide into each other as she organizes the piles into three larger ones. Donate, toss, keep. She's dragged the empty planters out into the yard, forearms straining, dirt streaked across her bare legs. It was hours ago when Dano called to tell her Stevie would be delayed. *Her wisdom teeth were impacted*, he'd said, and she almost laughed to hear the judgment in his voice. He has been looking after the girl for less than a week but already he makes it sound as though he is superior in his care and feeding of her.

She asks if Stevie's OK.

She's fine. She's had emergency surgery. He'd gotten his mother to call their family dentist to get her in the schedule.

What about her birthday?

Their birthday is in two days.

They've never spent a single one apart.

He isn't sure she's fit for travel. He puts it exactly that way. *Fit for travel.*

Fit for duty. Fit for service.

She checks the time. She will need to eat eventually. She walks back across the lawn, smelling the night-blooming jasmine in the air, looking up at the Big House, its eyes lit up, alert.

Once upstairs, in her bathroom, she puts on eyeliner, thinking how many thousand times she's swiped the ink on her lids, blurred face up close constant, only the backgrounds changing. She'd perfected the twin swoops in eighth grade with waterproof Maybelline liquid liner in a white pot that has been discontinued for decades. And when she slides off the sink, looking at herself, suddenly recognizable as the version that is ready for everyone else, she thinks how much her mother had hated her eyeliner.

Sunny had loathed it as much as Moon's pencil-lined brown lips and her chipped Hard Candy polish, the way she'd plucked her eyebrows into single-file arcs, constantly surprised, looking like a clown, *like a leper*, her mother called it. As if Sunny had ever seen a leper. She'd said the eyeliner made her look wild, like a lunatic, the way the black line extended way past Moon's eye, painted as though it were a chisel-tipped graffiti marker.

Sunny had gotten an upper blepharoplasty, the double-lid surgery, slits cut into her by big hammy white-man hands in some military hospital years ago, and Moon had always thought that they'd captured too much in the incision, making a fat sausage roll of a crease that lowered itself over her eye, obscuring her sight as Sunny aged until she had to undergo a brow lift to tuck it all back up again. Eyeliner is around the time the fights had become truly spectacular.

Moon slips into jeans, remaining braless in her shredded T-shirt. She pads downstairs, stepping into Vans, and grabs her keys but then changes her mind, reaching for Dano's keys instead. And just as she does, she feels a tremor. It is so minor and fleeting that she would dismiss it if not for the barking dog in the distance and a car alarm going off. She remains frozen. Listening. One hand hovering in the air as though she will see it tremble. She waits a minute. Then another.

Staring at the door, stock-still, she recalls the brawls she and Sunny would get into whenever she left the house. *Barn burners*, her stepfather would call them. Moon pictures her mother screaming, yelling about her makeup, her clothes, getting close to her face, blocking her egress as her ride, some dude, honks with all entitlement from the driveway, but now, and she doesn't know why or how she's able to do it, when Sunny's spit hits her face, instead of pushing her mother away full of rage and shame, Moon looks at her mother, startled, and her mother looks back, and then the two of them laugh.

This Moon lifts her forearm to her cheek, wiping off the saliva showily, and Sunny is doubled over, howling, one hand clutching Moon's forearm, the other on her thigh. The Sunny in Moon's memories never laughed. Moon isn't even sure when she would have seen her mother laugh so hard, broad face concertinaed, breathless, tears streaming out of her eyes, but the image rises now as the love for her mother fills her to the brim.

She waits for another tremor but there isn't one. She shoulders her purse, checks the time again, and gets into the car. On day sixteen of Stevie's stay in NICU, they'd felt a tremble, another small earthquake, *barely anything*, the women said, the nurses who calmly held the babies' beds still, so capable, they seemed to Moon like a coven of witches under the casting of a protective spell. And once it passed, they showed Moon and another mother (thirty weeks and two days; twin girls) a closet of fireproof aprons with large pouches, a kangaroo's solution for evacuating the babies, showing them how they would slide their small, warm bodies, one into each of the three pockets so they could walk them outside and to safety. Moon had been moved by their selflessness even as she'd been horrified by the forethought and its necessity.

Driving west now, she wells up thinking about the kindness of strangers, imagining Stevie in a nurse's apron, and regrets her rudeness to Dano on the phone. Her earlier anger at him feels distant. Cooled like a forgotten cup of tea, but she's glad that he's away. He is looking after Stevie no matter how intrusive this feels. She just wishes Stevie would call her and worries they won't speak on their birthday.

But then her mother pops up in her head again, teasing Moon's sullen sentimentality. And Moon thinks how she now loves her mother lawlessly. And how the grinning apparition of warmth and good humor exists without fidelity to the person she knew. It is a gift, and not one that she has earned, but she will take it. And then she thinks of Mac. Recalling for once that he's dead the moment that she conjures him. She sits with him in her thoughts. He is wearing shorts. Knees bared. Socks pulled up. He is a child who has yet to earn long pants. And he keeps her company as she drives. He tells her about all the dull things he'd told her in life but without any of the onerous gravitas. He chatters about the octopus documentary they'd watched together years ago; Mac had called it sophomoric, describing the filmmaker as an anthropomorphizing sap, but she also remembers how he'd quietly stopped eating octopus in restaurants despite having loved it. The little Mac in her head reminds her that octopi have nine brains and three hearts.

She drives to Melrose, and there's an open spot for street parking, the flashing meter like a sign from God. She parks and crosses the street, toward the scalloped black awning over Pee Wee's glass storefront that attempts to make the exterior appear quaint or down-to-earth, family-owned. Mac accompanies her, like a tottering child keeping someone company as they run errands. In life, their greatest breakups revolved around his selfishness, his inability to consider her. Mac had known that Dano's episode fee was higher than hers and not told her. She'd found the betrayal unforgivable. He hadn't seen it as betrayal. She'd thought they were family and they had been. He was exactly as he'd been in every family he'd known. Mercenary. Moon had thrown it in his face that he made a terrible Airman. Who would ever trust him in their six? At least she knew how to play a light bird's wife. All she had to do was pretend to be her mother. But now she sees all of Mac's shortcomings, his temper, his cowardice, his inability to speak honestly unless he was drunk. It all seems so frightened and small.

The interior of Pee Wee's is a shock. It is the clinical aesthetic of venture capitalism. Lit with bright-white LEDs, every screen highlighting the menu and the number they are serving. The dining area is as inviting as eating at baggage claim or the sales floor of a Sephora, all the surfaces stainless steel or hard molded plastic with curved edges. Closed in by the woman behind her, Moon moves toward the cafeteria line manned by polo-shirted workers and looks up at the menu with the apprehension of getting in line for a water park slide.

The line moves faster than expected. It is a strangely tense operation.

The tiniest bit, says one, holding out her index finger and thumb to denote how few beans she wants.

A lot, says another. *Like, a lot, a lot. Yeah more than that. Like tons. Psychotic amounts of cilantro.*

It gives Moon the sense of the claw machine in arcades, the taut attention of each customer frowning through the glass at the gloved hands they've been assigned. Attuned to the movements of the workers as though their scrutiny held the power to administer small electric shocks. She hates the divide. The sneeze guard. The demarcation between the serving class and the patron class. The lie of the wall's transparency. As though the see-through partition makes the caste distinction palatable, as if it doesn't exist at all.

Again, she's assaulted by memory. Her mind neatly divided into a split screen. A Brian De Palma movie. Carrie drenched in pig's blood. The leering teens in the crowd. A hit of oniony steam wafting into Moon's face from chafing dishes full of organ meats. The liver special at Luby's, her high school fast-food job. That hadn't been strictly fast food either. It was cafeteria style. She'd worn gloves too. Like Stevie.

And a hairnet. Like the lunch ladies at school. She hated how they saw her. The old people who came in at five p.m. Telling her they'd seen *Crouching Tiger, Hidden Dragon.* Moon's first acting job had been putting on a folksy accent for these seniors with their veteran's discounts, all those *y'alls*, *ma'ams*, and *sirs*, just so she could be told to her face how well-spoken she was.

She'd been servile to all of them with their fading war tattoos from 'Nam or even as far back as Koh-reeea, with that hard-ass Koh, asking if she was from the North or South, free to ask her as many questions as they wanted, their little China doll who was serving them meat and potatoes, all those boys at school asking if she'd heard of the special massage parlor off 410, where if you paid with a fifty-dollar bill they wouldn't just give you a standard happy ending but a really spectacular one. Moon recalls how she would drive home in her Ford Festiva, reeking of fried food and boiled vegetables, furious at the wrongness of her life, fuming every time a raised extended cab or a semitruck would swerve near her on the stretch of 35 that was always under construction, and she can't believe that Stevie is doing the same thing now.

The man ahead of her moves aside, indicating that it is Moon's turn to step up to the twentysomething girl with dark purple lipstick. Moon orders the chicken burrito.

The girl gives her tortilla a quarter turn and asks what beans she wants.

"Refried," says Moon, because they are the beans she knows. Tex-Mex beans. The only beans she likes. She walks back to the car, foil-wrapped burrito in hand, heavy and warm as a newborn. But then, at the meter, she can't find her keys. She searches all her pockets, then hitches her bag high on her thigh to check its cavernous belly. She's relieved Stevie isn't with her to sigh and glare. But then she calls up the moment in the car, how Stevie had called her Mom. Unprompted. And it's an arrow straight through her heart and she's stupidly happy again.

Sunny in her mind laughs at her. But with affection. Moon asks her mother what to do about Stevie. She finds that she doesn't need to sound out any words, she doesn't have to translate or wait turns, it's understanding and being understood at once. Sunny tells her that Stevie is soft. That she has fight in her but that it is blocked. That she will only come into her own once she knows her marching orders. This makes sense to Moon. She had always thought of herself in the same way.

There are times when Moon doesn't know how to behave outside of a scene. The presence of a camera has always allowed her to feel. Allows her to trace the path of her emotions and the reasons behind them more closely. There have been occasions when she'd been fighting with Mac and in reconciling in a scene no matter how unrelated to their argument in life, it would seem as though they were both pacified. It somehow functioned as the opposite of being wronged in a dream and being angry with a person in waking life.

So Stevie needs directions; cues. And Moon allows herself to wonder how it would have felt if Stevie had ever been on the show. If they would be closer. If they would know each other in a deeper way. Or if instead there would be more artifice. Competition or separation. She recalls Stevie's endless pining for attention when she came to set, to fit in with Dano and Mac and everyone in production. Her never-ending audition to belong, to be in showbiz.

It was Mac who hadn't wanted Stevie on the show. Not even as background.

At least this had been the party line.

He'd known Stevie's presence would distract Moon, but he'd also known it was Moon that didn't want Stevie there. That Moon needed a place not to be Stevie's mom. A space Moon didn't have to share.

I'm a terrible mother, she'd tell him.

Not the worst, he'd respond.

He'd been willing to take the hit for her, she remembers.

And she wonders what other kindnesses she's forgotten.

Moon would give Stevie everything, but she wasn't willing to give her that. Stevie would have to find her own way. This has always been the only path forward.

Finally, Moon finds the hard black miniature car that is Dano's key.

She gets in the vehicle, exhausted by her efforts. She can't believe that she won't see Stevie for her birthday. She still has so much to do. She will have to wash all their bed linens. Put up the blackout curtains in the Pool House again. She doesn't know why she'd taken them down in the first place, recalling their installation, how she'd stood on a chair, arms shaking from the effort, glue-gunning the heavy shower curtains right onto the joist. Long spiderweb strands of glue falling into her hair.

But the Pool House is another partition, she realizes. With Moon and Stevie servile to the tenants, the curtains only serving to conceal their labor. She'd always told herself the Pool House was an investment. That she was raising the property values. It's why the kitchen is so modernized, why the Pool House is so opulent. She'd made the joke that if a sports car was the dick of a man, a house was the dick of the lady of the manor.

When Moon first renovated the kitchen, she'd made it with her mother's kitchen in mind. She'd even made a private Pinterest board, *what not to do*, that she'd shown no one else, of Sunny's cheap tile, the crown molded particleboard cabinets, the curlicued faux Victorian bail pull handles on the drawers, the scroll corbels. All the mass-produced flourish of her mother's provincial tastes. But in thinking of the gold swan spigot in the bathtub, all Moon remembers is how much her mother had loved her home. How proud she'd always been of it. How she pleasured in the wall-to-wall carpeting, even in her bathroom. Moon had fantasized about the day her mother would visit, how she would take in the high ceilings, the real marble counters, the accents that Moon had seen in magazine pictures or movies. But now Moon sees how much Sunny would not care.

All those years she'd thought she was impressing her mother by sending her money and her mother had not even known. And now she laughs, the mother in her head laughing. And she recalls Mac. How hard he'd laughed when Moon confessed that she'd only gotten the jointed gold faucet on the backsplash because Gwyneth Paltrow had one. How they'd laughed together about how much Mac actually hated living by the beach. The traffic. The damp. The stickiness of his hands. How he loathed sand more than anything. How he always wore socks in the house because actually the idea of sand between his toes was anathema to him. *Glitter made of fucking rocks.* They had laughed until they cried and it warms her to think of their closeness. How they'd been real friends.

Moon wonders if it's at all possible that she'd held steadfastly onto the house thinking that if her mother ever visited she would stay in the Pool House. Sunny would have hated it. Mac *had* hated it. And now, sitting in Dano's car it occurs to her that she might hate it too.

Squatting in her own Pool House as though it is a miniaturized Hermitage, only now with her daughter, their situation despairing. But it is also hilarious. Hysterical. She's been living in the Pool House, miserable, and now with Stevie gone, she can't even sleep alone in the Big House.

She thinks of what Mac would think of her life and laughs. That she is getting kicked out now from even the Pool House, the tenants driving her and her children off her land at the behest of their dog. Mac laughs too. But then tears slip out of her eyes. Mac should have come to see her, not him. She wants the memory for her own. To scan those final days for clues. Instead she has to rely on Dano, the most fallible witness there is, and Corinna, who can't possibly know. And it's then that she asks Mac to forgive her.

Moon starts the car and removes her high heels, thinking of Mac and Stevie. Wanting Stevie to have a gorgeous life full of art and love and excitement. To be free. And as she pulls out of her spot, remembering the warm babies slung safely in oversized pockets for the earthquake vests, she flips down her sun shield and hears a loud, indignant honk. She brakes hard. And as the woman in the silver Prius gestures at her, Moon watches her precious, infant-warm burrito slide down her windshield, having been left on the roof.

She howls with laughter, a sob still lodged in her throat.

She pulls out her phone, remembering now that they had spent a birthday separately once. On the day she was born, she'd held Stevie for a moment, but then they'd both been whisked to their corners. Apart. To mend. And she goes to her phone, to the rental app, remembering that when she'd ripped the blackout curtains down it had been with the satisfaction of someone who'd hoped never to return, and Moon cancels the tenants' stay. She will be fined. They will leave nasty messages, but she will not hear them. She deletes the app and drives home.

DAY TWENTY-EIGHT

ADAM

STEVIE AND MOON'S BIRTHDAY

He sleeps when she sleeps. Eats only after he's fed her. They watch an inane dating show on an island. The house where the couples live has no roof. They must always be outside. Visible. They are rarely allowed to leave and don't know what time it is. It reminds him of L.A. Of the Pool House. And as Stevie's mouth heals, he can't believe he'd stayed there so long or what he'd done with his days there.

On the morning of her birthday, Stevie comes downstairs wearing the white cotton nightgown he'd bought her, creased from where it's been folded, and she looks like a Victorian ghost.

"I want pancakes," she announces, so he teaches her how to make them from scratch, sifting flour, using baking powder. "It's such a toxically masculine trait," she says of how he turns everything into a lesson. She burns the first one, but as it had been with driving, once she becomes absorbed in the task, she does well. She is cautious and methodical, getting her phone for reference photos, forcing him to pull out his kitchen scale so she can measure what he usually eyeballs, writing down *medium heat* in her Notes app.

He loves being back in his kitchen, with all his things, the exact pan he knows best, his red spatula. Once they've made three pancakes each, they eat the spoils happily, Stevie swaying in her seat at his counter in a childlike trance. "Turns out I'm an amazing cook," she says, and he wishes he had birthday candles to stick one in her stack.

After breakfast, they walk out to the waterfront on the promenade, and it feels good to be outside, among the joggers and dogwalkers, all the neighborhood people about their business. He calls Moon on FaceTime as he'd warned Stevie he would. Happy-birthdays are exchanged but the call is perfunctory. It's loud where they are, the wind whipping around them.

"So this kids thing is mandatory in Brooklyn, I take it?" Stevie says as a pregnant couple crosses their path and another pregnant couple says hello to the first.

"This part of town? Kinda yeah," he says. "It's washed Brooklyn."

"Don't say washed," she says.

"Why?"

She crinkles her nose. "It's really millennial. Just say old." He laughs. She's wearing her coat over her nightgown along with her new boots and it gives her a fetching yet unhinged quality. Her short, mussed hair appears deliberate for once, somehow glamorous and unkempt.

"You'll have to come back and see other parts of town," he says. They've rebooked her return flight for tomorrow, and he wonders if she'd been serious when she'd asked about living together. He imagines how it would be if it were just the two of them, the siblings left to their own devices in the cottage in a fairy tale. They would watch TV together, order takeout, and over time, he would convince her to go to college and become invested in the lives of her friends and she would listen to him air grievances about professional squabbles or complain about his mother. His friends would embarrass him if his and Stevie's worlds happened to collide. If he ever saw her out in more adventurous parts of Brooklyn, Bushwick, Bed-Stuy, him on his way home from dinner, her only just heading out. Nobody would believe them even as they explained it, that they were siblings, that her mother is his best friend, that their love is deep and pure.

"Yeah, right," says Stevie. "You'll get busy. You'll probably be married tomorrow. Pop out some babies. Plus, your wife would hate me for my childless life of excess."

"Seriously, no kids for you?"

She shrugs. "I think life is too hard to just make someone else do it," she says. "Like, kids don't get a vote whether they want to be here or not and that's fucked up to me."

"And you don't think it evens out?" he asks, looking all around him. "Everything amazing is a bit shit and everything shitty at least ends." He can't help it. He worries about her then. "What about love? Not, like, romantic love but like loving people, friends, loving what you do, laughing."

"So, love, live, laugh?" she asks. "No, of course, that's all great. I just don't know that Mac was necessarily wrong about, you know"—she steals a sidelong glance at him—"wanting to be done? Not to say I'm about to, you know, *leave*, but mostly I wish I didn't even have to start in the first place. Philosophically, I know I sound like a nihilist from a meme. That weird guy at the party in the corner that's like, *They don't know I wish I could die without killing myself*, but that's how I feel. Actually it's not even death. I wish I could be unalive."

She stops walking and studies his face. "You look like you're about to tell me to go for a run or something, like my problem is endorphins." He laughs, finding her delightful despite himself, and he knows she just needs her brain to bash around with other brains in college. Holding forth in rambling, stoned, insufferable conversations about existence with other people her age while mostly just wanting to have sex with each other.

"You should go to college," he says.

"You should get a job," she tells him.

When they arrive at Union Market, she grabs her own basket and ventures toward the refrigerated aisles as he makes his way to the bakery for a cake. He considers a small, dense Brooklyn Blackout cake, iced with blue and white flowers. He signals the attendant, asking if they have candles, but the only ones they have are housed in a glass cookie jar, blocky numbers reminiscent of wild style graffiti that are sold individually at eight dollars each when all he wants are the standard-issue ones that are white-striped and come in a box.

With his hand in the cookie jar, he locates a 2 and a 1 but doesn't like the way the colors look together, orange and silver, wishing they had normal fucking candles, hating that he is so obviously back in Brooklyn that this is the nature of his problems. He changes his mind, he'll just bake something himself, but by then the bakery lady has already lowered the cake into a cardboard box.

"Dano!" says a voice from behind, and Adam's eyes close. He already can't bear it. He turns and of course it is Archer, an old friend from theater. With a frozen smile, he casts about for Archer's wife and their kid who is fine, cute, but with the entitlement of an only child born to overworked parents. But he's swept into Archer's hug, getting choked out slightly from the beefy shoulder at his neck.

"Wow," says Adam, pulling away. "You're . . . disfigured," he says, stealing Stevie's old joke. Archer is outlandishly yoked, likely for a role, and as he laughs, Adam thinks how he hasn't worked out in a week and concentrates not to furtively touch his own bicep.

"Yeah, work," Archer says, rolling his eyes. "Protein farts that would clear out a room," he adds, looking over at the bakery counter with longing. "Man, I could fuck up this entire display right now." The bakery attendant asks if she can get Archer anything as she hands Adam his box. Archer declines, a palm laid flat against his rock-hard abs. And that's when Stevie rounds the aisle, stopping short, a single apple rolling to the corner of her basket, and gives Adam an uncertain smile.

She looks as strange to him as the first time he'd seen her in the purple polo shirt and hat back in California. Again, he gets the sense she's in costume. Her long coat looks suddenly conspicuous, sliding off one shoulder, spilling and gathering at her wrist, suggestively revealing her white nightie. She looks as though she has tumbled out of bed, her short hair tousled as though from sex, highlighting her obvious, extreme youth. Under the bright lights her skin is a little oily, face seeming unwashed. It's the Union Market on Court, in Cobble Hill, where high schoolers and college kids still live with their parents, and he feels implicated, as though he has draped his jacket over Stevie in an attempt to make her presentable. He knows how it looks. Food shopping is an intimate act, they're obviously returning to the same place.

But standing beside Archer in the overpriced neighborhood grocery store, he registers her observation of him as wry amusement. *Millennial.* Adam and Archer's similarities border on parody. Archer is a little older, in his early forties. They are both white. With dark, longish hair, thick-framed sunglasses, and clothes that are comedically prescriptive for the area. They wear chore coats over sweaters and destroyed wool pants and carry black canvas shopping bags. Adam's from a used bookstore. Archer's from a Japanese record label.

"Stevie, this is Archer," he says without providing further context. "Archer, Stevie."

"Are you all set?" the bakery attendant asks, and Adam steps aside with his box as Stevie's face lights up. "You got me a cake?" she says, then turns to Archer to tell him it's her birthday.

"Oh," says Archer, inspecting Stevie for longer than seems necessary. "Happy birthday."

She thanks him and asks Adam if they can have champagne and Adam watches the understanding pass across Archer's face that Stevie has only just turned twenty-one.

"Oh shit, Ang and Tahir are coming down tonight from Hudson," Archer says suddenly, friends of theirs from summer stock a million years ago. "Come. They'll shit. It's been so long. Bring your cake, Stevie." He gives her a sporting look. "We have champagne at our house. Please. We haven't seen you in forever. Sully would murder me if I didn't invite you."

Adam scrambles for an excuse but sees the hopeful look on Stevie's face.

"What time?" he asks, heart sinking.

STEVIE

They ring the doorbell of a brick building covered with ivy, on a tree-lined street that almost exactly resembles his. He is wearing the clothes he has worn all day, except now, hours later, his hair is dirty. He's grumpy and stoned, he'd been hitting a vape from the moment they got back, watching basketball downstairs at a deafening volume as she tried to figure out what to wear.

She cannot get a read on his mood, why he'd seemed so happy one moment then became sullen, responding to her questions with single-word answers as though he can't wait to get rid of her when it's her birthday. When it's their final night.

She's also been anxious all day about Pee Wee's. She was scheduled to work but never called in. She doesn't even know why. She has no remaining PTO or vacation days and could have at least called in sick but hasn't. In the morning as they were walking around, she figured she would do it when they returned. L.A. was three hours behind. She'd wanted to ask Adam to contact his dentist for a note but she'd put it off and now he's mad at her. It's midafternoon in L.A. and she'll have been a no call, no show. She feels helpless and trapped.

When the door swings open, they're greeted by a young blond child wearing a plastic flower crown and what appears to be a large chocolate milk stain down the front of her striped orange shirt. "Ni hao," bellows the girl, front teeth missing, then from inside the bright house, a tiny woman, also blond, presumably the girl's mother, shrieks with pleasure, streaking past Stevie, almost pushing the girl down to launch herself into Adam's arms. She clings to him like a howler monkey, her yellow sweatpants halfway off her small ass. Stevie understands with misery that she's overdressed. She's also appalled. She loathes the woman immediately.

"Missed you, duckie," she says right up to his face. "You can't leave me here with my family for so long I'll lose my mind." Her voice is hoarse and blood roars in Stevie's ears as she realizes who this is. It's the woman from that night. The one who'd come to the house, Stevie is sure of it. Adam still holds Stevie's cake, laughing as he walks in, the woman clung to him like a barnacle, kicking her tiny feet that are black with dirt, making a meal of the moment, until they stagger into her small daughter, the crown slipping off her glossy head.

Stevie stoops to pick it up and the girl snatches it from Stevie's hand to tear into the house screaming, "Ni hao! Ni hao! Ni hao!" at the top of her lungs.

The towheaded woman dismounts, gesturing vaguely to the coatrack behind them. "Jam your stuff wherever," she says, then grabs her daughter by the sharp little shoulder. "Zelda, what did we say about showing off in front of Mommy's friends?"

Zelda continues to glare directly at Stevie as though wishing her dead.

"Zelda?"

"We don't do it."

"And why is that?"

"Because kid's stuff is boring to grown-ups."

"That's right," she says. "And, honey, we can't just go around saying *ni hao* to people without knowing where they come from." She slings Stevie a rueful smile. "Zee's in Mandarin immersion school."

The woman introduces herself, *Sawyer*, *Sull*, *Sully*, she says, eyes sparkling, "Just don't call me Sally." And as she leads them in, Stevie can't help but be fascinated by the vision of chaos, by people who would treat their multimillion-dollar home in this way. Stevie has become fixated on money, looking at thumbnail photos of studio apartments in parts of New York she has never heard of, *Ocean Hill*, *Sunset Park*, *Bayside*, everything sounding strangely Californian. Nothing like New York at all. The cheapest unit cost $1,500 a month, which is about as much as her new purse. And when Sawyer takes the flowers from Stevie, flowers Stevie paid almost forty bucks for, she thanks her, but instead of putting them in a vase, she leaves them on a side table covered with mail and charger cables.

Stevie almost trips in the narrow foyer, over a dinner-roll-sized Croc. There are shoes everywhere, piles and piles, tossed together, mismatched as if they'd washed in on a tide, enough for several families. In the living room, there are splayed naked dolls with tangled hair, hard plastic tiles spilling out of upturned colored bins. And in the kitchen, Stevie's confused by the conspicuous lack of food or signs of preparation. The counter is laden with pickleball rackets, abandoned sacks of groceries that have not been put away, a scattered pile of crayons, and a large fruit bowl that contains takeout menus, twisted-off bottle caps, and a fraying, mud-stained dog leash.

"So Stevie, what brings you to town?" Sawyer asks. "Business? Pleasure?" She drops her voice at *pleasure*, grinning at Stevie in a brittle way. Stevie glances at Adam, unsure of how to respond, but when she looks back at Sawyer, at the way the woman is sizing her up, it becomes obvious that Adam hadn't told her about Stevie. And certainly not that she'd been upstairs that night.

"For fun, I guess," says Stevie. "Adam was staying with us in L.A., so when he was coming here . . ."

Sawyer smiles. "That *is* fun," she says.

Archer comes thundering down the stairs then, also in sweats and a T-shirt, picking up Zelda to swing her upside down as she giggles and screams.

"What can I get you guys?" he asks, noticing their empty hands, shooting Sawyer a look.

It is stiflingly hot in the house. Stevie feels herself growing faint in her warm clothes. She's worn a dark pleated skirt along with a dark gray triple-ply cashmere sweater. She'd wanted to redeem herself from the embarrassing run-in with Archer at the supermarket earlier when she'd been dressed like a Mennonite runaway.

When their clothes from Bergdorf had been delivered, she couldn't bear to try anything on again. Her face was still swollen, her left side somehow more misshapen than her right, her nose seeming altered, wider at the bridge as though she'd taken a direct punch, and purpling bruises at her jaw that were beginning to yellow. To add insult to injury, a new pimple had declared itself right in the middle of her forehead, the kind that is deep and painful that requires restraint not to dig out with tweezers.

She'd removed everything carefully from its wrapping, folding the bags as she went, the tissue too, flattening the boxes and looping the satin ribbons into neat spools, moving with a reverent slowness, placing the packaging on the floor of the room as she laid her new things out on the bed. Two dresses, a slip in dark green silk, the other patterned with small sprays of flowers. A purse. Two sweaters. The coat. Boots. Heels. Skirt. Two pairs of pants in austere colors, shrewdly cut. She'd calculated everything at close to $20,000. More than double what she has in her account, that she'd saved up for relocating, for the entire rest of her life. For the job that she is supposed to begin training for. The job that might now fire her.

She wonders if she should at least call Xan but her mind flashes back to their awkward hug, Freddie's cruel laughter, and she can't bear to.

"Are we the first ones here?" asks Adam. Stevie spent an hour googling every combination of *Adam Dano, Tahir, Ang, Angie, Angela, Sawyer, Sully, Archer, Brooklyn, New York*, to find out who these people were, to learn anything she could about their work. She'd wanted to look nice for his friends, and everything she's wearing is new, including the bra, underwear, and the purse, a half moon, in a deep purple, virtually indistinguishable from any other leather bag besides its subtle asymmetry and its price when she'd looked it up.

Sawyer laughs. "Yeah, and the last one. This ding-dong," she says, nodding at Archer, "got the dates wrong. That's tomorrow. We're having these amazing little lamb ribs with homemade yogurt."

Stevie's astonished. She stares at Adam and he widens his eyes but says nothing.

The food arrives. They've ordered in from a neighboring Korean restaurant.

"I don't know how authentic it is," Sawyer tells her as she cracks open the black plastic delivery containers, wet with condensation. "But they use Niman Ranch pork."

Later, getting drunk, Stevie can't decide if Sawyer is beautiful. Her eyes are dark blue, close together and deep-set, and with her long conniving nose, she resembles a possum at certain angles. Nothing like the woman she'd imagined when she'd spied on them, nothing like the other woman, the one at the funeral. She cannot reconcile if Adam Dano has a type and then the understanding descends all at once, that he has no type. That his type is whoever wants him first.

Sawyer tells them about an ancient tea house in Kyoto that has been overrun with TikTokkers. She keeps referring to them this way, *TikTokkers.* And Stevie can tell by the way she pauses, little hands held out in front, that she's told the story before and it kills.

Archer is attractive in a sturdy way. Huge. Someone who could convincingly play a Viking on TV. Or a merman. But his muscles are gym muscles. The kind of brawn that's most useful when guided into battle by a much more clever person. He watches Sawyer closely. Observes her in a simpering way.

So he just lets you leave the house at three in the morning? Adam had asked that night, and they'd laughed.

Archer is a cuckold, Stevie thinks. This impish crone trapped in a child's body has ensnared him. Stevie almost feels sorry for him. When he smiles he has strangely small teeth and Stevie idly wonders about the mechanics of the sex between them. He is a foot and a half taller. She imagines Sawyer scampering up him like a tree. Or him scooping her up to him, with her legs flung over his shoulders, drinking from her pussy like a coconut.

As Sawyer fills Stevie's wineglass, a little spills over the side. She's drunk, her words are lengthening as she speaks. Then, apropos of nothing, Sawyer abruptly turns to show Stevie her ass. "Shein," she says of her lounge pants. "You shop at Shein, right? All the little girls do." She pulls at a tangle of japchae from the serving bowl with her fingers and moans pornographically as she chews. The food is fine. They didn't bother heating it up when it arrived. Sawyer eats a piece of kimchi with a fork and tells them about a six-hour documentary on pickling by a Danish *lacto-fermentation god.*

Stevie's dying to take off her sweater but can't, she's wearing a tank underneath that's see-through. She asks for the bathroom anyway, desperate for a moment to herself, away from Sawyer's strangely prickly stories.

She shuts the door behind her and removes her sweater, sweat sopping the waistband of her skirt, armpits dripping. The hair on her brow is visibly wet. She runs her wrists under cold water, sighing, finally cooling, her chest slick with perspiration, holding the sweater between her legs, not wanting to put it down in the bathroom that is as cluttered and grimy as the rest of it.

Fuck these terrible people. She feels bad for their kid. She gazes at the tub filled with toys, the toothpaste streaks in the sink, the cabinet mirror with glow-in-the-dark stickers in the shape of whales that are dingy and peeling at the edges. When she dries her hands, the thick towel is damp already, and when she smells her fingers it smells like the mold of laundry left in the washing machine overnight. She stands in the bathroom unable to stop sweating. She takes off her skirt. She holds them, skirt in one hand, sweater in the other, radiant with heat. She opens the medicine cabinet, cartoon Band-Aids, Q-tips, children's allergy medication, multiple tubes of half-used travel toothpaste and a trio of orange prescription bottles, all with Archer's name. She searches for the Viagra but can't find it.

In the mirror now, her cheeks are flushed, her face shiny and damp. She hears their voices but can't make out words. She puts on her skirt and looks at herself in the mirror. Her lace bra is visible through her thin black camisole, but with the length of her neck and her flushed cheeks, she is appealing.

She returns to an empty table. As though the Rapture had claimed them or aliens beamed them up. She hears movement upstairs, Zee's thin voice and dull, heavy footsteps, then Sawyer and Adam come in from outside, the acrid smell of weed smoke trailing them in. Sawyer laughs, openly staring at her chest. Adam only touches his lips.

"I take it you're hot," she says, turning to Adam, who says nothing. But even with his gaze averted, Stevie can see how high he is. High and seemingly helpless. He only clears his throat.

"Where's Archer?" Stevie asks. The stupid obvious question. That she'd instinctively whispered it enrages her. She stares at them. Their carelessness is an insult. Their self-indulgence reminding her of Moon and Mac. It is boring and embarrassing. Stevie has no interest in middle-aged, suburban antics.

"He's with Zee," says Adam softly, which makes Sawyer laugh.

"Don't get excited, he only goes up when we have guests," she says. "You know he's been gone thirty-eight weeks this year."

When neither of them responds, Sawyer turns to her. "You having a good birthday?" she asks.

"Sure," says Stevie, and then has the sense to wait.

"Are you two fucking?" Sawyer says next.

Stevie's ears are hot. The provocation makes her mind go blank. She stares at Sawyer with no expression, strongly disliking her but giving no rise to it. Peering down, Stevie denies Sawyer. She withholds. She remains unblinking until the other woman sort of disappears, becomes a Shein-sweatpanted smudge against the rest of her cluttered house, a poisonous little performer in her claustrophobic life.

"Jesus, Sull," says Adam, but his voice sounds remote.

Stevie wants to smile but resists, a cool, dark, slithery place opening up inside her, satisfied by Sawyer's discomfort. Sawyer is openly glaring now and Stevie almost laughs but remains absorbed in her experiment of making time stand still. She can't believe the tension, the incredible electricity traveling between them; the other woman's pupils are massive, blacked out, and the knowledge that Stevie has made her feel threatened in her own home thrills her.

Stevie understands now the rage in the debris, the aggression in the entire evening. The impotent protest of the ordered-in meal, the threat display of the mess, and she almost feels sorry for Sawyer, for all of them, herself included, for all the things they all do without wanting to, their principles and desires in violent opposition to the circumstance as it unfolds. Stevie had wanted to leave the moment they'd arrived. She'd wanted a different night for her birthday.

Stevie turns away from Sawyer, travels to the foyer and picks up her flowers. "You'll want these in a vase," she says, pushing them toward Sawyer right in the moment Archer returns.

He hesitates on the final step, hand on the railing, regarding the three of them for a measure, until he goes, "Wait, did you change?" to Stevie. She can sense Adam and Sawyer's vigilance, the echo of intrigue hovering over them, but Stevie dispels it, uninterested. "It's broiling in here," she says, asking Archer to turn down the heat, but he can't, so instead he opens a window, cutting through the triangle of them as he crosses the room, breaking the moment.

Back at Adam's house later that night, in bed, spinning from the champagne and staring at the ceiling, Stevie gets up. She checks the time. She doesn't recall the walk home. Only that she'd passed out immediately, throwing her clothes on a chair. She has slept exactly an hour.

She's reminded of parties from when she was younger. How she'd always been the only kid. The sadness of being banished to her room at bedtime. The devastation of listening to an entire house full of people who weren't ignoring her but had cleanly forgotten she was there.

She feels for Zee. The asshole kid to asshole parents. Stevie wonders what will become of her. Drugs, probably. Minimally, drinking. Her friends will likely be real bitches. Against her will, Stevie thinks about going through the motions of leaving tomorrow. She's only halfway packed, she doesn't want to crush her new clothes in her duffel. The thought of flying alone, of landing at the airport, returning to the Pool

House, all of it makes her frantic and desperate. She can't breathe, her misery is so powerful.

She recognizes that she isn't entitled to feel this way. She is returning to the previous state of a life that belongs to her. But she also recalls the soaring sensation that took flight in her body when Adam mentioned college. And how easily he could make it real. Throughout the trip, she'd been delivered lesson after lesson on worth. Value. In the same way Stevie couldn't reconcile what about her bag made it so expensive or the business-class flight or the wood chair that Adam had placed in the guest room that a Google Image search revealed to be $17,000, it escapes the scope of Stevie's imagination, how she might deserve Adam's generosity if he were to financially support the next chapter of her life.

And allowing herself to think about it in his house, in his guest room, staring at her new clothes, it becomes real to her. More than an intellectual exercise or an idea. He's not like Mac, transactional or petty. Or like Moon, the constant underdog, embittered and entitled. Adam would give anything to her freely. She knows it. She's seen it. Stevie doesn't have to earn his kindness to receive it.

Adam's bedroom is empty and the lights are on downstairs. She moves heavily. Slowly. She has the sense that she wants to surprise him, and when she discreetly brushes her teeth in her bathroom, she leaves the lights off and runs the water as quietly as possible. She stoops and sees his bare feet jutting out from beyond the couch, lying on his back on the floor. There's a fire burning beside him. She pauses on the stairs but he doesn't stir. When she is standing directly above him, his eyes are closed, hands, one on top of the other, on his chest. She can tell he's awake, there's an alert quality to his stillness, and for a second she wants to shout, to see him startle.

Instead, she sits down next to him, regretting having been so mean to him earlier. She'd ignored him the whole way back, satisfied that he was penitent, certainly no longer annoyed with her. But now when he still doesn't acknowledge her presence, she lies down beside him. She feels emboldened. She presses her body against his side, making a game of it, as close as she can possibly go, but still he keeps his eyes shut. She wants to pull his eyelids open with her fingers, pinching the thin skin between her thumb and forefinger, like opening a tiny chip bag, and she remembers it as something she used to do to her mother. And she longs to feel close to another person's body with as much freedom.

Stevie wants to do so many things to him. She props herself up, supporting her weight, one hand on either side of his broad shoulders, and leans over him, hair spilling around her, enclosing them. He opens his eyes but she says, *Shhhh . . .* until he closes them again. She dips down to press her lips against his and then, when he doesn't move, she inserts her tongue in his mouth, feeling herself inside him.

He tastes smoky.

Nothing else reaches her consciousness.

Then she pulls up her nightgown, lifts the whole thing above her head, and lies back down because he would let her.

ADAM

Behind his closed eyes, he remembers her naked body in the Pool House. Mythic in the silvered light. She'd looked beautiful. Supine and unmoving. As though she were arranged for a painting or had been immortalized, a nymph rendered in white marble statuary. He'd known the sleep to be a pretense. Her stillness, the shallowed breaths gave her away. She was lying there, flaunting the soft gleaming intimacy as a test. By then he'd known how Stevie was wired. Not so unlike her mother in their motives, just a whole different way to get there. Her inhibition hid a clamorous need for attention, preening and goading but quick to become defensive if you addressed it directly. He'd toed the line, trod carefully, allowing for the mutual plausible deniability of that night.

But he'd been selfish too. Wanting to preserve the occasion in exactly the way that most appealed to him. Uninterested in what it might have been to Stevie, in reality, in the cold light of day. That night, he'd been reminded of his mother from a memory that is precious to him. When he was younger, he used to come home from school with only the help moving around on the other side of the walls, to the cheerless emptiness of his parents' apartment. And for a few months, he doesn't know why or when it started, he would take off his clothes, including his underwear, and get into her bed. He would stare at the light fixture on the ceiling, the domed smoky glass breast with its nipple, and deliberately not touch himself. An infusion of pleasure and guilt would travel through his body and he would get hard, painfully hard, his entire midsection seeming to throb in time to his heart but eventually as the glow spread, it would go away as he thought of his abstinence as an offering to his mother. That he would give her his restraint.

But one hazy afternoon, he'd found his mother's nude figure on top of the sheets. Her hair was out, loose, maroon and unspooled from their clips. She'd lain there sprawled, hair fanned out as though she were floating in a body of water. Ophelia. She rarely spoke to him with her full attention, examining him but rarely giving him her eyes, and the sudden appearance of her unconscious, entirely exposed body in broad daylight was so intoxicating, so rapturous that he stood there, legs trembling, fear coursing through him but helpless against staring at her, consuming her, unable to move.

Then, as it had been with Stevie, he'd known his mother was awake. This too had been a test. A sham test because they both wanted him there. Wanted him to look. Wanting to be seen because they were beautiful and knew they were beautiful but unwilling to admit their guilt and if that were the case, he would willingly eat their shame and also his own.

He'd observed Stevie's voluptuousness. Reveled in it and then covered her, almost brushing her thigh with his lips when he stooped to pick up her sheet. He marveled at the gentle slopes of her breasts, the lush roundness of her belly and thighs, how they weren't sculpted or willed into muscular cords the way it is with so many other women he has known, the youthful curve of her vulva, full and downy, and remembering this now his cock inflates, filled like an airbag on impact, trapped and struggling in his pants, abruptly alive, thrashing to live.

She eats his shame. He hears the telltale click of the mother of pearl buttons from her nightgown hitting the wood floor. He's pliant but blameless. She reaches for the band of his sweater and lifts until the fabric bunches at his armpits pinned to the floor at his back. She tries again but it won't go any further so she leaves it there, exposing his chest, his stomach, then presses her cheek against his torso and breathes deep. But then she roves, moving her face in sweeping motions, filling her lungs, smelling him and sighing pleasurably.

She explores him freely, hands nestling in his armpits, stroking her entire palms against his sides, gripping, then releasing him. Tactile experiments as though she has never seen another body or has any expectations of what to do with one. But then she sits up and he grieves the absence of her fevered head against him, breathing him, until her fingers unbuckle his belt, unzips him, then hooks into his waistband and yanks down. He's never been undressed in this way before, his hands are now beside him, but he eases his hips up ever so slightly as she tugs again and this time he is free, naked to the knee, jutting out at an angle like a spring-loaded zeppelin, indecent, unseeing but seeking, and this time she kisses his stomach, a warm trail that he cannot predict, not with his eyes closed, and then her hand encircles him, holding his engorged cock, and he almost reaches out to grab her by the wrist but doesn't.

He only wants to encourage her.

He senses her moving above him. Her thighs warm on his hips, and when she reaches for him again, he holds his breath. She kisses him, opens his lips with her tongue, and then her wet heat is on him below. She sinks down slowly, letting out a low guttural moan, and once she's taken all of him in, she does not move. Sheathed in the tight warmth of her, he is aching to grab her by the hips but doesn't. He doesn't shift against her. Exhaling raggedly. Determinedly. He wonders if he will come from just this. From the controlled connection. He feels tingling build, the sensation intense, as though rising from a region behind him, every nerve ending prickling urgently, and then he thinks, miraculously, joyfully, that his penis has never felt so vivid. He knows he could make himself come in that moment if he wanted to. But he doesn't. He doesn't even riffle through a kaleidoscope of images to forestall it or incite it, he just breathes.

After a while he softens and she unlatches herself to lie beside him.

She presses her body against his, her heart rabbiting wildly against his arm, and then touches herself, nudging him with her forearm as she moves. He keeps his hands still even as he gets hard again. And then she shudders forcefully, crying out, shivering. Afterward she lifts his arm to rest her head against him. And falls asleep.

DAY TWENTY-NINE

MOON

She watches out of her front window. Waiting. Stevie landed two hours ago but asked not to be picked up, she'll be taking a car, and Moon finds this funny. As though Stevie is trying to indicate how much she's changed in her short time away. The way year-abroad kids act when they've returned from three months in *Barthelona.*

She'd texted from the tarmac and Moon feels different knowing that she is back. That they are speaking again. While Stevie was away, she'd felt a nagging anxiety, as though she'd left the gas on or the tub running in an alternate universe. She wonders how Stevie will seem. She has so many things to tell her. That there'd be no more tenants. How wrong she'd been about everything. How Moon knows exactly what Stevie needs to do.

When her car arrives, Moon almost runs out into the street but stops herself, struck with shyness, grinning like an idiot. But when the car door opens her hand is on the front door, mouth open to call out, it's Dano who emerges first, gigantic knee the size of a skull, the length of him unfolding like a lawn chair, and Moon stops, taken aback, bewildered.

And when Stevie alights, Moon's stunned by her hair all over again, but this time the incomprehensible coincidence lands, their sudden shared resemblance. Of Moon with hacked hair, scratching from lice.

Of Stevie now in her dark strange clothes. It is either a miracle or an omen.

She watches Stevie watch Dano. Her daughter regards him with impatience, with none of the affection from before, and Moon wonders what it indicates, if Dano's return signals something unpleasant about their trip. And as he carries on with the driver, oblivious, laughing, talking, buddying up, campaigning the way he reflexively does, not knowing how else to be with other men, she watches Stevie yawn but stifle it behind a hand, a discreet gesture that is also unrecognizable. The men remove all the luggage from the trunk, more bags than they'd left with, and Moon thinks of how it isn't just the yawn or the clothes, she can see by the tilt of Stevie's head that she's exhausted but willing herself to wait, being polite, holding herself erect, shoulders squared, carrying Dano's coat on her arm, and Moon has the thought that she's being compliant. That Stevie is performing and Moon goes cold.

Finally, the driver is back in the car and Dano puts his coat on to free their hands, and as they approach they resemble each other. As though they are wearing a uniform. They pass the house to advance toward the Pool House, but then Stevie looks over her shoulder, as though attuned to her mother's presence. They lock eyes. First confusion, then a smile, relief, and Moon sees that Stevie is happy to see her and this fills her with a giggly delirium. Until Dano waves at her too with the eagerness of a great golden dog.

Moon doesn't know how to arrange her face as he strides in first to lift her up off her feet, delaying her reunion with Stevie with his big, earnest body. "Happy birthday, Moonie," he says, and she squeezes his arm, indicating to be let down, eyes fixed on Stevie, her daughter's hair casting her face in new angles.

"Wait, are we still in here?" Stevie asks her mother. "We don't have tenants?"

Moon has a speech prepared, but with every passing moment that Dano is there with them, her muscles become tighter. The sense of violation is so powerful that she doesn't know what to say.

"Not at the moment," she says, remaining circumspect, wanting to save the news of her plans for when it's just the two of them.

She turns to Dano. "I'm just trying to understand," she says to him, with a laugh to dull the sting. "Why you're back."

He stares at her with a strange blankness, but then glances at Stevie as though she might answer for him. And there's something in his fixed, bright smile that Moon immediately places. The understanding sweeping through her in a wave.

"Wait," exclaims Stevie, rushing for her backpack to pull out a crinkly white bag. Moon knows what it is even before she sees it and forces herself to laugh despite the dread in her chest. When people leave and return they bring gifts. It's why Jerry brought home pralines. Why Moon brought sweets for Stevie. It asks that the past be forgotten and for the future to be forgiven. It's always been a bribe.

"Happy birthday, Mom," says Stevie outlandishly, presenting the box of See's chocolates. They feel alien in her hands. This gift that signals change Moon won't consent to. And then, finally, Moon hugs Stevie, and it feels so good that she would cry, wishing she could unzip the cesarean scar that frowns up at her every time she sits down to pee to stuff her baby back inside.

Stevie pulls away first and Moon grabs her hand. Looking. Taking her in. Memorizing her. And then Stevie tells Dano to take their bags upstairs, dismissing him while she removes her coat to hang on the back of a chair, then washes her hands in the kitchen sink.

"I feel so out of it," she remarks. "Is this jetlag? Can a person get jetlag from three hours?"

Moon picks up the coat and holds it up, glancing at the discreet white label sewn into the lining. "This is nice," she remarks. Moon has a present for Stevie too. Clothes, but they're not new, possibly not as quietly luxurious, and she feels jealousy rip through her. She reaches for the tag on the back of Stevie's sweater but Stevie spins out of the way.

"Stop," she says. The sweater is a fine-gauge cashmere and the jacket from the same label prides itself on the timeless elegance that can be attained to the tune of fifteen hundred dollars for a sweater and upward of six thousand for a coat.

But then suddenly, she leans into Moon, glancing upstairs quickly before pulling her in by the arm. "Moonie, he's going to help us," she says. "To keep the house."

Moon nods along, finding it risible, and a fierce look darts across Stevie's face. "I'm serious," she says. "He promised he would."

But of course he would, Moon wants to crow, but before she can say anything, Dano is back downstairs and Stevie hands him the kitchen towel to wash his hands.

The kettle shrieks, startling them.

Moon opens the cabinet for mugs. "I went to Pee Wee's," she tells them, and Stevie laughs.

"When?"

"Few days ago," Moon continues. "I got the chicken burrito," she says, tying the teabags around the handles of their mugs and filling them.

"You hated it, didn't you," says Stevie, casting a meaningful look at Dano as she lifts her mug to blow on it. The water is too hot, the tea insufficiently steeped, not even close to ready, and Moon is reminded of Stevie as a girl and her obstinate little tea parties, milking the occasion for as long as she could, telling Moon where to sit, when to drink, ignoring her sometimes even as she held them all hostage, speaking to her stuffed penguin in a demented, quavering dowager's voice, elbow wedged against its windpipe just to keep its soft body propped up in its chair.

"Not at all. I just wanted to see it."

"Well, I quit," pronounces Stevie.

"Oh." Moon glances at the flat box of chocolates on the kitchen table.

She feels like a computer buffering. There's so much information coming at her all at once. She recalls the feeling of Stevie climbing on her, pushing her book to the floor, pulling at her face. How she would grope Moon's lips, her ears, jab at her eye, prying her mouth open only to cough into it, interrupting whatever it was that Moon was saying or doing so that Stevie could have her completely. Melting down otherwise. Wailing, stomping, outraged.

And whenever Stevie started crying in this way, Moon would carry her to the bathroom and hold her in front of the mirror and Stevie would watch herself, panting, tear-stained, and eventually stop, overtaken by the fascination with her own face. But when she turned three, the real tantrums came. It's then that she'd discovered the power of humiliating Moon in public. Hurling herself to the ground, shrieking, screaming, uncaring where they were, fueled by the commotion, the crowd, drawing power from the busyness of the supermarkets, restaurants, the chaos of the streets.

Moon remembers a brutally hot day when she'd botched an audition. They'd been visiting the grounds at Getty. They'd walked all over, Moon pointing out the flowers, reading the placards out loud for the names of the trees: Japanese maple, camphor, pepper. She'd hoped Stevie would tire out and nap but she'd been belligerent that day, announcing that she, Stevie Moon, in the third person, would ride the train back by herself. Not with Mommy.

They were both wretchedly overtired, waking up at five to get Stevie to her friend's house before pre-K so Moon could drive across town, wait for hours, then drive back for pickup. Moon tried to reason with her, pulling her away from the tracks as other children and parents stared. It is the look Stevie gave her that is indelible in Moon's memory. Stevie stared right at Moon, an eerie calm descending, and holding her mother's gaze, she lifted her dress in aggression, showing Moon her round belly as a threat, and then threw herself at her legs, tripping them both, sending them to the ground. Even as Moon landed on her tailbone, even as she felt murderous, she remembered laughing, impressed by Stevie's mettle. Her mother had been right. Moon had given birth to a girl exactly like her.

"It's so crazy how priorities can just shift once you get a little perspective," says Stevie. She shakes her head with a tight, bemused smile as if she can't believe her life from before. Then she carries her mug into the living room, intending for Moon to follow. She thinks of Stevie's hard little belly. Her underpants thick from the pull-up diapers.

"Did you give notice?"

Stevie bites her lip.

"So you didn't quit, you ghosted them."

"I didn't ghost."

Moon tilts her head. "No, I'm pretty sure that's exactly what you did. Which is embarrassing."

Dano settles in next to Stevie on the couch.

"Wait, you quit?" he asks her.

"I'm sorry, I didn't know everyone was so attached to that job," Stevie says, picking up her mug then putting it back down again.

Dano shrugs. His attention is squarely on Moon now. He places his hands on his legs and turns to her with a soft, hesitant look on his face. "Moonie, I really hate how we left things," he begins in an awful youth pastor voice, but then Stevie abruptly stands up.

"Actually," she says. "I should probably go over there. I need to pick up my last paycheck anyway." And despite it not being cold enough, she walks toward her coat, and Moon understands better than anyone that you don't waste a powerful outfit if you can squeeze multiple public appearances out of it.

"I'll call a car," Stevie tells them. "You guys talk."

When she leaves, Moon almost breaks. Almost laughs at Dano who has been left behind. But she doesn't. She can't, not right now. They watch Stevie through the window as she waves and then Moon turns to him, giving him grace, knowing that he doesn't know how predictable he is. And how true this is of anyone.

She takes a breath. She doesn't have to wonder what lengths she'll go to. It's all so fantastically clear.

"God, you must be exhausted," she tells Dano, with a smile, and then reaches for his hand, larger than hers but deserving of compassion too.

ADAM

The joke is that Moon is his mother. The painful reality is, he was in love with her, his crush immense and complicated by how much he wished she was his mother. An aunt. Sister. Any family that would have made his life easier, warmer. She'd given him such access, letting him follow her, enduring all his questions, ignoring everyone's jokes about his crush, but Adam wanted more. He was in love with her but she was also essential to him, he wanted to be her.

He'd known it was a violation to watch her first film but he'd done it out of devotion. Ripped the *Volumes* and played them in the background of his life over a strange few days where she'd loomed like a specter in the room of his mid-city apartment share, bleeding into his head, filling out the emptiness of his L.A. life.

Sometimes he would fall asleep with her playing in his headphones and dream of her and even when he opened his eyes, still stoned from strong California weed, he'd tap his laptop into wakefulness and she'd be there, frozen, sometimes asleep in the grainy footage, as though she was in the bed beside him. In those bleary vertiginous days she'd belonged to him, an eighteen-year-old Moon making her best work, her most important he still believes, exhibiting a persistent, painful frailty that was terrifying and ravishing even in her quotidian movements.

It is obvious in the movies that they are starkly poor. And bored. Mostly they read. Smoked. Slept. Brushed their teeth. Put a puzzle together. They seem to eat only cereal or sliced bread. He'd seen her pee. Clip her nails. And on a particularly joyful day when the Hermitage had their hot water returned to them, he'd watched her take a bath and fantasized about sliding into the water with her. He would tell her what he knew of her future. He would warn her against voluble redheaded men. He would teach her about movies and books that she herself as an adult decades later would have taught him.

He'd known the sex scene was coming. Her defilement. He could have watched the scene on its own but felt he'd owed it to her to watch it all. With her white, old-fashioned nightgown, hair unbrushed, feral and potent, she is a ghostly virgin with many teeth, and he has somehow fallen in love with this version of her too. The two dark-haired boys, monstrously tall, cast shadows like haunted trees on her small white frame, and he'd felt sick with fear. Unable to fast-forward, fearing it would be abandoning her. He'd watch her, smoking himself catatonic in his apartment watching the boys circle her, edging closer, dreading whenever she would goad them, climbing into their laps to study their hands, stealing freshly rolled cigarettes directly from their mouths or rushing toward them with her whole body, wrestling them to the ground, legs bare, underwear showing, screaming with laughter until they quickly overpowered her.

When they finally have sex in an otherwise unremarkable scene, Moon reaching for one on the couch as though out of boredom, the other entering the scene as if cued, Adam had masturbated all day, unable to eat, despondent and ashamed despite the brilliant sun outside, jerking off until the tip of his dick stung and his eyes ached in his skull. All he knew was that he hadn't been able to protect her but also that he had paid for it with his witnessing.

When he returned to work, having gone to hell and back with her, he'd said nothing. But there are other times when he wishes they would talk about it. How important the work is, how internet, surveillance, social media, all of it had aligned to make her contribution inviolably unique, inimitable, where it ceases to be film or documentary or performance art because it is everything all at once. But even that is a ruse. A cover. What he wants to tell her, what threatens to burst out of him when she looks at him, when she touches his face with her wet hand in the pool, when she says his name with kindness, is that he has loved her for so much of his life but that this doll version of her, the eighteen-year-old Moon trapped in the black-and-white footage, belongs to him. Is his forever.

The old joke of the show is not something they ever discuss. And it's with a rapid succession of warring sentiments—loneliness, humiliation, relief—that he takes her hand and allows himself to be led to the Pool House.

It is 67 degrees and the Air Quality Index is at 122. The sky holds the particulate quality of Los Angeles smog where it seems as though it has been rendered in soft colored pencils on textured sketch paper. Each tiny pixel containing its own poisoned sky. And as they walk together in the sun holding hands, him carrying her robe because she asks him to, he knows she knows. And she forgives him.

STEVIE

Her entrance couldn't have possibly gone better. The blocking was perfect. When she'd arrived, Freddie was right there in the alley standing with Mel smoking. They'd watched her car pull in but turned away to resume their conversation until Mel did a double take. Mel in her cheap lace miniskirt and hair ribbons. Freddie in her work polo.

Holy shit, went Mel, choking she was so surprised. Stevie could have kissed her then. Her reaction had been priceless. *Your hair*, she'd said, swallowing. They'd hugged, laughed, and Stevie could have been returning from war. *I didn't recognize you.*

She'll never see any of them again, she thinks with peculiar bittersweetness on her ride back home. It is absurd that only a few weeks ago they'd all been going to some stupid party. She passes Hollywood Boulevard and cannot imagine living outside of this. And for a moment she'd wished she could return to the simplicity of the time of the party, but everything is different now. The sky is a brownish ochre. Gas is $4.73 a gallon. She passes a cluster of three-wheeled office chairs, beat up and discarded on the street, the armrests tied together with string, the chairs facing each other as though in conversation.

She's stuck in rush-hour traffic, it's almost six, and she checks her phone to text Adam a heart. Thinking about Adam now, she feels full, a heaviness that is almost indistinguishable from sorrow. Not the infatuation of movies or books but something more immense. He loves her. She'd seen it in his response to her. He'd called her precious that morning, crying. Laughing as he cried. He looks so much like a boy when he cries. He'd told her that they couldn't make love. Calling it that, *making love*, a term that makes her shiver with embarrassment.

They'd spent most of the early morning planning. He'd wanted to return to L.A. to tell Moon in person. Suggesting that he'd have to ask her permission.

Permission? she'd asked.

We need her blessing. If we're really going to be together.

Stevie doesn't know what this formality implies. Blessing. Being together, really together. She wonders incredulously if he means marriage. She's stunned and disbelieving that it could mean marriage. A ring. A dress. A wedding. All those people looking at them all at once.

Even Freddie could see how altered she was. *I'm moving to New York*, she'd told her, waiting as she finished her cigarette.

What about Yarmouth?

Stevie shook her head. *Fuck Yarmouth*, she'd said before heading in through the back.

When Stevie knocked on Xan's door, her former boss hadn't seemed surprised. She hadn't remarked on her appearance or her absence but she had stopped typing instantly.

I have something for you, she'd said, pushing herself back from her desk, and for a moment Stevie expected paperwork, some official document to sign forfeiting her future, but instead there was crinkling and Xan produced a plastic bag from her bottom drawer. It was a paperback copy of Judy Blume's *Forever* and the Tupperware from Stevie's locker, washed.

I gave you until the end of the week before we tossed it, she'd said.

You didn't have to wash it, Stevie added, touched.

It was a vermin issue, responded Xan.

I'm sorry about Yarmouth, Stevie told her. *I'm moving somewhere else.*

I wouldn't worry about it, Xan said cheerily, not asking where she would go.

And finally, when Xan rose to her feet to see Stevie to the door, Stevie had blurted out, *My dad killed himself*, adding, *Things have been really hard.*

Xan told her she was sorry for the loss, then opened her door.

Xan's indifference might have been an act, but it doesn't even matter anymore. It's remarkable how unchanged they had all been. She imagines Xan's days, the loud demonstrative typing, Truck Day, throughputs, digital kitchens. She thinks of Freddie's week, scrolling on her phone, swiping on the apps, making excuses to go to Canter's whenever Sage is sitting out front. It's all past her. Such ancient history.

Stevie is transformed. Her life is finally romantic. Unbelievably romantic. She doesn't even know how the idea had come to her, to climb on top of Adam and not move. She'd meant it as an experiment. She hadn't had to tell him to stay still, he was so restrained, utterly submissive. It was as if he'd known by instinct that the only thing that would ruin the innocence of their bodies was movement.

She laughs out loud and the driver looks at her in the rearview. They'd just lain there. They'd been tested and managed to resist.

When Adam had offered to return to L.A. with her, she'd buried her face in her hands she'd been so happy. She's never experienced it before, a sweeping, devastating romance, and now she can't imagine her life without him. Everything has a sense of inevitability now. When he speaks, she barely listens, the overwhelm of his handsomeness is too loud. She can't believe he wants her. She feels beautiful in the eye of his interest. The depth of his concern in every aspect of her life moves her. He is so doting. So obsessed with her. She feels the burden of it. This lavish liability.

She considers the engagement ring he might get her. How she would touch her face lightly, laughing in the photographs. She wonders where they will sleep tonight. How Moon will feel. Whether they will remain separated, throbbing with lust but chaste.

She thinks of New York and is filled with fresh dread that flutters around the edges of her joy. She worries about making friends. School. But then she conjures babies and she envisions herself pregnant, the vision delivered to her with clarity. Stevie in her white dress. She doesn't want it but he does and maybe that will change her mind.

Stevie passes the sun-bleached strip mall signs, the ragged rat-filled palm trees, and her eyes fill with tears. Stupidly, she will miss all this. She cannot imagine Moon visiting them only a few times a year, how that will feel. The misery of making up a guest room for her, the pillowcase and sheets smelling of her once she leaves.

She runs into the Big House, eager for them. Wanting to call out for her mother, calling her Mom. Laughing when she has the deranged thought of Moon as a grandmother. How she would pick out a nickname. Gammy Moon. Mimi Moon. Or more likely just Moon. Both their cars are out front but they aren't home when she lets herself in, the blinds noisily clattering against the frames. The windows have been opened and the cross breeze is cool and fresh.

She calls into the kitchen and then up the stairs. She is starving. She sets her phone down, going into the kitchen to wash her hands. She looks into the Pool House, the buttery shards of light on the tile floor, the harsh dark shadows. From where she stands, she can still see the blackout curtains folded in a pile on the floor.

And then Moon walks into the frame. Naked. Her nudity unadorned. Her pubic hair surprisingly unkempt as is the hair on her head. Stevie holds her breath and takes a step back. Her first instinct whenever she sees her mother exposed will always be to hide, to spare Moon shame. But when she looks again, her mother remains there, looking out, her nakedness seeming almost incidental, but then she turns and the question of Adam's location is answered when he brings Moon her robe.

He is also completely naked. She has seen them through glass so many times, cooking, typing, talking, passing each other utensils, or onscreen, dancing, laughing, and for a second their individual nudity registers as less strange than why they are in the Pool House while she is standing here.

Moon puts the robe on, still talking, and then Adam reaches to Moon from behind to kiss her temple. And in that moment, as though Stevie has been able to hit her mark, Moon looks up.

She's caught like a fish by the hook of that gaze. She thinks of her mother on another morning, in the same robe, the good robe, watching Adam swim as Stevie watched Moon.

And in the next instant, Stevie is mother-bound, flying out the door, down the stairs, straight across the lawn, crossing the panes and into the scene she'd only just been watching. Moon holds her position but Stevie sees Adam dash into the closet and slam it shut.

Stevie is screaming. She cannot hear herself but she can feel it, the tightening everywhere, gripped by horror. She throws herself against the flimsy door, watching it leap off its hinges but not giving way. She keeps screeching his name. Emptying herself. Wanting all the glass around them to shatter over their heads. Shredding their skin, veins, arteries, all the major organs, killing them.

"What did you do?" she screams. "What did she do to you?"

She knows this is all Moon. She'd thought to bring her robe, a prop belonging to the Big House to stage such a scene. She'd planned it. Adam is guileless. He has to be. And Stevie throws herself against the door again, pounding, wailing, smashing with her fist, splintering the bones, throat burning. For a moment, she floats above, watching herself carrying on, hysterical, ridiculous, and again she has the sense of telling someone about this in the future, and then she is returned to herself and the agony of the moment, when her mother pulls her shoulders from behind, the scent of her, the roses and gasoline of her, and the other smell, her mother's smell and sex, him, and Stevie shoves Moon down to the tiled floor.

"Why can't I have anything?" she screams, striking Moon now with her fists. Moon escapes and Stevie gets up after her, slapping, hitting, the soft landing of Moon's robe enraging her. "I just wanted one thing!" Moon falls this time and Stevie falls on top of her, the cold hard tile against her legs. It is all so eerily repulsive. Stevie's stomach roils and she slaps her hand down on the cold tile, the white pattern of the caulk crossing her eyes. She opens her mouth to retch. Heart, lungs, and stomach convulse, but nothing comes except a long trail of spit and a horrible keening wail.

"Please," says Moon, getting to her knees, pulling up Stevie's hands in her own, holding them firmly as if to protect them, putting her face near Stevie's. "You don't know yet, but he's not it. It's not him." Stevie tears her hands away and Moon pulls at her, crying now too. "You have to go. You know how to go," she says. Stevie pushes her again and Moon's expression is collapsed, anguished, as if this is somehow more painful for her, and Stevie slaps her mother's face. Moon touches her cheek, the flush traveling up her neck, but then frighteningly Moon smiles. "Good," she says. And then, she says, "Now go."

Moon presses something hard into her palm but Stevie kicks her mother off. "No," she says, crawling on her hands and feet on the hard floor, banging on the door again, saying his name. Begging. Pleading. "Adam! What did you say to her? Did you tell her?" She shoves her fingers under the door, trying to reach him. But he won't face her, won't even say anything until Moon is grabbing at her hands again. "Look at me," she commands. "You can do this." Again she shoves something into her fist, peeling Stevie's fingers back, and it is a hard black key fob. The key to Adam's car.

Stevie pants. She stares at the slit beneath the door and says his name. "Please," she says. Then she says it again. Screaming. She screams it again and again until the word loses meaning. And a third time her mother reaches for her, pulling her back, and when they rise together, with heavy arms and grappling fingers, Moon's bathrobe falls open, the flash of hair, her ragged C-section scar, the puckered white of her skin nightmarish but tender, and Moon is saying something to her, but Stevie can't hear for the pounding of her heart. Her mother. "엄마," she moans, and it hurts her to say it, but she wants to hurt Moon too. Now Moon is sobbing, begging, smoothing Stevie's hair, trying to hold her face in her hands, the tip of her mother's finger is in her mouth and Stevie spits at her, disbelieving, ravaged, but she takes the key.

She presses her forehead on the door, her voice illusory and echoing inside her. "Adam," she says. Quieter. So he hears that she forgives him. She can't see, can't breathe, she feels that she will die but still he doesn't come out.

"Stevie, I can't," he says finally from the other side. And her fist flies up again, banging, she knows he is kneeling on the sad mattress on the closet floor, in the dark, and she knows how he feels, how much he hates himself, but still he doesn't come out. Moon grabs her again by the shoulders and shakes her gently. "Go."

DAY ONE

And then Stevie is driving.

She heads toward the freeway and her chest is tight. It is the anxiety of every possibility suddenly presenting itself, spatchcocked and spread-eagled before her. The spaghetti of highways that can fling her out of town and clear across the country. The steering wheel trembles in her palms and Stevie feels a puncturing of momentum as she tears through the skein, the fatty webbing, the membrane that keeps her connected to Moon.

She starts crying again. Hot awful tears. It is the difference between almost knowing and almost forgetting. The traffic gives way suddenly and the light is painfully bright. Purifying. For a fraction of a moment, she forgets where she is. That she is driving. The loss of herself is so black and complete like the cigarette burn, a cue mark, blotting out a frame of film, and she is horrified when the car lurches, a spooked mare, but she steadies it. She laughs, a deranged little burble of relief, and then slows her breath. She looks in her rearview. She is free of Moon's orbit. It is miraculous how convincingly she can move along with the other cars that deftly, somehow, avoid her.

The sudden lightness is unimaginable. The motility of her. Her capability. The flat, broad path ahead leading to I-5 north, the Verdugo Mountains rising in the horizon as she goes.

ACKNOWLEDGMENTS

As with teeth, this list only grows longer with time.

I'm grateful to so many people for their love and friendship while I wrote this book. To Megan Lynch at Flatiron for your unwavering support. For your confidence. Your patience. For understanding *milk teeth*. Kara McAndrew for fielding my many questions. Thank you, Sarah Barley, we will dance together properly someday.

Thank you, Jason Richman, you've been so good to me for so many years now. So reassuring and hilariously unflappable. To Duvall Osteen, for adoring phone calls as much as I do. For knowing exactly when I need one. To Daniel Beracha and Isabella Byrne for verbing all the nouns with so much care.

To Priya Verma and Stratton Vasquez for wisdom and precision. Edward Orloff. Jermaine Johnson, my friend. Mary Pender-Coplan.

Thank you to the people who hold my hand in this life. Who fill my heart to bursting. Asa Akira; Dawn Astronaut, thank you for having that "thing." Best gift ever. No contest. Leilani Arita for celebrating each milestone with joy and reverence. Also, beauty. Phil Chang the bestie. Eric Chang and Irene Lee for matinees and advice. Your brains make me feel less lonely. Kenzo Digital for perspective. Minya Oh for the answers. Julia Oh for discernment.

My sweetest Jinjamin, Jin Ha. Thank you for talking to me not just about *the business* and *the craft* but also the feelings. Anything that feels reductive or flat is on me entirely. To Bea Kim for the calls about performance. It's breathtaking to watch you take flight. Kathy Ito Kim for your grace and warmth. And modeling motherhood for me.

Sidebar: Zero mothers in this story are remotely inspired by the women in my life. Okay, maybe my own mother but only through the lens of projection and obsession.

To my L.A. family. Jayne Min. Please let me come live in your dollhouse. Steve Yeun for the conversation and the side quests. Carol Lim: I will never recover from you leaving New York but I know when to find you at Fraser Place.

Jenny Han. The juggernaut. The absolute legend with the singular vision. Thank you for caring deeply. For making me laugh so hard. Caroline Tsai and Victoria Storm; 4 p.m. chores forever. J. Wortham for your light. For the tendrils. For receiving me as I am. Allison P. Davis for the dispatches and the commiseration. Books, man. Why even? Collier Meyerson for being the mayor of the entire neighborhood and for the safe space to write. To Lulu Wang for breaking stories and sharing so openly about art.

Fisheries is inspired by my time at MacDowell. A magical space that goes incalculably hard. Thank you to David Macy, Courtney Bethel, Jenni Wu, Sarah K. Jordan, Jean Yoon. I'm grateful to Banks Studio. And especially to the James Baldwin Library. Thank you, Sadie Greene, for the chair advice and to Stef, Lamorna, and Porochista for the immaculate vibes. And to my entire cohort for being my very first audience. What a gracious, tender place to land.

To Kayla Min Andrews for the Katherine Min Fellowship in support of my time there. I'm so grateful for your mother's words and for your labor that delivers them to me. I can't wait to read more of you.

I owe so much to all the supportive spaces and gestational places for *Pool House*. I'm grateful to the Haus am See Foundation Board, Krämerstein, and the Municipality of Horw for the breathtaking lakeside residency in Lucerne. The water really does taste like Volvic. It's wild.

To the members of the *unofficial* Kastanienbaum Yacht Club. Remo Bitzi, you know how to live a life. I am indebted to Laura Breitschmid and the entire Breitschmid family. I continue to receive your kindness in multiple countries. Tenuta Palmeri in Avola and the *misterio delle chiave*. I took them! My *motivi* is plain and constant. I also long to be a *proprietaria delle cassette*. I hope we all live together someday.

Zur Neuen Apotheke Bio-Weinhandlung & Second Hand Üsé Studio and Kaffeekranz in Lucerne for letting me linger.

To bookstores! But especially my locals. Yu & Me Books and Books Are Magic. Thank you for the support throughout my career. But especially for this book. The scary one.

Kazumi Fish, Theresa Phung, Christine Jeon for the preorder campaign.

Michael Fusco-Straub at BAM. As well as Nicole Vasquez and Yeshim Kayim-Yanko.

To Lucy Yu for your friendship. For understanding me so totally. For movie recommendations and a safe harbor always but particularly during snowy nights. For being spiritually incapable of small talk.

To Emma Straub for your understanding. For so many texts and conversations about dads and what it is to miss ours.

To my early readers. Suze Webb, Maeve Higgins, and especially Melissa Albert. Thank for your grace while I ALL CAPSED about whether or not this was a book.

Mark Lotto, my longtime editor and other brain and my weighted blanket. Getting a "nice" from you in the notes is what I live for. Your "lol no's" are just as crucial.

To Erica Cerulo and Claire Mazur for the group hugs and your confidence and for doing Good Work. To Mira Jacob for the walks and the talks and the teas. Jami Attenberg for the encouragement. For understanding stories. And for the collective wisdom of your vast network.

Bryan Washington. Michelle Zauner. Lisa Ko. Rachel Khong. Traci Thomas. Miwa Messer. Shea Serrano for the advice. Jonny Sun for the hugs and the eats. Karen Chee for your spirit and glee.

To the U.K. Team. Sue Armstrong at C&W, Cathryn Summerhayes at Curtis Brown. Thank you, Francesca Main at Phoenix Books, for your invaluable note about stage directions and for believing that these weirdos will carry.

To the audio team at Macmillan. Katy Robitzski. Maria Snelling in marketing and Jessica Thurber in publicity. Joy Osmanski for giving voice to all my books. Thank you for your excellence. And for being Korean. It's an honor just to be Asian.

Thank you, Katherine Turro and Cat Kenney at Flatiron. Laywan Kwan for the beautiful cover.

Peter Do for the looks. Aaron Richter for the headshot that persists.

And finally to my family. To my father, Andrew Hyung-bum Choi. I'm told I resemble you even if I don't always know what that means. I feel your absence every day. To my brother Mike Choi, to Wylie and Ollie. Vicki. And to my mother, Veronica won-mi Choi. My reason for writing at all.

And for Sam. To whom this book is dedicated. Thank you for your companionship in the desert. Thank you for being my home.

ABOUT THE AUTHOR

MARY H.K. CHOI is a *New York Times* bestselling author whose work has appeared in *The Atlantic*, *The New York Times Magazine*, *New York*, *GQ*, and *Elle*. Formerly, she was the culture correspondent for *Vice News Tonight* on HBO, a columnist at *Wired* and *Allure*, and a guest columnist for the *New York Times* Opinion desk, as well as an executive producer of the *House of Style* documentary on MTV. She was awarded the Katherine Min Fellowship at MacDowell and has also written comics for Marvel and DC. She is currently developing her books for film and TV. Follow her on all social media at @choitotheworld, as well as the *choitotheworld* Substack that covers mental health, culture, and technology.